MAGIC
UNDER THE
BIG TOP

MAGIC UNDER THE BIG TOP: A Circus Anthology

Cover designed by Qamber Designs & Media.
Cover photo by Wendy Wild Photography.
Interior formatting by Key of Heart Designs.
Interior graphics by Vsevolod Petrov.
Illustrations by Sean Eddingfield, Ben Falco, Martina Localzo, Adriano Moraes, Marcella W.

Published by Snowy Wings Publishing
www.snowywingspublishing.com

ISBN: 978-1-958051-80-1

First edition: September 2024.

MAGIC UNDER THE BIG TOP

A CIRCUS ANTHOLOGY EDITED BY

MARY FAN

Snowy Wings
PUBLISHING

TURNER, OREGON

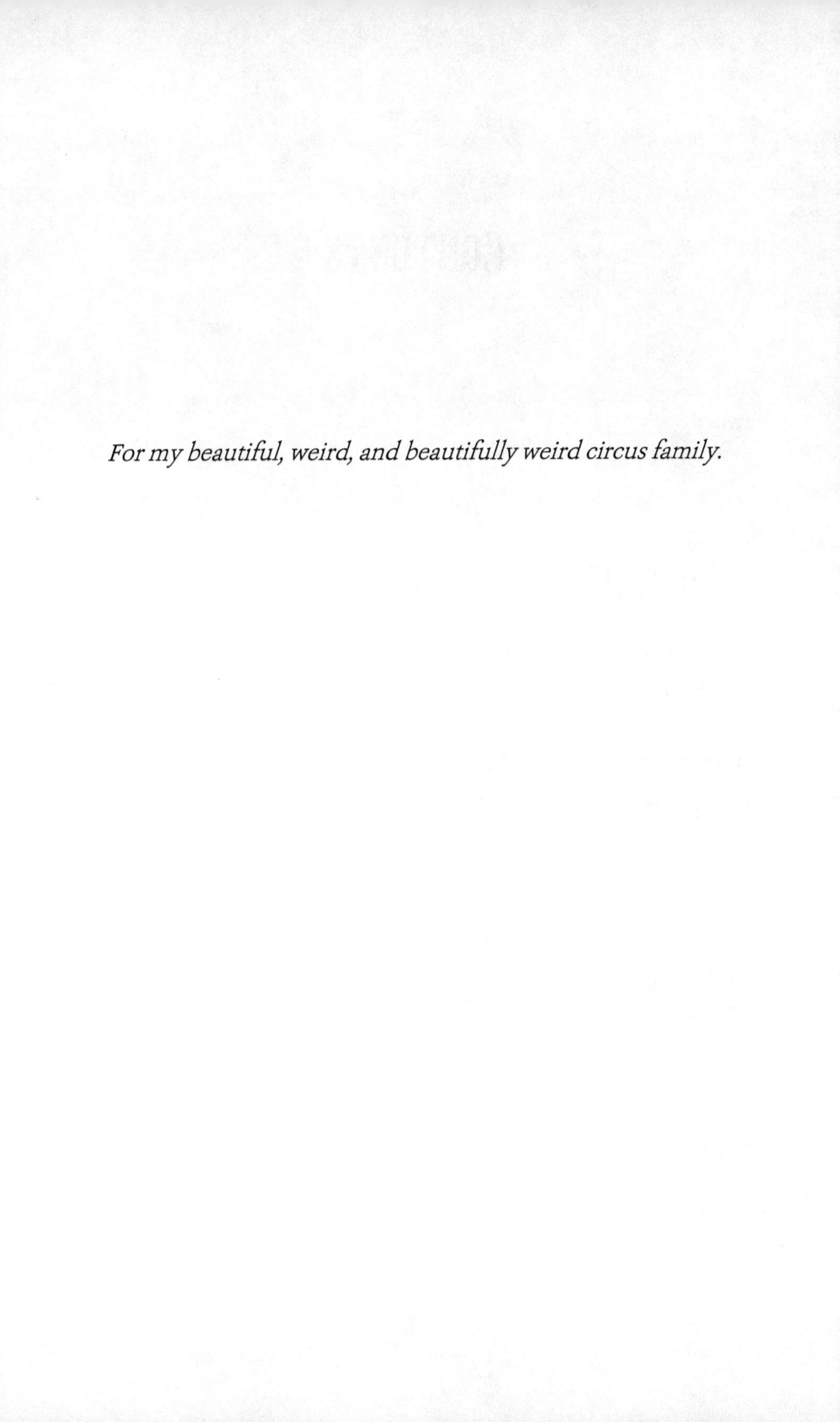

For my beautiful, weird, and beautifully weird circus family.

CONTENTS

FOREWORD
HOVEY BURGESS

orn one year and three months before the United States entered World War II, my earliest memories are those of being taken, as a toddler, to see two American circuses—Hunt Bros. Circus under a small canvas big top in Dumont, New Jersey, and Ringling Bros. and Barnum & Bailey Circus at Madison Square Garden in New York City.

As a pre-teen, having moved to Rockaway, New Jersey, I and a neighborhood friend walked to nearby Dover, New Jersey, to see Hunt Bros. Circus. As we walked back from the circus to our neighborhood, I told him that, after high school and during college, I wanted to join a circus for a summer. He said, "You can't do that." My heart sank. "If you join a circus," he continued, "you will get sawdust in your blood, and you won't be able to leave."

Another decade passed, and I was one of four prop boys for Hunt Bros. Circus.

Two months before becoming a teenager, on July 19, 1953, having moved far from Madison Square Garden and the Eastern seaboard territory of Hunt Bros. Circus, to Kankakee, Illinois, I saw a Sunday matinee-only performance of Ringling Bros. and Barnum & Bailey Circus in a sprawling

Foreword illustrations by Adriano Moraes

big top for the first, and only, time. So different from Madison Square Garden and on a gigantic scale that dwarfed the modest scale of Hunt Bros. Circus.

The following decade, I was teaching at Ringling Bros. and Barnum & Bailey Clown College in Venice, Florida, at the invitation of Bill Ballantine (Dean) and, later, at the invitation of Dick Monday (Director), at the Circus World Museum in Baraboo, Wisconsin.

In my day, Hunt Bros. Circus winter quarters were in Florence, New Jersey, and Ringling Bros. and Barnum & Bailey Circus winter quarters were in Sarasota, Florida. But originally, Barnum & Bailey winter quarters were in Bridgeport, Connecticut. Ringling Bros. Circus winter quarters were in Baraboo, Wisconsin.

One day, browsing in a bookstore, I came across a book entitled *The City of Baraboo* (1980) by Barry Longyear. "Baraboo?" Was it a circus book? Yes, it was. But it was not about the city of Baraboo, Wisconsin. It was about a traveling circus that traveled, not by horse and wagon, not by riverboat, not by railroad car, not by truck, but by spaceship. An absolutely logical extrapolation from circus history. A delightful science-fiction name for a spaceship that carries a circus from planet to planet: *The City of Baraboo*.

When I was in my mid-teens, in the summer of 1956, two circus events occurred that had a tremendous effect on me. Ringling Bros. and Barnum & Bailey Circus closed its tented season early, folded its big top forever, and, the following season, moved exclusively into outdoor and indoor permanent areas. An era had ended. To my dismay, a door had closed. At the same time, Burt Lancaster (1913-1994), a circus acrobat turned movie actor, produced and appeared in the motion picture *Trapeze* (1956), which was shot on location at the Cirque d'Hiver in Paris. Much as I loved the movie, I thought the idea of a one-ring circus in a permanent building was an outrageous example of poetic license. I could not have been more wrong. Not all circuses are American, three-ring, traveling, and under canvas. The Cirque d'Hiver had been built in 1852 as Cirque Napoléon and was briefly known as the Cirque National before finally becoming the Cirque d'Hiver. To my delight, a door had opened.

The modern circus is a worldwide phenomenon that can be traced back to three English equestrians of the late 18th century: Philip Astley, Charles Hughes and John Bill Ricketts. A former cavalryman, Astley was the first to build permanent circuses in London, Paris, and Dublin. Charles Hughes built a circus in London and was the first to bring circus to Russia. Ricketts built the first circuses in the United States and Canada. The modern circus was destined to spread throughout Europe, Asia, Africa, North America, South America, and Australia, becoming a worldwide phenomenon.

While horsemanship was at the very center, it was in combination with other elements that made circus *circus*.

First, and foremost, was the circus clown, derived from Italy's traditional, but universally popular, *Commedia dell'Arte*: "Pedrolino" (Italy), "Pierrot" (France), "Petrushka" (Russia), and "Clown" (England and the United States).

Second, were various acrobatic skills of ancient origin, such as rope-walking, tumbling, human pyramids, and juggling. Juggling can be traced back to the 11th Dynasty of Ancient Egypt. Other important acrobatic circus skills do not predate the modern circus. The flying trapeze was introduced at the present-day Cirque d'Hiver by Jules Léotard in 1859. The rola-bola was invented by a Brazilian hand-balancer in 1927.

Finally, there was the presenting of trained animals, other than, and in addition to, trained horses. Initially, there were dogs, but eventually there were also magnificent elephants, "fighting" tigers and lions, balancing sea lions, and even a motorcycle-riding polar bear. With loss of habitat, poaching, extinction, protective legislation, a disregard for animal welfare, animal rights protests, and outright legislative bans, non-human animals are rapidly vanishing from the circus scene. Another door is closing.

Because I bounced back and forth between five colleges and as many circuses, it took me about eight years to earn my undergraduate college degree. I started at the Pasadena Playhouse College of Theatre Arts as a certificate student, then Kellogg Community College in Battle Creek, Michigan, then Florida State University, where I participated in the extracurricular FSU "Flying High" Circus, then back to the Pasadena Playhouse College of Theatre Arts as a degree student, followed by special studies at New York University and Columbia University to complete the humanities component (Art History) for my degree.

Unlike today, college tuition was very inexpensive in the 1960s, but travel to Europe was not. Now, in my mid-twenties, I qualified for a seven-week Columbia University student charter flight to and from London, birthplace of the modern circus. From London, I made my way to Paris, where I was able see two historic circus buildings: Cirque d'Hiver and Cirque Medrano. I bought five heavy rubber dog balls and three small Indian clubs and did quite well busking as a juggler in the streets of Paris. I was traveling very light, with a single small suitcase. But in it was a veritable treasure: a pulp paperback of *The Circus of Dr. Lao*.

The Circus of Dr. Lao by Charles G. Finney had been published in 1935, five years before I was born, but I had known nothing of it previously. This was a Bantam Fifty 50¢ F2755 Science Fiction published April 1964, just one year before my sojourn to Europe. Dr. Lao is Chinese, presenting his circus of mostly ancient mythological creatures, to a bewildered American desert town in the Southwest. Charles G. Finney (1905-1984) became a newspaper editor in Tucson, Arizona after serving in the U.S. Army and having been stationed in Tientsin, China from 1927 to 1929. Literary critics have suggested that there is an influence here on Ray Bradbury (1920-2012) and *Something Wicked This Way Comes* (1962).

Returning from Europe, I had a clerical job at Brander Matthews Dramatic Museum in Low Library at Columbia University. There, I met Carlo Mazzone-Clementi (1920-2000) an Italian from Padua and expert on the *Commedia dell'Arte*, who got me an interview resulting in an opportunity to teach circus techniques to acting students at New York University's new School of the Arts. Although I was not on tenure track and never tenured, I taught there for over fifty years and for exactly one hundred semesters (1966-2017).

A year after I began teaching at NYU by day, I auditioned for, and got, a job at The Electric Circus, performing by night. It was an environmental sound and light discotheque with live bands, calculated to simulate a psychedelic trip. As a live performer, I did not perform on a stage. It was more intimate than that. Somewhat like busking in the streets of Paris. I performed right in the middle of a, sometimes crowded, dance floor. Whether I was juggling Indian clubs on a unicycle or juggling apples on stilts dressed as a chef, I was dependent on the follow-spot operator to help me "create" a performance space in the crowd. It was only when I juggled flaming torches that the audience gladly backed off to give me space.

Eventually, I would use elements of *Commedia dell'Arte*, busking in the streets of Paris, and performing at The Electric Circus, to create a Circo dell'Arte group that performed in New York's Central Park. This would eventually inspire and contribute substantially to the creation of The Pickle Family Circus in San Francisco, The Big Apple Circus in New York, and Circus Flora in St. Louis.

The aforementioned Barry Longyear's *The City of Baraboo* (1980) was actually the first of a science-fiction circus trilogy consisting also of *Elephant Serenade* (1981) and *Circus World* (1981). Likewise, Charles G. Finney's *The Circus of Dr. Lao* (1935) is an amazing circus fantasy. But, such works, in my experience, have been few and far between. I have no doubt that the anthology you have before you, edited by Mary Fan, and to which she has also contributed, is one of the largest collections of circus fiction ever to be published.

–HOVEY BURGESS

HUMMINGBIRD

DOROTHY DREYER

Exhilaration charged through her blood.

Leonie stood perched upon the top of her chest of drawers, her eyes trained on the mattress she'd dragged to her floor. She didn't even need the mattress, she thought. She'd jumped from trees higher than the dresser and had landed perfectly—gracefully—every time. She'd always been agile, her balance impeccable, and her aim on point. It was a blessing as well as a curse, for princesses were supposed to be proper and not engage in dangerous stunts such as this.

The mattress wasn't there to keep her from hurting herself, however. It was to muffle the sound of her landing. If her father were to catch her in such a reckless position, he'd have her head. Not literally. Though, being the king, he had the means and the men to carry out such a beheading.

Leonie scrunched up her eyes and stretched her arms out. The moment she leapt from the dresser, her chamber door opened. Leonie flipped once in the air, heels over head, before her feet planted firmly on the mattress—or as firmly as one could on such a malleable surface.

"My stars, Your Highness!" Beatrice, her handmaid, scrambled to shut the door behind her before rushing to the princess's side.

Illustration by Adriano Moraes

Leonie, feeling the high from the jump, giggled and performed an elegant cartwheel off the mattress. She faced Beatrice, half expecting her to applaud.

"No disrespect, Your Highness, but you'll be the death of me yet. Just think what such a sight might do to your father." Beatrice rounded Leonie, rushing through the routine of removing her nightgown and readying her for the morning meal with her parents.

"That was nothing," Leonie said with a sigh. "I've done double flips from high trees and triple twirls from swinging ropes into the river."

"Dear child, do not scare me with such images. The river? Your father's heart would stop on the spot."

"Which is why he will never hear of it."

Beatrice tightened Leonie's bodice. "Yes, ma'am, Your Highness. I just don't understand why anyone would go to such trouble to toss their bodies about like that."

Leonie sucked in a breath as Beatrice yanked on her bodice laces. "Because it makes me feel alive. And what's the use of being in this world if one cannot feel alive while living it?"

"You've talked me in circles, Your Highness. And you're late for your morning meal. The king and queen will start to worry."

"I suppose they're already upset with me as it is." Leonie sat at her vanity as Beatrice tended to her hair. "They believed Prince Henrick would be a perfect match, but he was too controlling. He wanted to stamp out my fire, and I couldn't have that."

"He was quite handsome, though," Beatrice said as she ran the brush through Leonie's dark tresses.

"I suppose so, but don't you think there's more to a lifelong commitment than staring at a handsome face?"

Especially the handsome face of someone who wouldn't let Leonie be herself. While he might have seemed charming and attractive on the surface, his true nature was much darker. Henrik was condescending and manipulative, with a strong desire to mold Leonie into the perfect princess, one that fit his own narrow definition of what was proper.

As they had begun their courtship weeks ago, Prince Henrick would often criticize Leonie for her love of acrobatics and other activities that he deemed unsuitable for a princess. He believed that her place was in the castle, not out in the world, and that she should be focused solely on her duties as a future queen.

Henrik was also jealous and possessive, not wanting Leonie to have any close relationships outside of their own. He would become angry if she spent time with her friends or family without him and would often try to control who she could see and where she could go.

Their courtship was, therefore, short lived. Despite her father's wishes, Leonie had refused to marry Henrik, knowing that he would never truly accept her for who she was. She was determined to live her life on her own terms, even if it meant defying tradition and breaking away from the path that had been laid out for her.

But her decision had caused strife between the kingdoms. Though her father claimed he supported her choice, Leonie couldn't help but feel she'd disappointed him.

Finally ready to leave her chambers, Leonie strode out into the hall. Her royal guard bowed to her as she emerged, walking beside her as she made her way to the meet her parents.

"Good morrow, Your Highness."

"Good morrow, Sir Isaac." Leonie wasn't quite sure if her cheeks were simply flushed from her acrobatic practice or if casting a glance at the young guard had caused the surge of blood.

He walked with purpose, each step he took full of confidence. His dark blond hair was pushed back from his face, and the morning sun danced in his deep green eyes. She noticed a smudge on the breastplate of his armor and had to restrain herself from touching it.

"How's my father's mood?" Leonie asked him in an attempt to alter her train of thought.

Slender sconces which half encompassed the basalt columns lit the hall, shrouding it in a dark orange radiance. The tapestries depicting the kingdom hanging along the stone walls danced in the flickering light as the princess and her guard continued on their way to the dining hall.

"His mood is indecipherable. I think one of the things people fear of King Gerald is his unpredictability."

"Some may call that stoicism. Others call it indifference." Leonie sighed. "I think he's still trying to decide whether to forgive me or not."

"Your Highness, you are his only daughter. He'd move mountains for you if he could. Anyone in the kingdom would. And since his aim is always to please you, he took your decision for what it was. There is nothing to forgive."

She stopped just as they approached the dining hall doors. "Anyone in the kingdom? Including you?"

A crease formed between his brows. "Pardon, Your Highness?"

"You would move mountains for me? If you could?"

Her breath hitched as his eyes searched her face.

"With certainty, Your Highness."

Before she could say more, Sir Isaac reached for the handle and pushed open the large oak door.

Leonie, momentarily unable to find her breath, nodded to him once before turning toward the room.

The dining hall was a grand space with high ceilings and ornate decor. Large windows let in the morning light. A crystal chandelier hung from the ceiling, positioned directly over the long, wooden table. Carved into the stone columns, gargoyles looked down upon the marble floor.

It wasn't the first time Leonie had been late for the morning meal, but her father gave her a disapproving look, nonetheless.

"Good morrow, Leonie," he said sternly.

King Gerald III was a tall and imposing figure, with broad shoulders and a commanding presence. His sharp features were defined by a strong jawline and high cheekbones, and his piercing blue eyes seemed to penetrate one's soul. He wore his dark hair swept back from his forehead, with a few strands falling loosely over his ears. His doublet of deep crimson was embroidered with gold thread, and a gold chain hung around his neck. He lifted his goblet, and the ruby on his ring gleamed.

"Good morrow, Father," Leonie replied, taking her seat at the table. "Good morrow, Mother."

Leonie was the spitting image of her mother. They each had long, dark hair that cascaded in waves past their shoulders and deep hazel eyes. Unlike King Gerald, Queen Elana did show her emotions. She smiled at her daughter, her love for her evident on her smooth features.

The breakfast table could accommodate twenty people with its ample length. Made of the most luxurious polished wood with intricately carved legs, it was set with fine stone plates and silverware, and crystal glasses that sparkled in the morning sun. A vase of fresh flowers sat in the center of the table, adding a touch of color and fragrance to the room. The chairs were plush and comfortable, with embroidered cushions that matched the tapestries on the walls. A large platter sat between Leonie's place and her mother's, overflowing with fresh fruit. The smell of newly brewed umber and warm bread filled the air, making Leonie's mouth water.

"I hope your studies are going well." Her father stroked a hand down his beard.

Leonie wasn't fooled by his attempt at small talk. She knew he was working his way up to discussing something more serious. Despite his stern demeanor, there was a warmth to his expression as he looked at his daughter. His posture was straight and proud, befitting of a king, but he leaned forward slightly as he spoke to her, showing a hint of concern.

"They're fine," Leonie said with a shrug. "I've been busy practicing for my upcoming exams." She played along, bracing herself for whatever it was he was about to say.

"That's good to hear. Good to hear." The king glanced at his wife and cleared his throat.

Leonie smeared jam on her bread and took a bite, watching her mother. It was obviously her turn to speak, judging by her father's expression.

"My dear," Queen Elana began. "Your father and I were just wondering if you might have had time to reconsider your decision to not wed Prince Henrick, now that you've had a chance to have a good sleep to help your thoughts."

Leonie set down her bread, taking a big swallow. "If it is your wish that I marry him, for the sake of the kingdom, for the sake of peace, I will do as you say. I do not wish to cause a war, and I do not mean to be selfish. I just wish I didn't have to sacrifice my happiness in order to pacify everyone else."

King Gerald and Queen Elana exchanged a look.

"Your happiness is important, Leonie." Her father shifted in his chair. "I support your decision. Your mother and I both do. And House Gloster will simply have to live with it."

She found it hard to believe, but she mustered up a smile for them. "Thank you."

"The Gloster Kingdom was at a crossroads, it seems. They need to choose allies to strengthen their army's efforts, and this marriage would have been a way to unite our houses. They could still be our allies, if they choose, but without a marriage to seal the deal, I'm unsure we will remain in their favor. That said, there seems to be some consequence we must be aware of."

Leonie blinked at her father. "Consequence?"

"Yes. Though there has been no formal declaration, rumor has it House Gloster may be siding with our enemy and plotting a strike against us."

"What kind of strike?" Leonie asked.

"I can't say I would know," the king answered. "But I do not wish to take any chances and risk your safety. I think it best—just until I know it's safe—that you remain within the castle grounds."

"But, Father!"

"Leonie, this is a matter of your welfare. Besides, where else must you need to be?"

"The cir—" Leonie cut herself off, not wanting her parents to know the truth. "Lady Seline's, I meant to say. Today is her name day. She's invited our small group to celebrate."

"I thought her name day was last month," Queen Elana stated.

"No," Leonie lied. "That was Felicity's. Please, I've been looking forward to it all week."

"Nevertheless, I do not condone it." Her father finished off his brewed umber and set down his cup. "I don't want you to attend any gatherings or events until we know more."

Leonie felt as if her heart had been pierced. She had been so excited to attend the circus, but now, it seemed her plans were ruined. "But Father, I'm sure it's safe," she protested.

"I'm sorry, Leonie, but my decision stands," her father said, his tone final.

Leonie sulked in her seat. Unable tell her father the truth, she simply muttered under her breath, "Fine."

Despite her father's suspicions, Leonie was unwilling to give up her plans for the evening. The circus was counting on her.

With Sir Isaac escorting her, Leonie made her way through the winding back streets of Cenios Village, avoiding the main roads to remain inconspicuous. Leonie's hood was pulled low over her face, casting her features in shadow, while Sir Isaac wore a cloak with a hood of his own.

As they approached the circus tent, they could hear the lively music and raucous laughter of the crowd inside. The tent was brightly colored, with red and yellow stripes swirling around its exterior. Sir Isaac led the princess to the rear of the tent, where the performers entered.

"I'll wait out here," he told her.

"Don't you want to see the show?"

"I think it best to guard the place. You heard what your father said about the Gloster Kingdom. If one of their spies were to come here—"

"Sir Isaac, no one knows I'm here. No one but you knows what I do here. I highly doubt House Gloster will think to come to the circus to find me."

He hesitated before he nodded. "Be careful."

Leonie flashed him a smile beneath her hood, and then turned to go backstage.

Inside, the tent was packed with people of all ages, seated on benches that circled the central ring. The air was filled with the smell of hay, sweat, and popcorn, and the performers were already warming up for their acts. The hairs on Leonie's skin stood on end with excitement as she took in the sights and sounds.

"Hummingbird," the main stagehand called to her. "Thought you'd never show up."

Leonie dropped her hood to reveal a wig of dark blue. Most of her face was disguised by an eye mask of silver glitter. She removed her robe to reveal her tight-fitting, blue-and-silver bodysuit. "Sorry I'm late. Had some trouble getting here."

The truth was, she'd had trouble sneaking out of the castle. If it had not been for Sir Isaac and Beatrice, she would have been stuck in her chambers all night.

As she passed a mirror, she checked her outfit. She smirked to herself. No one would know it was a princess in this garb. No one had any idea that Leonie had been practicing with the circus for months under the guise of a peasant girl with the stage name "Hummingbird." Even if her father was right, even if House Gloster had sent out assassins to attack, it would be highly unlikely that they would suspect she'd be performing in a circus, of all places.

Leonie peeked out into the center ring, where the strongman was exhibiting his strength, lifting heavy barrels attached to a metal bar. She knew him as Addam, who was a kind and gentle soul. But he'd never let the audience know that.

When she swung around to stretch before her performance, Leonie ran into Blaze, the fire eater. With flaming red hair appropriate for her act, Blaze gave Leonie a small smile.

Leonie adjusted her mask, feeling something was off. "Hello, Blaze. How are you?"

"I'm well, though a little disappointed with my act tonight."

"What happened?"

"I don't think I was concentrating enough. I nearly singed my hair."

Leonie frowned. "I'm glad to see you were unharmed. I'm sure the audience loved you, nonetheless. They always do."

"Thank you, Hummingbird. Your words do me good." With a more genuine smile, Blaze left her to change into a different costume.

The sound of applause caught her attention, and Leonie turned to see the strongman heading her way, having finished his performance. Addam's features turned softer when he spotted her.

"Hummingbird! You made it."

"Yes. Just in time to see the end of your act. Impressive, as always."

"You're too kind." He placed a strong but gentle hand on her shoulder as he continued farther backstage.

"Hey, you ready?"

She turned to see her counterpart. His name was Carl, but under the big top he was known as Hawk. She and Carl had spent hours together perfecting their act.

"Yes," she answered. "All set and ready to fly."

"You remember the order?" His accent made the Rs roll.

She tapped the side of her head. "Memorized backward and forward."

He smirked. "Don't mix those up."

She let out a small laugh and gave him a nod before turning toward her ladder. Leonie chalked up her hands and blew out a long breath before checking to make sure her blue wig was secure. If it were to fall off during her performance, her true identity could be exposed.

The ringmaster's voice blared through the tent as Leonie approached the ladder leading to the trapeze. Her blood buzzed with the thrill of the moment.

"And now, performing a death-defying act on the flying trapeze, high above our heads, the infamous Hummingbird and Hawk!"

Music played, and the crowd applauded, whooping and hollering for her as she climbed the rungs. The higher she got, the wider her smile became. One spotlight followed her while the other was trained on Carl, who was standing on the opposite platform. As Leonie reached the top of her platform, a drumroll sounded, and the audience held their breaths. All eyes were on her. She lifted her hands in the air, engulfed in their wonder. She turned toward the trapeze bar and wrapped her heavily chalked hands around it.

Carl took his bow, accepting the audience's applause, and then he gave Leonie the signal. Taking a deep breath, she launched herself into the air and swooped downward on the fly bar. Carl swung toward her at the same time. On the upswing, she did a half turn in the air. When she swung back to the platform, she brought her legs up and hooked one leg around the bar. Keeping her other leg straight, she leaned back, being sure to keep an eye on Carl. As the two of them swung toward each other again, Leonie let go of the fly bar and caught the stick Carl held out. She then unhooked her leg and swung down.

The crowd applauded, but the duo was not done yet.

Leonie bent her body so that she was ready to spring from the bar on the next upswing. Her heart raced as she watched the bar come closer, and at the right moment, she released the catch bar and propelled herself toward her fly bar. She caught the bar and swung back to her platform, landing perfectly.

"Can you believe it?!" the ringmaster shouted into his megaphone. The audience went wild.

Looking over at Carl, she imitated him, arms in the air. They bowed at the same time.

Hummingbird and Hawk performed three more stunts, the crowd watching their graceful and seemingly effortless maneuvers, before the show moved on to the next act.

As a man on high stilts juggled his way into the ring, Leonie descended the ladder, her skin glistening with sweat and her body buzzing with adrenaline. This was living. This was feeling alive. Her passion helped her escape from the pressures of her royal life. As Hummingbird, Princess Leonie was free to be whoever she wanted to be.

Leonie grasped Sir Isaac's arm. "Oh, I've missed this so much," she said. "Swinging through the air, the applause, the lion tamer, the clowns, the sheer thrill of it all."

Now in a simple dress, Leonie kept her cloak fastened with the hood low. Her costume, wig, and mask had been stuffed in a canvas satchel, which Sir Isaac had slung over his shoulder. They were almost back at the castle, and although Sir Isaac kept his serious demeanor, Leonie swore the corner of his mouth lifted slightly into a small smile.

"Yes, Your Highness. I see how it thrills you. But you mustn't forget, we need to be careful. There are enemies out there who would stop at nothing to get their revenge on you."

"It's a good thing I've got you at my side, then. The question is whether you'll be able to sneak me back into my chambers without my father finding out."

"I'll see to it. You have my word."

Leonie smiled, enjoying the feel of Sir Isaac's strong arm. She remembered when he'd first caught her sneaking out to the circus. He was determined to stop her, to talk her out of it. But she won him over eventually. When he'd seen her in her Hummingbird disguise, his jaw had dropped before he'd regained his composure. A blush rushed into her cheeks at the thought of his expression. Her outfit was quite snug, and she was sure he hadn't expected to see all of her curves in such detail.

Sir Isaac pulled open the hidden door that led to the secret passage to the princess's chambers. The tunnel was dark, and Leonie took the opportunity to squeeze closer to her guard. He had a musky smell that she'd grown fond of, and it took everything in her power not to lean her nose against his bicep to draw in more of the scent.

When they reached the secret panel that opened into her room, Sir Isaac checked first to make sure it was clear.

"You see," she said as she slipped into the room. "We made it, safe and sound. Don't we make a fine team?"

Sir Isaac needed to enter the chambers to cross over to the main door. It would take too long to go back through the passage and around to the castle gates. The sconces were lit and cast a soft glow on his features as he walked quietly through her room. Leonie was still riding a high from her performance, and though she knew it was not proper, she wished Sir Isaac could stay and keep her company.

"Goodnight, Princess." Sir Isaac locked gazes with her as he opened the door and crept into the hall.

"Goodnight, Sir Isaac. And thank you." Her voice was soft.

As the door closed, she whirled around, holding her hands to her chest. It had been a perfect night. She simply needed to keep her activities hidden from her parents.

Leonie woke with a start.

"Begging your pardon, Your Highness, but your father beckons." Beatrice pulled back the curtains of Leonie's room, revealing the morning sun.

"Am I late again?" Leonie stretched as she sat upright. "I was simply exhausted last night, and I'm afraid it put me in a very deep sleep."

"No, Your Highness. You're not late. But there's urgent news, and His Royal Highness has insisted you join him in the great chamber."

Panic rose in Leonie's throat like acid. *Oh no, he's found out I left the castle last night. He'll act out in anger and restrict me even more.*

Beatrice grabbed the princess's chamber robe and held it open for her.

"Shouldn't I dress first?" Leonie wanted to delay her meeting with her father. She'd rather go through all the motions of her morning routine, slowly, simply to stretch out the time before she needed to face him.

"Your father insisted you see him straight away."

Leonie didn't answer. She slipped on the robe and pulled it tight around her. Pushing her hair behind her ears, she crossed to her door. She supposed there was no avoiding the confrontation.

Sir Isaac waited for her in the hall. He gave her a solitary nod before continuing with her toward the grand chamber. Leonie's throat was too dry to make any comment. A million thoughts rushed through her head. If Sir Isaac had an inkling of what this meeting was about, he didn't give her any clues.

They've found out. And poor Sir Isaac will surely be sacked. Or worse!

When she entered the grand chamber, King Gerald was pacing. His forehead was scrunched, and his brows drawn low. Leonie's mother stood nearby, wringing her hands. Leonie swallowed hard, her heart pounding. Sir Isaac stood sentry by the door, overlooking the room.

"Good morrow, Father, Mother." Leonie clasped her hands together in front of her.

"Leonie, my dear." King Gerald took big strides as he crossed the room to her. He placed his large hands on her shoulders, his expression severe.

"Y-Yes?" *This is it. My life as Hummingbird is over. I shall never feel free again.*

"There's been a development. Late last night, an assassin from House Gloster was captured outside the castle gates. He carried daggers and a vial of poison."

Leonie couldn't move. This was not the news she'd expected.

"He's been secured in the dungeon, so do not fret. But my advisor warns me this may not be the last we encounter from the Gloster Kingdom."

"But... What was his intention?" Leonie wrapped her arms around her waist.

"He's being interrogated as we speak." The king glanced at his wife for a moment. "But we know you were the target."

"Is that what he said?"

"I believe the exact wording from that sack of dung was, 'If Prince Henrick can't have her, no one will.'"

Leonie couldn't feel any stability in her knees. As she wavered, Sir Isaac rushed over to ensure she wouldn't fall. As she righted herself, her mind rushed with thoughts. *Had he been there when I was outside the castle? What if he had seen me? What if he had bested Sir Isaac and kidnapped me, and I was never to see my parents again? What if he had ended my life on sight?*

"It's a good thing you were safe in your chambers," Queen Elana stated, coming over to hold Leonie's hand. "Imagine if you had gone to your friend's name day celebration and he'd found you."

"Yes," King Gerald agreed. "That would have been catastrophic. You should never doubt my wisdom."

Leonie blinked, nodding to appease him. "What happens now?"

"With the assailant?" her father asked.

"No. I mean, what happens politically? Was this an attack on the kingdom? Is it cause for war?"

King Gerald sighed. "For all we know, this cut-throat could have been acting of his own accord. Or perhaps the young prince sent him on a personal mission. An inquiry will be sent to House Gloster, but until their response, we cannot act on the basis of one man's actions."

"Until we know more," her mother added, "you *must* remain on the castle grounds. Better yet, please do not leave the castle itself."

"I'll see to it that more guards are assigned to you." The king gestured to the commander of the kingsguard. "We can't take any chances."

Leonie pulled a dress over her Hummingbird costume. She was expected at the show that evening. Hawk and the others were counting on her. Despite her father's warning, despite his demand that she remain in the castle, she had to get to the circus. Her audience would be waiting. And she couldn't very well tell the circus crew that she couldn't attend because her life had been threatened. None of them knew she was the princess.

Aside from that, she refused to allow anyone to take away something she cherished. Rejecting Henrik was her way of breaking free from a life she had no desire to live, and she wouldn't permit him to restrict her to the castle out of fear.

Besides, in her disguise, the enemy would never find her. They'd never imagine the princess would be swinging from a suspended bar and flipping through the air. They'd expect her to be sitting in her chambers or having tea in the grand parlor with the ladies of the court.

The trick would be convincing Sir Isaac.

Leonie paced back and forth in her room, a sense of restlessness taking hold of her. But she couldn't wait any longer. She cracked her door open slightly and took in the sight of Sir Isaac. There were three more guards standing sentry in the hall. The gears were turning in her mind as she tried to decide what to say.

"Sir Isaac." Leonie straightened her back, forcing herself to appear confident. "May I have a word with you in my chambers?"

Sir Isaac looked between her and the other guards. It was quite unorthodox for one of them to be alone in her room, but it was also a request of the princess, and he couldn't very well turn her down.

Once he stepped into her room, she shut the door and faced him. "I need your help."

Sir Isaac raised an eyebrow. "Your Highness?"

"I need to get back to the circus. I have to perform tonight," Leonie said, her voice beseeching. "Please, Sir Isaac, I need you to help me sneak out of the castle."

Sir Isaac frowned. "Your Highness, with all due respect, it's not safe for you to go out."

"Are you disobeying an order?"

Sir Isaac took a deep breath and let it out slowly. "I have to insist that it would be unwise for you to leave the castle."

"But I have to, Sir Isaac," Leonie insisted. "The circus is my life. You know that. And besides, I will be in disguise. No one will know it's me. No one ever suspects that it is me. The only risk is leaving the castle and returning undetected."

"Your safety is my top priority, Your Highness," Sir Isaac replied firmly. "I cannot allow you to take unnecessary risks."

Leonie sighed, knowing that Sir Isaac was only looking out for her best interests. "I understand that, Sir Isaac. But you know me. You know how important this is to me."

Sir Isaac's expression softened. "I do know you, Your Highness. And I know how much the circus means to you. But please, don't make me choose between my duty and your wishes."

Leonie hesitated, then reached out to take Sir Isaac's hand. "I'm not asking you to choose, Sir Isaac. I'm asking you to help me do what I need to do. We can make sure I'm safe. We can take precautions."

Sir Isaac looked down at their joined hands. When his gaze came back up to Leonie's eyes, there was a warmth in them she didn't expect to see.

"Very well, Your Highness," he said. "I will escort you back to the circus. But if I sense even the slightest danger, we are returning immediately."

Leonie's smile was small but sincere. "Thank you, Sir Isaac. I knew I could count on you."

To her surprise, Sir Isaac gave her hand a gentle squeeze before releasing it. "Of course, Your Highness. My loyalty is to you, after all."

Sir Isaac and the princess crept through the darkened streets, moving quickly and quietly to avoid detection. The princess had wrapped herself in her heavy cloak, but her heart was pounding with both excitement and fear. They were so close to the circus now, but she couldn't shake the feeling that they were being watched.

A snap sounded behind them, and the princess whirled around, her hands clasping her cloak tighter around her. Sir Isaac stepped in front of her, his hand on his sword hilt, scanning the shadows for any sign of danger. They waited, holding their breath, but the only sound was the rustling of leaves in the wind. Sir Isaac relaxed his grip on his sword, but Leonie still held her breath.

"Maybe we should go back," Sir Isaac whispered. "It's not worth the risk."

Leonie finally sucked in a breath of air and shook her head. "No. I must perform tonight. I won't let enemies scare me into hiding away and not living my life."

Sir Isaac hesitated, and then took her hand. "Very well."

Leonie kept a firm hold of his hand. Her stomach did little acrobatic acts of their own feeling his fingers on her skin. With Sir Isaac's nod, they continued on their way in silence.

The circus tent loomed ahead, its colorful banners flapping in the night breeze. As they approached, the princess's heart skipped a beat. She wasn't sure if it was the anxiety of knowing there might be someone out to get her or her anticipation to take to the trapeze, but either way, the rush of adrenaline coursed in her veins.

"I'll be at the front access," Sir Isaac said as he escorted her to the back of the tent. "I'll keep a careful eye out."

She wanted to hug him, but it wouldn't be proper. "Thank you, Sir Isaac."

She slipped into the tent and readied herself for her performance. Backstage was buzzing with activity. Leonie was sure it had always been this way, but being on edge made her acutely aware of everything everyone was doing. It overwhelmed her to the point of making her dizzy.

No. I need to concentrate. Once false move and I'll fall.

Though there was always a safety net below them when they practiced, it was lowered considerably when they performed to make the act more impressive to the audience. It was awfully close to the ground, and Leonie was certain her body would still feel the impact if she were to miss the catch bar or slip from the trapeze.

The time had come. Hummingbird and Hawk were announced, and Leonie stood on the platform high above the circus ring. She raised her arms to present herself to the onlookers, her heart racing as she waited for her cue. Down below, the crowd murmured in anticipation.

The music began. Leonie held the fly bar and sprang into the air, flying toward Carl, who hung upside down from his trapeze bar. They met mid-air, and Leonie released her bar. Hummingbird and Hawk clasped their hands tightly as they swung together. The crowd gasped in amazement as the duo spun and twisted through the air, their bodies perfectly in sync. Carl released Leonie's hands at the perfect time, and she did a flip before grasping onto her trapeze bar.

As Leonie completed her final flip and then arched hard to swing and land gracefully on her platform, a wave of exhilaration washed over her. She felt a rush of adrenaline and a sense of accomplishment; that itself was a reward for executing a challenging and awe-inspiring routine. Her heart continued to pound in her chest, and blood rushed through her veins. Her muscles buzzed with the effort of the performance, and she was acutely aware of a satisfying ache in her limbs. A sense of peace and fulfillment engulfed her. Looking out over the crowd, she spotted Sir Isaac at the entrance, his eyes locked on her. Taking a deep breath, she smiled at him.

But her smile faded as two dark figures emerged behind him.

Panic bubbled in her throat. She wanted to shout out to him, but the music and the audience were too loud. Since his gaze was on her, however, he could see the fear on her face. He stiffened, checking behind him.

Sir Isaac immediately drew his sword from its scabbard as the two attackers stepped closer. The music stopped, and the crowd's clapping ended.

"House Gloster demands its promised princess. Where is she?" The taller of the men pulled out two long daggers, holding them out at his sides, ready to utilize them. "We followed you here. We know she's with you."

Sir Isaac didn't answer. He held his ground as the two men, now both wielding daggers, slowly circled him.

"Where's the princess, pretty boy?" the shorter man asked, sneering.

Leonie couldn't control her breaths. She wasn't sure how, but she needed to help Sir Isaac. Clambering down the ladder, she prayed in her head that he wouldn't be harmed. Her panic caused her to rush, and her foot slipped from the rung. She let out a yelp, her knuckles turning white as she held onto the ladder with her hands alone.

Sir Isaac must have noticed. "Your Highness!"

The crowd gasped. The circus performers and the cut-throats from House Gloster followed his gaze. The looks on her assailants' faces told her she'd been discovered. Leonie struggled to get her feet back on the rungs.

Sir Isaac shifted his position so he stood between the Gloster assassins and the path that led to the princess. The first man lunged forward, his dagger flashing through the air. Sir Isaac deftly parried the blow with his sword and countered with a swift thrust. But the man was quick and agile, dodging his counterattack. The second man came at him from the side, and Sir Isaac spun to defend himself.

Leonie finished her descent as she watched, her heart pounding in her chest. As she reached the ground, a hand clamped around her arm, causing her to jump.

"Princess?"

Leonie turned to see Carl. He searched her face, certainly wondering if it was true. Her blue wig had loosened on one side, and she pushed it off her head as she nodded, her heart still racing.

The other circus performers gathered around her, realization dawning on their faces.

"It's true," Blaze said. "She's the princess!"

"The enemy is at hand!" Addam, the strongman, shouted. "Protect the princess at all costs!"

At the sound of Sir Isaac grunting, Leonie focused her attention on the fight that was still underway between him and the offenders. Her eyes widened when the performer on stilts made his way toward the skirmish, stepping in front of the shorter man with his stilt and effectively separating him from his partner. The man tried to go around the stilts, but he was faced with a flash of fire, breathed at him by Blaze. He turned on his heel and ran in the opposite direction, but stopped short when he came face-to-face with the circus lion. Backing up, he attempted his escape. A sharp *whoosh* sounded, and the shorter man reached for his chest. It bloomed with red liquid. Leonie turned her head to see the knife thrower, Marcel, standing from where the weapon had originated. Marcel raised his jaw, satisfied with his aim. The Gloster assassin stumbled backward, blood welling from his wound. He twitched for a moment and then lay motionless on the ground.

Sir Isaac parried with the taller of the culprits, but he proved to be a worthy adversary, his advantage his swift footwork. As their battle took them deeper into the center ring, the Gloster man quickly picked up the juggling clubs that lay on the ground, throwing them hard at Sir Isaac. One of the clubs hit Sir Isaac in the head, knocking him down.

The assassin didn't hesitate. He whirled around and charged toward the princess. The clowns tried to confuse him with chaos, but he swiped at them, slashing one of them across the face. Eyes wide, Leonie backed up until she hit the ladder. He was getting closer. She turned and climbed the ladder, faster than she'd ever done before. Looking down, she could see he was still after her and would reach her in a matter of seconds.

Leonie grabbed the trapeze bar and leapt from the platform, but there was no one to catch her and help her across. Hawk was still on the ground with the others. Her breath stuck in her throat as she realized the swing would propel her back to her waiting assailant.

Thinking quickly, Leonie flipped around, her feet aimed at the man. His scowl changed to a dropped jaw as he understood what was about to happen. Leonie screamed as her feet rammed into the man's chest, thrusting backward off the platform.

He wailed as he fell and then hit the ground with a thump. Though he groaned and moved with less precision, he managed to get to his feet, daggers still clutched in his hands. Sir Isaac rushed to him. The man swiped at him, dazed and staggering. With a swift move, Sir Isaac disarmed the man and knocked him back to the ground. The man lay there, gasping for breath, as Sir Isaac stood with his sword at the ready.

Leonie quickly made her way down the ladder, her head spinning from the harrowing events.

Addam marched over and hovered over the man. "You have failed your quest." The strongman grabbed the cut-throat by his arms and lifted him.

Carl then fastened the man in thick rope to keep him bound.

"Send your kingsguard," Carl said to Sir Isaac. "We'll keep him entwined until they arrive."

Sir Isaac nodded to Carl before turning to Leonie, his face grim.

"We need to leave, Princess." He sheathed his sword and extended a hand to her. "I must get you to safety, in case there are more."

She took his hand, closing the distance between them. Knowing he would protect her at all costs, Leonie melted into his arms.

A week later, King Gerald III and Queen Elana sat in prominent seats in the front row of the circus. They had a clear view of the ring. The ringmaster appeared and bowed to them.

"Your Royal Highnesses, it is my honor to have you as special guests tonight. We are all excited to perform for you. It is with great pride that I present to you our very first act of the evening, performing graceful yet daring acts of flight, Hummingbird and Hawk!"

The crowd cheered as Leonie raised her arms, smiling at the crowd. She wore her blue wig, but her mask was not on. There was no need to disguise herself anymore.

The music swelled, and the crowd grew quiet. The two performers jumped into their synchronized routine, swinging back and forth on their trapezes. They gracefully flipped and spun in the air, passing each other mid-air and catching the other's trapeze bars with their outstretched arms. Leonie swore she heard her mother gasp.

By the time they finished their routine, Leonie was glistening in sweat. She and Carl took their bows, the sound of applause filling the tent. Leonie descended her ladder to find Sir Isaac standing guard. He reached out his hand to help her off the final rungs.

"Brilliant as always, Your Highness."

Leonie blushed. "Thank you, Sir Isaac."

He escorted her backstage, and soon the king and queen appeared. They found Leonie, still in her Hummingbird costume, surrounded by her circus family. She was flushed and exhilarated from her performance, but her smile widened when she saw her parents.

"Father, Mother," she said, bowing. "I hope you enjoyed the show."

King Gerald was the first to speak. "Leonie, you were magnificent. Though I have to admit it frightens me to see you fly through the air like that, I do understand the beauty of it. I did always have dreams of flying when I was a child."

"It looks incredibly dangerous," her mother added. "But I can also see the joy in your face."

"I hope you can understand what it means to me to be able to perform. And the people here, they are like extended family to me. They all helped protect me the night of the attack."

"I'm aware," her father said. "And they won't go unrewarded." He turned to the performers and crew. "We owe you a debt of gratitude for your assistance in thwarting the assault against my daughter. I've spoken with my master of coin, and a generous donation will be granted to the circus so that it may go on for many a year."

The performers gasped and voiced their gratitude as they bowed to the king and queen.

The king then turned to his wife. "Let us go, Elana, and enjoy the rest of the show."

"We are proud of you, my dear. You are truly gifted." Leonie's mother came forward and placed a kiss on each of Leonie's cheeks before she turned to join the king.

As they left the backstage area, Leonie let out a sigh. She could never imagine that it would have come to this, being able to live out her passion with her parents' approval. She turned to go change and found Sir Isaac waiting for her. His gaze was tender, and heat rose in her cheeks. Something told her that being a circus-performing princess was not the only departure she would make from the conventions of traditional royalty.

2023

RUNAWAY RENEGADE

JANINA FRANCK

A discordant melody disturbed the calm of the forest. Hauntingly jolly, with just enough dissonance in its sound to create a stark contrast to the gentle breeze, making the luscious greens of the trees sway gently and letting the warm spring light dance with shadows along the ground.

Caleb was deaf and blind to it all—each of his crunching, energetic, and hurried steps covering the faint tune, his mind much too occupied with thundering thoughts, and his eyes glaring steadfastly at the path as though he blamed the dirt and gravel personally for everything happening to him.

He wouldn't go back. He couldn't!

That world didn't want him, so he didn't want *it!*

With an absentee mother and a father who had neither time nor mind for him, bullies at school, no money, and living as a permanent scapegoat who was met with nothing but demands by the people in his life, Caleb had finally blown up. Quietly. Internally. But nevertheless, he'd finally hit the resolve to run away, to grab his things and walk out of the apartment, with every intention of leaving and never looking back. He was sixteen; he could make it somehow. No one would come to look for him anyhow, and even if they did, there was his fake ID proclaiming him to be nineteen and giving him a different last name. The picture was old—it had been taken last year, before he'd cut his dark hair short, but his brown eyes still looked back with the same intensity as they did now. He now had a little more muscle too, and his growth spurt was tapering out after bringing him to six feet. Despite all of that, it still ought to work. People never looked that closely.

All he had to do was get far enough away. He didn't want to risk someone seeing him get on a bus to leave in Laragh—so he needed to at least go as far as Rathdrum first. And the best way to get there without being seen was cutting through the forest, so here he was, filled with anger, but on his way to freedom.

A dog's sharp, echoing bark pulled Caleb from his thoughts and, with a start, he finally acknowledged the tune he'd been hearing all this time. Not so much by listening to it as by its sudden, inexplicable absence, as if the ordinary sound of a canine had re-established reality.

The dog barked again, this time a little closer, and Caleb found himself noticing the faint sounds of distant conversation. Of course. He should have known better than to assume there would be no strollers in the forest on a pleasant day such as this. There was only one thing for it—if he wanted to avoid being seen, he'd have to leave the path and trust his instincts to keep heading in the right direction. Well, that and the GPS on his phone.

Determined, Caleb left the path and ducked behind some bushes, careful not to step on any twigs that could give him away and thankful for his mud-green jacket that helped him blend into the thicket just a little. He trudged on quietly for a little while, listening out for the dog's periodic barks as he went. When it seemed quite close, Caleb remained rooted to the spot, ducking behind some bushes to remain out of sight from the path, and waited to let the group pass, though he couldn't hear their conversation anymore.

After realizing that the dog hadn't barked again for several minutes,

Caleb silently and slowly counted to fifteen before resolving to continue his journey. He needed to get at least as far as Dublin by tonight, after all, if he wanted to be able to take a ferry to England in the morning. And he knew too well that it was his only chance.

He scarcely managed to take a single step before he saw a giant, scruffy-looking black dog staring straight at him with piercing yellow eyes. While the deep colouring was unusual, Caleb identified the breed as an Irish Wolfhound, though he wasn't used to them looking as menacing or deranged as this one managed without so much as showing its fangs or growling.

Frozen in his tracks, Caleb stared back at it, his muscles tense lest it should lunge at him. Clouds had shifted in front of the sun, and a cool breeze rustling through the treetops brought a chill with it, almost an ominous feeling. Stories, legends, and myths Caleb had heard about black dogs, or creatures that sometimes appeared like dogs, came to his mind, though he wasn't clear on the details anymore. In the stories, had they helped, or had they killed?

Drizzling rain pattered against the cover of leaves, letting only a few solitary drops fall to the mossy forest floor. The dog, at last, lifted its head slowly as if to whiff the air suddenly rich with the earthy scents indicative of rain in the countryside. Then suddenly, it turned and bounded back toward the direction of the path.

Caleb remained frozen for a moment longer, mentally clawing at fragments of tales he'd heard before, tales of the unseen parts of Ireland.

He wasn't superstitious, exactly. But everyone knew the stories, didn't they?

And everyone followed the *rules* to a certain extent, because it didn't do any harm if the stories weren't real, but… you didn't want to chance it in case they were.

Rules such as "don't look back when you're on a country road alone and hear steps behind you, because it's death following you"; "greet a stranger on the country road so death knows that you are polite"; "don't cut down the faerie trees"; "never step inside a faerie circle"; "always offer your visitors tea and biscuits, because you never knew if they might be fae and would hold it against you if you don't"…

A lot of the rules were really just about manners, so they were easy to follow. Everyone knew they were poppycock, just stories, but… *to be sure to be sure.*

So, he wasn't superstitious. Not really. But a black dog met in a forest… It could have been a sign. If the stories were real, of course, which they weren't.

Nevertheless, doubt entered Caleb's mind. Maybe he shouldn't have left home. Maybe he was making a mistake. Maybe he should have stayed on the path.

Yes, the path. It was safer, anyway, staying on the path, even if he did come across people, wasn't it? What were the chances that he'd come across anyone he knew? They probably hadn't even noticed his absence yet.

Just as Caleb decided to take the sign—whether it was one or not—and head back toward the path, the music started up again. A jolly tune, the individual notes sounding as if they were played by a music box, with that small amount of dissonance so typical for the older variety when the metal had begun to rust. Even through the rain that was progressively getting heavier, the melody rang clear, though distant.

Any thought given to his original path was gone in an instant. Instead, Caleb could only think of that melody, who was playing it in the middle of a forest, and how it could only be terribly, terribly interesting.

His feet began to move almost of their own accord. They walked on, breezing through the leaves, climbing over fallen logs, skirting around bushes, and pushing through brambles without hesitation. Forgotten were the *rules*, forgotten was the dog. What remained were the problems Caleb knew he was leaving behind, the life he wanted to escape, and the view in front of him—the forest in all its natural beauty: mosses and ferns cascading from tree trunks, luscious grass and bushes only dotted and juxtaposed by an occasional vibrantly coloured flower, a million shades of green, be it veridian, forest, olive, cadmium, or phthalo greens, blending together to paint a fantastical landscape. It seemed to Caleb that the soft rain only enhanced the colours' saturation. Every breath he took was full of the forest's heavy yet fresh fragrance. Caleb might have wondered why his allergies weren't kicking up, but in this situation, with the melody beckoning him through the forest, it just felt *right*.

It wasn't until he came across two trees leaning against one another, shaping something of an arch, that Caleb faltered in his step and regained some autonomy over his thoughts and actions.

Creepers had wound and weaved their way around and across the two stems, inadvertently merging them. The melody drifted through the forest from beyond this biological gate, but every fibre in Caleb's being warned him against taking a step through it. It was the *rules* again. Things like this, in stories… they could take you to the realm in which the fae lived. And even if Caleb didn't believe in the stories—Who in their right mind would? There was no scientific foundation or proof, really—he still wouldn't take any chances.

Back in command over his actions, and annoyed that he was giving in to a superstition, Caleb trudged around the trees and went on his way, following the sound of the melody. Pulling out his phone, he resolved to check his location to make sure he wouldn't get too much off track, but as soon as he unlocked the screen, he was met with the realization that he had no reception. Though it was annoying and inconvenient, it wasn't that surprising. There were many places in this area where it was nigh impossible to get any signal. It might have been the twenty-first century, but there were still plenty of areas in rural Ireland lacking infrastructure.

Just following the sound seemed therefore like the best course of action one way or another.

Dutifully skirting a circle of mushrooms around a fallen log, Caleb continued on his path, ignoring the mud that was beginning to stick to his trainers, and huddling deeper into his coat to protect himself from the rain that showed no signs of stopping.

Over time, not only did the tune get louder, but he started to believe that he could hear voices. They were beginning to remind him of the sounds of the fairgrounds that visited the towns every year, like an announcer in the beginning of a show.

Suddenly excited, Caleb surged forward, past several bushes, and dodged a few trees, only to find himself in full view of a large, empty clearing.

Still enraptured by the whisps of sound carried in the mild breeze, Caleb left the cover of the trees and took a few steps toward the clearing's centre. Immediately, he was battered by heavy rainfall. In an instant, his jeans and grey hoodie stuck to his skin, and his hair was pushed flat down his head, making his fringe obstruct his view.

Even though he looked around the edge of the clearing and listened intently, Caleb found it impossible to locate the origin of the music he'd been following.

"Hello?" he asked, his voice uncomfortably loud and clear.

No reply reached his ears, but he nevertheless felt someone's eyes on him. *Someone* was watching him. Some*thing*, perhaps. No matter how much Caleb strained his eyes, he found nothing in the fringes of the forest. No movement, no sound other than the strange music filling his ears. A shiver ran down his spine as he realized something was wrong about this picture, but it wasn't until several moments later that he became aware of exactly what was bothering him.

Even though he could still feel and see the rain, he could no longer hear it over the music. Additionally, the leaves of the trees didn't move under the sudden weight of raindrops as they continued to pelt down. Instead, the trees stood motionless, as though they had been carved out of stone.

A primal instinct deep inside Caleb's chest made him take a step backward. As soon as his foot touched the forest floor once more, the world around him changed.

Suddenly, the music, which had felt like an ethereal whisper just a moment before, rang loudly in his ears. The sky transformed into a dark fabric, stretched above him like the roof of a massive tent, sprinkled with glowing, slowly pulsing lights seemingly mimicking stars.

A loud, booming voice announced, "And now, esteemed guests, visitors from realms far and near, behold, the enchanting Damhán Alla!"

From the shadows of the corner of Caleb's vision, a trapeze brought a girl with long, flowing black hair swinging into the centre of what had just a moment earlier been the forest clearing. At the top of her flight's arc, she let go of the bar, her spinning allowing the clear crystal lines on her black leotard to catch the light and sparkle like dewy spiderwebs in the twilight.

Caleb blinked, stunned by the unexpected sight, and where a moment before, there'd been nothing, a set of golden silks now fell from the fabric sky to the floor, a mere five feet from him. Startled, he stepped back again, but his foot caught on a root, and he dropped onto his bum. All the while, his eyes continued to be glued to the girl now wrapping herself into the golden silks, creating beautiful and daring shapes, stretching languidly on some occasions and spinning rapidly on others. When she let go of the silks and dropped, Caleb's breath got caught in his throat, and a sigh of relief escaped when she was caught by the silks wrapped around her. Her movements were so natural, so *right*, that it appeared as though the silks weren't something she was using so much as something that was a part of her.

Slowly, Caleb got back to his feet, though his gaze never left the girl on the silks.

Damhán Alla. Spider.

Her name echoed through his mind, encompassing all his thoughts. Her expressive black eyes met his, her enticing smile beckoned him, and before long, he found himself reaching out to her.

Damhán Alla climbed back to the top of the silks in easy, fluid motions, that made it look like she was walking on air, when an empty trapeze flew toward her from somewhere above or behind Caleb. She caught it in one hand, let go of the silks, and twisted around to hook her legs over the bar as the trapeze flew back toward Caleb. She reached out a hand to him and found his still-outstretched arm.

The unexpected impact Caleb felt in his shoulder as he was suddenly lifted from the ground knocked his breath away for a moment, but he recovered quickly, taking hold of the second arm Damhán Alla was offering him.

Cold wind tearing through his soaked clothing, his legs dangling freely with no hold as he swung back and forth, Caleb somehow remained free from fear. He was too preoccupied with the beautiful girl holding him, his only lifeline, without which he would surely die.

She smiled at him, sweetly, her deep black eyes almost mischievous and otherworldly in their stark contrast to her fair skin.

Then, without warning, she let go of both his arms at once, and Caleb, in his surprise, failed to make up for the lost support, and his own grip slipped. Without control or awareness of up or down, he flipped backward in the air. Before he even had the chance to realize what was happening, he landed in a finely woven, sticky net that bounced when absorbing his impact.

Stunned, Caleb hung prone at an angle to the ground in the net, his heart racing and his head stumbling to keep up. Damhán Alla had swung back into the darkness and disappeared, but the music—the strangely dissonant and eerie, yet jolly, tune, so hauntingly familiar—played on.

"Esteemed guests, runaways and vagabonds, the lost and the forgotten, welcome to our little renegade show!" the booming, bodiless voice announced. Caleb didn't get the impression that the speaker shouted, or amplified their voice, but the sound nevertheless resonated around the space and reached him unimpeded. "This is *your* opportunity to test the boundaries of what you believe you can do. Your chance to reimagine and reinvent yourself."

Caleb's eyes were fixed on the starry roof above him as he let the words echo in his mind. There was an itching feeling in his fingertips that made his breath quicken. It was as if the voice was speaking to his innermost desire— as if it was presenting him with the solution to his problems.

Now the voice had become almost like a whisper in Caleb's ears. "All you need to do is to take to the stage."

Take to the stage.

An invitation, an offer, for seemingly nothing in return.

A sharp bark cut through the music, pulling at stories of fae from the depths of Caleb's consciousness once more. Stories that told of strange occurrences in Ireland's woods, of unsuspecting wanderers in the wild.

At once, his hands and face felt clammy with heat and cold flooding his body simultaneously. This couldn't be real. None of it could be. His mind must have been playing tricks on him.

And yet, even while he desperately tried to persuade himself, the wet clothes clinging to his body, the strain in his shoulder from unexpected impact, and the sticky feeling of the net that seemed to hold him in place all felt too real to deny.

As strange as it was, it was happening.

Calm. He needed to stay calm and in control. While he had never heard stories of a faerie circus, that didn't mean it couldn't exist. The important thing was to remember the *rules.*

Never use words of thanks unless he wanted to be indebted to them, but always remain polite so as not to anger them.

Never give out his name, because names held power.

Turn down any offers, even transactions, because there was always the chance for an unforeseen catch.

Never eat in a fae realm if he didn't want to be stuck there forever.

"I appreciate the offer," Caleb said to his surroundings in general, unable to keep his voice from trembling, "but I really had better head home."

There was no response, but the tune kept playing undeterredly.

Hairs on Caleb's arms and neck suddenly rose upright, as though his body were warning him of impending doom.

They're watching, he thought to himself.

He glared into the darkness, to get a better view of his surroundings, understanding the scope of this place and how he could return to the forest, but aside from the bare, earthy floor and the starry fabric above him, he could only make out vague, shadowy silhouettes of trees at the edges of the clearing. The silvery netting he stuck to, only illuminated by the faint glow from above, stretched from the ground in the centre of the clearing all the way to the trees, but Caleb was unable to free his head from its grasp to see clearly. Struggling against these constraints proved futile swiftly. He was stuck.

Frustrated, he blinked. In an instant, thousands of eyes, no two alike, appeared in his surroundings, their attention fixed on him. Then, as if by some inaudible queue, they all flicked to another part of the clearing. Instinctively, Caleb followed their gazes and saw a tall man: legs long and slender, shoulders broad and muscular, the face young, only sporting plumes of what could one day be a beard, and hair as white as a sheet. The man, poised on tiptoes, launched into a pirouette, and produced two balls on long strings—poi.

"And now," the booming voice announced, "behold the marvellous wonder of Aéd! Watch closely as he brings a little light into tonight's performance, but be careful not to get too close, or you might get burned…"

The man with the poi, Aéd, began spinning them in individual circles alongside his body, one on the left, the other on the right. He clicked his tongue, and the two poi were set alight, as if by magic. Now creating a flaming visual, like two shields of light, Caleb could see nothing else except the orange of the fire. Aéd's performance drew him in, much like Damhán Alla's had done.

The poi's movement never stopped. Sometimes, they were both in one hand; other times, they were separate. They seemed to cross each other's path without getting entangled somehow, but Caleb couldn't follow their movements. The flaming lights lingered for an instant longer than the poi themselves, creating shapes and images in their wake that imprinted themselves on Caleb's retinas. And even while the poi were swinging wildly and beautifully, Aéd himself shaped graceful pose after pose, twirling and leaping across the ground as though the poi were not something he controlled, but an aura that was attached to him. Caleb didn't know a lot about ballet, but this performance would have left him with the deepest respect even if it had not involved poi or fire.

Aéd leaped again and, this time, let go of his poi. Still twirling around each other, they soared above Caleb and landed on the netting that was holding him in place. In an instant, the entire web was shrivelling into black fragments, and Caleb was dropped to the floor in a rain of ash, a lingering sense of heat on his skin even though the flames had never licked him.

Jumping to his feet, Caleb looked around, but Aéd was gone, as were the webbing and the poi. The eyes were still there, looking down at him from the ceiling and from the trees. Caleb took a step forward, and they followed his movements.

The music that had been playing unrestingly finally slowed, as though a music box had been wound and played to its last tones.

His inner voice told Caleb that once it ended, he'd be free to go home, that he'd have held out for long enough, but the thought was immediately followed by a painful pang.

That place wasn't a home. It was a place he'd been living, but not a place that could be called home. Not anymore. Not for a long time. Remembering it was enough for his throat to close and his shoulders to tremble.

Any energy he'd been feeling, any desire to escape and to *go home*, was suddenly replaced with an empty sense of loss and loneliness. Where would he go?

The music played its last notes before silence fell over the clearing. All eyes were on Caleb; it felt to him like the world itself was holding its breath. He shut his own eyes and breathed deeply. Then, he slowly opened them.

Nothing had changed.

Eyes above him, waiting expectantly, watching with interest, shadowed trees in the darkness, nothing but himself in the middle of an empty clearing.

And still, it was silent. Only the sound of his own heartbeat rang in his ears. The music had stopped, and there was still no way out, was there? Unless, of course, all he needed to do was leave the clearing.

Just as Caleb had resolved to follow his hunch, a squeaky, rusty sound made him turn. A unicycle, unmanned, made its way toward him from the darkness, the pedals moving on their own, the seat only swaying a little with its movements.

Stunned, Caleb stayed rooted to the spot, even when the unicycle stopped dead only a few feet away from him.

"You have a choice, dear runaway." It was the voice that had been announcing the acts thus far, except it was no longer booming around the clearing without a clear source. No, this time, it belonged to a body that was peeling itself from the trees, cloaked in reds and blues, skin so pale it almost appeared green, long, braided hair a platinum blond, and deep, black eyes. Their features were fine, their lips curled into a soft, yet knowing, smirk. "This renegade show can only be found by those who desire to leave everything behind, and it will find those who have no way to turn back. You may watch more of the performances, if you wish, or you can join the troupe and take up an act yourself. Which will you pick?"

Caleb looked down at the unicycle.

"Can I go home instead?" he asked.

The announcer's smile broadened. "You have no home to return to, else you would not be here."

They were right. Caleb knew they were right. And yet…

"I can find a new home," he argued, his fists clenching by his sides. "I can make a fresh start."

"Yes," the other agreed. "You can make a fresh start. Nothing is stopping you. All you need to do is to reach out and grasp your future in your own hands." Their voice was soft now, almost a whisper, and Caleb could only look at the unicycle. It just stood on the spot, and yet, it felt like it beckoned him. Like he needed to take it and mount it. "You can be happy here, you know. You can do whatever you want to. Be free. Be a *renegade*."

Yes. He could be a renegade. He could be happy.

He reached out to the unicycle, but a moment before he touched it, a sharp bark echoed from the clearing's edge, making him freeze. There, growling, stood the black dog—no, hound—that he had met in the forest earlier, its yellow eyes set on him, almost glowing in the darkness.

Ah, Caleb thought. *So that's why. It was a warning.*

The stories—there was always a reason why they were passed on.

Slowly, the hound padded toward them, fangs bared, head low. It positioned itself between Caleb and the announcer, as if its intention were to protect Caleb from them.

Caleb, his hand frozen in the air, inches away from the unicycle that seemed to be shivering with anticipation, looked from the hound to the announcer. He still had a choice. This scruffy creature was here to stop him, he realized. The announcer was still smiling, almost self-satisfied, their arms crossed as they waited for him to make his choice.

With a start, Caleb pulled back his arm. He should think about this.

"What if I don't choose?" he asked. "Can I decide later on?"

He had no home. But should he really choose to become part of a fae circus instead? Caleb couldn't deny to himself that against all his better judgement, it was still *tempting*.

He could belong somewhere. Be a part of something. Live through an *adventure*.

The announcer's smile broadened. The hound turned its head and sniffed the air before suddenly howling, ears flattened against its head.

Startled, Caleb took a step back, only to bump into someone. Two small hands with long, slender fingers crept across his shoulders and over his chest as several strands of long black hair draped over his shoulder as well.

"But you already made your choice," a soft feminine voice muttered into his ear. "You took my hand, didn't you?"

A glance to his left showed Damhán Alla's face, her teeth too white and sharp, her smile too broad.

"All that's left is to choose your act," Aéd agreed, from his right.

Caleb hadn't heard either one approach, but he suddenly became aware of more figures approaching from all sides, all of them equipped for various performances.

So many.

Panic suddenly overwhelmed him. This was a bad idea. He needed to get out! Away!

He pulled away from Damhán Alla's embrace and found, with surprise, that she was holding him less forcefully than expected. This left him stumbling forward. He tried to reach out to the hound, but it had disappeared. Instead, the unicycle waited for him. He tried to stop himself, but his momentum brought him forward, and his hand found the seat.

"Welcome, dear runaway, to the renegade show."

When the Circus Comes to Town

PAIGE DANIELS

Colorado, 1934

Always packing up and moving away, from one town to the next. It was the life he'd always known. Most just blended into one another. The circus performers would come into various towns with their tents, costumes, and toys in a patchwork of assorted bright hues that would liven up the bleak, dusty landscape. It was rewarding work, knowing that he played a part in making the townspeople forget about their troubles, if only for a few hours.

But this next stop was different. This was no ordinary town; this was a special stop that Nic had been looking forward to since the beginning of the journey.

The large, muscular man ran a comb through his thick blond hair then checked his suit for the hundredth time as the train rocked back and forth on the tracks. He checked his watch.

Why does time have to move so slow?

Behind him, a snicker caught his attention.

He narrowed his eyes at the small man lying on the bottom bunk in their cabin. "What are you laughing at, Barton?"

"You. You're the biggest, strongest man that I know, and yet that little lady makes you more scared than all the lions and tigers in our circus."

"I'm not scared," Nic said as he took one more look in the mirror. "I just want to make sure that I look my best. I haven't seen her in a while."

"Ha, you're rich! You're scared."

The train slowed then came to a stop. Nic's eyes grew wide, and he turned to his best friend. "Do I look okay?"

Barton waved at him and blew a raspberry. "My friend, you're six foot five, two hundred and fifty pounds, with a head full of hair. I should be so lucky," he said as he rubbed his bald head. He smiled and continued, "Don't worry, Ella will be happy to see you."

"Thanks, friend," Nic said as he left their cabin.

Nic weaved through the narrow walkways of the train cars, intent on his destination. As he walked, he heard various murmurs and ribbings about where he was going and who he was seeing. The circus folks were a tight-knit group. Everyone knew everyone else's business. Nic loved his large circus family, but they were also exhausting.

"Nicolae, where are you going? Like I have to ask." A woman's voice rang through the halls.

Nic stopped in his tracks, took a long breath, then turned on his heel. "Mother, I think you know where I'm headed."

Selina tucked her thick, black, curly locks behind her ear then crossed her arms across her chest, a sure sign that a lecture was coming. Nic looked at his watch and tried to muffle a sigh.

"Nicolae, we have a lot of work to do to set up the show, and you have responsibilities. You can wait to see your girl."

"Mother, I'm just going to see Ella for a little bit. Have I ever let my responsibilities slip? Besides, I have plenty of time before they need my help."

Selina pursed her lips together and tapped her toe against the wooden floorboard.

Nic sighed. "Mother, you know that I won't let anyone down. Please, just let me see my friend."

A sad smile grew on Selina's face. She squeezed Nic's arm and nodded. "I know. You're a good boy, and she's a good girl. I just want you to be cautious, that's all. The world isn't always kind to people like us. Just be careful, okay?"

Nic bent down and gave his mother a peck on top of her head. "I will, Mamma."

As he walked away, he heard his mother reminding him again not to be late to set up the tent.

Nic knew his mother had his best interests at heart. She was not one of those overly protective mothers. His youth had been spent exploring all the circus had to offer. Being an inquisitive young man raised in the circus had meant finding himself in many precarious situations, none of which had seemed to bother his mother much.

He knew that his mother was worried about him getting his heart broken, like she had many years ago. She didn't talk about it much, but he knew that his father lived in one of the towns they frequently visited. She wouldn't speak of his father; she only said that it had been her choice to live the circus life with Nic. His mother was not one to be tied down to a traditional life. She was a free spirit and loved her life on the rails, but there were times when her loneliness shone through.

Nic's thoughts turned to the present as a gust of dry, dusty wind hit him in the face. At the train station, the townspeople were gathered to see the brightly colored circus cars. Nic craned his neck to find the person he was looking for.

A smile appeared on his face when he saw a diminutive woman with freckles.

Ella paced along the walkway of the train station. She stopped then smoothed down the white dress decorated in pale blue flowers. It had taken her six months of saving up flour sacks and trading with neighbors to get enough matching fabric to make this dress. She was sure that compared to the flamboyant circus fare Nic was used to, it would look boring and drab.

But that was how it was out here: boring and drab. The omnipresent dust covered this town and hundreds of other towns just like it. There was no escaping the dust. It was everywhere you sat, walked, and touched. It was almost enough to drive a person insane. But the circus offered a respite from these troubles, and man, were there ever troubles for Ella.

Before she could think about them any further, her heart lifted when she saw a glint of a train in the distance. Her heart skipped a beat, and her palms started to sweat. She was taken back to the moment when she'd met Nic just a few years ago. Her father had taken her and her mother to the circus as a reward for a long, hard crop season. Ella had been awestruck at the lights, colors, and fantastic feats of the circus performers. Her favorites were the aerialists spinning in the air, defying gravity. They were like leaves sailing on the wind, hypnotizing and exotic.

When she and her family were leaving the show, a pylon holding up one of the circus tents came loose. It would have crushed her father if it hadn't been for Nic, the strongman, being there to catch it. Thankful for what Nic had done, Ella's mother had invited Nic over for dinner. It hadn't taken long for Ella and Nic to drum up a friendship. Nic wasn't like the other men in her town. He didn't care that Ella liked to work on the farm's tractors and get her hands dirty in the soil. He even didn't seem to mind that Ella swore, smoked, and occasionally enjoyed a little contraband alcohol. He was the best friend that Ella ever had. Every time he left, a piece of her left with him, too.

The train stopped on the tracks, and after a moment, people started to exit the train. She saw some familiar faces, but not the one she was looking for. Then, after a few long minutes, the large man came into view. Before she could take him in, he was off the train and had her in his arms.

"Good to see ya," Nic said as he held her in an embrace.

She nestled into his warm body. She loved his smell—it was something between sweet grain and pachouli.

She pulled away with a smile on her face. "It's good to see you, too. I didn't ever think you all would be back this way."

Nic offered her his arm, and they started to walk toward town. "Well, we were offered a few more shows en route to see you. We never turn down a paying gig. It's hard times. We need all the shows we can get, since fewer and fewer people turn out these days. How's your ma?"

She sighed. "She passed a few months ago. It's all this damn dust. She was weak anyway, and after Papa died last year, I just don't think she had it in her to fight. She missed him too much."

Nic gave her a gentle squeeze then stopped. She turned to face him as she wiped the tears forming in her eyes. She hated being vulnerable, and she didn't want Nic to see her like this. It was supposed to be a happy time.

He flicked a piece of her auburn hair out of her face then took one of her hands. "I really liked your ma, and I know you two were close. It's going to hurt for a long time because you loved her so much. I realize there's nothing I can do or say to make it better, but I can be here for you as long as you want me to."

After so many platitudes offered by the townspeople, this bit of honesty was refreshing. It also didn't hurt that she had her friend here to talk to, even if it was just for a few days.

The pair strolled along the streets of the town, catching up on each other's lives. As they walked, they saw the townspeople and the circus folks also catching up. This town was always welcoming to the circus. Many friendships, like Nic and Ella's, had been made in the years that the circus had come to town.

After a few minutes of walking, Ella stopped in front of a drug store. "Can I interest you in a soda?" she asked, motioning to the door.

Nic opened the door and waved Ella in. At the counter, a portly man sidled up to the pair and smiled.

"How are you, Sam?" Nic asked.

The man's mouth turned down into a frown. "Not great. Since Mr. Alastair passed, it's all gone to hell, because his son took over. It's tough times for us all, but one thing that kept our town going was that we all pooled our resources to keep each other upright. But now, I'm not sure what's going to happen."

He set two sodas in front of the couple and walked to stock his shelves. Nic rubbed his head, thinking of the kind man. Mr. Alastair had been the richest man in town. According to Ella's parents, Mr. Alastair had owned more than half the town, but you'd never know it to talk to the down-to-earth fellow. Nic would always see him laughing with delight at every show the circus put on. He would even buy tickets for the town's poorest residents. Mr. Alastair had always made time to talk with all the circus performers, to tell them what a wonderful show they'd put on.

Nic sighed. "Why didn't you tell me about Mr. Alastair?"

Ella shrugged. "Dunno. I was going to, but I figured I laid enough on ya with my ma's death. I didn't want to sully our visit with all this talk of dying. I'm sorry, I should've told you sooner about everything. But it's so hard to tell if you'll even get my letters. Besides, I thought news like this should be told in person, not in a letter."

Nic nodded. "You're right. I'm not mad. Just in shock. What did Sam mean about not being sure about what's going to happen?"

Ella started to answer, but she was cut short by the ringing of the bell over the door. Ella grumbled when she saw a skinny blond man with a pencil mustache. He looked out of place with his fancy double-breasted suit and fedora. But that was how Chris Alastair was. He wanted everyone to know he was better than them. He was nothing like his father.

Chris sidled up to Nic and Ella, smirking. He took off his hat, showing his perfectly pomaded hair. "Well, looks like the circus freaks are in town once again."

Ella grumbled, "No one asked your opinion. Why don't you get out of here?"

Chris scoffed. "My dear, this is my property now, and I can do whatever I damn well please."

Nic bolted up, towering over the skinny man. "Do not use that language in the presence of a lady."

Chris laughed. "You're talking about Ella? The girl who works on tractors and has more dirt under her fingernails than my mechanic? She is no lady."

Nic growled, and his face contorted in anger. Chris almost looked intimidated.

Ella took Nic's hand and beckoned him to calm down. "It's okay. It's not like he knows what hard work really means. Unlike his father."

"You do not have permission to talk about my father," Chris said. "And you are just like the rest of this town, Ella. I am not going to be as forgiving as my father of the town's debts to him. He was too soft-hearted, and it's time someone had a backbone. Consider yourself on notice. You have one month to erase your debt."

Without another word, Chris turned and exited the store, leaving them in silence.

Nic's back ached, and his hands burned as he tugged on the massive ropes attached to the tent decked out in a patchwork of red, gold, and purple. The sounds of the workers chanting in time as they raised the tent filled the air. After sitting long hours on the train and his encounter with Chris Alastair, this sweat-inducing work was definitely what the doctor had ordered. As he gave another tug to the rope in time with the other workers, the tent came to life, towering over all the people. He smiled at the sight.

He took a long drink of water then turned to see Ella petting a horse and talking with Pearl, the animal handler. Nic couldn't help but smile at the woman with pink cheeks and freckles decorating her face. He loved that she was plain-spoken and industrious. Every time he left her, his heart broke, and he just knew that one of these times when he came back into town, she would have her heart stolen by another. It was unfair for him to think that she would wait around for him forever. But how could he leave his mother?

Now that both Ella's parents were gone, leaving her weighed on him more. But Ella was an incredibly smart, capable woman. She didn't need him.

He shook all those thoughts from his head when she approached him.

"No matter how many times I see you all do that, it amazes me," she said with her head craned up to see the tent.

"I've been helping with it as long as I can remember, and I'm always amazed too. So, tell me about what's been going on at your farm."

Ella sat in the dry prairie grass, and Nic followed suit.

She grabbed a handful of soil then let the wind blow it from her hand. "This is what has been going on. I'm sure in your travels, you've seen it all over."

Nic nodded in agreement.

Ella continued, "Our farm is struggling, like everyone else's. Mr. Alastair helped my parents with a loan against their property. All things considered, our sugar beet farm is doing okay, but it's not enough to make good on the loan payments. Mr. Alastair was understanding and just told us to pay what we could. But now…" Tears came to her eyes, and she stopped.

Nic wiped the tears from her eyes and feathered a soft kiss on her lips.

Ella smiled. "I'm glad you're here," she breathed.

"I'm glad I'm here too. I hate seeing this. I just wish there was something that I could do." He paused for a moment then blurted out, "Come with me. When we leave, get on the train with me."

She looked at him with her mouth wide open.

"I'm serious. You're handy with tools. You could fix any of our mechanical issues that come up. If you're worried about what people will say about us being together, I'll marry you. Just come with me."

"I… I… I didn't think I'd ever get a marriage proposal. Well, at least like that, anyway." She hugged him.

"So, it's settled, then? You'll come with me?"

Tears came to her eyes again, and she shook her head. "Nic, I can't. It's not just about me. I have workers who rely on me. If I gave up on the farm, at least ten families would be affected. Chris Alastair would win. It's not right."

Nic sighed. "I knew what you were going to say. It was worth a try. I meant every word, though. You have my heart, Ella Klein."

"I know you meant it. But you need to understand, I have to fight for what's right. I'll sell every last piece of furniture in my house and sleep on the floor before I give up."

Nic gave Ella a kiss on the forehead and smiled. "And that's what I love about you."

He leaned in to kiss Ella again. As his lips brushed against hers, a commotion in the distance stopped them. Both bolted up and rushed in the direction of the noise.

In a few seconds, they were face-to-face with five large thugs yelling and pushing the circus folks.

"Mr. Alastair says he don't want you freaks here. Get on outta town," one dark-haired goon with a handlebar mustache growled.

The circus's ringleader and owner sauntered up between the goons and the other circus folks to break the tension. He stroked his black goatee and said in a loud baritone, "Gentlemen, I'm sure there's been some misunderstanding. We reserved this area months ago with Mr. Alastair for the show. He's always been accommodating to us."

The goon sneered. "Yeah, well, that Mr. Alastair is dead. The one that counts wants you outta here."

"Gentlemen, you must understand, we rely on this income. Can't you see your way to…"

"No. Get out, or we'll burn this all to the ground."

Nic started for the thugs, but Ella grabbed his wrist and shook her head firmly.

She whispered, "You don't need to be starting nothing. Let them go, and we'll figure this out later."

Nic growled and took a long breath. She was right. Starting a fight right now wouldn't solve anything. It would probably make things worse. He balled up his fists as he watched the goons leave the area, throwing jibes at the circus folks.

There had to be something he could do.

Selina sat in her tent, unpacking boxes of brightly colored hoops and wands for her act. It was a craft passed down for generations, and she loved it. Unfortunately, it seemed as though this craft would die with her. Nicolae had never taken a liking to illusions and fortune telling. He'd said it was all hogwash. He preferred to work with his hands. Fortunately, he'd inherited her family's large stature. Years of manual labor had honed his physique to where he could take over for the strongman who'd retired five years ago. She knew that the circus wasn't in his blood like it was in hers, and that her time with him was coming to an end.

As she set out the last of her colored handkerchiefs, she jumped at a shadowy figure in her doorway.

"Can I help you?" she asked cautiously. As the figure walked closer to her, she was able to make out who it was, and she smiled at the burly red-headed man. "Marcus, how are you? It's been a while."

He took off his bowler and gave her a nod. "That it has, Miz Selina." He paused for a moment then asked, "I s'pose you've heard the news about Mr. Alastair by now?"

She sat in a red velvet chair behind a table. She pointed at a crate for Marcus to sit on.

He took a seat, facing the woman, and gave her a sad smile.

"I have heard the news," she said. "He was a good friend, and my heart was broken when I heard. When did it happen?"

"Not too long after you left last year. I'm sure you noticed that he wasn't well the last time you were here."

Selina nodded. "Yes, he looked very frail. When I asked about it, he just gave me some drivel about being under a lot of stress. I knew he was sick, but I didn't want to sully our time together, so I didn't say much about it. If I'd known it was the last time—"

Marcus patted the top of her hand to offer some comfort. "That man could be a pigheaded SOB."

Selina laughed as she dried her tears. "Yes, he could. We had some good times, didn't we?"

"That we did."

Selina cleared her throat and straightened her back and shoulders, giving herself a sort of aristocratic air. "So, what brings you here, Marcus? I assume this was more than just a social call."

"Yes, ma'am." He reached into his coat pocket, produced a fat envelope, and deposited it into Selina's hands. She knitted her eyebrows, and he said, "He never held the choices you made against you. But he wanted there to be other… options, if you all wished."

Selina's breath caught as she read the contents inside the envelope. Her reading was interrupted by a ruckus.

Outside, Marcus and Selina saw the thugs walking away from the circus folks, spitting insults.

Marcus shook his head and started away from Selina. "It's a shame what that boy is doing to this town. Maybe something can be done."

Selina looked down at the letter and whispered, "We have options now."

"Are you sure it was a good idea to go on with the show, Mamma?" Nic asked as he put the last of his props for his strongman act into place.

Selina smiled and patted her son on his shoulder. "I'll explain everything after the show, but it will be fine. We can't let people like Chris Alastair and his thugs scare us and the town. Mr. Alastair wouldn't have wanted it that way. The circus was special to him and to this town."

"I trust you, but I do think we're playing with fire, though."

As if to emphasize his thoughts, a ball of fire from the fire-eater filled the tent, followed by *oohs* and *ahhs* from the crowd. The duo watched as the trapeze artists floated deftly through the air over the fire-breathing act. It was almost as fun watching the crowd's reactions to the acts as the acts themselves.

Nic looked down at his props one last time to ensure that everything was in its place. He didn't see what the big deal was about his act, really. He'd start by bending a few metal bars, then some of the clowns would try to pick up his weights while comedically failing, and he'd come to their rescue and fling the weights overhead effortlessly. He'd usually round out his act by lifting a large yoke on his back, and then, one by one, a few of the circus folks would sit on the yoke as Nic paraded them around the ring. Afterward, he'd pose for a few pictures with kids. It wasn't a real skill like the aerialists or his mother's magic act. He just happened to be strong. He loved his circus family, but many times, he felt like he just didn't belong.

Before he was able to think about that further, a murmur from the crowd caught his attention. From the ring, there was yelling. Not that of the ringleader, but someone else: Chris Alastair.

Anger welled in Nic when he finally looked out to see the source of the commotion. The same thugs from earlier that afternoon were in the crowd, bullying people to leave while Chris Alastair stood in the ring and shouted at the crowd. The fire breather had moved to the side, trying to steer clear of them. The aerialist had stopped her act and was slowly climbing down to the safety of the ground.

"This ends now," Nic said as he stomped out to the ring.

"You've all been warned," Chris Alastair yelled at the crowd. "We told you to move your act. We told you people not to come to the circus. Now, we're going to have to show you that we were serious about this."

Nic sidled up to the man and looked down at him as he said, "You need to leave my circus now before things get… heated."

Behind Nic, a host of circus folks started to gather.

Chris laughed as his gang drew closer to him. "What are you and your freaks going to do? You have no right to be here. We told you this afternoon to clear out. This is my property, and you'll do well to get out."

Before Nic could say anything, his friend Barton scrambled from behind him then stood in front of Chris and sneered. "You don't scare us. We've seen a lot worse than that, you lily-livered folks. You wouldn't be so tough if it wasn't for your goons."

Chris laughed then kicked Barton. "What are you going to do, little man? Bite my ankles?"

"That's it!" Nic bellowed.

Without another thought, he reared back, but before he could land his fist in Chris's obnoxious face, one of the goons pushed Chris out of the path of Nic's fury and landed a punch in Nic's gut.

Nic just laughed, picked up the thug by his collar with one hand, and flung him across the ring like little more than a piece of garbage.

The other goons started for Nic. One after another, they started to assault him. Seeing this, the circus folks began to intervene, attacking Nic's assailants.

"Quiet!" a voice shouted over the cacophony of screams filling the tent.

Then a flash of light and a plume of smoke appeared with a loud *bang*. The tent went eerily silent, and the melee stopped as everyone stared at the mysterious cloud of smoke.

Selina strode out of the smoke, wearing baggy purple pants and a gold lamé top that shimmered in the lights of the big top. Her dark curls cascaded all around her, making her look wild and fierce. She stared at the thugs with her emerald eyes, daring them to speak.

"You will leave now!" she shouted.

Chris confidently walked over to the woman and folded his arms across his chest. "This is my property. You cannot tell me what to do."

"I beg to differ." She pulled out a thick envelope from a pocket. "This town has always been special to me, because when I was a young woman, I met a kind man here. He loved the circus. Every time I left him, I felt that my heart would break." She paused for a few seconds as she glided over to her son. She touched him on his arm and then continued, "Twenty-five years ago, he left me with something very special."

Nic's eyes went wide. "Mother! What are you saying?"

She handed Nic the envelope. "I'm saying that Mr. Alastair was your father. He tried to get me to stay here when he found out, but that is not the life I wanted. I didn't see how I could fit in here. We both agreed that we would tell you the truth when the time was right. It just got harder the longer we waited. I am truly sorry."

"You're lying!" Chris bellowed. "He loved my mother!"

Selina shook her head. "He did love your mother, and I was very glad he found someone to make him happy. His love for me didn't diminish the love that he had for your mother."

Nic looked up from reading the contents of the papers. "Am I reading this right?"

"Yes, son, your father always ensured that you were taken care of, and he wanted to ensure this after his death. Half of his estate is now yours. You have options now. You don't need to stay with the circus any longer. You can follow your heart," she said as she looked over to Ella, who made her way down from the seats.

"No!" Chris hollered. "I will talk to my lawyers about this. I will not let this stand."

Marcus appeared at the entrance of the tent and walked over to Chris. "Your father made sure everything was ironclad with the lawyers. You can still live very comfortably."

"You haven't heard the last from me," Chris said as he stormed out.

Nic looked at Ella with tears in his eyes and said, "I guess I can do something now."

He took her in his arms, thinking about the future they would have together.

Nic and Ella waited on the platform as a brightly colored train barreled down the tracks. Nic looked down at Ella with her auburn hair flying in the wind and smiled, thinking about the whirlwind of activity that had surrounded his life in the last year.

Before his circus family had left, Nic and Ella had married in the weirdest, most colorful ceremony ever. Then, he'd flung himself into learning as much as possible about Ella's farm and all the businesses Mr. Alastair had willed to him. When he wasn't busy with that, he and Ella fought Chris Alastair's efforts to reclaim his wealth. Fortunately, Chris knew his father was a savvy businessman and soon gave up and moved himself and his money to a much less dusty landscape.

It had been an exhausting year, but also one of the most rewarding in Nic's life.

Ella touched his hand then smiled as she patted her swollen belly. "What do you think your ma will say about this?"

Nic chuckled as the train squealed to a halt. "Why don't you ask her yourself?”

In the distance, a woman's voice filled the air. "Nicolae!"

Before they had time to react, the couple was engulfed in a warm embrace.

"I missed you so much," the woman cried.

"Looks like someone's been busy," a voice snarked from behind Nic.

Nic pulled away from the embrace and gave his friend a playful shove. He turned back to his mother, who was patting Ella's tummy with tears in her eyes. "Come on, guys, I got a great space reserved for y'all. I can't wait to catch up with everyone."

Nic's heart pounded in his chest as he saw his family gathered around him. This is where he was supposed to be. He took a few heartbeats to take it all in then drew a long breath and led his family into town.

FOR YOUR ENTERTAINMENT

JAMIE KRAKOVER

At the edge of the galaxy, a circus draws many in, but no one ever comes out. It lives inside the black hole Signe. The very black hole my ship heads right for.

Outside my window, the alluring swirl of red and white wisps hypnotizes me with its beauty. But the alarm bells in my head tell me to turn back and never return. I ignore their pleas as I power down the engines.

Last chance to turn back, Astra. The quiet voice in my head taunts. I close my eyes and indulge it for a brief moment.

"Not without Cassian," I whisper to the void to set myself straight. I open my eyes and stare into the spinning abyss. The red and white gasses twirl around each other like a dust storm.

A hail comes over the comms, drawing my attention back to the control panel. "Unidentified craft, what brings you to Signe?"

My brother. But I can't tell them that. They'd never let me in. And I have too much riding on this to screw things up now. It's not like I can go back to my old life. Sure, being a thief pays the bills, but stealing a ship from the boss puts a target on your back. Despite that, I'd do anything for Cass. He's the only family I have. We've relied on each other for the last six years, ever since I turned fifteen. And being able to pay the bills means nothing without Cass.

The good news is no one will follow me here. They don't know exactly what happens in this place, but they do know that what goes in, never returns. The pressure is on to get this right. My brother is the only thing I have left to lose.

I twirl my long ponytail, a nervous habit, then press my thumb to the comms button. "The promise of entertainment and an escape." Hopefully, that sort of bullshit was enough to pique their interest.

"Power down your controls, and prepare for scanning."

I flip off all the unnecessary systems and lean back in the captain's chair. It's like talking someone into cotton candy for dinner.

I smile. I shouldn't. But this is the easiest part. They want most people to come. They don't want us to leave. Leaving would be the adventure. A challenge I curse and relish all at once.

I spent the better part of the last two months retracing Cass's steps. Each one leads me here. When I could no longer deny the reality of what happened to him, I finalized my plans to steal this ship and worked through how to rescue Cass.

A trip that would only lead to insanity.

Attempting the one thing no one has ever done successfully—escaping the allure of Signe.

Honestly, I don't know what all the hype is about. Circuses kind of creep me out. But this is supposed to be a premier experience. The galaxy's worst-kept secret. If Signe is so great, why has no one returned to talk about it?

The hype over something no living person could share is equal parts confusing and intriguing. Regardless, I'm about to get my answer.

The cockpit lights up with a pink glow as the scanner inspects my craft.

"Nothing to hide," I say into the void. More to break the painful silence than to anyone specific.

"Singular lifeform, please proceed to the docking bay," says the ethereal voice over the intercom.

"You got it." I mock salute the control panel then engage the engines. Full speed ahead.

Turn back, says the voice in my head. But there is no going back. Only one way in and no way out.

The black hole swirls around me in a tunnel-like fashion, guiding my craft to the docking bay. Inside, hundreds of ships of all shapes and sizes are locked to the various ports. My ship glides past the *Orion*, the famed explorer ship, that went missing two decades before I was born.

"So that's what happened." The only question is: Will I live long enough to escape and tell the tale?

The variety of ships sends a wave of awe over me. It's a shipyard museum. There's technology that hasn't been seen in millennia all the way to the latest state-of-the-art ships fresh off the build yards.

"Such a waste of a great ship." I silently pick out the ship I'd steal if given the chance then pull up next to the *Perseus*. The freighter my brother was last seen on. Its untarnished hull and shiny engines are as pristine as the day I waved him off.

I wish I'd never let him join a shipping crew. I should have nagged him more about his choice, but it wouldn't have mattered. He's as stubborn as a thief on a banking ship. But I'd heard the infamous stories of the *Perseus*'s peril. Its curse of a million targets on its deck. I'd repeated them all to Cass. Even sent messages once he left. He ignored me still. Now, I know why. If we escape this prison, I'll kill him myself.

The ship slides into the dock with some small bumps. The airlock hisses, telling me it's safe to exit.

I grab my utility belt from the hook at the rear of the craft and stock it with my knives, and a stun stick for good measure. Slamming my hand on the airlock release, I curse into the air. "Stars, Cassian, why do you have to be such a stubborn fool?"

I march down the ramp, only to be met by a curiously tall, ghostly white creature in a blue woolen gown running from their neck to the floor. There's no shape to the garment, just a giant tube. It seemingly hangs on by sheer magic. Unlike my leather pants, close-cropped, armor-lined corset, and boots that hide a series of lockpicks and an array of poisonous darts. Equal parts practical and alluring in a pinch.

"Please check all weapons larger than utility knives at the weapons bay. They will not be needed here." The creature waves their lanky arm off to the right where a small shack sits. Guns, lasers, swords, and weapons of all kinds cover every spare inch of the walls. Some are so old, they're rusty. Others contain a nice layer of dust.

I snort then pound back up the ramp, removing my stun stick from my belt. I place it in the ship's safe and use my fingerprint to lock it. Like hell if I'll let them confiscate it.

I hold my hands up in surrender as I pad down the ramp. "Happy? No weapons."

The creature only nods slightly then walks silently toward a large tent with silver, white, and maroon silks draping off it.

As we approach the entrance, the creature extends their arm. "Enjoy your stay."

"Not going to give me the grand tour?" I ask, more for my own amusement than theirs.

The creature blinks but says nothing. Minimal engagement. I can get on board with that. I duck under the silks and walk down the darkened entrance toward the light and noise of voices.

I emerge in what appears to be a small city. Vendors show off their food and wares as I stroll by. The aroma of cinnamon fills my nose. I close my eyes and inhale deeply, instantly reminded of my grandmother's baking. I open my eyes and proceed toward the big tent straight ahead. That's where I expect to find Cass.

Patrons bustle by, stocking up on goods, stuffing sweet desserts and candies into their mouths, and laughing at jokes. There are jugglers in the street throwing everything from balls to flaming swords.

"No weapons." I huff but make note of the number and location. *Only in a pinch.*

I pass by a magician pulling coins from a child's ear while another makes cards disappear and reappear.

On the awnings above, contortionists painted like statues periodically shift into new poses, each appearing more painful than the last.

A man rides by on a unicycle, followed by a trio of women balancing plates on long thin poles.

I spin, taking it all in. It's glamorous and engaging. I'm in awe of the talent and the sheer number of acts around me, each performer with a unique costume on its own that somehow blends in harmony as one with the others. No one appears sad, or here against their will. In fact, it's the happiest I've ever seen a crowd in my entire life. No fighting, no sticky fingers, no yelling. Maybe it's the food?

Note to self: Don't stay long enough to need refueling.

The atmosphere is almost unnatural, against the nature of the universe. Maybe it's more than the food.

But the smell of popcorn overwhelms me, drawing me off the main path toward a series of arcade games I remember from my childhood.

"Throw until you win." A tall, bearded man in striped pants and a purple vest holds a small magnetic ball out to me.

I blink but say nothing.

He angles his head at the tower of metallic rods stacked four levels high. He throws the ball. It knocks the entire stack down. The ball returns to his hand like a boomerang, and the stack magically restores itself.

"See, simple." His voice has a quiet calm, drawing me toward him.

I extend my hand for the ball. *Focus, Astra.* The voice growls in my mind. I shake my head and withdraw my hand, rubbing my temples. "Maybe later," I mumble before stumbling back to the main path. The man hands the ball to another unsuspecting customer as I force my feet toward the main tent.

The music grows louder as I step underneath the awning. It's soft and low, a series of chimes and deep horns. It thrums at a rhythm mismatched to my pounding heart. It's so deep I feel it in my chest, but it's more like a giant hug then a crushing blow.

Inside, the tent is much larger than the outside implies. I step into a rounded vehicle that instantly floats. It guides me around the main ring and past numerous other pods that have been locked into place. In total, thousands of viewers fill countless pods. All are focused on the main event.

Giant bubbles of various sizes and colors float around the tent. Flying trapeze and silks artists soar around the bubbles, periodically grabbing the edges and pulling them in different directions or changing their shape entirely.

In the center of the room floats the largest bubble with two performers inside. One with shimmering purple skin, the other a bright turquoise. The dim light periodically catches their skin and makes it glisten like diamonds. They swing and flip around each other at varying speeds. It's utterly mesmerizing to witness the near misses.

My vehicle hisses and jolts as it locks into position halfway up the tent. I don't pay it much attention and focus back on the center, where the two bodies slide over each other like well-oiled engine parts. They seemingly stay in place by sheer magic, or maybe the lack of gravity. It's hard to tell.

My mind wanders, wondering how they're so graceful with only the support of the other's body. It defies logic and physics.

Astra. The voice in my mind hisses at me. I blink and force myself to search the crowd for Cassian. He must be here. I can feel it. I examine the panel on the front of the vehicle, looking for controls, but there are none beyond providing seating and adjusting the angle of it. I activate the seating button. A purple velvet lounger materializes. I hit the button again, and it shifts into a black leather recliner. Much more my style.

Don't get too comfortable. I hit the button again, and a metal chair appears. Closer. I hit the button a third time, and it becomes a small wooden stool. Perfect.

I squat on the stool, then pull my bio binoculars from my belt. Pressing my eyes to the lenses, I scan the crowd in search of Cass's wild brown hair. It was long when he left. He likes it that length. Unless the crew forced him to cut it, that would be the best way to locate him.

I shift the binoculars from pod to pod. Couples making out, children in complete awe of the show, adults equally hypnotized. No Cass.

What is with this place?

A quiet voice comes over the speaker in the floor beneath my seat. "Can we tempt you with some kettle corn or nectar juice?" The voice is lyrical, like a lullaby.

"I'm good," I bark back, silently cursing them for interrupting my search.

"No cost, we can get you anything your heart desires."

"Blue milk?" I laugh to myself at the thought of them tracking down the rarest delicacy in the galaxy.

"Coming right up." The voice replies without hesitation.

"No, I—" It was a joke, but the connection severs before I can finish.

I tap my fingers on my knives. It usually helps me think, but the music slows my brain. My eyelids grow heavy, and I yawn.

"Stay awake," I growl then pinch myself hard on the arm.

I need a new plan. Searching the thousands of people in the room individually is not going to help me find Cass. I close my eyes in an attempt to focus better, but my head pounds to the beat of the bass in the music.

Maybe I'd be better off returning to the street fair, among the performers and crowds. I shake my head, remembering the allure of the popcorn out there.

A panel on the front of the vehicle hisses, and a tall glass of blue milk appears with a yellow straw. I stare at the glass. My mouth waters, but I don't move toward it. I can't. This was supposed to be an in-and-out job.

If I can't find Cassian, maybe I can make him come to me.

A loud voice booms throughout the tent. "For your entertainment, please direct your attention to the center ring."

My gaze glides toward the giant bubble seemingly against my will. I blink in disbelief as the bubble expands to ten times its size and a dozen small mechanical crafts appear out of thin air.

They spin around each other, change colors, and make mesmerizing patterns. I want to look away but can't. The shapes slow my heart rate, and I breathe deeply. Five minutes. That's all I'll allow myself, then it's back to finding Cassian.

I step to the edge of my craft so I can get a better view. The acrobats from before appear near the roof and lower into the giant bubble without the aid of wires. They dodge and twist around as the small crafts whizz by, barely missing them. Then the turquoise-skinned individual steps onto one of the crafts and leaps from craft to craft, pushing them into a new design.

A scream tears through the calming music. My head whips in the direction of the noise, even though the scream sounds feminine. Not Cass. But as I locate the source, I gasp.

In a pod half a dozen over from mine, a young woman in a gold-sequined unitard collapses into the arms of a shaggy-haired guy in dark pants, a loose-fitting tunic, and a utility vest I'd recognize anywhere. Cassian.

His face contorts into a mix of surprise and confusion as a pool of red radiates out from her left side.

I jump onto the control panel of my pod then launch myself to the next pod. The individuals inside don't acknowledge my presence. They're still focused on the main event. Which is fine, because I bolt across it, climb onto the control panels, and launch into the next pod over.

My heart pounds as I pick up speed. When I'm two pods over, I scream, "CASS!" But the sound evaporates into the music around us. I pick up the pace and launch into the pod closest to his.

"Cassian!"

This time, his head lifts from staring at the pool of blood around him. He drops the girl as if suddenly realizing what happened. He stares at me in shock, like he's seeing a ghost. As I launch into the air toward him, he steps to the edge of his pod.

Two tall white creatures, like the one who greeted me on arrival, fire a long black weapon at him. He instantly goes rigid as five metallic bands wrap around him, securing his arms, legs, and mouth.

I land next to him and reach out, but with lightning speed the creatures levitate him out of my grasp and send him over the edge of the vehicle.

"Nooooo!" I scream as I rush to peer over the side of the craft. Cass floats in a bubble several stories down. His clothes have changed into a blue-and-gold unitard. He's gliding and twisting in an ethereal way. Unnatural for the guy who trips over his own feet.

I glance toward the pod in search of the mysterious creatures, but they've disappeared along with the body and the blood. Like it never happened. The patrons watch the show in silent admiration, completely unaware that someone just died mere feet from them.

I open my mouth to scream to Cass again, but I choke on his name. No sound comes out. I try again but get the same result. I grab my throat.

"For your entertainment, direct your attention to the far side of the ring." The voice booms again.

All eyes, including mine, focus on the spotlight directly ahead of the pod. Cassian's bubble rises toward the ceiling. He's performing intricate poses and graceful moves like he's been part of the show the whole time. He's so consumed by the music and the act, he doesn't seem to notice the crowd.

He really is in his own little bubble. My gaze scans for the quickest path to him. But as I find it, my mind shifts. *What if I joined him?*

The alluring pull inside me propels me forward. I stand on the controls. As the bubble floats closer, I leap toward it.

As I pass through the cool material, it wobbles briefly before I'm floating inside. Suspended without need for a floor or a harness.

I look down. I'm wearing a unitard that matches Cassian's. It's gorgeous and accentuates my curves in all the right ways.

He grabs my hand and spins me. It's graceful. My arms and legs move in a fluid fashion, as if I've been doing acrobatics my whole life. I smile at Cass. He smiles back, but it's not his casual smile that I'm used to. It's the one he uses when he's about to con someone out of something good. It's all an act. Or is it?

We tumble around each other in a peaceful bliss. The motion's hypnotic and calming. My mind clears. The only thing I desire is to flip and float more. I have my brother. I don't need anything else in this world.

You need to leave.

The deep voice jolts me back to reality. The audience comes into view. I gasp as I see the ground so far below.

I twist to face Cassian.

"Cass, wake up!"

But he keeps spinning then grabs my wrist and twirls me again, sending me to the far edge of the bubble.

I struggle to rotate back. With nothing to push off of, I can't make my way to him. As I hit the edge of the bubble, it ripples and morphs but feels solid enough. I kick off it and rocket straight toward Cass. As I pass into range, I grab his shoulders and spin us in uncontrollable circles. I squeeze his arms hard, digging my nails into his skin.

He doesn't flinch. Too far gone, maybe. My mind spins, trying to figure out how to get through to him. And then I see it: a missing sequin on his unitard. A hole between the glistening colors. I focus on it. It helps me regain control of my surroundings.

But as Cass rotates in the air, the sequin magically reappears, filling the void. I blink and focus on the spot, but it's no use. It's been filled.

It's an illusion.

I allow a few seconds to pass as the thought processes then look toward the center of the performance area. A large section is missing. Performers are cut in half, and parts of their bodies float in and out of view.

"It's not real," I whisper.

Several of the audience pods disappear and reveal a section of wires. The same crisscrossing wires used for elaborate holograms. *A simulation?*

My brain runs at a thousand miles per hour as Cass grabs my arm and twists me into a death spiral. I'm spinning so fast, I can't focus on a single thing. But as the room twirls around me and the colors blur together, the pods start to vanish.

More and more of the wires appear.

"It's not real," I repeat, this time louder and more sure of myself. The room spins faster.

Wake up. The voice inside my head nudges me. I fight it. I'm not asleep. Or am I?

WAKE UP.

I cough. Then my head explodes in pain. I squeeze my eyes shut in an attempt to stave off the pain. When my eyes fly open, a blinding white light floods my vision. I blink rapidly until everything comes into view.

The circus tent is gone. The pods have evaporated. The performance bubbles are nowhere to be found. I'm in a glass tube. Surrounded by thousands of other glass tubes. Each containing a single lifeform.

"Where am I?"

But my head explodes in pain again. I rub my temples to alleviate it. My fingers brush against a series of sensors attached to the sides of my face. I rub my hands over my head and discover more in my scalp and at the base of my neck.

My vision goes white again. Slowly, the bubbles with performers start floating past.

"NO."

I yank the leads from my face and the back of my neck. The images instantly disappear.

A red light fills the glass tube, and an alarm blares. I grab my ears, but it does nothing to muffle the sound. I pat myself down, taking inventory, but all of my usual hiding places for a variety of weapons are empty. Whoever runs this place really knows what they are doing.

How did I get here?

Craning my head upward, I search for a way out of the tube, but none is readily apparent.

I crouch and inspect the metallic base capping off the glass tube. Glass and metal. The connection between the two can't be that strong.

I stand. I jump. The metal clangs. I jump a few more times. The metal clangs more, as if it's starting to separate from the glass of the tube. I brace myself with a hand on either side of the glass tube. Pushing upward, I lift my feet so they are pressing against the sides of the tube. I scale the sides until I'm crouched up near the top of the tube, which is not much larger than the height of my body.

When I'm positioned as high as I can go, I pause to reposition then release and slam into the metal base with a loud *bang*. The metal shifts and shrieks under the weight of my impact. Enough to see a crack forming between the surfaces. It's working.

I scale the walls again and drop a second time. The crack expands. A few more times should do it. After three more climbs to the top, I slam my body down toward the metal platform once again. It gives way with a horrific crash. I fall onto the tube below me, landing hard. The air rushes from my lungs.

I groan as spotlights hover over me. Several small, uncrewed crafts are circling me, daring me to run so they can take me down.

Get up. NOW.

Despite the voice in my head prodding, I lie on the metal surface for a few moments longer, using the break as an opportunity to search the surrounding tubes for Cassian. There are too many to count. Column after column of creatures from every corner of the universe.

Miraculously, across the way and several levels down, I locate him. His eyes are closed. His hair is longer. He looks serene, like he's sleeping. Now, I know better.

I close my eyes, trying to come up with a fast plan, but my brain races with disastrous possible outcomes. A large craft approaches, one similar to the flying pods in the circus tent. It has four passengers. Two drivers and two others who are armed with an arsenal of weapons. They must be security.

Ignoring them, I stand and judge the distance between my column of tubes and the one across the way that holds Cassian. It's too far to leap on my own. I eye the crafts circling. They're spaced out at approximately the right intervals to make a series of small jumps.

Backing myself against the wall holding the tubes into place, I take two giant steps across the metal platform and launch into the air, reaching for one of the small crafts. My left hand grazes and misses the hold, but my right closes around a small bar on the bottom of the craft. I swing a few times before I'm able to slow my momentum, reach up with my left hand, and grab another anchor.

Once I'm hanging, I search the remaining crafts for a good place to move to next. But the craft I'm holding must be aware of the extra weight. It flies erratically, using short, jerky movements in an attempt to shake me off.

My gaze darts, looking for a new craft to swing to. When I find it, I swing my legs a few times to get enough power then launch toward it. This time, I stick the landing with both hands and waste no time looking for my next move before the craft can try to shake me. But the other crafts are firing at me. I swing more to evade the blasts than to gather momentum. After two more jumps, I land on the metal platform several tubes above Cassian.

The firing stops. Curious. They must be afraid to break the tubes. They don't want to let their collection of creatures go. But why?

I inspect the controls on top of the tube. The symbols are unrecognizable to me. I hit a series of buttons at random. Several of the controls turn red in protest, but one button blinks with a red light, daring me to press it. So, I do.

The tube hisses and fills with smoke. The cover I'm standing on rises into the air, and the smoke comes with it. The hairy creature inside jolts. Its eyes fly open. It thrashes in confusion then looks up at me and growls.

"Don't look at me."

The creature doesn't seem to understand and thrashes more.

I point to the crafts circling around us. The creature looks out the glass tube and seems to understand my meaning, because it starts punching the glass in anger. Then it looks up at me as if judging the jump out of the tube.

I bow and wave my arm, inviting it up.

But before it makes a move, I slide down the side of its tube to the next tube down. Banging on the controls again, I release a second humanoid creature with glimmering pink skin. This creature is less confused and instantly jumps from the tube. It launches at one of the crafts, trying to dismantle it.

Alarms blare all around us now, with red lights blinking.

Time to go.

"Not without Cassian," I mumble.

I slide down another couple of tubes, releasing the lifeforms as I go. There are half a dozen loose. Several are releasing others, while some are attacking the crafts. A warning message rings out in a language I don't recognize, but it's clear I'm running out of time.

When I finally land on Cassian's tube, I slam my hands over the controls and release the cap.

"Please be okay," I whisper into the void.

Cassian gasps and blinks, trying to get his bearings. He looks up in confusion. When he finally recognizes me, he smiles widely the way he always did growing up.

He checks out his surroundings, and when his gaze returns to mine, a question forms on his face.

"No time to explain. We gotta go, now." I extend my hand to him.

He yanks the leads from his head and accepts my hand. I pull him from the tube. We embrace. Despite the chill around us, it's warm. It's home.

"So, what's the plan for getting out of here?" He laughs, but when he sees my face, he stops. "Got it. Fly by the seat of our pants."

"You know me so well."

Then we both laugh and take in the chaos around us.

More and more tubes are opening. Creatures are flying around, taking out the increasing number of crafts showing up. There's shooting, but never in the direction of the glass tubes.

An explosion erupts beneath us. The whole room rocks. I reach for something to brace myself, but the only thing I can find is Cassian. He grabs my arm and uses his other to hold onto the center column that secures all the tubes.

I breathe a sigh of relief, but it's short lived. Fire shoots from some of the ducts connecting to the glass tubes. Another announcement blares, but I can't understand it. Cass shrugs his shoulders.

The circling crafts that can break free from the fight disappear into a large duct.

"Why do you think they're leaving?" Cass asks, trying to make sense of the chaos.

Before I can answer, an entire column of hundreds of glass tubes detaches and collapses to the floor like a building imploding. The heat from the fireball plumes toward us. The whole building shakes violently. While the quaking slows, the building still sways.

"I think that's your answer." But I bite the inside of my cheek, afraid to share my theory. The more tubes are destroyed, the faster the building seems to crumble, which further reinforces my conjecture.

Cass nods then offers me a boost to climb to the next level before joining me.

"This place isn't going to last much longer. We need to find a ship." I'm breathing heavily now with a combination of exhaustion and fear.

We keep climbing, taking turns pulling each other up until we reach the duct the crafts disappeared through. It's large and not well lit.

Cass and I exchange a look. He shrugs then bolts down the tunnel. I follow close behind. The tunnel rocks. We pause to brace ourselves against the walls.

"This place seems to be falling apart faster and faster." Cass extends his hand, and I accept.

"That's exactly what I was afraid of," I mumble as we pick up the pace. The more creatures are released, the bigger the quakes become, and the more everything crumbles.

We skid to a stop at the edge of the tunnel, which opens into another large room filled with glass tubes. It's completely intact, but some of the tubes have large cracks in them, no doubt from all the shaking.

I scan the room, looking for an exit. "There." I point across the way: another duct, but this one is smaller than the one we're standing in. My gaze traces a path back from the duct, identifying a climbing path.

I lean around the tube and reach for a handhold.

"Hold on a minute." Cass pries open a panel. There's a large keypad. He hits some of the keys in a seemingly random order, but shortly after, a large, empty pod flies over.

"How'd you know how to do that?"

He smiles as if remembering another life. "Let's just say the *Perseus* was more than just a shipping freighter."

I smack him across the arm. If we had more time, I would have killed him right on the spot. It didn't fully explain everything, but it's enough of a hint to point to why Cass refused to give in to my pleas that he not join the crew. Given this mess, I know I'm still right. But being right feels like a dull knife in my belt.

We step into the pod without any more words on the matter. Cass pilots it toward the duct. We zoom through it into another room with glass tubes. These are of a much older design than the previous rooms.

"See if you can find a map." He points to a series of buttons on the far side of the control panel.

I hit a couple at random. The pod jerks in protest.

"Not that button."

"I figured that out, thanks."

"The one that looks like a spiral with a star in it."

I scan the buttons and find the one matching his description. When I push it, a giant holographic map appears in front of us. It tilts on its side and marks our current location. Cass yanks the controls. We whip around a corner through another duct. The red dot on the holographic map does the same.

"There." He points to an open space on the map. "That must be the docking bay."

I nod in agreement, then glance behind us. "But we've got company."

Several large pods filled with uniformed guards are speeding toward us. One fires a long blast. Cass looks behind us then maneuvers our pod out of the way. The blast blows a hole in the duct, and steam pours out.

"There's a weapons panel back there. Start firing."

"Which button?" I ask, panicked I'll do something to damage the pod further.

"Doesn't matter, just pick one!"

The pod buzzes louder beneath us and speeds up as I hit my first button. It's shaped like a spider web. A large net shoots out from the back of the craft and wraps around one of the pods chasing us. The latter spirals out of control and slams into the wall of the duct.

"Brace yourself!" Cassian shouts.

I grab hold of the control panel and slam my fist down on a button shaped like a snowflake. An icy blast erupts from the back of the pod and coats the tunnel with a thin layer of ice. Too bad the next pod is too far away to be caught in it directly. But when it passes over the frozen area, it loses its momentum and drops out of the air.

Three more pods appear, seemingly out of nowhere, to replace the fallen pod. "They just don't quit," I mutter under my breath.

"What was that?" Cass asks.

"Nothing. How close are we?" I ask in an attempt to distract him.

"Another minute."

Five more pods appear inside the duct. "I don't think we have another second."

Cass hazards a glance behind him and shoves the controls forward. We sink so fast, my stomach drops. Two of the pods sail over us as we scrape the bottom of the duct. Cass yanks the controls upward, and we level off. He fires at the two pods ahead and destroys them instantaneously.

My body warms as we pass through the smoke plume from the explosions. But we still have six more to deal with. I press buttons with more frequency. A giant bubble encapsulates one pod and lifts it to the ceiling while a series of bullets rips through two more pods. I hit a button with what look like comets on it and take out two more pods before the ammo runs out.

Cass yanks the craft around a sharp corner. "How are things looking back there?"

"One left." I slam my fingers down on a flame-shaped button. A giant fireball erupts from the back of the pod and takes out the remaining craft. "And we're clear."

Cass sighs in relief but increases the speed anyway. We take one more duct before emerging into a docking bay filled with ships. It's very different from what I saw when I arrived. How much of this was a hallucination?

But I don't have time to think through it. The docking bay is in complete chaos. All kinds of lifeforms are scrambling to get engines up and running and crafts loaded with supplies. I scan the room before I lock onto my ship.

"There." I point.

Cass nods and angles the pod toward my ship. "I never pegged you for a

J-class."

"It's all I could find in a pinch."

He laughs, knowing I'd rather have a faster K-class ship.

Despite the chaos in the docking bay, the corner where my ship sits is abandoned. Maybe my crappy ship was my four-leaf clover. It was so old no one in their right mind would touch it.

Cass sets the pod down, and we bolt toward the ship. He runs to the captain's chair while I search for supplies. But those jerks stripped my ship clean of all weapons, including the one I thought I'd left on board. Or was that all part of the hallucination, too?

By the time I make my way to the co-captain's chair, Cass has the ship running.

"Find anything?"

I shake my head. "They scavenged it for anything worthwhile. I'm surprised the ship is intact enough to fly."

"About that…"

"Don't tell me they took the hyperdrive."

"No, but they might as well have. They stole the nav computer."

"Stars. So, we're flying blind." I look out the cockpit and search for another option, but all the ships appear to be occupied. An explosion erupts from one of the ducts. The docking bay rocks, confirming that we are out of options and time.

"Punch it, Cass."

I plop into the co-captain's chair and buckle in as Cass lifts the craft into the air. He doesn't wait for clearance but follows a larger craft outside the force field.

Once in space, the craft smooths out, but only briefly. The black hole swirls and spews gas in all directions. The tail whips around faster and faster.

Cass engages the main engines, which groan under the pull of the black hole.

"I don't think we're going to make it."

"We have to engage the hyperdrive."

"It could be a death sentence. Or we could end up lost in space." But Cass doesn't seem scared. He's smiling. Ready for the next adventure.

"At least we'll be together." I smile back at him.

"Together," he says, engaging the drive and freeing us from the pull of Signe.

THE SHADOW MENAGERIE

KARISSA LAUREL

enevieve groaned and rolled over, ignoring the persistent knocking at her caravan door. She dragged her coverlet over her head, but the quilted cotton couldn't muffle the clatter of knuckles rapping against wood. "Genevieve… wake up. *Please.*"

"Go away," Genevieve mumbled. The darkness in her cabin and beyond her small windows told her morning was still far away, and she held strict personal convictions against rising before the sun, especially after a long day of performing—and not merely one long day, but an entire week of them.

Le Cirque du Merveilles Mècanique had set up exactly seven days before at the fairgrounds on the outskirts of Menshin, one of the largest cities in Dreutch. While not the capital in terms of government or commerce, most Dreutchish citizens considered Menshin their country's cultural center. If Steinerland was Dreutch's head, then Menshin was its heart, and a self-propelled, mechanical circus was the type of spectacle the Menshin populace adored.

The circus had enjoyed sold-out shows every afternoon and evening since its arrival. With sales and attendance showing no signs of waning, Falak Savin, ringmaster extraordinaire, had settled in for a long-term stay—or "long-term" by circus definition, meaning Falak could change his mind any moment, but probably not before three or four weeks at least.

"Genevieve, this is an *emergency*." A familiar voice full of genuine panic broke through the fog in Genvieve's sleep-addled brain.

She sat up, rubbed her face, and tossed aside her bed covers. "Coming. I'm coming, Svieta. Hold on."

Genevieve stuffed her feet into felt slippers and shrugged on her silk robe, knotting its sash around her waist as she opened her small caravan door. Tendrils of cool night air caressed her cheeks, and Genevieve blinked as she focused on the familiar face of the circus's master mechanic. "What is it, Svieta?"

Svieta's mouth worked, but no sound came out. She flapped her hands. "I can't—" She shook her head. "I don't—" The wizened little mechanic, with iron-threaded curls and an experience-lined face, was clearly upset by something. She gestured at the red-and-white striped tent housing the circus's mechanical menagerie. "Please, you must see for yourself."

Cold slivers of dread pricked the back of Genvieve's neck as she glanced at the tent. Ynnua, the mechanical unicorn with whom she performed trick-riding routines, resided in that tent between performances. Svieta's contagious panic crept into Genevieve, constricting her heart. "Ynnua? Has something happened to my sweet girl?" Genevieve launched herself from her caravan's short steps and raced the distance between her wagon and the menagerie, leaving Svieta to follow at her own, slower pace.

Upon reaching the tent, Genevieve flung open the door flap and charged to the controls for the gas-powered lighting. When the overhead lanterns flared to life, she examined the scene. The animals were all there and, upon first glance, appeared in perfect condition. Their bronze and steel exteriors gleamed, metallic feathers, trunks, tails, wings, and ears catching and diffusing the glow of soft gaslight. But to an experienced eye such as Genevieve's, something was obviously amiss.

Panting, Svieta trundled into the tent and stopped at Genvieve's side. Her hand, flat like a knife, sliced the air, gesturing at the elephant and peacock. They stood side by side, utterly motionless. "Do you see?"

With her breath frozen in her throat, Genevieve nodded. Leaden footed, she trudged to Ynnua, who was as unmoving as marble. The single bronze horn in the middle of her forehead flashed from the gas lamps, but no spark of life animated her. She was a beautiful statue but nothing more, and that was absolutely, completely *wrong*.

Genevieve stroked her faithful companion and found her steel skin cold and inert. No thrum of animating spirit responded to her touch. "What…?" She paused and swallowed, forcing down the swell of emotion in her throat. "What happened?" Glancing around the room, Genevieve confirmed Ynnua was not alone in her perplexing condition. No other animal showed signs of awareness or life. Usually they were always moving, shifting, chirping, flapping, trumpeting, neighing, roaring.

But the menagerie tent was silent.

Still.

Lifeless.

An involuntary whine of distress seeped from Genevieve's throat.

"I found them like this only a few moments ago." Svieta crossed to the elephant that stood over twice as high as she did. She ran a hand down his limp trunk. "I was assigned to security patrol for the second half of the night, and I came here as soon as my shift began. I do not know how long they have been like this."

"What do you think happened?" Genevieve stroked her unicorn again and grieved Ynnua's lack of response. Normally, the mechanical beast sighed, or leaned into Genevieve's touch, or sniffed her pockets in search of treats she could no longer truly eat, but that her animating spirit—retrieved by Svieta from the Shadowlands of afterlife and installed into this clockwork avatar via a dubious Magical procedure—still sought out of instinct and memory.

Svieta closed her eyes and inhaled a deep breath. She spoke quiet words, barely a whisper, as she twisted her fingers into complicated configurations. Genevieve recognized those actions, knew they were signs of Svieta working her peculiar brand of Magic. Mechanic, or Tinkerer, was too humble a title for what Svieta really was, but Magician wasn't quite right either. There really was no name for her unique amalgamation of technology and supernatural craft. "I do not know much, yet," Svieta said, "but I do know that they are gone. All of them." She extended a pointing finger in a wide arc, indicating each animal in the menagerie. "The bodies are empty. Their spirits have… *departed*."

Genevieve gasped, her hands going to her mouth as hot tears rose in her eyes. "Dead?"

Svieta clicked her tongue. "They were already dead. They cannot die again."

"But it feels the same."

The mechanic nodded. "Indeed."

"Can you fix them?"

Svieta glanced at Genevieve, revealing wide, gray eyes full of doubt and worry. She waggled her head in a way that meant neither no nor yes. "Depends."

"On what?"

"On discovering what happened in the first place."

Genevieve rubbed Ynnua's chin, as if still hoping for a response. "I appreciate that you told me about this, Svieta, but why? Why me and not Falak?"

"I will tell him." Svieta sidled up to the peacock and traced his splayed tail feathers, a blend of brass and other metals tooled as fine as the real things. Add "artist" to the many of Svieta's insufficient titles. "But while he will be motivated to find answers because of what it means to his wallet, you will be motivated to find out what has happened because of love." She turned her troubled gaze upon Genevieve again. "If we want to fix this problem, love will be the way we do it."

It sounded unlikely to Genevieve, but what did she know? She was a circus performer, a trick rider, and a runaway from a royal family who ruled hundreds of miles away in another country. Love had mostly been a stranger to her in that place.

Genevieve cared very specifically for Ynnua and for the bond they'd built over their previous year of performing together, training together, often eating and sleeping together, too. One might call that love if they were being generous. She certainly cared for her circus family, as well, though it had taken her a while to lower her guard enough to acknowledge her softer feelings for them. The loss of anyone, and especially the animals, was unacceptable, but she had no idea what she could do about it. Once upon a time she'd had the best education gold could purchase, but that certainly hadn't included training in intricate mechanical engineering, and definitely not lessons in Magic. That knowledge was reserved for a sacred few, such as Otokar, her family's Magician. And for Svieta, outcast though she was.

Svieta seemed to have read Genevieve's mind, hearing her doubts. "Whatever has happened here, I will not be able to fix it alone. I am too old, too slow. You, though…" Svieta shuffled closer to Genevieve. "Fast, agile, clever. You have much at stake here. Too much to lose, I should think. Together, we have the necessary skills and knowledge to solve this riddle."

Skeptical, Genevieve squinted at the mechanic. "I don't know if you're right. But I'm willing to try. I don't know what I'd do without Ynnua. Where would I go if Falak decided I had no purpose here anymore?" Convincing Falak to accept her into the circus in the first place had taken more effort and intention than Genevieve wanted to admit. If she could no longer work for the circus, how quickly would he send her packing, running back home with her figurative tail between her legs?

Svieta patted Genevieve's shoulder. "This is why you will be the best one to help me."

Overwhelmed and uncertain, Genevieve scoffed. "Where would I even begin?"

Gritting her teeth, Svieta gave Genevieve a pained look. "We begin by telling Falak."

As they trudged toward the circus master's wagon, however, a realization formed in Genevieve's mind, though with great reluctance. *No, I really should begin by telling Otokar.*

Falak took the news of the menagerie's dilemma as well as Genevieve had expected. He had stormed into the mechanical animals' tent wearing only his jodhpurs, stretching suspenders over his scarred chest and shoulders as he went. In bare feet and with his uncovered black hair gleaming under the gas lamps, he took in the grim scene, mouth agape and blood rising in his umber-colored cheeks. "I'll have their head."

"Whose head?" Genevieve asked.

With his back to Genevieve, Falak flexed the fingers of his flesh-and-bone hand at his side, clenching and unclenching. His mechanical hand mimicked the same movement, quietly clicking and whirring. Shoulders stiff and spine ramrod straight, he looked as though he wanted to punch something, or some*one*. Genevieve had known Falak to be passionate, stubborn, bossy, and sometimes angry. At this moment, though, she believed he also had the potential for violence.

"Whoever it is who has done this." He marched to the inert mass of metal that had once been a fiercely loyal lion named Sher-sah. The lion had suffered the indignity of quasi-death once before. That he should have to experience it again, and so soon after his most recent trauma, seemed like sacrilege. Life, even the strange mixture of existence motivating this unconventional collection of beasts, was sacred. In Genevieve's opinion, whatever had been done to them was miles worse than the Magical taboos Svieta had violated in crafting these creatures in the first place.

Hands now fisted on his hips, Falak spun on his heel and faced his mechanic and prize trick rider. "Who do you suspect is the culprit?" His wrathful gaze shifted between the two women. "Who is capable of such a deed? Magicians, surely. Who else would have the ability? Not Le Poing Fermé, though. I believe they have been all but demolished by now."

Svieta nodded. "I suspect a Magician is involved, but who and for what purpose, I cannot yet say. But no, not Le Poing Fermé. What is left of that vile cabal is scattered to the winds like ashes."

Falak's attention turned to Genevieve. He raised an expectant eyebrow.

Genevieve resisted the urge to curtsey. His imperious manner reminded her so much of her sister. *Old habits die hard.* "I don't know, either. But I think I know where to start looking."

Falak rolled his hand, urging her to continue.

"Otokar," she said, simply.

Falak's face hardened, eyes narrowing, mouth pinching. "Do you really think that's a good idea? You and he do not have the best history—"

Genevieve threw up a halting hand. "You don't have to tell me. I know this. I lived it." Genevieve's transition from a princess of Bonhemm to a proletariat circus performer had not come without a great deal of resistance. Not from Genevieve, but from her sister, the Empress of Bonhemm, and, more specifically, from her Magical bloodhound, Otokar. "But he is the best scryer of his generation. If anyone can discover the culprits, it will be him." Based on the way her old scars itched, Genevieve feared she already knew who the culprit was, and she was walking right into his trap.

Falak's heavy, dark brows drew together as he flapped a hand at his mechanic. "Svieta, can you not scry as well?"

The older woman shook her head, and her curls bobbed, echoing her dissent. "My Magic is best suited to material, practical applications. Scrying is too…" Her fingers patted the space before her, as if seeking to pull the right word from thin air.

"Theoretical? Metaphysical?" Genevieve suggested. "Abstract?"

"Yes." Svieta nodded. "All of those things."

Falak's dark gaze flitted back to Genevieve. "What if he demands your return home instead?"

An oily sickness swirled through her gut. A similar fear had possessed her the moment she'd realized what she might have to do to get Ynnua back. "Let's go one step at a time," Genevieve said. "I'll reach out to him and see what he has to say."

Svieta patted Genevieve's shoulder and offered a weak, unconvincing smile. "Perhaps he will help you out of the kindness of his heart."

Genevieve rolled her eyes and started for her wagon. "He has no heart. Maybe you can build one for him from iron and spirit like you did for Lady Stormbourne."

In reply, the little mechanic merely snorted. "How will you contact him? Whatever happened to the menagerie has taken out my homing pigeons as well."

Spinning on her heel, Genevieve continued toward her caravan, walking backward into the darkness. "Then I guess I'll have to send a telegram, like other mere mortals must do."

At first light, Genevieve borrowed one of the circus's few real horses and rode it to the closest telegraph station. Telegrams were a rare commodity, but both Menshin and her home city of Prigha were large enough to justify maintaining infrastructure for the technology. After depositing several coins in the telegraphist's palm, Genevieve produced the message she wished to transmit. Then, she followed her nose to a cozy teashop, paid for a pot of oolong and a basket of pastries, retrieved a tattered novel from her pocket, and made herself at home at a streetside table. She had no idea how long it would take to send her message, or how long before Otokar responded.

So, when she retrieved them from the telegraph office several hours later, she found the contents of his response were only somewhat surprising.

Genevieve,

Your communique was received by the castle and dispatched to me forthwith. Will gladly assist in attaining the solution for your misfortune. Only require that you make your request in person.

Luck favors you. Currently in Steinerland on a research project at the university. Will tell steward to set a place for you at my table tomorrow evening.

Essen Supper Club.

Seven o'clock sharp.

Come alone.

—O. Kouzlo, Imp Mgn, Bonhemm

That Otokar wanted her to appeal to him in person was no great revelation, but to find out he was nearby, in Steinerland, was enough of a shock to chill her blood and make her old scars burn. A tingle of trepidation skittered across her shoulders, raising fine hairs along her neck and arms. Was his proximity merely coincidence? Perhaps. But Genevieve knew better than to assume anything but the worst when it came to her old nemesis.

He wasn't asking her to come home, to the castle in Prigha, to her sister and the torments of her past. Because of that, she was willing to risk meeting him in person. Otokar would not underestimate her, though. Not this time, not after her previous escapes. Theirs was a tentative truce, her freedom as fragile as glass. Surely, this meeting would shatter their peace.

But Ynnua was worth it.

Svieta was worth it.

Even Falak was worth it.

For the sake of *Le Cirque de Merveilles Mècanique*, Genevieve would stand in her house of glass and throw every stone she could find.

Convincing Falak to lend her a horse the next morning for her half-day journey to Steinerland had been relatively easy. Easier than convincing him to let her leave on her own. Genevieve had packed a small valise full of essentials and graciously accepted a pouch of coins from the notoriously tight-fisted ringmaster.

"This mission might be personal to you," he had said, chuckling at her wide-mouthed look of surprise, "but it is a matter of extreme importance to me. This undertaking is circus business, and therefore must be considered a circus expense."

Genevieve said nothing, merely closed her mouth and nodded. She stowed the money pouch deep in the saddle bag of her moth-eaten mount, a chestnut mare of indeterminate breeding named Brenna. Svieta and a few others had gathered to see her off. They wished Genevieve well as she and Brenna plodded away from the circus on a dusty pathway. She kept her eyes glued to the road ahead, afraid she'd lose her nerve if she looked back.

Traffic on the main thoroughfare was heavy, and she took some comfort in the crowds. *Safety in numbers, hopefully.* She did not, however, let down her guard. Even among the nameless, faceless throngs of travelers, she might seem a good target for anyone—thieves, pickpockets, confidence scammers— looking for an easy mark. A year in the circus had worn down her naiveté, and she had developed a protective layer of cynicism, skepticism, and intuition that was at least as useful as the coins in her bag. Maybe even more so.

By sunset, Genevieve had reached the outskirts of Steinerland a few coins lighter—she had paid for a lunch of cold meat pie and warm beer from a roving food wagon halfway along her journey—but mostly as well off as she had been when she'd left the circus. Her cold shoulder and unfriendly nature had seemed to deter attention. Also, the old horse and worn tack beneath her probably implied she wouldn't be worth the effort of robbing.

When she reached the inn Falak had recommended—humble lodgings on the edge of Steinerland that wouldn't take too many coins nor leave her with too many fleas—she paid for a single room for herself and boarding for Brenna. With little time to spare, she washed off the road grime, combed her dark hair and re-braided it, and changed from her traveling attire into a more elegant frock the circus's costumer had lent her. The gown was fine silk, the color of peridot, that brought out the green swirls in her hazel eyes. She didn't want Otokar to think her a desperate vagabond, but beyond that, she didn't care about his opinion. She certainly didn't want his regard or admiration. That was what circus audiences were for, and she was eager to get back to the peculiar little niche in the world that made her feel most like herself.

After tucking a few coins into her pocket and hailing a hansom cab, Genevieve was on her way. Catching herself tapping her foot and biting her nails, she fisted her hands in her lap. "Dammit!" It wouldn't do to let Otokar see her nervous. A year of living on her own—earning and managing her own money, taking care of herself, making her own decisions—had matured her, given her more self-assurance and better judgement. *Hadn't it?* No longer the dependent little brat she'd been when he last saw her, she would not be manipulated, now, as she had been before. She wouldn't let him wrap his clever fingers around her again.

The cab arrived at her destination sooner than she'd expected. It stopped with a jolt, and she rocked forward, nearly slipping to the floor. Grabbing the door handle, she steadied herself and smoothed her hair. When the driver opened her door, she descended to the street as elegantly as if dismounting from Ynnua after their final stunt. She paid her fare, including a tip, bobbed a curtsey to the driver, and sashayed to the dark doorstep of what the driver insisted was the Essen Supper Club.

It didn't look like much: a dowdy brown-and-white, half-timbered, two-story cottage in the classic Dreutch style. No sign advertised the cottage's purpose. A dim gas flame burned over an even dimmer doorway swathed in ivy and cobwebs. A few grimy glass panes leaked milky light from a thick wooden door. She lifted the heavy ring gripped between the teeth of a grimacing chimera—half lion, half ram—and clacked it against the door twice.

Several moments passed before a shadow interrupted the meager illumination. The door opened inwardly with a quiet groan, and a small man with a balding head feathered in wispy white hair bowed perfunctorily. "Princess Karolina, I presume?"

An involuntary wave of panic and anger washed over her. "Don't call me that. My name is Genevieve."

The old man merely nodded, stepped aside, and waved her in. "Imperial Magician Kouzlo is waiting for you."

The aroma of fragrant herbs, baked bread, and roasted meat greeted her as she stepped into a dining room filled with small wooden tables. Oil lamps flickered on the walls, and tealights on the tables struggled to hold the room's inherent gloom at bay. Only a handful of people occupied the space, most pointedly ignoring her and focusing on the dishes before them. Like a visual magnet, Otokar's tall, lean frame drew Genevieve's gaze. He looked the same as when she had last seen him, nearly a year before. With his dark hair cut in long messy waves, some found him handsome. His long nose added character to a face that might have been too pretty, otherwise. He wore a dark shirt, and Magical symbols in gold thread embroidered the high, banded collar. His black coat and pants seemed to absorb the room's scanty light. Hands folded together on the table before him, the Magician smiled—really, it was more of a smirk—but he did not stand to greet her.

The little steward who had opened the door ushered Genevieve to the table and pulled out her chair. Once she sat, he placed a linen napkin in her lap and poured wine from a bottle already sitting on the table. Clearly, Otokar had started without her.

"I took the liberty of ordering for you," Otokar said after the steward had left. "I know what you like."

Genevieve bit back her retort. *Making power plays already? I should have known.* She plastered on a smile and batted her lashes. "How gracious of you."

Otokar raised a long finger, and a basket of crusty bread danced across the table toward her. "The supper club is not particularly elegant, but the food is palatable at least." He gestured to the plate of seasoned oil between them. "Please, help yourself."

Genevieve vibrated with the need to dismiss pleasantries and get to the point of their meeting. From experience, however, she knew Otokar didn't work that way. If she pushed too hard, too soon, he would shut down. To have any hope of influencing things in her favor, Genevieve would have to play by his rules, despite her deep aversion for such games. She selected a slice of bread, sopped it in the seasoned oil, and nibbled a corner. The bread was palatable, as Otokar had said, but nothing compared to the fresh rolls Geppenio, the circus cook, baked every day.

Otokar's heavy, black-eyed gaze rested on her as he lifted his wine glass to his lips. Genevieve knew what lay beneath his equanimous mask, though, and it made her want to shiver.

Quiet chatter from the other patrons filled the silence between them. Neither dared to speak, as if being the first to do so would tip the scale of power in the other's favor. So, Genevieve bit her tongue, met Otokar's stare, and held it as she sipped her wine. Her hands were steady, but, inside, her heart quaked, and she feared he could sense it.

Eventually, a waiter arrived with their meal, breaking their stalemate. She released a long, silent breath and studied her plate's contents. Potatoes and meat, probably chicken, swam in pale pink sauce smelling vaguely of tomato. Her mouth watered. The pasty and beer from lunch had long since faded from her stomach, and she eagerly dug into her supper. Otokar could read whatever he wanted into her actions. She had never been one to turn away a meal, not even when she had been a spoiled princess. *Hmph, as if I didn't pay for every ounce of everything I was given. Paid with my own flesh and blood…*

"You always were an enthusiastic eater." He picked up his cutlery and sliced into a breaded pork cutlet.

"Life is short." She shrugged. "Might as well enjoy the best parts of it." Her chicken was tender, if also a little bland, but the sauce was warm and heavy in a comforting way.

He ran his gaze over her. "You do not look as though you've had to skip too many meals."

"Why should I?" She forked another piece of chicken. "We're successful at what we do, and everyone enjoys the benefits of it."

"The circus, you mean? I've heard discussion of it even here in Steinerland. People are willing to travel quite a long distance for a cheap thrill."

Ignoring his jab, Genevieve slid her fork tines into a hunk of potato and lifted it to her lips. "Not so cheap. Entrance tickets seem reasonably priced at first, but once you're through the gates, you find everything else comes at a separate cost, and that's not including the concessions. We've emptied more than a few pockets in a matter of only minutes."

Otokar chuckled. "Your ringmaster is a shrewd businessman. I'll give you that much."

He wasn't wrong in his assessment of Falak, so Genevieve said nothing and bit into her potato.

Another moment of quiet eating passed between them before Otokar exhaled. The tension in his broad shoulders eased. He might have been relaxing his guard, or he might have been setting a trap. Genevieve was wary. "Are you happy?" Otokar pinched the bridge of his nose. "Your sister is worried for you. I've assured her you were quite where you wanted to be."

"*You* assured her?" Genevieve scoffed. "You, who were so determined to force me back to the castle. Back to the laboratory. My contentment has not been in your interest, now or ever."

Showing no reaction, he casually cut another piece of meat. "You and I were a team, Genevieve. Together, we were solving the riddle of restoring your family's divinity."

"The word 'team' implies consent." She stabbed a piece of chicken and swirled it through the pink sauce. Her appetite was waning as her anger waxed.

"You were not a prisoner." Otokar clicked his tongue. "Your life was not without luxury, beauty, pleasure…" He drained the last of his wine. "So many in this world would've happily traded places with you."

"Then let them. Find someone else for your experiments."

"You know it doesn't work that way. Your bloodline cannot be substituted."

"We've had this argument too many times. The old ways are dead." She pushed her plate aside, mourning the loss of her appetite. "The old *gods* are dead. It's time you and Tereza let them go. You have amazing power, Otokar, yet you continue to waste your time on pointless pursuits. I'll never understand it."

The Magician leaned back in his seat and folded long fingers over his flat belly. He arched one thick, black eyebrow. "Is that really what you came all this way to discuss with me?"

She refrained from rolling her eyes. "You know it isn't."

"Just a year ago, you made it clear that you wanted nothing to do with me or your sister, and out of love and respect for you, we have abided by your wishes." Otokar caught a waiter's eye and motioned for him to approach. "Yet here you are, in a borrowed costume and minding your manners… The reason for your presence here must be something quite important for you to swallow your pride and put yourself in this position."

The waiter cleared away their half-empty plates. "Anything else, sir? Aperitifs? Tea? Coffee?"

Otokar nodded. "Coffee, yes." He glanced at his dining partner. "Will you have some?"

Genevieve nodded. "Please." She waited for the waiter to leave before returning to their previous discussion.

Both of the Magician's eyebrows arched this time. "What sort of coincidence?"

"What are you researching?" she asked. "What was worth leaving the castle and coming all this way to discover?"

He snorted. "Steinerland is not so very far from Prigha."

"You've never been fond of travel."

"You know of the history of birthright exchanges in the Stormbourne family?"

Genevieve shook her head. "Lady Stormbourne never brought it up in our limited discussions."

"The Stormbournes' roots are in Steinerland, as you may know, and the University library has extensive records on their history."

"You think there's something in those records that could be applicable to my sister's… situation?"

Lady Evelyn Stormbourne could command lightning and thunder as though they were her pets. Genevieve's family had once possessed the ability to command and manipulate metals and minerals in a similar fashion. But that way had been lost long ago, and she didn't believe it could be recovered, despite Otokar's and Tereza's insistence otherwise.

The waiter returned with a pot of fragrant coffee. He set cups and saucers on the table and poured. Then he placed the pot between them, along with the sugar and cream. "Anything else?"

Shaking his head, Otokar waved him away.

Genevieve inhaled deeply, savoring the brew's rich fragrance. She might have lost her appetite, but she could almost never refuse a cup of fresh coffee. After stirring in sugar and cream, she sipped. Then she sighed. *Bliss.*

"Perhaps…" Otokar said, responding to her earlier question. "But, again, the issue of your sister's divinity is not why you are here."

Genevieve narrowed her eyes and studied her opponent, looking for a tell. Did he really not know, or was this more manipulation on his part? "The menagerie animals are dead. *Dead*, dead. Their spirits have… departed. They are inert. Inoperable. Unalive." She summarized her experience with Svieta of discovering the mechanical animals in their dire state.

Otokar swallowed his coffee. He had added nothing to it, preferring to drink it black. *Just like his soul.* "How unfortunate," he said.

"Did you have anything to do with it?"

He pursed his lips, as if tasting something sour. "Some, particularly those in the Magical realms, consider that circus mechanic's creations to be an abomination. Reaching beyond the veil, bringing back the souls of those who have passed on…" He clicked his tongue three times and shook his head. "Verboten, some would say. Wicked, even."

Genevieve leaned forward, her gaze intent on her adversary. "What would *you* say?"

He shrugged. "Necromancy is not my area of expertise, but I'm in no position to judge." Fast as a striking cobra, like Ajej, the circus's mechanical snake, Otokar's hand shot across the table. His fingers gripped Genevieve's wrist with bruising pressure. With his other hand, he pushed back her cuff, revealing scars lacing her inner arm from wrist to elbow. "I am comfortable treading on the path of the verboten, as you well know."

Genevieve yanked free and arranged her sleeve in place. Glaring, she nearly snarled as she spoke. "Just answer my question. Was it you?"

He sat back in his chair and smoothed his jacket's lapels. "Such occurrences do not happen without stirring interest in the Magical world. Gossip abounds. But rather than telling you who may or may not be the culprit, I can, instead, offer you the necessary procedure for retrieving your missing souls. It's simple enough that even your circus's strange little mechanic can do it."

Genevieve took a deep breath and willed her pulse to settle. He was right that the culprit didn't matter so long as there was a remedy, but the fact that he had the solution so readily at hand all but verified his guilt. And to get that solution from him, she'd possibly do something very stupid and desperate. "Will you tell me?"

His nostrils flared. "Why should I?"

Her anger surged, and her jaw clenched. "You owe me."

A surprised chuckle escaped him. "I do?"

She held her tongue. She did not need to justify herself. Truth was truth.

Again, they stared each other down. Genevieve had everything to lose, and for that reason, she knew she would win, though she would pay dearly for it. Otokar's entire livelihood wasn't at stake the way Genevieve's was. No matter whether he found the solution to Empress Tereza's lack of divinity or not, Tereza would never abandon him. She loved him too much.

Otokar would relent to Genevieve's demands because he wanted something from her. His wanting something from her was the whole reason he'd invited her to dinner in the first place. His wanting something was most likely the reason the menagerie was the way it was, even if he wouldn't admit he was the mastermind behind it. He certainly hadn't invited her here because he missed her less-than-charming presence at the castle.

"I'll tell you," he finally said, his gaze cutting away. "But the information will not be given for free."

"I expected as much." She slumped back in her seat and rubbed the scars on her arms. "What will it cost me?"

He raised a single, slim index finger. "One month."

One month in his lab, subject to his experiments again. The contents of her stomach turned to sludge. She shook her head. "No way."

"Then you may leave this place with exactly as much knowledge as you had when you came in." He poured more coffee for himself. "Good luck continuing your circus career without an act."

"One week," she countered. "I'll give you one *week*."

He scoffed. "That's not enough time to even be worth the effort."

"Take it or leave it." She shrugged. "I can learn to do my routine on a regular horse." She didn't know if that was true, but she'd try anything if it meant she could stay with *Le Cirque*.

"Three weeks."

She gritted her teeth and studied his countenance, the firm set of his jaw, the harness of his obsidian eyes. The was no softness there, and there would be none even after she consented to his offer. There was no naivete left in Genevieve when it came to Otokar. She knew exactly what she was getting into, and even then, Ynnua and the circus were worth it. *Dear gods, they'd better be worth it.* "Two weeks. And only if your information is useful."

Without hesitation, Otokar's head bobbed. Having concluded his dealings, he dispensed with niceties and stood in a swift and elegant motion. "My information is solid. I accept your terms. I will send a coach for you soon."

As Otokar strode from the dining room, a folded piece of parchment dropped into Genevieve's lap, as though falling from thin air. On it was a collection of alchemical symbols she recognized from her time in his lab, though she did not understand them. She certainly hoped Svieta would.

After a restless night of almost no sleep, Genevieve had given up her rented room, retrieved Brenna from her boarding stables, and set out on the road before dawn. Arriving in Menshin in the early afternoon, she returned to the circus eager to find Svieta. Falak, however, encountered her first.

He opened his mouth, presumably to ask for a report, but Genevieve waved him off. "Let's get Svieta, so I only have to tell this story once."

Nodding, Falak escorted Genevieve to the mechanic's wagon. He skipped up the steps and drummed on the door. "Svieta, Genevieve's back. And by the look on her face, she has news." He glanced at Genevieve and frowned. "Can't tell if it's good news, though."

Svieta's door swung open, and the little tinkerer waved her guests inside. Her wagon was mostly all worktables, mechanical parts and pieces, tools, cans of grease, and a small bed obscured by a half-finished project: something with tentacles, by the looks of it.

Genevieve pointed to the incomplete creature. "Is the circus considering a mechanical aquarium? Gears and grease and water sound like a bad combination."

"It is merely an experiment." Svieta waved her hands, as if brushing away Genevieve's interest. "That is not why you are here, though."

Genevieve chuckled as she retrieved the parchment from her pocket and handed it to Svieta. "You're right. *This* is why I'm here."

The mechanic snatched the paper and unfolded it. Her eyes shifted back and forth as she skimmed Otokar's scribbles. As Svieta read, she muttered strange words under her breath, quirked an eyebrow, pursed her lips, wrinkled her nose, and, finally, looked up. She glanced at Falak first, then at Genevieve. "Yes. I think this should work."

Genevieve's body sagged as relief surged through her. "Thank the gods. I was so worried he was pulling a trick. I didn't expect him to let me have the solution so easily."

Svieta snorted. She sucked a tooth. "Easy?" She shook her head. "Nothing about this is easy. But it is *doable*." Her gaze slid to Falak. "With some luck. And money."

He groaned and rolled his eyes to the ceiling. "Of course. Nothing ever comes freely, does it?"

Svieta scurried to a worktable. Sorting through the junk, she rustled up a nub of charcoal and a mostly blank scrap of paper. "I will make you a shopping list, ringmaster."

"Is there anything I can do?" Genevieve asked.

"Oh, yes." Svieta barked a cold little laugh. "But you aren't going to like it."

"I promised Otokar I'd give myself to him and his laboratory for two weeks. It can't possibly be worse than that."

Svieta gave her a sad, piteous look. "I wouldn't be so sure. One must never take lightly all the dangers inherent in a journey through the veil between life and death."

A ball of ice formed from nothing and lodged in Genevieve's throat. "Journey?" she croaked. "*Through* the veil?"

"Indeed." Svieta nodded as she handed her shopping list to Falak.

"But you never crossed the veil to retrieve spirits for your creations before. Didn't you just sort of…" Genevieve hooked a finger and dragged it through the air as if latching onto something and towing it into place before her. "Call them forth?"

Svieta bobbed her head. "Yes. But those spirits were free." She motioned to Otokar's formula lying on her worktable. "This would indicate our animal friends are *not* free. Quite the contrary. To succeed in reviving our menagerie, we must work as a team. I will pierce the veil and keep it open, a feat requiring my constant vigilance and concentration. Meanwhile, you will cross to the other side, locate our missing companions, and release them from their Magical snares."

Genevieve's mouth gaped as blood drained to her toes, leaving her lightheaded and woozy. "Magical snares?" She swallowed, but the ice in her throat did not budge. "On the *other* side of the veil. I'm not sure I'm cut out for this."

Since the beginning of time, people had told frightening stories of the horrors to be found in the Shadowlands. Monsters who had once been human, and terrifying creatures born of dark Magic who had never known true life, who fed on misery, fear, and the energy of lost souls. Those stories were told sometimes as entertainment, or to explore one's darker feelings in a safe setting, or, more often than not, as a warning. No one could say for sure if any of those stories were true, but Genevieve was on the verge of finding out.

"If you aren't," said Falak, patting her shoulder lamely, "then I'm not sure anyone else is. I'd say this is a job for a lion tamer, perhaps, but since Lady Stormbourne returned to her home in Inselgrau, we find ourselves sadly shorthanded in that department."

Genevieve coughed and flapped her hand, as if trying to wave off the responsibility Falak was imposing on her. "I don't see how the next one in line is me."

Falak gripped both of Genevieve's shoulders, positioning her so he could face her fully. His dark gaze bored into her hazel eyes. "If not you, then who? Who else loves those beasts as much as you? Who else would risk themselves for them?"

Genevieve dropped her gaze, accepting the truth of Falak's words. She already knew it had to be her but admitting it in the face of her growing fear wasn't easy. Ynnua was her responsibility, and, by default, so were the other animals. Svieta's duty to the menagerie might have been equal to her own, but the mechanic's part in this scheme was one that only a Magician could play, and no one else in *Le Cirque* even came close to possessing those sacred and arcane abilities. The rest would be up to Genevieve. She had sworn to do whatever it took to save Ynnua.

"At least I can look on the bright side…" She offered a limp smile to her ringmaster, who quirked a questioning eyebrow. "If I don't survive this, then I won't have to spend two weeks in Otokar's lab."

It took nearly another whole day to gather the necessary supplies. Piercing the veil was metaphorical in some ways and quite literal in others. Procuring a golden blade transmuted from lead was the greatest challenge, but not impossible… or cheap. Svieta performed the alchemical process herself, following Otokar's precise formula using ingredients purchased in the city, to Falak's extreme financial dismay. She spent the rest of her time creating the method for unlocking the spirit animals from their entrapments. The result was something half potion and half iron skeleton key, a physical manifestation of the Magical words and abilities a true Magician would have used in Genevieve's place.

After a night of fitful sleep, Genevieve dressed in her most comfortable leotard and stockings, braided up her hair, and met Svieta at the menagerie's doorway an hour before dawn. Curious onlookers—workers and performers from Le Cirque drawn by the rumors of what was about to happen—watched from the shadows. Fearing her own failure and being a disappointment to them all, Genevieve tried her best to ignore the spectators and focus on the overwhelming task before her.

"Often, Magic is a balance between the real and the symbolic, as you have seen." Svieta raised her golden knife and the potion key for emphasis. She pointed the knife at the tent's flap, which Falak was holding open, and then at the dark sky overhead. "The tent's doorway is the real side of the coin, and the veil is the symbolic side, yes? Dawn is the time when the transition between the two sides is thinnest—the scale between real and not-real is most balanced. Understand?"

Genevieve nodded. Whether she understood or not mattered little, though. Her part required little cognizance and a great deal of courage and action. This quest would appeal to her strengths, at least. She was no dunce, but her talents tended to be more physical than academic.

Svieta slashed her knife downward. "Once I cut through the veil, you will step through to the other side. If your Magician's instructions were correct, the key will act as a compass to lead you to the animals. Move quickly. It will become harder to keep the veil open as morning progresses. If the doorway were to collapse, it would be at least eight hours, the time of gloaming, before I could open it again."

Cold clamminess washed over Genevieve, and her stomach rolled. To be stuck on the other side... How she wished she didn't have to do this alone. How long would it take to send a request for assistance to Lady Stormbourne? This would be an adventure the demigoddess would be willing to undertake for Sher-sah's sake alone. No... Genevieve shook herself, trying to discard her dread. *Focus on the task, save the animals, save Ynnua, save myself. I can do this.* "Let's get on with it. It's not going to get any easier by waiting."

Svieta gave her a hard, assessing look before nodding once and stepping to the doorway of the open tent flap. She motioned for Genevieve to join her. With no fancy words or pronouncements, Svieta raised her knife and slashed. As the knife cut through air, a split in the fabric of space and time seemed to open along the blade's course. Even darker than the night sky, blackness spilled forth, bringing a frosty breeze scented with the dank odor of rot and decay, like a swamp.

Svieta motioned to the Magical opening. "Time is short, Genevieve. Do not hesitate."

Genevieve gripped her potion key in her fist and glanced at Falak. His eyes burned brightly in the glow of his lantern. He still held the tent flap aside with a determination that seemed to indicate he believed he could also hold the veil open, indefinitely, if he were strong enough and stubborn enough. If anyone could, it would be him.

But Genevieve didn't want to chance it, so she took a deep breath and…

…Stepped through.

Her vision adjusted to the darkness, revealing a dim moon illuminating a drab landscape. Or something that resembled a moon, hanging in a sky—*is it actually a sky, though?*—devoid of stars. An odd feeling, like dizziness but not, churned through her, making her feel disoriented and heavy. Breathing slowly, she inched forward, moving further into the strange land. And strange it was, because as she shuffled onward, she recognized her surroundings as a mirror image of the living world she had left moments before.

Slowly, she spun and found herself facing a shadow version of the menagerie tent, stripes dull, gaslights nearly nonexistent. Each step after crossing the veil had carried her further away. She glanced at the potion key in her fist, now exuding a pale purple glow. As she backed away from the shadow tent, the glow seemed to fade. *Hmm? Interesting.*

Genevieve approached the menagerie again, and the glow brightened. The key's illumination increased with each step toward the tent's doorway, and Genevieve held her breath in anticipation as she stepped around Svieta's Magical opening and into the shadow menagerie's interior. There before her they stood, each creature in its place, but instead of mechanical, metallic beings, all the animals appeared as they had been in life—fur and feather, skin and tusk—devoid of Svieta's artistic license and mechanical applications. Genevieve's presence seemed to excite the animals, and they responded with caws and roars and trumpeting that lacked their usual tinny echoes.

A familiar whinny drew Genevieve's gaze, and her heart soared when she spotted Ynnua. Her beloved horse was missing the unique horn she usually wore, but Ynnua's muscles rippled under what might have been a chestnut-colored hide in regular light. Coiled around the horse's fetlock was a fine silver chain held in place by an elegant padlock. The chain's other end encircled a large stake embedded deep into the ground.

Genevieve exhaled with relief and started toward Ynnua, but before her first footstep landed, a piercing shriek shattered the comforting cacophony of animal noises. Genevieve spun around, searching for the source of the dreadful cry, but it must have originated outside the tent, from somewhere beyond the flimsy walls. Her heart shuddered, dreading the discovery of whatever had created such a horrible sound. *Move fast, and maybe you won't have to find out.*

With both hope and a little panic lightening her feet, Genevieve raced to Ynnua and crouched beside her ensnared hoof. Shaken by nerves and fear, she bumbled her grip and dropped her potion key. "Gods blight it!" She retrieved the key and inserted its toothy head into the lock. It popped open with little resistance, and the chain fell away. Ynnua reared on her hind legs, neighing with clear delight.

Hoping her instincts were right, Genevieve pointed at the tent doorway, to the opening to the world of the living, and slapped Ynnua's haunch. "Run, darling. Run home, now!"

Ynnua dropped to all four hooves, lowered her head, and bunched her muscles. In a single, powerful stride, she crossed the distance and hurtled into the Magical rift between the Shadowlands and the living world. Genevieve's heart soared as she watched Ynnua disappear into the light, but sobriety returned when she glanced around the room and realized the enormous task still awaiting her. Freeing the dozens of remaining creatures would take a while, and before she could settle on the next in line, the cursed shriek from outside tore through the tent again, much closer this time.

Genevieve's nerves tingled as she reached for the shackle around the elephant's ankle. The earth beneath her shook as if a massive oak had fallen, slamming into the ground a few yards away. She was sure no falling tree had created that earthquake, though, and her hands trembled as she worked to free the elephant. An intelligent creature, the elephant needed no goading when the chain slipped away. He trumpeted once and headed for the doorway, but his heavy footsteps were nothing compared to whatever was steadily pounding the ground outside the tent, coming ever closer as Genevieve hurried to release the dragon, and then the peacock.

Genevieve's terror tasted sour as she reached for the lock holding Sher-sah, the lion, in place. She had formed no plan other than to free as many animals as possible as quickly as she could, but some subconscious part of her must have told her to put off releasing Sher-sah right away because she might need him to help her fight. Her subconscious was smart, because the moment she inserted her key and released the lion's padlock, the entire tent was torn away as though a cyclone had snatched it.

Darkness enshrouded Genevieve and the remaining animal spirits as the increasingly familiar roar of whatever was stalking them battered her ears again. Sher-sah bellowed, but even his fierce cry was no match for whatever awaited them in the darkness.

The ground shuddered.

The air itself trembled.

But instead of a giant, fearsome monster, in rolled a thick fog, glowing green like the bioluminescent mushrooms in the forests outside of Prigha Castle. The odor of swamp—mildew, putrefaction, and rot—came with it, stronger than Genevieve had noticed when Svieta first cut through the veil. Sher-sah roared again, but distant and muffled, as though the fog had gagged him. In the corner of Genevieve's vision, a shadow—humanoid, but moving in inhuman ways—shifted and disappeared.

The hairs on Genevieve's arms and neck rose and prickled.

The shadow streaked past her again. Then came a cackle. A wailing cry.

"Sher-sah," Genevieve hissed, searching for a sign of the powerful beast. She knew the lion's ferocity and strength, had come close to being his victim herself not so long ago, but he did not respond, and she didn't know if any shadows in the green swirls of fetid mist belonged to him.

Uncertain of what to do, Genevieve considered her options. Wait and see what was coming for her, or try to find Svieta's portal and return home? They could make a new plan, couldn't they? Come back in numbers, maybe with weapons, or at least more hands and maybe more spell keys? But... as she wavered on the verge of deciding to retreat, the fog parted, and a figure stepped through. Genevieve gasped and stepped back, but the apparition raised its hand in a halting gesture. She responded instinctually, stopping in place.

The mist's green glow illuminated him well enough to reveal a human face and features—an old man with sparse white hair and beard, deep wrinkles around his nose and eyes, and his thin frame draped in a black tunic and robes resembling the garments worn by Genevieve's royal ancestors in the portraits lining Prigha Castle's walls. Something in his countenance was familiar, and the feeling that she had seen him before nagged her.

"Great-granddaughter," he said in her native tongue. "Do not fear, for I bring you good news."

Despite his reassurances, Genevieve's heart lurched, and she stepped backward again. "Wh-who are you?"

He placed his hand over his heart and bowed slightly. "What a shame you do not recognize me, but I'm sure my appearance is unexpected, to say the least."

"You called me 'Great-granddaughter.' Does that mean—"

"Yes, though perhaps our lineage is more than a few generations removed from each other. 'Great-granddaughter' is the closest term for what you are to me."

Genevieve was no scholar, but neither was she stupid. Her gaze narrowed as she clenched her jaw. "Your presence in this location, at this particular time, is no coincidence, is it?" Another ghostly howl echoed through the surrounding fog, but at least the earthquakes had settled.

Her great-grandfather's expression brightened, his eyes widening, lips curling into a smile, though one with a sinister edge. "I'm glad to know my descendants haven't devolved into a bunch of inbred twits."

"Otokar is somehow behind this family reunion, isn't he?" Genevieve glowered at the elderly spirit standing—floating?—before her. She should have known freeing the menagerie wouldn't have been so easy. She had thought her two-weeks-in-Otokar's-lab agreement had been too suspiciously simple.

Her great-grandfather moved closer. He gestured, gnarled fingers reaching toward her. "A great opportunity has been bestowed upon you. A chance to reclaim our family's heritage and honor. Open yourself as a vessel to me and my power, and you will be remembered as the great redeemer of the Jagiellon Empire."

Genevieve looked over her shoulder, hoping for a sign of the portal. How long had she been here, and how much longer could Svieta keep it open? But her brief glance revealed only more fog and no sign of Sher-sah or what remained of the menagerie. Meeting her great-grandfather's strange gaze again, Genevieve resisted the urge to shiver or curl her lip in disgust. "I'm not sure what this 'opportunity' entails, but it sounds vaguely incestual to me." She remembered Otokar saying that he'd been studying the Stormbourne family in Steinerland, and he'd mentioned something about how their birthrights—their ability to command storms and lightning and thunder—had been transferrable. Was this how Otokar thought it would happen for her own family? Receiving the spirit of her great-grandfather, and, presumably, his divine powers, and then being forced to convey them to her sister?

"Besides, knowing Otokar is involved is also enough for me to know that I must, unfortunately, express my deepest regrets." She took three quick steps back. Even if her movements were taking her further away from home, she suspected letting this apparition come any closer would be worse. "The only things I care to be remembered for are my astounding performances with *Le Cirque du Merveilles Mècanique*. The Jagiellon Empire will just have to go on without my participation."

Former Emperor Whoever Jagiellon growled in a wholly inhuman way. The wrinkles in his face deepened to black crevasses. Malice glittered in his now fully obsidian eyes, and he no longer resembled any of the ancestors in Genevieve's family portraits. "Such words are traitorous, girl. No grandchild of mine—"

"We can talk about family treachery if you really want, but I think neither of us will be convinced today." Shifting her weight, Genevieve prepared to turn and run. Even if she had no hopes of finding the portal, she at least had to get away from the old man who was transforming into a beast before her. With each beat of her heart, he grew, gaining mass and muscle, claws and fangs, until he towered over her. A giant. An earthquake in monstrous form.

Genevieve ran.

Blind in the fog, Genevieve focused on nothing more than remaining upright and putting as much distance between herself and the monster as possible. The ground shook again as he chased her. She hoped the fog provided her some cover, but perhaps the monster could see through it with his beastly eyes.

"Sher-sah! Please, if you're out there, if you can hear me…" She heaved several breaths before calling out again. "King Lion, I'm begging you!"

Instead of a roar, though, a familiar neighing, almost as fierce as a lion's snarl, cut through the monster's bellows. A different vibration, the pounding of hooves, shook the ground beneath her. She was afraid to hope, yet her heart soared. A metallic flash reflected the green bioluminescence that had become the only source of light in the gloom. Another whinny sounded, closer this time. Genevieve stopped, breath held, and searched the fog.

She had almost rotated a complete circle, spying only emptiness and more mist, before the utterly magnificent figure of Ynnua in her metallic menagerie body erupted from the gloom. Someone had taken the time to saddle and bridle her, and her single horn seemed to tear the fog to shreds as she galloped closer. Without a conscious thought, Genevieve responded. Her body moved with muscle memory built from hours and hours of training. She launched herself, grabbing the unicorn's reins and saddle, and mounted Ynnua's back.

"YAHHH-HOOO!" Genevieve cried, heart soaring, tears of relief stinging her eyes. Tightening her legs, Genevieve held fiercely, trusting Ynnua to take them home. Behind them, her great-grandfather roared so deafeningly, she had to clamp her hands over her ears. The heat of his breath burned her neck and shoulders. "Run, Ynnua, run!" she urged.

Already galloping impossibly fast, Ynnua picked up her pace. A gleam of what seemed to be daylight appeared before them as nothing more than a sliver, a nail paring, but it was the way home, and unicorn and rider raced toward it with every ounce of skill they possessed. Fine hairs prickled along Genevieve's neck and arms like a warning signal. She glanced back in time to see her great-grandfather swiping at her with his huge, beastly fist. Reflexively, Genevieve hooked her leg through a trick loop in Ynnua's saddle and threw herself over until she hung upside down. Without slowing, Ynnua shifted her weight, adjusting for her rider's unusual position. This was a familiar trick, one they had practiced hundreds of times.

From her flipped vantage point, Genevieve watched her great-grandfather reach for them again. Terror surged inside her, both cold and hot at the same time, but her body knew what to do even as her mind panicked. She swung her leg and twisted, throwing herself upright, and squeezed her left thigh tight against Ynnya's side. The unicorn responded instantly, turning a sharp angle in time to avoid the giant's fist. Several paces later, Ynnua readjusted, aiming again for the tear in the veil that Svieta had somehow held open all this time.

Heart pounding, lungs pumping, Genevieve resisted the urge to close her eyes as she curled close to Ynnua's neck and body, making herself as small and aerodynamic as possible. The seam between worlds blazed before them. Another few strides would bring them through. Ynnua stretched forward and…

Genevieve flew through the air and landed in the dirt with a crash, her ribs screaming from the blow that had blasted her from Ynnua's back. Gritting her teeth and panting, Genevieve cried out as she rolled over. She had little fight left in her, but she wouldn't be a coward, back turned, refusing to see what was coming for her. Her great-grandfather loomed over her, a giant creature from her nightmares with fangs and black claws and coarse gray skin. Howling, he reached for her, but his rage was answered by a feline roar of equal ferocity.

Sher-sah's metallic form soared over her, briefly blocking her vision. Genevieve screamed as she sat up, ribs stabbing her side as she watched Sher-sah's metal fangs latch onto the giant's forearm. He swung his body and twisted his head, tearing flesh, ripping muscle. The giant shrieked as black gore oozed from the wound.

"Genevieve!" Someone shouted nearby. Looking behind her, she discovered another vaguely familiar figure standing at the doorway between worlds. He was pale, elegant, and handsome, his long silver hair cascading over his shoulders. She thought she should know him, that his presence here meant something significant, but consciousness had become a nebulous thing. She was too exhausted and in too much pain to place the young man in the right slot in her memory.

Ynnua stood beside him, impatiently stamping the ground. None of the other animals remained in the shadow menagerie, however, and Genevieve wondered how the last ones had made their escape without her spell key.

Slim muscles bulged under the young man's suitcoat as he grasped the veil's nebulous edges in his fists. "I can't hold the doorway much longer. You have to cross now."

Genevieve's great-grandfather bellowed again. She glanced at him in time to see him shake Sher-sah off like a bothersome gnat. The big cat twisted in mid-air and landed on all four paws. He hunkered down, gathering himself for another attack, but Genevieve's plea caught his attention.

"Forget him, King Lion. Take us home, now."

At first, Genevieve thought the lion had decided to ignore her, but as he launched toward the giant, he executed another elegant mid-air twist. He landed at Genevieve's side and slipped his massive maw around her bruised torso and hips. She screamed as he lifted her, and the pain from what were certainly broken ribs made her dizzy and faint. As the lion bounded toward the doorway between worlds with the Bonhemmish-princess-turned-circus-trick-rider cradled in his mouth, Genevieve passed out.

Before she did, though, she heard the pretty young man say, "Tell Lady Stormbourne what I did today. Tell Evie that Jackie Faercourt was there to help you all escape."

Genevieve stood in her backstage dressing room, watching herself in her vanity mirror as she pressed her fingers into her side.

Falak had hired a Magical physician to tend to Genevieve upon her return from the Shadowlands, and the doctor's spell work and physicking had quickly healed her worst injuries. Genevieve still felt the ghost pains of her wounds at stressful times, such as in the moments before a performance. The physician had suggested such sensations were only her imagination, lingering emotional trauma from her ordeal. Whatever the reason, the pain felt real enough, but Falak assured her that time was the truest remedy of all. Genevieve tended to believe him, since he spoke from acute experience. But how much time would be impossible to guess, and she was growing impatient. *It's been* months *since that day…*

Months spent recuperating amongst her dearest friends—family, really. The circus could never be just a job to her, and its people could never be mere co-workers. Months spent recuperating in her own wagon and not in the laboratory of Bonhemm's Royal Magician. Genevieve figured the agreement she had made with Otokar was revoked the moment her great-grandfather had appeared and attempted to… possess her? Inhabit her? Was there a proper technical term for allowing a spirit to enter her body and take control of her for the purpose of transferring a divine birthright?

That transaction had not been part of the deal, and if Otokar had mentioned it in their original negotiations, she never would have agreed. *Which is likely why he didn't mention it.* Either way, she had not gone back to Prigha Castle, and Otokar had not attempted to enforce their contract. But she didn't believe for a moment that he had given up so easily. *He would only give up when he was dead.*

Someone outside her dressing room curtain cleared their throat. "M'lady, Genevieve, you have a visitor."

She recognized the voice as one of the stagehands who performed general labor duties behind the scenes. "Who is it?" Genevieve asked.

"It's me, Princess," another voice said. The curtain swept open, and Evelyn Stormbourne, former heir to the throne of Inselgrau and current Lady of Thunder, stepped into the small space. She wore humble clothes, a modest linen split-skirt and muslin shirt and vest embroidered in the Fantazike style, but her identity was as unmistakable as the crackle of static electricity surrounding her. "Your friendly neighborhood lion tamer."

Genevieve gasped, jumped from her seat, and threw herself at Evie. The two young women embraced, laughing with unbridled joy. "I wasn't entirely sure I would ever see you again," Genevieve said, squeezing her friend close.

"Did you think your circus could travel all the way to Inselgrau and I wouldn't come see you?"

Genevieve released Evie and stepped back to get a better look at her friend. The young Lady of Thunder looked happy and a little better fed and less stressed than the last time she'd seen her, but otherwise mostly the same. "We're hours from your home, though."

"You think mere hours would keep me away?" Evie shrugged and glanced at the imposing young man behind her. He wore a green military-style jacket with brass buttons, and he stood ramrod straight, at least until he began to smile.

"Gideon!" Genevieve squealed and threw herself into his opening arms. "You came, too?"

"Can't go anywhere without him," Evie said. As the Lady of Thunder met her Captain of Security's gaze, her eyes twinkled. The two were so obviously in love, it almost hurt Genevieve to see it. Love like that was rare, and she doubted she'd ever know it herself. She had family, though, and she supposed that was enough. Many people in the world weren't even that fortunate.

"Well, I'll put a little extra flair in my performance tonight…" Genevieve bent over her vanity table, picked up an open tin of lip color, and swiped a dash of red onto her lips. "Just for you." Satisfied with her appearance, she flounced the ruffles of her short riding skirt and struck a pose.

Evie chuckled and poked Genevieve's shoulder. "I can't wait to see it. But I'm sure you can guess that watching your performance isn't the entire reason for my visit."

The warm mood in the dressing room faded. Genevieve's shoulders sagged, and her smile drooped. "You heard about my, erm, *adventure*, did you?"

Evie took Genevieve by her shoulders and guided her to the vanity table. With a gentle push, she directed Genevieve to take a seat. As if reading her mind, Gideon retrieved a nearby footstool, and Evie sank onto it. She gathered Genevieve's hands and held them between her own in her lap. "I wish I could've been there to help you. What a horrible thing to endure on your own."

Genevieve looked away, unable to hold the gaze of an intensely concerned demigoddess. She shrugged one shoulder. "At least it was over relatively quickly. It could have been worse. Fortunately, I had some help."

Evie smiled sadly. "Svieta, and Falak. Sher-sah, and Ynnua."

Taking a deep breath, Genevieve gathered her courage and met Evie's gaze. "There was one more person there who helped. In fact, I'm not sure I or the rest of the menagerie would have made it out without him."

"I've heard whispers," Evie said, tapping her chest over her heart—her iron heart that had provided a home to the spirit of her own however-many-greats-grandfather. Their union had worked out for the best, but Genevieve had no doubt her own great-grandfather had no benevolent intentions when it came to her. She suspected she would have been used up and discarded after her value came to an end. "But I just wanted you to verify it."

Genevieve swallowed and nodded. Her eyes fluttered closed as she exhaled. "Until he spoke and confirmed his identity, I wasn't sure who he was. I knew his presence was meaningful, but I was too senseless at the time to make the proper connections in my memory. But he was there, Evie. It was definitely him."

The Lady of Thunder gasped. Genevieve opened her eyes. Gideon's big hand rested on Evie's shoulder reassuringly, but the Lady of Thunder's face had gone pale and wan.

"Jackie Faercourt was there," Genevieve said, resolving then and there to help Evie with the return of this menace, the Lady's own greatest nemesis. Faercourt had perished during his cabal's violent attempt to overthrow Lady Stormbourne's kingdom, but it seemed even death could not diminish his obsessions. "The most powerful Magician that Le Poing Fermé ever knew was holding open the doorway between the living world and Shadowlands, and he wanted to make damned well sure you knew it."

You can read more about Lady Stormbourne and Genevieve in
The Stormbourne Chronicles.

Three Brothers Circus

SELENIA PAZ

When Grandfather started to forget, I began racing home after school and sitting next to him. I had heard my aunts talking about it, and I didn't want him to forget my name. I didn't want him to forget who I was.

It happened so fast. Over the next few months, he stopped driving, and if he wanted to go walk anywhere, another adult had to accompany us. It was as if they were afraid he would forget who I was as we were walking and would not want to return with me. I don't know what scared me more: the idea of Grandfather forgetting me, or the thought that it could happen while we were doing something as simple as taking a walk.

We started sitting on the metal rocking chairs on the porch in the evenings, after the heat from the sun had almost disappeared. Grandfather started to ask me to bring his photo album over, and I would turn the pages as he furrowed his brows.

"He might not remember everyone," my aunt said quietly. "Don't worry if he doesn't know who some of the people are. Just nod and encourage him to try."

"Okay," I said, my throat tight.

Illustration by Adriano Moraes

Midway through the photo album, Grandfather would motion for me to stop turning the pages. Gently, he would brush his fingers over the only photograph in the album that featured my grandmother.

Subconsciously, I reached up and tugged at a small patch of white hair that never failed to grow back. No matter how many haircuts I'd had or how short my hair had been cut, there was always that bright white streak in a sea of brown. My grandmother had the same streak, but hers was long and fell down next to the right side of her face. That was the only thing I had inherited from her; the rest of me was almost a copy of my grandfather in his youth. Brown eyes and skin, tall but unfortunately not elegantly tall—more lanky and awkward. Even now, Grandfather only stooped slightly due to his age, yet he still towered over me.

As a little boy, I had always thought that she had passed away long ago. But now, at sixteen, I began to pay closer attention to my aunts' gossip. She had not passed away, they whispered. She had just left. One day, she'd walked out and never came back.

Grandfather started to peel back the clear film that protected the photograph in the album. Bringing the photograph closer between us, he ran his index finger over the background. There was a large tent behind him and my grandmother, and she was wearing a black, slim-fitting tuxedo and a top hat. Behind and to the right, an older gentleman in a dark suit was passing by, carrying a large stack of books.

"We can go," Grandfather whispered.

"Go?" I asked.

Grandfather flipped the picture over.

I recognized his scrawling print. *Estela, Three Brothers Circus.*

Grandfather raised his hand and pointed at the calendar.

October 30.

"We can go tonight," he said, his voice coming out in a rushed whisper.

I started to rise, to call for my aunts.

Grandfather placed his hand softly over mine.

"It isn't far, Andres. I have not forgotten the way."

I thought about the countless times I had seen this photograph, the many times I had walked in on my grandfather looking through the photo album. But never had I been to this circus. I had not even seen any advertisements for it in the town. How could I know whether it still existed?

What if Grandfather was just imagining it? What if he thought it was a different year than what it actually was? Valle Hermoso was such a small town in northern Mexico, perhaps he was even thinking about a circus across the border, in Texas.

"She is there," he said quietly.

I was startled out of my thoughts.

"Who? Grandmother?" I said, my voice barely above a whisper.

Grandfather looked into my eyes and nodded.

"She didn't leave," he said, reading my mind. "She is there, at the circus, tonight."

"But Grandfather…" I began. How could I put into words that, perhaps, Grandmother had passed away? It had been so many years. What if he was in another place?

"No," Grandfather interrupted. "She is not gone. She will be there, at the circus. She lives forever."

As luck would have it, my aunts decided to make a last-minute run to the store to get some candles and ingredients they needed to prepare for their trips to the cemetery over the next few days. As soon as their car was out of sight, Grandfather stood with an energy I hadn't known he still possessed and walked inside the house, the screen door slamming behind him. Returning a minute later, he handed me the keys.

He had been giving me driving lessons before he became too ill to drive himself, and since then I had not really driven his old truck, afraid I would hit something and cause damage to it.

Grandfather held up the keys.

"I… I don't know, maybe we should walk?" I said cautiously.

"Nonsense. You know how to drive. You've done it many times before," Grandfather answered. I began to reach for the keys, my mind rushing through the millions of possibilities, of things that could go wrong.

"Some things you never forget," Grandfather said quietly.

I reached over and grabbed the keys, making sure to lock the door behind us. My heart began to beat faster as I realized the trouble we would be in when my aunts came back.

The soft rumble of the truck as we pulled out of the driveway calmed my nerves slightly, and I was grateful that there were not many cars on the bumpy gravel road. Grandfather instructed me to turn right at the end of the street.

I kept turning to look at him, just to make sure he wasn't asleep. He stayed quiet and only nodded when I would glance at him, indicating I should keep going. We reached an area that had not been developed yet, and Grandfather motioned for me to turn right. I turned on my signal and slowly drove into an overgrown gravel road. Tall trees grew close together on both sides of the path, blocking out the moonlight that had begun to shine down.

I slowed down, hesitating, my heart racing again. What if this was a bad idea?

Grandfather reached over and placed his left hand on my arm. "Try not to worry so much," he said.

He motioned forward with his hand. "Just a little more."

Darkness fell around the truck, and I reached down and turned on the headlights. For a few seconds I couldn't see anything, and I pressed down gently on the brake, afraid I would accidentally crash the truck into a tree.

Just as suddenly, there was a blinding brightness. I covered my eyes with my arm and felt as the light began to fade away. I lowered my hand and gasped.

We had arrived in a large clearing surrounded by tall trees. I could see the full moon was out, the source of the bright light.

Strange, I thought. *It didn't seem this bright a few minutes ago.*

Off to the right, cars were parked side by side, and I released the brake gently and began to drive toward an empty space. People were headed toward the entrance of a large circus, the moonlight illuminating numerous tents and a small booth near the entrance.

I had only just shifted to Park when I realized Grandfather was already out of the truck, the door shutting behind him. I hurried to catch up with him as he zigzagged through the crowd, heading straight for the small booth.

I felt a strong push, and the truck keys flew out of my hand, landing a few feet away. As I reached down to grab them, I tried to avoid the crowd passing by me, amazed that so many people were arriving at this circus. How had they heard of it? My hand touched something cool and metal, and I picked up the keys and placed them carefully in my pocket. The last thing I needed was to lose them. I could only imagine how angry my aunts would be for that, on top of everything.

I pushed my way through the crowd, trying to find my grandfather, a sinking feeling growing in my stomach. The wind began to blow, the leaves of the trees rustling all around. I stopped a few feet from the ticket booth, realizing that my grandfather was nowhere in sight.

"Excuse me, sir," I said, walking up to the gentleman at the booth. He wore a red-and-white-striped shirt that matched the red and white stripes of the tents behind him, a small number "3" stitched on the pocket of his shirt in red thread.

"Did you happen to see an older man pass by, wearing brown pants and a brown-and-white plaid shirt?"

The man looked at me curiously before answering. "I believe I did. He went inside—he must not be too far ahead."

Looking at the ticket prices, I reached for my wallet and pulled out two pesos. As I handed them over to the gentleman, I realized something. Grandfather hadn't had any money with him.

"I can pay for his ticket," I began, pulling out another two pesos.

The man raised his hand to object. "No worries," he said, tearing off a ticket and handing it to me. "He already had one from a previous visit."

I frowned. "But... he hasn't been here in years."

The man smiled, and there was something odd about the way he did so.

"Tickets to the Three Brothers Circus are always good. You should hang on to yours... you never know when you might want to come back."

I took the ticket from his hand and began to walk away. Soon, I melted into the crowd, not sure which direction I should go. One thing was clear: I couldn't spot my grandfather anywhere. With a growing feeling of dread, I realized I had lost him.

I tried not to get distracted, but as I looked around at the booths and the tents, I couldn't help but notice how odd they were. There were some that had familiar games such as balloon darts and ring toss but mixed in among those games were tents and booths offering other services.

A booth offering a drink from the fountain of youth, just five pesos to age backward one year.

A tent offering the opportunity to relive one memory. One hundred pesos to step back in time to a special moment in your mind. I hesitated in front of this booth, imagining the possibility of reliving a moment once more.

A fortune-telling tent: *Las Tres Hermanas*. This tent had one of the longest lines as people took out their coins to pay for a glimpse into their future. As I passed the tent, I wondered if these three sisters were related to the three brothers the circus was named after.

The wind grew stronger, and I began to wish I had brought along a jacket. Even more, I wished I had thought to bring my grandfather a jacket, and I hoped with all my heart that he wouldn't catch a cold.

As I walked, a panic began to rise up inside of me, and I had to take deep breaths to calm myself and keep going. As the crowds began to thin out, I finally allowed myself to do something I had been dreading: I looked at the watch on my wrist. The second hand ticked by. How was it almost ten o'clock?

A large crowd was exiting the main tent, which was several times larger than the others. Managing to squeeze in, I realized a performance must have just ended. The last performance of the night.

Several employees were clearing out tables from the center, sweeping up small scraps of paper and trash that had fallen from the audience. Three men in dark tuxedos stood near the center of the tent, helping to roll up a heavy rope.

I walked slowly up to them and gave a small wave in greeting.

"Hello, I'm sorry to bother you," I said, my voice echoing in the empty tent. "But I'm looking for my grandfather. We were separated at the entrance, and I really must find him." My voice came out with a slight tremble, and I tried to calm myself as I realized just how worried I was.

The men stopped rolling the rope and came toward me.

I could see that each had a word stitched in red on the front left pocket of his suit: *Memoria. Amare. Mors.*

"Your grandfather?" one of the men asked as they got closer. "Perhaps he is waiting for you at the entrance." He looked at his watch. "It is nearly ten o'clock, and the circus will be closing soon."

I shook my head. "It's just…" I paused. "My grandfather has difficulty remembering things. I know he remembers this circus. He wanted to come tonight, but I'm just not sure if he will know what to do once it closes."

The gentleman with the word *memoria* stitched on his pocket spoke up. "He has been here before?"

I nodded. "I believe… many years ago. He… he met my grandmother here. That's actually why he wanted to come tonight. I don't think he realizes what year it is, because he believes she will still be here."

One of the gentlemen, the one with the word *amare* stitched on his pocket, dropped the rope gently on the ground and walked toward me, his eyes taking in my face, then stopping at the patch of white hair on my head.

"Your grandmother?"

I nodded. "Yes. But I'm not even sure she would still be here," I said.

"Estela," the man replied.

My eyes widened. "Yes," I finally said. "How did you know?"

The man motioned to the spot of white in my hair.

"She is here," he said, turning to the other two men. "I will ask Ignacio to take him." As he walked away, the other two men put down their ropes and came closer.

"Estela's grandson," one of them said, nodding. "Yes, I can see that now."

"What is your name?" asked the other.

"Andres," I said, a million thoughts filling my mind. Grandfather was right. My grandmother was here. But why did she leave, then, so long ago?

I shook my head, trying to push away the thoughts.

"Are you the three brothers who own the circus?" I asked slowly.

They nodded.

"Your names…" I said, motioning toward their pockets. "Are those your names?"

They nodded again.

The man motioned in the direction in which the third brother had headed. "Amare. Or Love."

Pointing to himself, he said, "Memoria. Or Memory." And pointing to the third gentleman, "Mors." A pause. "Or Death."

"Love, memory, and death," I repeated, largely to myself.

Memoria nodded, silent.

"The only three things people need to live a good life," said Mors, the tallest of the three brothers.

"Death?" I asked, almost immediately wishing I hadn't.

"Oh, yes," he answered without hesitation. "Perhaps the most important. Because, if it were not for Death, can you imagine how many people would never know to appreciate what they have? I can think of no better reason to appreciate every moment, can you?"

I swallowed.

The other man rolled his eyes. "True, but one could argue that memory is the most important. What else is there that gives life so much value, that you appreciate it because of the looming guarantee of death?"

The men looked at me, as if waiting for me to answer.

The man continued. "Even love. How can you love something you do not remember? If you have memories of a person or a place, that is how you love them. And if you have no memories, well…"

A knot tightened in my stomach. What were these men talking about? I thought about my grandfather, about his fading memories. But this memory hadn't faded. He'd known exactly how to get here.

"Here we are." Amare had returned, a tall, thin gentleman carrying a stack of books trailing behind him.

Something clicked in my mind, and my eyes widened.

"Ignacio will take you to Estela," Amare said. "Her tent is not too far from here."

Ignacio peeked over his tall stack of books.

"Yes, well, we had better get going. The circus is closing soon," Ignacio said, his voice rushed. Turning, he began to head to the back of the tent.

I stood for a moment, the three brothers watching me carefully.

"Thank you for your help," I said, rushing past them with a slight nod.

As I trailed behind Ignacio, I fought the urge to look back at the brothers, who I felt had not moved and were watching us as we left. A strange feeling crept up behind me as I realized that I had seen Ignacio before.

He was the man with the books in the background of the photo that my grandfather looked at so often. The one he had taken with my grandmother.

Almost fifty years ago.

And he looked exactly the same.

There were now only a few persons here and there. Families with small children who were still trying to win that one big plush toy. Couples on dates that they did not want to end.

Despite the tall stack of books in his hands, Ignacio was several feet ahead of me, and I struggled to keep up.

The wind now had a cooler chill to it, and every so often, I would hear the crackling of leaves as the last remaining stragglers headed toward the entrance.

As we neared the edge of the circus, the tents were more widely scattered. A strange gold-and-gray tent sat near the edge of the trees, almost separate from everything else. I thought for a moment that this was a private tent, but there was a sign outside advertising services.

"Prolong your life! Works better than the fountain of youth!"

I smiled, thinking it must be a jab at the booth I had passed at the front of the circus.

Parts of this tent were slightly tattered, and it had an older, more faded appearance compared to the other tents. If I squinted my eyes, I could almost pretend it was part of a black-and-white movie.

I wondered if this was what the tent had looked like when Grandfather was my age. I stared at Ignacio's back, noticing now that his black tux was also slightly faded, with some of the threading loose in a few spots. The hairs on my arms began to rise as I remembered the photograph, where Ignacio was passing by in the background, his appearance unchanged.

I opened my mouth, about to ask how long he had worked here, when Ignacio stopped abruptly at the entrance to the tent.

"Estela, you have a visitor," he said, his voice loud and crisp.

Silence.

"Estela, you have—"

Soft footsteps approached the entrance to the tent, and a hand moved the tent flap aside.

"Ignacio, it's not—"

Her eyes spotted me. Without thinking, I took a step back.

This was Estela, my grandmother. And just like Ignacio, she looked just as she did in Grandfather's photograph.

She stepped completely out of the tent, and I noticed she was wearing the same suit and top hat she had in the photograph. Either the same one, or an identical one, I told myself.

She nodded toward Ignacio, who turned and began walking away.

A part of me wanted to reach out, to say, "Wait," because I could not understand how it was that he looked the same. My mind, trying to make sense of it, tried to convince me that perhaps he was not the same man. Perhaps he was a son or grandson.

But then, what about Estela?

"You must be looking for your grandfather," she said gently, stepping aside and opening the tent's flap even more.

Are you the woman in the photograph? I thought. *The same one?*

I cleared my throat, holding back the questions I wanted to ask, and then shuffled slowly through the entrance of the tent.

I felt the tent opening close behind me, a warmth enveloping me as we came in from the chilly night.

Grandfather sat on a wooden chair in front of an old wooden desk, his hands clasped together on his lap. He smiled when he saw me.

"Andres," he said with a slight laugh. "Did you enjoy the circus?"

I nodded slightly and returned his smile.

"I am sorry," I said, turning to the woman. "I have been searching for my grandfather all evening. He seems to think that you are my grandmother, who he met here many years ago."

I turned to look at the woman. Her eyes sparkled in the candlelight as she waited for me to continue. I saw the same streak of white in her hair, but it was impossible. This had to be a daughter or a granddaughter.

"You must be Andres," she said, taking a step toward me. "Your grandfather has been telling me about you."

She eyed my hair curiously, her gaze stopping at my own patch of white hair.

I looked down at my watch. It was past ten now. My aunts were going to be furious. But I needed to know.

"You look very much like my grandmother. He has a photograph of her, taken in front of a tent just like this one. You look just like her. You even have her name.”

“It *is* her,” Grandfather said, smiling.

I looked at my grandfather. He was sitting upright and alert, but also very calm. Calmer than he had been the past months. Was there really anything wrong in letting him believe that this woman was my grandmother, the woman he fell in love with so many years ago? If that brought him some kind of peace, what was wrong with that?

But something nagged at the back of my mind. How could two people at this circus look exactly as they had decades ago? That would be a big coincidence. But I didn’t have time to figure that out now.

“Grandfather, we must be getting back home. Everyone will be worried about you.”

Estela’s smile faded a little. “Why worried? He used to visit the circus all the time.”

I turned toward her and lowered my voice a little.

“Grandfather has been… forgetting things. He does not always remember people, or where he is. It is… happening more often now,” I said in a low voice.

Estela’s eyes widened.

“He remembered this circus, and its location. But I think that is why he feels that you are my grandmother. Your resemblance,” I said. “I am so sorry for any trouble.”

I turned and walked toward my grandfather, but her hand caught my wrist.

“It is no trouble. I have always wanted to meet my grandson.”

I stood there listening as Estela tried to explain to me, my heart speeding up as I imagined the ticking of the second hand on my watch.

"This is a very unique circus," she said, motioning around her, "as I am sure you have noticed."

I nodded.

"There are persons here who have been part of the circus for decades, and some who have been here for centuries, traveling around the country, trying to evolve with the times as they continue their crafts." She paused, then continued. "A little bit of youth here, a bit of good fortune there, nothing too much or too heavy to harm anyone."

"But it's just for fun, right? I mean, how can you gift youth?"

"For a few pesos, you'd be surprised what people can gift," she replied.

"Is that… is that what you did? You… you purchased youth?" I said cautiously, not wanting to offend her.

She laughed. "Oh, no," she said. "No, my gift… is a little different."

Grandfather looked over at her. "Estela lives forever."

She closed her eyes for a moment. "I am unable to age."

The candles on the wooden desk flickered.

I opened my mouth to respond, but found I couldn't.

"Are you—?"

"Telling the truth? Yes."

I shook my head, the *tick tick tick* of the second hand of my watch playing continuously in my head.

"I'm sorry, but we really must go. My aunts, they must be very worried about my grandfather."

I moved closer to him, but Estela placed her hand on my wrist.

"He has not forgotten me," she said.

I nodded, unsure how it was possible that I believed she was my grandmother. That she had not aged since the photograph was taken. Or since, well, who knew how long before that? "No, he hasn't."

"But he is forgetting." This last statement sounded far away. I looked at my grandfather, his eyes sadly returning my gaze.

He nodded.

He knew.

Watching him over the past months, I would catch small moments where Grandfather would forget minor things. He would forget to turn off the faucet when watering the plants, where he left his silverware or his cup of coffee and then turn around to make a new cup, where the items in the cupboards were or where he had left his books. But I had also seen him forget other things.

He began to mix up my aunts' names, and they gently reminded him. He forgot to eat his lunch, and might only eat dinner because we were all home to nudge him toward the kitchen. He would forget the year and imagine himself much younger, inviting me and my aunts over to his house so that his parents could make us some dinner. And when we tried to explain what year it was and where we were, he had started to become upset at times. My aunts had explained to me what would happen, and I had looked up some information at the library before I needed to put the book down.

"I can help him," Estela said.

Tick. Tick. Tick.

I didn't understand. I didn't understand how this circus existed in the middle of these trees, and I had never heard of it. I didn't understand how she could not age, how it seemed perhaps this circus did not age. I didn't understand how my grandfather's memory was so clear with this circus, with my grandmother. But perhaps that had to do with a certain kind of love, one I had not experienced yet.

Looking at my grandfather, I did not want to understand how it was possible that he would one day forget me, too.

Spending time with him and seeing him change, I did not know what was worse. Losing your memories, or watching someone you love lose theirs.

The seconds were ticking by, and we were in this impossible circus that I had begun to doubt was even real. But I did not want my grandfather to forget.

"How?"

Ignacio's books spilled all over the table in the tent as he looked around to find the right one.

"And you are sure?" he said, not looking up, as if he already knew the answer.

"I am," Estela replied.

She reached over and grabbed my grandfather's hand.

I looked down at my watch. It was almost midnight now. Almost October 31. My aunts were going to kill me.

"A-ha, here," Ignacio said, pulling out an old dusty volume from the bottom of the pile of books.

"And, is he—" Ignacio said, motioning with his head toward me.

Estela nodded.

"He understands?" Ignacio said again, more loudly.

"He gets the gist," Estela said, her voice rushed.

Ignacio turned to me as he carefully eyed her. "Do you know what is going to happen?" he asked me clearly.

I nodded.

He waited for me to continue.

"Estela is going to help my grandfather with his illness, and in exchange, something might get passed on to me. But it's okay, I don't mind forgetting some things."

"Forgetting?" Ignacio repeated, confused. "You must not—"

"Ignacio, there's no time," Estela said, giving him a pointed look.

Ignacio watched her for a few seconds.

"Are you sure?" he finally asked her, and I got the feeling he was asking her about something completely different.

"We are," she replied.

"You are sure?" he asked me.

I nodded. "If this will help my grandfather. If it is what he wants."

Grandfather turned toward me and smiled, but it was a sad sort of smile. The type of smile you give someone when you are leaving for a trip, and you might not come back.

Ignacio nodded, then opened his book. Reaching into his pocket, he took out a small red candle, placing it at the center of the table, and lit it with a match.

As he began to read through the book, I realized everything he was saying was in Latin. The only words I understood were the names of the brothers.

Memoria. Amare. Mors.

He repeated them several times and then fell silent.

I looked up to see my grandfather watching me.

"Thank you for bringing me tonight. I am so glad I did not live long enough to forget you."

The wind began to swirl around the tent, and as my grandfather reached out to grab my hand, I saw that he was fading away. I tried to grab his wrist, but my fingers went through his hand.

"Wait," I called out, my voice tight. "Wait, I didn't know he would leave."

"If he stays, he will only forget," Estela said over the sound of the rushing wind. "If he goes, we go together."

I took a step forward, then stopped.

Grandfather looked at me with a sad smile. "I will never forget you now."

The candles flickered and went out, and the wind stopped. When Ignacio reignited them with a match, he looked at me with sadness in his eyes.

"You were here," I said. "You were in the photograph, in the back. The photo my grandfather took with Estela."

He nodded as he gathered his books.

"But, how?" I was not sure exactly what I was asking. "How was she the same?"

As he stepped toward the entrance of the tent, Ignacio stopped.

"Estela lived a very long time. She could give away her years in small increments, and yet she would never age. It seemed she was meant to live forever. That is why she could not stay with your grandfather. What would happen when people realized…" He trailed off.

"They're gone," I said.

Ignacio nodded. "They have moved on to the world beyond this one."

"But, how?"

Ignacio stepped closer to me, and I saw what seemed like pity in his eyes.

"She had to find someone to gift her life to," he said quietly.

"Someone?" I repeated.

"She had been searching for some time. And I think she finally succeeded."

The ticking of the second hand fell silent in my mind.

"But—"

"Good luck, young man. Living forever is certainly not what these circusgoers think it is."

Turning, he headed out of the tent and disappeared into the night.

My aunts were furious.

I tried to explain what happened, and while they struggled to believe me, I knew they really didn't.

Not until the years began to pass.

And I didn't age.

ON MOONLIT WINGS

MARY FAN

Georgia, 1910

Clutching the rope, Anna swung her legs over her hands until she hung upside down. The yellowing canvas of the big top glowed from the early morning sun beating down outside, and the scents of animal and human bodies thickened the air. She hooked her knee onto the rope, released one hand, and reached down—

"Point your toes!" Marcelle's sharp voice, which carried a light French accent, called up to her.

Anna tried to remember her feet as she grabbed the bottom part of the rope and wrapped it around her free leg and her waist. But, weary after two hours of practicing, her body dropped abruptly, and she barely managed to keep her grip.

"That's enough for today."

Disappointed, Anna climbed down and landed roughly in front of Marcelle, billed as "The Empress of the Skies."

"I'll get it next time," Anna said.

Marcelle nodded, her thick black curls, streaked intermittently with silver, bouncing by her thin, snowy white cheeks. "Your inverts are looking good. You only need a little more stamina."

Wiping sweat from her forehead, Anna smiled. Escaped tendrils from her gleaming black bun clung to her sticky neck.

Though the audience seats were empty, the ring was bustling with activity. Jugglers practicing their tricks. Clowns rehearsing their stunts. Trapeze artists warming up their swings. Instrumental voices swirled over the noises of people chattering and grunting.

Maja Lozanac, an acrobatic dancer billed as "Fortuna" for her abilities to dream of the future and see things others didn't, entered. Already dressed in her blue-and-yellow costume, she tied her signature blindfold over her eyes. "The ringmaster is on his way. You had better go get into costume."

Anna started to leave, but agitation scratched at her heart. She hated that the last thing she would do on the rope that day was a failed wrap. She rushed back to the apparatus.

Marcelle pursed her lips, exaggerating the thin lines by her mouth. "I told you, you are finished for today."

"Let me do one last climb." Anna grabbed the rope.

Marcelle shook her head but didn't object.

Anna scissored her legs and scooped the rope over her hips. If this was to be her last climb of the day, she wasn't going to make it a boring one. After reaching above, she repeated the motion, then prepared to try turning upside-down again.

"Time to set up! Everybody out!" William Andley's voice boomed through the big top. Both co-owner and ringmaster of the Albers & Andley Traveling Circus, he commanded immediate attention.

Anna scrambled down the rope.

"You!" Mr. Andley, a blond man with a thick mustache dressed in a red waistcoat, glared at her. "What are you doing here? Go get dressed!"

"Yes, sir." But as Anna tried to rush past him, he grabbed her arm.

"I had better not catch you wasting time here again, understand? Stay with the ethnological exposition, where you belong."

Clenching her fists, Anna sped away without a word.

The moment she arrived at the costume tent, Kirsten Sigrist, an animal trainer, ran up to her with Rosie, Anna's two-year-old daughter, in her arms. Kirsten's blond hair looked as if she'd tried to gather it in a bun but only managed half, and her green-grey eyes were frenzied. "Thank goodness you're back! Rosie's a delight as always, but I need to get my dogs ready for the show."

"Mama!" Rosie reached out with her tiny hands, which carried a cool brown tint that bore little resemblance to Anna's pale gold complexion.

Anna gathered the child in her arms with a smile. Though her shoulders ached from practice, she never tired when holding her little girl. Yet looking into Rosie's soft brown eyes caused sorrow to drip into her heart. Every day, Rosie looked more like her father, and every day, Anna wished he could have met his daughter.

She made her way to the costume rack and grabbed her and Rosie's outfits for the ethnological exposition, more casually known as the human zoo. Though Anna had worn the same "Chinese Princess" costume for the past three years, she'd had to modify Rosie's every few weeks. The girl sat surprisingly still as Anna dressed her. Adorable as she looked in the pink-and-gold outfit with its flower-covered headdress, guilt stung Anna each time she dolled up her child for circusgoers to gawk at.

It wouldn't be long before Rosie was old enough to ask why she was made to spend all day in a fenced enclosure, forbidden to say a word of English, while onlookers stared and pointed.

Because some don't see us as people, Rosie. Anna dreaded the day she would have to explain that.

"What's troubling you?" Charles Sasaki, already dressed in his "Chinese Warrior" costume, approached her.

Anna whirled toward him. "How do you accept this? Your family came to America from Japan fifty years ago, yet you're made to masquerade as a Chinese man in his 'natural state.' I don't understand how you're never angry."

"This is the best-paying job I've ever had." Charles shrugged then smiled, his friendly black eyes crinkling. "Cheer up, Anna. You're royalty."

Anna made a face. "I'd rather be seen for what I can do than what people think I look like."

Tanya Mizrahi, a blue-eyed woman with short, shoulder-length hair, arched her brows at Anna. Though, like Anna, she was barely more than five feet tall, she seemed to take up more space with her strong presence. There was a reason why she was billed as "The Amazon Queen."

"If you want to defy their expectations, you have to be better than they imagine the best could be," Tanya said. "You must think about what you want to achieve more than what you want to escape. I did not become the only female lion tamer in the country by moping."

"Why are you not in your exhibits yet?" Mr. Andley stormed through the costume tent. He paused and stared at Rosie. "No. This is not working anymore." He snapped his fingers. "Sarah! Wrap this girl in one of your shawls. She's your daughter now."

"What?" Anna clutched Rosie to her chest as Sarah Barnes, a majestic woman with dark brown skin already dressed in her "African Priestess" costume, approached.

Mr. Andley huffed. "It was fine when the baby was swaddled and no one could see her face, but it's becoming too obvious now. I can't have customers asking why there's an African baby in the China exhibit."

"Because we're *American!*" Anna's voice rose. "She's *my* daughter! You can't—"

"Hand that girl over to Sarah, or I'll sack you right now." Mr. Andley glowered. "I can find another Chinese Princess in a heartbeat."

Sarah held out her bracelet-covered arms. "It's okay, Anna. I'll take good care of her."

Blinking back tears of fury, Anna complied. She wished she could storm out and never look back, but she barely had enough money to live off of as it was.

"Mama?" Rosie stared at Anna with round, confused eyes as Sarah took her.

"Hello, little one." Sarah's mouth curved. "Your Aunt Sarah has a new costume for you. Won't that be fun?"

Anna tried to give Rosie a reassuring smile as Sarah walked off. But she couldn't help feeling as if she was losing her daughter.

California, 1907

The aerialist spiraled downward and stopped inches above the ground as her skillfully wrapped rope caught her. Anna gasped and clutched John's arm, both terrified and awed.

John flashed her one of his heart-melting grins. "She really is a sensation, isn't she?"

Anna nodded. "I wish I could do that."

"Well, why not? Let's run away with the circus!" His brown eyes danced, and the spring sunlight brightening the tent warmed his brown complexion. "You can dance in the chorus until you learn enough tricks to do an aerial act, and I can build sets or anything else they need."

As the aerialist climbed the rope for her next trick, Anna dared to imagine herself in the woman's place. She'd loved to dance as a child, but her father had ordered her to stop a few years ago, since he considered it inappropriate for a young woman of marriageable age. How wonderful it must be to dance in the air!

"You want to, don't you?" John's breath whispered across her face. "In all seriousness, what's keeping us here? I have no family, and yours will never see you for who you truly are."

Anna sighed. The future her father envisioned for her—full of domestic chores and obedience to a man just like him—felt like a nightmare. Now that she was almost twenty, she wouldn't be able to avoid it for much longer. Scarcely a day passed when he didn't bring up the topic of marriage. Yet if he knew about the man she wanted to spend the rest of her life with, he would kill them both.

She longed to agree to John's fantastical plan. But she shook her head. "Don't be foolish. We would run out of money and starve to death."

A heavy look descended on John's face. "Whatever happens, know that I love you."

The music swelled, but Anna didn't see what the aerialist did next, for her eyes closed and her lips found John's.

Georgia, 1910

Seated in a chair carved with dragons, Anna tried to focus on her calligraphy and ignore all the eyes staring at her. She hated that the skills her mother had so painstakingly taught her to honor their ancestral traditions were now being used to entertain the ignorant.

A few feet from her, Charles, her "husband," swung a prop sword in graceful arcs, punctuating each move with a fierce, "*Ha!*" No one would know that his movements were an art form he'd developed himself and not the "ancient Chinese sword-fighting techniques" advertised on the posters. At least he enjoyed performing.

And as much as Anna had grown to detest her ornately embroidered costume, at least she had chosen to wear it. She wasn't sure if the same could be said for the aboriginal Australians in the enclosure to the left.

Anna looked past the gawking crowd and glimpsed Rosie, now wrapped in a colorfully patterned shawl with her textured black hair teased out, playing with a cloth doll inside Sarah's enclosure. Several people leaned against the fence and pointed at the toddler. Through the mutterings of the crowd, Anna caught the word "savage." Her blood boiled.

I have to get us out of this "exposition." She gritted her teeth. *Tomorrow, I'll practice harder on the rope.*

California, 1907

Silvery moonlight spilled through Anna's open window and traced the perfect contours of John's regal cheekbones. Lying in his arms and surrounded by a pool of her unbound hair, heart racing and skin tingling, she finally understood what true bliss felt like.

"Tell me one of your stories," she whispered.

"What kind?" Soft yet resonant, his voice felt like a gentle rain.

"Any kind."

In the blackness of midnight, she felt rather than saw his smile. "Once upon a time, there lived a fairy princess with beautiful gossamer wings. She loved to fly across all the realms, including those of mankind. One day, she met a man who had no such powers, but whose voice soothed her soul. Though they fell deeply in love, it was forbidden for her kind to be with his, and the fairy king threatened to lock her in a tower if she ever saw her lover again. Desperate, the two sought the advice of a sorceress, who told them that the only way for them to be together was if the princess cut off her own wings."

Anna frowned. "Where did you hear this story?"

"I made it up. I call it 'On Moonlit Wings,' but I haven't written it down."

"Why not?"

"I can't decide how it ends. What do you think of it?"

"It's sad, but I like it. Maybe you could sell it to the papers—"

A scream exploded outside Anna's door. She bolted up, recognizing her mother's frantic voice. Heavy footsteps approached.

She scarcely had a chance to react before a booted foot kicked down the door. Her father stood beneath the frame, a gun in his hands. His long black queue swayed behind him like a snake.

"What they said was true," he growled, raising the weapon.

"*No!*" Anna rushed toward her father.

Chunks exploded from the wooden wall as a bullet pierced it. Anna's mother grabbed her father's arm, pleading with him to stop. He shoved her off, sending her to the ground, and took aim again.

"John, run!" Anna tried to block her father, but he threw her aside. She fell in a heap on the floor.

As John scrambled out the window, Anna grabbed her father's ankle and pulled. He tripped but didn't fall. A bullet tore the window frame.

"He will not get far," her father said darkly. Five other men—her father's kin—appeared in the hallway outside. He turned to them. "Let us hunt down the beast that defiled my daughter."

"No, please!" Anna started to get up.

Her father seized her wrist with a cruel scowl. "You will return to China on the next ship and live with my brother's family until he can find a man willing to marry you. No one will ever speak of this shame again."

New York, 1910

The Albers & Andley Traveling Circus wouldn't open its doors to the public for another week, but already the big top was full. Hopeful performers waited in the audience seats for their turn to try out for the show. Anna waited among them, dressed in a glimmering leotard and tutu she'd borrowed from Marcelle, who sat beside her. Rosie was perched on Anna's knee, happily watching a trick rider do somersaults on the back of a running horse.

Henry Albers, a portly man with a thick gray beard, strode across the ring, observing. William Andley walked alongside him with the air of a king observing his subjects.

The rider flipped off the back of the horse, landed before the two circus owners, and curtseyed, the colorful ribbons woven into her curls tumbling forward. The men nodded to each other.

"We'll take the act," Mr. Albers said.

The young woman clapped her hands with delight. "Thank you!"

"Next!"

Drawing a deep breath, Anna rose from her seat.

Marcelle marched ahead of her with a proudly lifted chin. "*Messieurs!* You know me as the Empress of the Skies. Now, allow me to introduce my protégé, the Princess of the Skies." She gestured at Anna, who scrambled to approach as Rosie fidgeted in her arms.

Mr. Andley snorted. "What is this?"

Anna handed Rosie to Marcelle and quickly patted her hair, some of which had come out of its updo after her daughter had tugged on her ribbons. "Sirs, I've been training with Marcelle for almost three years now. I—"

"You already have an act." Mr. Albers pointed one meaty finger at Anna.

"I won't be displayed like an animal anymore!" Anna inhaled deeply. "Sirs, imagine how much the crowds would love a double aerial act. Let me show you what I can do."

"You have some nerve," Mr. Andley growled. "I hired you for the ethnological exposition, and that's where you'll stay."

Marcelle ignored him and approached Mr. Albers with a smooth smile. "*Henri*, I was your most popular performer long before you brought *Guillaume* on board." She gestured at the other man. "In all these years, I have never disappointed you, *oui?* I wouldn't let *Anne* audition unless I thought she was ready. She could be great—someday, she could even be better than me. Give her a chance."

Anna's heart skittered. She was used to Marcelle lecturing her about crooked knees and clumsy inversions. This was the first time she'd heard such high praise.

Mr. Albers relaxed. "I suppose it can't hurt—"

"No!" Mr. Andley's brows gathered. "Henry, you came to me because your family's circus was about to go bankrupt, and you needed a fresh perspective. I brought this circus back from the brink. I know what it needs, and it's *not* the whims of an aging aerialist." He glared at Marcelle. "You were past your prime before I even joined. You're lucky that Henry is a sentimental man."

Anna scowled. "How dare you?"

Mr. Albers sighed. "I'm afraid William has a point. I'm sorry, Marcelle, but your talent is not what it once was, and, I fear, neither is your judgment."

Marcelle stared at him.

Mr. Andley took a threatening step toward Anna. "I told you to stop wasting time here. I will sack you the next time there is an incident like this."

Hot anger churned through Anna's gut. After years of hard training—and countless bruises, burns, sprains, and aches—to develop the strength and skills to appear weightless, she would not even have the chance to try performing.

She refused to go back to that garish enclosure, pretending not to understand the insulting comments directed at her. She could not watch people ogle her daughter and speak of Rosie as they would a captive cub.

"There will not be any more incidents because I'm leaving." Anna took her daughter from Marcelle. "Thank you for all you have taught me."

Marcelle narrowed her stern green eyes but didn't speak.

Cold pricks of fear pierced Anna's stomach as she wondered how she and Rosie would survive alone, but she did not regret her decision.

Mr. Andley laughed. "Where will you go?"

Marcelle gave him a withering look. "This is not the only circus in town." She turned to Mr. Albers. "And it is not the circus it once was. Good luck, *Henri*. When you see the papers lauding the phenomenal new aerial act that is the Princess of the Skies, remember this day and all you lost when you let this buffoon"—she glared at Mr. Andley—"start making the decisions. Come, *Anne*. Let us seek out a circus that still knows what talent looks like."

Anna blinked and followed as Marcelle marched out of the ring. "I… didn't expect you to leave, too."

Marcelle arched her narrow black brows. "Did you think I would let you take everything I taught you to another circus and not come with you?"

"I…"

"Enough stammering, girl. Go pack your things and say your goodbyes. Let us not linger here a moment longer than we must."

"Yes, ma'am."

California, 1907

So many tears had poured from Anna's eyes, she wondered how she hadn't drowned in them yet. An unrelenting pain crushed her heart. Though a week had passed since her father and the others had murdered John, it remained as acute as the moment she'd learned the news.

She wasn't sure how or why she was even still alive. Every day, she would cry until her body collapsed from exhaustion then wake only to cry even more. Unable to eat and barely able to drink, she felt as if she was fading to nothing.

She couldn't bear the thought of her John—her kind, beautiful, intelligent, imaginative John—lying dead at the bottom of the river, where her father had dumped his body. Locked in her room, whose window had been boarded up, she lay on her side with her knees curled in. If there were any mercy in the world, death would soon take her, too.

The door creaked open, but Anna kept her face buried in her hands. She recognized the sound of her mother padding softly across the floor, probably with another bowl of soup she hoped to entice Anna to eat.

But this time, a new sound accompanied the usual steps and sighing— that of metal jangling.

Tempted by curiosity, Anna peeked over her fingers.

Her mother rushed up to the bed, a large sack on one shoulder and a small bag in her hand. She shook Anna's shoulder with an urgent look. "Get up! Hurry! We do not have much time before your father returns."

Anna blinked, puzzled.

Her mother shoved the two bags at her. "I packed some food and spare clothes for you, and I gathered as much money as I could. Go to the station. Take the first train out of the state, wherever it is going."

"What… What do you mean?"

"I will not watch my daughter waste away." She paused, hesitating. "I did not want to marry your father, but I had no choice. That will not be your fate. Run, *Xiao An*. Live."

Anna tentatively took the small bag of coins. "What about you?"

"I will be all right. I have often wanted to run as well, but I have your brothers and sisters to care for. Now, get out of here! You can cry more after you board the train."

Nodding, Anna stood and slung the large bag over her shoulder. Terrified as she was of facing the unknown, at least the road ahead held possibilities. "Thank you."

"This country was built for opportunity. I agreed to accompany your father here because I wanted that opportunity for my children. You are American. Do not let anyone make you forget that."

Illinois, 1910

As the hoop in her hands spun faster, Anna counted out four beats in her head and then hooked her knees onto it. Holding the other side of the apparatus, Marcelle did the same and released her hands, reaching for Anna, who took them.

Imagining the lilt of violins, Anna counted out another four beats, then, in sync with Marcelle, took one leg off the hoop and arched her back.

A child's babbling sounded below, and Anna tried not to think about what Rosie might be doing in the arms of the assistant who had agreed to watch her while the Empress and the Princess of the Skies auditioned for the Stein Family Circus.

As the piece progressed, Anna struggled to stay with Marcelle. A double act required precise timing to keep the hoop balanced. But she kept getting ahead, and she felt the apparatus wobbling.

By the time she and Marcelle finished, she was dizzier than she'd been in a long time, which seemed odd after all the hours she'd spent practicing to grow accustomed to the spinning. She nearly tumbled forward while giving her bow.

"Ah, Marcelle, you will always be a wonder." Eugene Stein approached with a wistful smile. "Ten years ago, I would have paid a pretty penny to steal you away from Henry Albers. But I'm afraid time withers even the brightest bloom, and while I was intrigued by your new 'Princess,' she is not as skillful as you were in your youth. I am sorry."

Disappointment dug its claws into Anna's chest. After eleven auditions in three towns, she should have been numb to hearing the same things each time.

Mr. Stein gave Anna an appraising look. "I am, however, putting together an 'Around the World' act and could use a representative of the Far East. Perhaps you could be my Chinese acrobat. And you, Marcelle, could represent France."

Anna's gut balked at the proposal, but she bit the inside of her cheek. After two months of searching for work, this was the closest she'd come to an offer that would allow her to perform. However, she hadn't left Albers & Andley to end up in yet another job that would treat her like an exotic animal. "No. I can't."

Marcelle scowled at Mr. Stein. "We are not museum pieces. We are artists. If you cannot appreciate that, then we will go someplace else."

Anna took Rosie from the assistant and rushed to catch up as Marcelle stormed away. *What happens now? Another city, another circus? What happens when we run out?*

The money she and Marcelle had spent on rooms and trains had been meant to sustain them through the winter hiatus, when circuses paused their traveling and performance jobs became scarce. Though Marcelle claimed she had substantial savings from a lifetime of fame, even that couldn't last forever.

If no one hired them soon, they wouldn't be able to feed themselves, let alone keep roaming.

Texas, 1907

In the days since she'd left her childhood home, Anna hadn't thought at all about where she was going. But now, she found herself in a state she'd never been to before, frightened and lost in a way she'd never imagined possible. What money she had left wouldn't be enough for a room that night.

Seeing a sign for the Albers & Andley Traveling Circus, she thought back to the joyful times when she and John would sneak away to explore menageries of amazing animals and watch acrobats perform incredible feats. She wandered toward the spot where workers were setting up tents, the sack of clothes and near-depleted food on her back. She could already imagine what the place would look like when it was completed—a portable town full of colors and delights. With the bright morning sun shining in her eyes, she could almost see John waving to her amid a sweaty crowd, greeting her with a beautiful smile that left her helpless to his pull.

"What are you doing there, girl?" A blond man with a heavy mustache scowled at her from several feet away.

Startled out of her reverie, Anna quickly turned to leave.

"Wait!" The man strode to her, looking her up and down. "I'm in need of a Chinagirl. Last one quit without warning."

"What are you talking about?" Sweating from the heat, Anna suddenly felt sick.

"The ethnological exposition. It's a good job. You'll get a place to live, three meals a day, and decent pay, and I won't even ask what you're running from. What do you say?"

Whatever this job involved, at least she wouldn't have to sleep on the street. "Yes… Yes, sir."

"Excellent. I'm William Andley. What's your name, and how old are you?"

"My name is Anna Song. I'm nineteen—" Overwhelmed by a flood of nausea, she fell to her knees and vomited onto the dry grass.

"Whoa!" Mr. Andley jumped back. "Ah, so that's why you're running." He chuckled. "Not a problem. I'll have the seamstress make your costume extra-large and loose. A family exhibit would be nice, I think. Yes, this could work out well."

"What?"

He pointed at a large train car. "Go on, then. You have no time to waste if you're going to be ready for opening day. Tell them I sent you." With that, he walked off, leaving Anna kneeling in the grass.

She touched her belly, her eyes widening. She'd suspected but hadn't dared think about it. But now, she couldn't pretend any longer.

Trembling, she staggered to her feet and headed to the car.

Illinois, 1910

Seated on one of the narrow beds in their rented room, Anna stroked Rosie's hair as the toddler played with her cloth doll. *Whatever becomes of me, you will grow up to be a capable and independent woman. I will make sure of that.*

Marcelle paced from the window to the door and back again. "Nobody values skill and experience anymore. All they want is spangles, spangles, spangles." She paused. "*Désolée, Anne.* I let you down today."

"What do you mean?"

"I could not keep up with you on the hoop, and that ruined our chances with *Eugène*. He was right about me. I am not the performer I once was."

"You are magnificent." Anna stood. "I'm lucky to perform with you."

Marcelle shook her head. "We must abandon the partner routines. You and I will each perform individually, side by side but on different apparatuses. I may not be able to invert as smoothly as I once could, but I still know what makes a good act."

"Marcelle…" Anna hesitated. The seed of idea had planted itself in her mind a few weeks back, but she hadn't spoken of it. Now, with their other options close to exhausted, she decided it could be worth the risk. "You have been performing longer than I have been alive, and you know more about creating a show than Stein or Albers or Andley put together. Perhaps, instead of seeking the approval of men who want spangles, it's time to start your own circus."

Marcelle paused, her brow furrowing. "I cannot deny that the thought has crossed my mind. I know enough performers who might be willing to take the risk. But even if I could corral them all, even if I could convince a bank to give me a loan, I could hardly build a menagerie, a museum, a sideshow. How could we convince the public to come to our tiny show when they're accustomed to so much more?"

"You could make it different from what they've seen before. Give them a story. Instead of only tricks performed by acts that have nothing to do with each other, make it like a play, or an opera, but with aerialists and acrobats instead of Shakespeare and Mozart."

"That would be interesting." Marcelle stroked her chin. "The public does love a good story. I have a pianist friend who has for years told me he wants to compose an opera. I could write to him."

Anna's pulse hummed with excitement. "It will not be easy, but if we succeed, we could give the world something truly beautiful."

She could practically hear the gears in Marcelle's mind clicking as the older woman began pacing again. "My name still means something to the world. It will be difficult to obtain a large enough loan or find investors, but perhaps I could convince the performers to accept an equal share of the profits in exchange for a lower payment. You and I are not the only ones who have grown tired of those smarmy bosses. Yes... this could work. Did you have a particular story in mind?"

Anna smiled. "Let me tell you a tale about a fairy princess who falls in love with an earthly man..."

Kansas, 1907

"The Empress of the Skies" was a well-deserved name. Sitting in the empty audience stands, Anna watched Marcelle rehearse. The aerialist held the rope high above her with her hands wide and her legs free. She twisted her hips and bent her knees one at a time, as if walking on the air.

Thinking of the life growing inside her, Anna pressed her hand to her belly. A little piece of John, a little piece of herself, a little piece of the future.

Though the thought of being a mother still frightened her, she already loved this child whose face she'd never seen. She couldn't wait to show the baby wonders like what she witnessed.

Marcelle twisted the rope around her waist, spread her arms and legs wide, and spun down toward the floor.

Anna couldn't help thinking of the last show she'd attended with John. Sadness blossomed in her heart. If only she hadn't so easily dismissed his idea of running away. She'd had to do so anyway—if she'd listened, he might have been there beside her, encouraging her to try learning to fly.

"You're the new girl." Marcelle lowered herself from the rope and waved. "You're always here when I'm rehearsing."

Anna stood with a self-conscious smile. "I love watching you perform, but, of course, I can't attend any of the shows. I hope I'm not intruding."

"Not at all. After a month of watching you watching me, I decided I should introduce myself properly." She held out a hand. "Marcelle Brodeur."

Anna took it. "Anna Song."

"You are part of the human zoo, *oui?*" Marcelle crinkled her nose. "Good luck with that."

Anna sighed. "I wish I could be a performer instead, but I don't have any skills."

"Why not learn, then?" Marcelle tilted her head. "I don't usually take on students, but you've watched me every day since you arrived here, and that shows you have dedication. I could teach you."

Anna brightened but then shook her head, placing her hand on her belly. "I can't. It's not safe."

Marcelle narrowed her eyes. "*I* will tell you what's safe. We'll begin with skills that can be done from the ground and start building up your muscles. After the baby is born, then I'll let you go up in the air."

Anna's lips split. "That would be wonderful."

Ohio, 1911

Anna wove through the bustling backstage area. With the show's opening night only a few days away, the atmosphere was growing more and more excited. She was supposed to play a background fairy in the next scene, spinning on a hoop behind Marcelle, who would be performing on the rope as the fairy princess.

After nearly a year of hard work—and Marcelle contacting every friend she'd ever had—*On Moonlit Wings* was about to become a reality. The rented theater had been transformed to accommodate aerial apparatuses and animal cages, and enough people were interested in the Empress of the Skies' new show that papers across America had written about it.

Standing by her lion cages, Tanya Mizrahi waved. "Have a good rehearsal, Anna!"

"Thank you!" Anna squeezed past Charles Sasaki, who would be playing the warrior who fell for the fairy princess, and Sarah Barnes, who would be playing the fairy queen.

They were hardly the only defectors from Albers & Andley. Kirsten Sigrist had arrived with her ten dogs; they, along with Tanya's three lions, would separately perform animal acts to represent parts of the fairy kingdom. Numerous dancers and singers had also joined the show, as well as new acts eager for a chance to shine.

Maja Lozanac, who would, with her blindfolded acrobatic dances, play the role of the sorceress, stepped in front of Anna. "I had a dream about the show."

Intrigued, Anna asked, "What did you see?"

"If you are brave, you will carry us all."

Unsure what that meant, Anna continued on her way. When she arrived, Marcelle was already waiting on a catwalk above the stage. Her routine would begin with her climbing down, representing the fairy's descent to the earth.

"What took you so long?" Marcelle clapped. "Let us begin!"

Anna climbed a rope ladder to reach the hoop. She wished she could watch Marcelle bring her character to life with her famed strength and grace but had to focus on her own movements.

A thrill shot through her. She still couldn't quite believe that she and Marcelle had succeeded in putting this show together. Whether it was greeted with great fanfare or fizzled after a few performances, at least they'd created something that was their own.

A thudding noise and a cry interrupted her concentration. Startled, she looked down. Marcelle lay crumpled at the bottom of the rope.

Gasping, Anna rushed to climb down. "Marcelle!"

"I'm all right." Marcelle sat up, rubbing her ankle. "My grip isn't what it used to be. I may have been too ambitious with the choreography." She tried to stand but quickly plopped back down, cursing. "I won't be able to climb like this."

"What are we going to do?"

"You have to take the role. I should have given it to you in the first place. You are ready." She placed a hand on Anna's shoulder. "I said you could be great, and I meant it. This is your chance to prove me right, Princess of the Skies."

Florida, 1908

Anna wasn't sure who was crying louder—her baby or her. Clutching the two-month-old to her chest, she tried desperately not to scream.

With the wet heat, it was easy to forget that it was still winter. Albers & Andley had called everyone back to prepare for the upcoming spring and summer tour. Anna had hoped that by now, she would have figured out how to be a mother. But with Rosie refusing to stop wailing, she wondered if she would ever learn.

"Shut that thing up!" Storming through the costume tent, Mr. Andley glowered at Anna. "Or I'll feed it to the lions!"

Tanya Mizrahi looked up from the costume she was mending and sniffed. "My lions do not eat infants. However, they do enjoy eating pigs." She gave Mr. Andley a pointed look.

"What's going on here?" Marcelle approached. "*Guillaume*, stop scaring the baby and let us do our jobs."

Mr. Andley's face purpled, and he walked off with a huff.

"Thank you," Anna said between sniffles. Having spent the winter moving between the homes of whoever had a bed to spare, Anna was beyond grateful for all the support she'd received from her fellow performers. She only wished she didn't have to be such a burden. "I-I'm sorry for all the trouble."

"Nonsense. Here, let me take her." Marcelle reached out for the baby. Rocking her gently, she sang a quiet French lullaby.

Anna wiped her eyes, watching in awe as Rosie quieted and eventually fell asleep. "How did you do that?"

"Experience. I may not have children, but I've looked after many over the years. We take care of each other here. Now that Rosie's asleep, I think it's time I teach you a drop. Tanya, would you mind looking after the baby?"

Tanya took the infant and cradled her. "What a sweet girl!"

Anna smiled. "Thank you… Thank you all so much."

"Someday, it will be your turn to take care of us," Marcelle said.

"Yes, of course. I won't let you down."

Ohio, 1911

Every seat of the theater was filled. The audience, promised an exciting new show from the great Empress of the Skies, watched breathlessly as Charles, playing the warrior, fought his way through various acts representing dangers in order to reach the enchanted fairy kingdom.

But they wouldn't get the Empress. Instead, they'd get the Princess—an announcement Marcelle, fearful of requests for refunds, had saved until after everyone was seated.

Waiting on the catwalk for her musical cue, Anna tried to still her quivering heart. Over the last several rehearsals, she had put her body through more than she had imagined it capable of. Her glimmering blue-and-white leotard, reminiscent of moonlight, and pale pink tights hid countless bruises and rope burns, and dull pain covered every muscle. If she wowed this audience, it would all be worthwhile. Everyone was counting on her to make their show a sensation, and she wouldn't let them down.

They all looked so amazing on stage.

Maja, with her blindfolded acrobatic dance. Dressed in a sleek black-and-silver leotard, she flawlessly transitioned from balletic spins to athletic tumbles as the narrator spoke of the power of fate and the sorceress who knew its secrets.

Kirsten, with her ten playful dogs. Her long red skirt opened like a blooming rose as she whirled this way and that, directing the dogs to perform flips and jumps as the narrator described the delights of the fairy kingdom.

Tanya, with her three lions. Wearing her famed Amazonian armor, she commanded them to run over and under obstacles on cue as the narrator warned of the kingdom's dangers.

Upon hearing the opening melody of the song that would accompany her first performance, Anna gracefully climbed down and came into view of the audience from above. Still near the top, she swung her legs and lifted her hips to twist the rope around her waist. After wrapping it around her body a few more times, she let go, spinning downward at a dizzying speed. She stopped inches from the ground, caught by her precisely wrapped rope, and posed with an arched back as the audience screamed their approval.

It was the same drop she'd once gasped at while watching a show with John. It felt like a lifetime ago, yet she still remembered his smile as if it were yesterday. *I did it, John. I wish you could see me now.*

Her wings might have been invisible, but the audience had seen them nonetheless. As she climbed back up, turning upside down, hooking her knee, and grabbing the rope above in a spider-like ascent, she wondered how he would feel if he knew she'd turned his story into a show.

She held the rope with arms wide, as Marcelle once had, and released her legs, pedaling them slowly. As the rope spun, she glimpsed the audience.

For years, people had stared at her, but never like this—never with awe and admiration. Though her hands were starting to burn, she felt she could stay in the air forever.

A face caught her eye—obscured by the shadows yet unmistakable. The gentle curve of his brow, the flawless contours of his cheeks… but it couldn't be John. It had to be her imagination putting his face onto someone who looked like him from a distance.

She wrapped her legs back around the rope, suddenly wanting to cry.

California, 1906

Even inside the museum tent, Anna still looked around warily, fearful of spotting someone her father knew. He would never forgive her for wasting money on the circus. But having spent her entire life in his house, she'd yearned to glimpse the wonders of the world.

Behind a glass case sat an exquisitely decorated helmet—a relic of the ancient Greeks, according to the sign. It seemed impossibly old, and she marveled at its majesty.

A young man her age stared at it from across the case. Open-faced and handsome with the most beautiful brown eyes she'd ever seen… she blushed when he looked up and his gaze caught hers.

Flustered, she moved on to the next exhibit, an ancient sword. He wandered over to a nearby case containing a painted vase. As she wove through the exhibit, she kept glimpsing him and chastising herself for being so drawn to a good-looking stranger.

She was in the middle of observing a set of baubles that supposedly belonged to an ancient queen when he appeared beside her.

"That looks like something Helen of Troy would have worn." A soft voice, flowing like a clear creek, rippled past her ears.

She looked up with a start.

He smiled at her. "I apologize if I startled you."

"Not… not at all."

"My name is John Maxfield." He held out his hand.

"I'm Anna Song." Uncertainly, she reached toward him.

He took her hand and lifted it to his lips, sending delighted chills over her skin. "Pleased to meet you, Miss Song. Are you here with your family?"

She shook her head. "They think all this"—she gestured widely—"is frivolous, but I find it wonderful. It's all so amazing… so far from the ordinary life I'm expected to live."

"That's why I came, too. The world is so big, and our lives are so small. At least here, we get to experience a piece of all that's out there. And at least here, what's different can be celebrated. For someone like me, who doesn't belong anywhere, that feels special."

"I understand. I want more than I was born to have, and because of that, I'm considered strange. Here, everything is strange, and I'm no longer alone."

Their eyes met again, and for a long moment, they didn't speak.

Then, John jerked his head toward the tent's entrance. "Are you going to see the show in the big top?"

"Of course."

"Forgive me if this is too bold, but I would be honored if you would let me escort you." He held out his arm.

Blushing, she took it. "That… would be nice."

Ohio, 1911

Cheers and laughter swirled backstage. Glass bottles clinked as performers drank to their wild success. Anna squeezed past them, aiming for the dressing room so she could change out of her leotard.

"*Anne!*"

Hearing Marcelle's voice, Anna turned around.

Marcelle rushed up to her with a grin. "You were magnificent tonight. You are no longer the Princess of the Skies—you may now claim the title of

Empress. I relinquish it gladly."

Anna shook her head. "I can't. That's your stage name."

"You are a worthy successor. All the critics are saying so. I've spoken to a few investors, and they are very interested in our continued success. Soon, we will be able to tour the country."

"That would be wonderful."

"If you will excuse me, I must return to them. I just wanted to tell you before you left to go celebrate." Marcelle vanished into the crowd.

Anna's heart danced, but she wasn't in the mood to celebrate with the others. A heavy feeling still weighed on her as she thought about the one person she wished could have been there—and how impossible that wish was.

"Excuse me, I'm looking for Miss Anna Song. Have you seen her?"

Anna froze. That man's voice, watery yet firm, sounded just like John's.

"Yes, she went that way." It was Kirsten who replied. "You look familiar. Have we met?"

"I don't think so, ma'am. Thank you."

Anna almost didn't dare turn around. When she finally did, tears sprang to her eyes.

He was there—right there before her. Alive. Real.

His eyes widened at the sight of her. "It's—It's really you. I didn't dare hope…"

"John?"

He nodded.

The next thing she knew, they were in each other's arms. She held him close, scarcely able to believe what she was seeing and hearing and feeling. Questions tumbled through her head, but she couldn't stop sobbing long enough to ask any.

"If I'd known you were alive, I would never have stopped looking." His breath whispered across her hair.

"Wh-what?"

"While running from your father, I fell into the river and was swept downstream. By the time I made it back to town, word had spread that you'd killed yourself. Since then… no place felt like home. I wandered from town to town, picking up whatever work I could. Then I saw in the papers that the Empress of the Skies was putting on a show with the same name as the story I once told you… and that one of the performers had the same name as you… It seemed impossible, but I traveled two days to get here in case it was true, that you were still alive. And then I saw you dancing in the sky…"

"My father told me he killed you." Anna wiped her eyes. "I-I never stopped missing you. That's why I asked Marcelle to turn your story into our show."

He smiled. "I like the ending, how the fairy princess discovered the magic to give the man wings, how they flew off into the night. Did you come up with it?"

"Yes. It was my way of letting them run away together… like I should have with you."

"It's not too late, if you'll still have me."

Anna's heart leaped, but she stopped her tongue from answering too quickly. Rosie… he still didn't know about Rosie. Would he—

"There you are!" Maja rushed toward her, carrying a squirming Rosie. "I was asked to return her to you. I'm sorry, I would look after her, but she keeps trying to tear my costume."

"Thank you." Anna automatically took the child.

"Mama!" Rosie grabbed at Anna's face.

John stared with eyes rounder than Anna had ever seen them. Her heart clenched. What was she supposed to say?

He nodded at Rosie. "Is… Is that…?"

Anna lifted her chin and adjusted Rosie to face John. "John… this is

Rosaline Maxfield Song. She's… she's yours."

A broad smile spread across his lips. "Well, isn't she a gift?" His expression sobered. "Please, Anna, wherever you go, let me come with you. Let me be there for you—and for our daughter."

Tears of joy streamed from her eyes. "Yes. Yes, stay with us."

He wrapped an arm around her waist and pulled her in close, kissing her deeply. Her heart hammered, and she thought she might dissolve in a swirl of light.

A sticky hand grabbed her bun, pulling her back to reality. Before her, John bent over sideways, Rosie's other hand tangled in his short black hair. The toddler giggled delightedly.

Anna and John both burst out laughing, their voices and Rosie's braiding together into a cord of happiness.

THE CIRCUS MEMORIES OF A CARTOONIST

BASED ON REAL FACTS

STORY AND ART BY ADRÈNO   EDITED BY MARY FAN

EARLY 2016

I DO REMEMBER WHEN I ARRIVED.
DETAILS OF HOW DON'T MATTER MUCH. IT INVOLVED
TRYING TO MAKE SENSE OF MY LIFE, SEEKING THAT
FRAGILE BALANCE BETWEEN FINANCIAL SURVIVAL, PRO-
DUCING ART, AND HOLDING ON TO MY SANITY.

SO I DID WHAT ANY LOGICAL PERSON
WOULD DO UNDER THOSE CIRCUMSTANCES:
I JOINED THE CIRCUS.

THIS WAS THE HOUSE OF THE SQUIDLING BROTHERS
CIRCUS IN PHILADELPHIA. THE SQUID'S HOUSE.

THIS IS WHERE THIS STORY BEGINS.

JASON WAS AN ACTOR, WRITER, POET, MUSICIAN, AND PAINTER. ARGUABLY HIS DEATH IN 1998 WAS THE CATALYST FOR JELLYBOY AND MATTERZ TO COMMIT TO THEIR MUSIC AS A MEANS TO PROCESS THEIR GRIEF, AND THAT LED THEM TO START A BAND, *THE HYDROGEN JUKEBOX*, EVENTUALLY GETTING INVOLVED WITH SIDESHOW AND TURNING THAT INTO A CAREER. THE BAND EVENTUALLY STARTED INCORPORATING DANCERS, SIDESHOW AND BURLESQUE PERFORMERS AND TURNED INTO *THE CARNIVOLUTION SHOW*. THE BAND ENDED IN 2010 WITH A FISTFIGHT BETWEEN JELLYBOY AND THE DRUMMER, STYX LATTE, ONCE THE SIDESHOW PART TOOK OVER.

MATTERZ AND JELLYBOY FIRMLY BELIEVED HAD HE LIVED JASON WOULD HAVE BEEN A GIANT AMONG PERFORMERS AND HIS PRESENCE WAS FELT THROUGHOUT THEIR LIVES.

JELLYBOY WAS A SIDESHOW CLOWN, RINGMASTER AND A GOOD FRIEND FOR ABOUT 2 YEARS AT THIS TIME. HE HAD BEEN MENTORED BY PERFORMERS ENIGMA AND RED STUART IN THE SIDESHOW ARTS WHICH INCLUDED SWORD SWALLOWING, FIRE BREATHING, BLOCKHEAD, AND ELECTRIC STUNTS, AND HAD BEEN PERFORMING PROFESSIONALLY FOR 10 YEARS AT THIS POINT.

MATTERZ, THE INDESTRUCTIBLE CHICKEN MAN ALSO FROM A MUSICAL AND THEATER BACKGROUND, MATTERZ WOULD PERFORM FEATS OF PAIN RESISTANCE LIKE BED OF NAILS, MOUSE TRAPS ON HIS TONGUE, AND ALSO RUNNING DRESSED AS A CHICKEN. HE WOULD DIRECT HORROR FILMS WITH THEIR SIDESHOW FRIENDS PLUS TAKE CARE OF ALL THE AUDIO AND LIGHTING TECHNICAL PART OF CARNIVOLUTION. MATTERZ WASN'T LIVING AT THE HOUSE ANY LONGER BECAUSE...

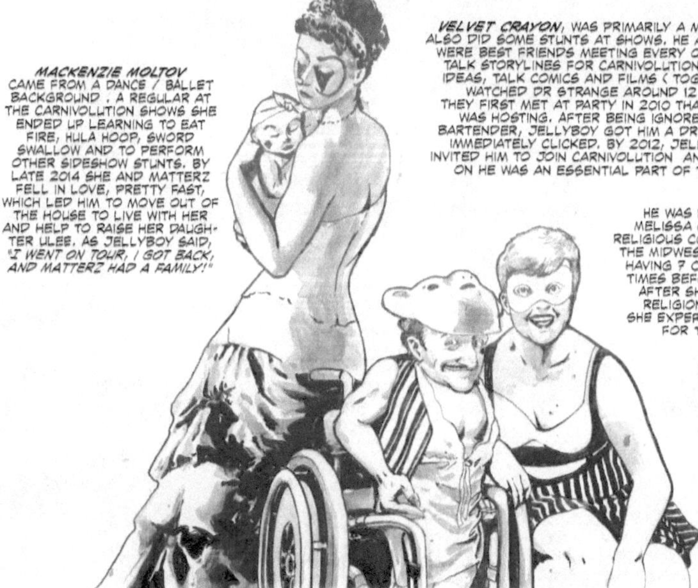

MACKENZIE MOLTOV CAME FROM A DANCE / BALLET BACKGROUND . A REGULAR AT THE CARNIVOLUTION SHOWS SHE ENDED UP LEARNING TO EAT FIRE, HULA HOOP, SWORD SWALLOW AND TO PERFORM OTHER SIDESHOW STUNTS. BY LATE 2014 SHE AND MATTERZ FELL IN LOVE, PRETTY FAST, WHICH LED HIM TO MOVE OUT OF THE HOUSE TO LIVE WITH HER AND HELP TO RAISE HER DAUGHTER ULEE. AS JELLYBOY SAID, "I WENT ON TOUR, I GOT BACK, AND MATTERZ HAD A FAMILY!"

VELVET CRAYON, WAS PRIMARILY A MUSICIAN WHO ALSO DID SOME STUNTS AT SHOWS. HE AND JELLYBOY WERE BEST FRIENDS MEETING EVERY OTHER DAY TO TALK STORYLINES FOR CARNIVOLUTION, EXCHANGE IDEAS, TALK COMICS AND FILMS (TOGETHER THEY WATCHED DR STRANGE AROUND 12 TIMES). THEY FIRST MET AT PARTY IN 2010 THAT JELLYBOY WAS HOSTING. AFTER BEING IGNORED BY THE BARTENDER, JELLYBOY GOT HIM A DRINK AND THEY IMMEDIATELY CLICKED. BY 2012, JELLYBOY HAD INVITED HIM TO JOIN CARNIVOLUTION AND FROM THEN ON HE WAS AN ESSENTIAL PART OF THE SHOW.

HE WAS DATING MELISSA. MELISSA CAME FROM A VERY RELIGIOUS CONSERVATIVE FAMILY IN THE MIDWEST WHICH, ASIDE FROM HAVING 7 CHILDREN, MOVED 60 TIMES BEFORE SHE TURNED 21. AFTER SHE WAS FREE FROM RELIGION AND HER FAMILY, SHE EXPERIENCED THE WORLD FOR THE FIRST TIME.

AMONG OTHER THINGS HER JOURNEY INCLUDED DRINKING COFFEE WHICH WAS FORBIDDEN IN HER HOUSE AND VISITING NY. THAT'S WHEN SHE MET VELVET PERFORMING AT THE CONEY ISLAND SIDESHOW. SHE WAS NOT A PERFORMER HERSELF, NOR DID SHE WANT TO BE, SHE ENJOYED HELPING OTHERS PRODUCE THEIR ART.

I WOULD STAY IN THE ATTIC WITH MY DRAWINGS, MY BOOK, COMICS, COMPUTER AND STORIES.

JIM WAS A JAZZ/ COUNTRY/ PUNK MUSICIAN WHO TENDED TO LOCK HIMSELF IN HIS ROOM WITH HIS RECORDS PLAYING FOR HIMSELF MOST OF THE TIME. NO TV, SMARTPHONES OR "ANYTHING THAT COULD CONTROL HIM".

THE PUPPET ROOM

JELLY SHARED HIS ROOM WITH FIBI EYEWALKER, A SELF TAUGHT ISRAELI PERFORMER. INITIALLY JELLYBOY WASN'T INTO DATING OR MENTORING ANOTHER PERFORMER.

ONCE THEY GOT THROUGH THAT THEY STARTED HAVING DUO ACTS TOGETHER

BORIS WAS A PHOTOGRAPHER/ BDSM ENTHUSIAST.

THAT ROOM WAS TAKEN LATER IN THE YEAR BY POLYANNA HIGHGLOSS, BELLYDANCER/ SIDESHOW CLOWN.

TITANO ODDFELLOW. A TRADITIONAL STRONGMAN WHO USED TO LIFT PEOPLE WITH HIS BEARD OR TEETH, HOLD A JACKHAMMER AN INCH FROM HIS FACE WITH ONE HAND, BEND OVER METAL AND SWORD SWALLOW.

HE HAD TWO DOGS: RICKY AND EVE. TITANO WOULD GO ON TOURS AND ASK A FRIEND TO COME WALK THE DOGS.

IT WASN'T ANY SURPRISE WHEN SUDDENLY RICKY WOULD WALK UP INTO MY ROOM OUT OF FEELING ALONE. I DIDN'T MIND ANOTHER SOUL NEEDING COMPANY.

THE LIVING ROOM WAS THE "GUEST ROOM". THERE WERE ALWAYS FRIENDS OF JELLYBOY AND OUT OF TOWN PERFORMERS STAYING FOR A SHORT OR LONG TIME. RICHARD, A DISABLED WRITER WORKING ON HIS TORI AMOS THESIS WAS THERE WHEN I MOVED IN. HIS HEALTH WORSENED AND, BY FALL, HE MOVED INTO A HEALTHCARE CENTER.

A CLEARLY MORE APPROPRIATE PLACE FOR HIS CONDITION THAN A CLOWN HOUSE.

Kunst und Wunderkammer

FIBI, JELLYBOY AND TITANO HAD
COLLECTIONS OF SWORDS AND RELATED
PROPS FOR SWORD SWALLOWING. THERE
WERE BANNERS AROUND THE HOUSE THEY
USED AS BACKDROPS FOR SHOWS MADE
BY TOMMY TOONZ, SYD TORCHIO AND
OTHER ARTISTS. BY THE WALLS, POSTERS
OF DIFFERENT PERFORMANCES AND INDIE
HORROR FILMS
PRODUCED AND DIRECTED BY MATTERZ. AS
JIM WOULD TELL ME THEY COVERED THE
WHOLE PREVIOUS HOUSE WITH FAKE BLOOD
TO SHOOT A SCENE TO THE
LANDLADY'S DESPAIR

A FEW JAR BABIES STOOD BY THE BOOK-
SHELVES, ONE OF THEM WAS A MIX OF
CHICKEN AND SQUID IN A JAR FILLED WITH
ETHER, THE SQUICKEN. WHETHER IT WAS
PROP FOR A SPECIFIC SHOW OR JUST A
HOUSE DECORATION I NEVER ASKED.
BY THE WINDOWS, JELLYBOY WOULD MAKE
LITTLE SHRINES.

THE SHRINES WERE ALL MADE BY
ME WHILE LATE NIGHT DECORATING
ON LSD AND I TRIED MY BEST TO
MAINTAIN THEM AS OBJECTS
FLOWED INTO THE HOUSE LIKE
DRIFTWOOD ON A RIVER. SO MANY
PEOPLE COMING AND GOING, SO
MANY SHOWS, I JUST FELL IN LOVE
WITH ALL THE COOL OBJECTS AND
STARTED MAKING SCULPTURES OUT
OF THEM.

AND FINALLY THERE WERE
PAINTINGS BY THEIR LATE
BROTHER JASON.

BY MAY, FIBI WAS PERFORMING WITH HER EUROPEAN FRIENDS, THE DEMENTED DOLLS, AND THEY BRIEFLY STAYED AT THE HOUSE. I PAINTED A BANNER FOR THEIR TOUR AND IT WAS A GREAT TIME.
SIDESHOW PEOPLE CAN BE VERY SENSITIVE., ADRIANO.
"WE PERFORM TOGETHER, AND WE ARE ALL CONNECTED WHETHER WE LIKE IT OR NOT."
"WE LOVED EACH OTHER, WE ALL SUPPORTED EACH OTHER."
"TRIED TO INSPIRE INSTEAD OF STEALING FROM EACH OTHER'S ACTS."
MY HEART IS BIG, THESE THINGS DON'T NEED TO BE HARD.

MY PREVIOUS CIRCUS RESIDENCE
HOUSE OF YES
BY APRIL 2015, RYAN UZI AND ANYA SAPOZHNIKOVA ASKED ME TO PAINT THE COMIC BOOK BATHROOM AT THE NEW HOUSE OF YES, A NIGHTCLUB/ CIRCUS PERFORMANCE SPACE RUN BY AERIALISTS KAE BURKE AND ANYA SAPOZHNIKOVA SINCE 2007. RYAN, AT THE TIME, WAS PARTICULARLY OBSESSED WITH ONE SPECIFIC GRAPHIC NOVEL...
JOHN DIFOOL
NOT LIKE I MADE ANY OF IT EASIER ON MYSELF.
ANYA, IT WOULD BE BETTER IF I HAVE THE COMPLETE 300 PAGES OF THE GRAPHIC NOVEL IN THE BATHROOM SO PEOPLE READ THE COMIC.
YOU WANT ME TO REPRODUCE 30 PAGES OF THE INCAL GRAPHIC NOVEL BY MOEBIUS AND JORODOWSKI?
HOW LONG WILL YOU TAKE?
3 DAYS...
IT TOOK 3 MONTHS.
THE INCAL BATHROOM
I BROKE DOWN THE 6 ISSUES, 300 PAGES, TO DISTRIBUTE AMONG THE WALLS. LARGE IMAGES WOULD STAND OUT WITH SMALLER FRAMES AND CUT OUTS OF THE GRAPHIC NOVEL IN A WAY THAT LET YOU FOLLOW THE STORY.
IT WAS A MADMAN'S JOB. AS ANYA SOON ENOUGH FOUND OUT.
ADRIANO, ARE YOU OK?
THIS COMIC IS SO FUNNY!
ANYA, DON'T WORRY. I AM AS SANE AS I HAD ALWAYS BEEN.
HAHAH HAHAHAHAH HAHAHAHAHAH
HAHAH HAHAHAH HAHAH

BY 2005 THE HYDROGEN JUKEBOX BAND LOST THEIR ARRANGE-MENT PERFORMING AT PARADES IN SOUTH ST ONCE THEIR SHOWS TURNED TOO POLITICAL FOR THE TASTE OF THE ORGANIZERS.

IT DIDN'T TAKE LONG THOUGH TO FIND A PERMANENT RESIDENCE FOR THEIR SHOWS.

THE TIBERINO MUSEUM IS A COMPOUND OF HOUSES WITH A HUGE BACKYARD OF MURALS, SCULPTURES, AND PAINTINGS BY DIFFERENT MEMBERS OF THE TIBERINO FAMILY IN WEST PHILADELPHIA. IT WAS FOUNDED IN 1999 BY JOSEPH " JOE" TIBERINO AS A MEMORIAL TO HIS LATE WIFE ELLEN POWELL TIBERINO (1937-1992).

THE CARNIVOLUTION SHOWS STARTED HAPPENING THERE BY 2005 WHEN THE SQUIDLING BROS PERFORMED THROUGH SEVERAL OTHER OPEN ART STUDIOS AND ENDED UP THERE WITH CLOWNS, JUGGLERS, AND MUSICIANS TO JOE TIBERINO'S DELIGHT. HE INVITED THEM TO PERFORM AND FOR ALMOST A DECADE THEY WERE THERE EVERY SUMMER. ONCE THEY HAD A FIXED RESIDENCE WHAT WAS INITIALLY A VARIETY SHOW PERFORMANCE OF THE HYDROGEN JUKEBOX BAND EVOLVED WITH WHOLE WRITTEN SCRIPTS, MORE PLANNING AND MORE PRODUCTION BUT NO LESS MADNESS.

AFTER JOE'S FU-NERAL IN 2016, THE TIBERINO FAMILY AGREED TO HAVE NEW SHOWS THERE IN HIS MEMORY.

THAT WAS WHEN I FIRST ATTENDED. IT OPENED WITH WHAT SOUNDED LIKE A WHOLE BAND BUT IT WAS VELVET CRAYON ALONE WITH HIS GUITAR AND SAMPLERS, OR AS HE TOLD ME "WITH HIS GHOST BAND".

WELCOME TO THE SQUIDLING BROTHERS' CARNIVOLUTION! WHERE WE ADVENTURE THROUGH TIME, SPACE AND INTERDIMENSIONAL POCKETS TO FIND THE STRANGEST ACTS IN THE UNIVERSE!
THE SHOW WAS AROUND 3 HOURS. THERE WAS SWORD SWALLOWING, BED OF NAILS, FIRE PERFORMANCE, FEATS OF STRENGTH, AERIAL ACTS, TRASHY MERMAIDS, PUPPETS GALORE, BELLYDANCE, AND OCCASIONALLY SUSPENSION AND I WOULD PRODUCE AROUND 40 DRAWINGS OF THE PERFORMANCES.
EACH SHOW HAD A SPECIFIC ONGOING STORY. VELVET CRAYON WAS THE PRESIDENT FIGHTING AN EVIL EMPIRE LED BY STAR COMMANDER. BIG MAMA MADOODI WAS THE WEIRD SPIRITUAL LEADER THEY WOULD GO TO FOR ADVICE AND GUIDANCE.
STAPLE THE CLOWN!
ONCE DRIVING ME BACK HOME, MACKENZIE OPENED UP HERSELF A BIT:
MY WHOLE WEEK I ONLY WORK AT A STORE, DEALING WITH @##* CLIENTS
THIS IS THE ONLY TIME WHEN I CAN BE MYSELF.
IT WAS A GREAT SPECTACLE WITH A PUNK ROCK DIY BUDGET. SOMETIMES IT EVEN BROKE EVEN OR MADE PROFIT. IT WAS CIRCUS LIFE.

HOUSE OF YES

I HAVE TO BRING THESE BODIES BACK TO THAT CRAZY B**** FROM AMOK!

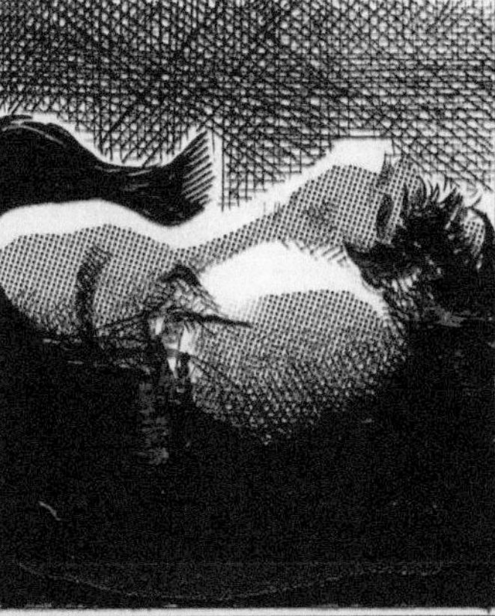

WHAT MADE AN AUDIENCE?

- IT IS NOT WHAT YOU ARE THINKING! WE WERE DRINKING LAST NIGHT, JELLYBOY NEEDED A PLACE TO CRASH AND...
I DON'T REMEMBER LAST NIGHT...
YOU ARE NOT HELPING!

THE BUSHWICK OPEN STUDIOS WAS HAPPENING THAT WEEKEND. HOUSE OF YES, STILL UNDER CONSTRUCTION, DIDN'T HAVE EVEN THEATER CURTAINS OR A FINISHED STAGE; BUT THEY WOULD HAVE A SHOW NONETHELESS.
ANYA, HOW ARE YOU GONNA GET PEOPLE FOR THE SHOWS? NOBODY DID ANY PROMOTION!

WE ARE GONNA HAVE A PARADE.

AND IF THERE WAS ONE THING I LEARNED IN LIFE IT WAS TO TRUST ANYA ON THIS. HOUSE OF YES WASN'T A SUCCESS BY ACCIDENT BUT DUE TO SOME KEEN OBSERVATIONS AND INTUITION ABOUT CIRCUS PRODUCTION FROM ANYA AND KAE.
THEY CAME FROM NOWHERE. PEOPLE MERELY SAW THE STILT WALKERS, JUGGLERS, CLOWNS, AND PEOPLE DRESSED AS MUPPETS AND JOINED US TO FORGET THEIR STRUGGLES, TO REMEMBER THEIR CHILDHOODS. MAYBE FOR SOME THIS WAS A MERE LIGHT ON A DARK DAY BUT STILL A LIGHT NONETHELESS.
AS THE SONG I HEARD GROWING UP IN BRAZIL WOULD SAY...
I WAS LAZING ABOUT IN LIFE MY LOVE CALLED ME TO SEE THE BAND PASS BY SINGING SONGS OF LOVE MY LONG-SUFFERING PEOPLE BID FAREWELL TO PAIN
THE SERIOUS MAN WHO WAS COUNTING MONEY STOPPED THE SAD ROSE THAT WAS ALWAYS CLOSED OPENED UP THE WEAK OLD MAN FORGOT ABOUT HIS WEARINESS AND THOUGHT THAT HE WAS STILL A BOY; TO GO OUT ON THE TERRACE AND DANCE
THE CHEERFUL MARCH SPREAD OUT ON THE AVENUE, AND PUSHED ON THE FULL MOON THAT WAS ALWAYS HIDING CAME OUT MY WHOLE CITY GOT ALL DONE UP TO SEE THE BAND GO BY SINGING SONGS OF LOVE

'NO SURPRISE THERE. TITANO IS A GUINNESS WORLD RECORD STRONGMAN."

EVENTUALLY, MORE DETAILS STARTED COMING IN, SO WE GOT A BETTER PICTURE OF THE WHOLE THING.

Frank Walsh
Underground poet
staying at the house

SOMEONE KNOCKED AT THE DOOR CLAIMING TO BE THE CENSUS. I OPENED IT, GOT SUSPICIOUS, AND TRIED TO LOCK HIM OUT...

YOU DON'T LOOK LIKE THE CENSUS!

HELP!

Laila Poché
Clown-adjacent
friend

MY FRIEND LIVES TWO DOORS DOWN. HE SAW THE WHOLE THING. HE FIRST HEARD SCREAMING, BELLOWING AND THEN...

AND FINALLY ONE DAY I ENDED UP GETTING THE BUS TO NEW YORK WITH TITANO. HE WAS FULLY PAINTED BLUE; HE HAD A GIG IN NEW YORK AND WOULDN'T HAVE TIME TO PAINT HIMSELF THERE.

I ASKED HIM ABOUT THIS.

Mine is a tale of woe and sorrow, Adriano...

WHICH I REPRODUCE HERE WITH THE MINOR ARTISTIC LIBERTIES THAT PERTAIN TO A CARTOONIST...

The Prose Odd
HOW THE BRAVE TITANO ODDFELLOW DEFENDED OUR DOMAIN FROM INVASION
WITH HEIGHTNED SENSES, FROM HIS BEDCHAMBER, TITANO RECOGNIZED THE CALL TO BATTLE!
Help! I need a mighty warrior!
As it had been foretold...
So my time has come!
HIS HEROIC SOUL, UNABLE TO YIELD TO FEAR OR DOUBT, HASTILY CHOSE HIS WEAPON!
To me, my hounds, Rigry and Eve, if we meet Valhalla this day, we must die with honor!
PREPARE TO MEET THY FATE, EVIL SCOUNDREL!
HOLY @#@!! IT'S CONAN, THE BARBARIAN!
RETURN TO FACE THE PRICE OF THY MISDEEDS!!

Come Back Here, you little Shit!
TITANO RAN AFTER THE POOR GUY FOR 4 BLOCKS BEFORE HE ESCAPED.
And such an epic tale had been retold several times by all who lived in that house...

2017
BETWEEN ALL THE SHOWS VELVET AND MEL GOT MARRIED BUT MORE CHANGES WERE COMING.

FIBI DECIDED TO MOVE TO NY TO LIVE WITH HER FRIEND FRANÇOISE VORANGER FROM THE HYBRID COMPANY, AN AERIALIST/ ACRO YOGA/ CONTORTIONIST GROUP SHE HAD BEEN PERFORMING WITH.
AMTRAK eTicket
PRESENT THIS DOCUMENT FOR BOARDING
RESERVATION NUMBER 325D96
One-Way
PHI ► NYP
PHILADELPHIA, PA   NEW YORK PENN, NY
1:50 PM   4:53
2260

THINGS WERE GOOD ON THE STAGE BUT EVERYTHING ELSE WAS FALLING APART.
651

WE WERE HAVING FEWER SHOWS, AND I WANTED TO MOVE TO NY BUT JELLY WAS TOO ATTACHED TO THE HOUSE. I FELT THAT I WAS WALKING ON EGGSHELLS LIVING THERE, BUT THEY WOULD BE RESENTFUL IF I MOVED OUT AND THAT TURNED INTO A SCAR ON MY CREATIVITY.

I LEARNED A LOT ABOUT HOW TO PUT A STORY TOGETHER FROM CARNIVOLUTION, HOW TO MAKE IT PSYCHEDELIC, FUN, AND USED IT IN OTHER SHOWS. THERE WERE GOOD THINGS THAT HELPED MY GROWTH BUT ALSO DARK MOMENTS

elcome to New York
IT IS THIS MIX OF PAIN AND BEAUTY THAT MAKES REALITY. NOT EVERYTHING IS CUTE, PERFECT AND WITHOUT PROBLEMS.

BY MAY THE LANDLORD TOLD US TO MOVE OUT JULY 1ST. HE WOULD SELL THE HOUSE. WE HAD A FINAL BIG HOUSE PARTY AND I PAINTED A GIFT TO OUR TIME LIVING TOGETHER.
THE TIMES ARE A-CHANGING
BUT THINGS WOULDN'T END WITHOUT ONE FINAL MYSTERY.
WHILE BREAKING DOWN THE HOUSE MATTERZ AND JELLY FOUND A ROOM IN THE BASEMENT NOBODY KNEW ABOUT. IT WAS COVERED WITH OLD COMPUTER SCREENS COVERED WITH DUST LEFT BY A PREVIOUS TENANT.
ALMOST AS IF SOME GHOST HAD LIVED IN THAT ROOM THE WHOLE TIME WITHOUT ANY OF US BEING THE WISER.
WHILE WE LEFT THE HOUSE AND THOUGHT ABOUT THAT STRANGE MYSTERIOUS ROOM A NAME EVENTUALLY CAME TO MY MIND:
JASON?
YOUR DREAM, WHAT'S YOUR DREAM?
WHAT ARE THEY?
ANY ONE OF YOUR MOST BEAUTIFUL DREAMS TO OPEN UP.
BLOOMING, RIGHT INSIDE OF YOU
"MANY TIMES IN LIFE I FACED AN INSTANT THAT SHIFTED MY WHOLE PERSPECTIVE, ADRIANO."

THE NOT SO SECRET ORIGIN OF THE HOUSE OF YES

2023 INTERVIEW WITH ANYA
I MOVED FROM ROCHESTER WITH KAE TO STUDY FASHION AT FIT.
STILT WALKER
LADY CIRCUS
I LEARNED TO STILT WALK; I GOT REALLY INTO IT, MET OTHERS, LEARNED TO DO AERIAL. AND SOON ENOUGH FORMED LADY CIRCUS - AN ALL FEMALE CIRCUS
ONE NIGHT I WAS COMING BACK ON THE SUBWAY AND AN OLDER MAN APPROACHED AND GAVE ME A CARD TO LEARN STILT WALKING. HE THOUGHT I'D BE A GOOD CIRCUS PERFORMER. I CALLED HIM THE NEXT DAY AND I WAS IN. THAT WAS HOW I STARTED.
WHILE LOOKING FOR A SPACE TO PERFORM I CAME ACROSS A WAREHOUSE THAT WAS EMPTY; THEY HAD JUST EVICTED EVERYBODY. IT WAS A LABYRINTH OF WALLS THE JUNKIES HAD BUILT
AND THAT WAS THE FIRST HOUSE OF YES.
KAE, LET'S MOVE TO THIS CRACKHOUSE!
YES!
WE HAD TO BRING DOWN WALLS, REBUILD THE WHOLE SPACE AND START HAVING SHOWS THERE.
BUT DESPITE ALL THE FIRE PERFORMANCES AND ALL THE CIRCUS ANTICS; AFTER A YEAR, IT WAS A BAD TOASTER CLOSE TO A GIANT PUPPET MASK THAT DOOMED THE PLACE.
- I WAS WATCHING DESPERATELY AND SCREAMING WHILE THE WHOLE BUILDING BURNT TO ASHES.

IT WAS WHEN I LOST THE SPACE THAT I REALIZED. WE WERE JUST LIVING, BEING CREATIVE, DOING WEIRD SHIT. THE OLDER PEOPLE THOUGH SAW IT DIFFERENTLY.
WE WERE PART OF A LINEAGE OF PERFORMERS WHO CAME BEFORE US AND WILL COME AFTER. IT WAS A COMMUNITY SPACE TO PRESERVE AN ART FORM.
THEY SAY YOU SHOULDN'T LET YOUR JOB DEFINE YOU BUT WHEN YOU ARE AN ARTIST YOU ARE YOUR JOB. YOU GOTTA PUT YOURSELF INTO IT.
Erma Ward 1928 WORLD'S CHAMPION AERIAL GYMNAST
IT STARTS WITH A DESIRE FOR CHAOS, TO ESCAPE CONVENTIONS. THE SPARK OF BEING CREATIVE COMES FIRST. THEN YOU LEARN THE SKILLS UNTIL YOU ARE ABLE TO PERFORM AND LAST FIND THE SPACE TO PERFORM. AS YOU KEEP PERFORMING AND MAKE YOUR NAME, YOU GROW, GET MORE REFINED, AND WORK FROM BETTER BUDGETS. THAT'S HOW IT USUALLY WORKS WITH EVERYBODY.
WE NEEDED TO REBUILD THE HOUSE OF YES. AND WE DID.
I ALWAYS BELIEVED WHAT WE DO IS REALLY IMPORTANT. THIS HAS TO HAPPEN.

SOMETIMES WHILE WRITING, TIME CRASHES UPON ITSELF. DIFFERENT MEMORIES FROM PLACES, PEOPLE AND SITUATIONS OUT OF ORDER FOLLOWING A DREAM LOGIC OF ITS OWN TO SUDDENLY ARRIVE WHERE YOU NEEDED TO BE.
WHY WAS I ALLOWED TO SEE THIS? WHO... WHO AM I?
YOU ARE THE ETERNAL WITNESS. THE DROP OF WATER THAT WILL NEVER BECOME ONE WITH THE GREAT OCEAN.

THIS IS WHERE THE STORY ENDS. THE FIRST NIGHT SLEEPING HERE AND OBSERVING EVERYTHING AROUND ME.

THE MOMENT THIS MAD ARTIST WAS HOME.

THAT'S SOME REALLY WEIRD PEOPLE, MY LIEGE...
THIS INFORMATION WILL SUFFICE! PREPARE THE SHIP!
ENEMY APPROACHES, STAR COMMANDER!!!
THE TIME HAS COME FOR OUR GREATEST BATTLE!!!
SMVSV!!
WER!
SEND IN THE CLOWNS!

WALKING AN EMOTIONAL TIGHTROPE

AMY BEARCE

The big red tent towered in the evening air, with glowing lights lining the edges. My heart sped up, and I laughed, just because. We were finally becoming high schoolers after the longest year ever, and who didn't love a circus? The death-defying drama, the lights, the skills, the popcorn?

I used to hate it, actually. As a secret psychic empath, all the fear around me during acts like the high wire made me chew my nails down to the nubs. When you can literally feel other people's fear and pain like your own, you learn to avoid the bad stuff as much as possible. But finally, my mental shields were under control, and I could go and enjoy a fun night on the town.

Excitement and happiness floated in the air, so strong that it had a scent to my empathy, like perfume, drizzling the evening with extra sweetness each time I dropped my shields a little. It wasn't like our little Texas town had lots of big events to enjoy. Just because my friends and I had secret psychic abilities didn't mean we didn't like to relax just like everyone else. I'd even curled my wavy blond hair and worn my favorite jeans for the occasion.

I didn't expect it to be quite so crowded, though. I zipped up my mental shield, which was a bummer, but touching others always amplified what I received from them. I didn't want any nasty surprises.

"Hey, watch out," my best friend, Avery Portman, said as I accidentally stepped on her flowered combat boots.

"Sorry, but petite people are at a severe disadvantage here," I called back as another big dude pushed between us. Ugh.

Suddenly, a small space opened up in front of me, as if I was holding a battering ram or a knight's shield. The people coming at me sort of just melted to either side with the flow of traffic. A few looked surprised, but most didn't notice at all.

"No one squashes my Parker," a voice whispered in my ear, and then Ethan Kwon took my hand.

"Thanks for the help!" I winked at him. It was nice having a boyfriend who could move things with his mind, which included solidifying air. It was also nice having a boyfriend who was so kind and funny. His tousled black hair, devilish smile, and amazing drumming skills were the icing on top.

We made a pretty good team, my besties and I: me, the empath with emotional sensing, Ethan, the telekinetic, and Avery, who was psychic and got warnings of the future. There were a few others like us in town, but they weren't with us tonight. Which was too bad, because they were a ton of fun to be with, too. They were out of town at various camps and summer trips, so it was just the three of us for the whole week.

"Let's get front-row seats!" Ethan crowed. Music was pumping from big speakers as showtime grew closer. Big spotlights swooped up and down the canvas tent walls and the bleacher seats.

"What if they pull up volunteers from there?" Avery asked, twirling her red hair nervously. "Shouldn't we be more discreet?"

I responded, "No one can tell what we are unless we let something slip. And we won't... right?"

They both nodded firmly. We could never forget Avery once had a vision of some government agency grabbing us all to experiment on. Or to use us as weapons.

Admittedly, we could do a lot of damage together if we wanted. But we don't, of course. We're the good guys. Or, we try to be. We use our psychic gifts to help others when we can, though we've got to stay subtle about it. It's safer that way.

We're a handful of secretly gifted kids surrounded by normal people who mostly don't believe that psychic abilities are real. Our parents had all met while getting treated with a new "cutting edge" fertility drug that later got banned. The end result was a small group of babies who each manifested a different psychic power as we grew up. The unethical fertility specialist burned all the documentation and disappeared, but thankfully, our family friendships had stuck.

We settled in the front row, munching on popcorn that Ethan had the wisdom to buy on the way in. The show began with clowns, which were a little creepy but otherwise fun, followed by a trapeze act that was truly impressive, super pro.

Avery leaned over. "I'd be so afraid up there, wouldn't you?" We studied the woman, graceful like a dancer, flipping in the air.

"Definitely would rather keep my cute shoes on the ground," I replied. "Wow, they're really good. Even better than the ones I've seen on TV."

A funny dog act came next, with all kinds of breeds from Chihuahua to Great Dane wearing tutus and playing instruments with their little feet and noses. Totally adorable. That act was followed by a lady who fit herself into a small box. I shuddered. "No, thanks."

When the high-wire act began, I didn't think much about it. It was just as scary and amazing and fun as the rest of the evening. But then—

Fear. Fury. Fascination.

The emotions hit me hard, one after another, and I gasped, struggling to strengthen my shields even further. I wasn't fast enough to stop the knife-stabbing pain to my chest and heart. "Ow!"

"What?" Avery looked at me, eyes dark with worry. She knew what that sound out of nowhere probably meant.

"That girl up there's having a lot of big feelings. It's razor-sharp." Was it any wonder that I'd spent half my life trying to make everyone around me happy? It hurt to be around hurting people, at least it did until I finally mastered my shielding. And then this girl managed to get past them anyway.

I studied the tightrope walker. She was younger than some of these others, maybe barely out of high school. Her tawny brown skin and straight black hair spoke of a heritage closer to Ethan's than mine. Her name was Belinda the Brave, according to the signs. She didn't use a parasol or balancing pole to cross, so far up that our necks hurt from the angle after more than a minute.

I turned to Avery. "You're our crystal ball. Why don't you focus on the future for her, and see if you can figure out what her problem is?" I asked.

Avery's gift didn't always answer when called, but she was a lot more reliable these days. And the last time someone was able to break through my shields like this, they were one of us, as in, psychically gifted, too.

With a nervous look over her shoulder at the cheering crowd, Avery closed her eyes and focused. A moment later, she swayed in her seat, and her eyes flashed open, seeing a future that none of us could witness. "She's in danger. She needs help. And I get the feeling she has a special… talent… beyond the tightrope walking."

I sighed. "Of course she does. Dang it."

Ethan nudged me. "So much for a fun night out. It's always work with you people."

As soon as Belinda the Brave finished her high-wire act, we slid from our seats, heading to the back of the tent, hoping to grab her before she went to wherever circus workers changed.

She was fast, though. She slipped out of the back of the tent and moved quickly to a trailer. She said something to a guard.

Ethan said, "I think she told him she's not feeling well and is going to skip the bows tonight."

I didn't want to miss the rest of the show, but this poor girl needed help. I had a plan.

I put on my brightest smile. Have I mentioned that I have a fantastic smile and know how to use it? "Hey, there." I glowed at the young man guarding the trailers. "Belinda told me to find her when she was in town—can I say hey? We're old friends."

He glanced at me. "Nice try. We don't need any crazy fans back here, thanks anyway."

I snorted, affronted. "Crazy fans? Was I impressed by her skills? Yes. Am I crazy? Maybe, in the best way. But I just saw her for the first time tonight and wanted to ask her how to get started myself. I'm super psyched about trying out for the circus."

Avery looked at me as if I'd grown a second head, but Ethan caught on fast. "Me, too. We're very good with our act."

"You'll have to talk to the ringmaster after the show." He waved his hand at us. "I'll tell 'em you stopped by."

I debated using my empathy to make him want to go away, but playing with people's feelings never ended well, so I huffed a sigh.

We returned to our seats in the big tent, but the rest of the circus was just a stream of noise and color as Ethan and I frantically debated what our "act" could be.

"What about shooting you out from a cannon?" Ethan winked at me.

I smacked his shoulder. "I'm a very good dancer. We could dance with flaming batons?"

Avery laughed. "Then let me just go round up a couple dozen fire extinguishers in the next fifteen minutes. No, think simple. You don't have to actually *do* a whole routine, but he may want to see a demo, you know."

"But the pitch is just an excuse to get near the high-wire walker, right?"

Ethan asked, suddenly sounding a bit more worried.

Avery shook her head. "All I'm saying is, it'd better sound good, or you'll be drawing the wrong kind of attention to us."

Shoot. I hadn't thought about that in my moment of brilliant inspiration.

"Well, what about *her* job?" Ethan asked, gesturing at the high wire. "Parker, I could solidify the air under that wire so even if you weren't balanced, I'd hold you up. And if you fell, I could catch you before you hit the ground. Probably."

"Probably? Very comforting."

"They have nets, guys." Avery rolled her eyes.

Yeah, but… I hated heights. Like… really, really hated them. I'd learned that the hard way when I had to play a pirate in our spring show, high up on a beam to simulate a ship's plank. And the idea of falling from *this* height—net or no net—was totally terrifying.

I gulped. "Maybe Ethan can be on the wire?"

"Too late, show's finished, and the guard's waving us over… The boss told him to send us right there to the circus floor," Avery whispered.

The ringmaster was taller than he even appeared from a distance. At least six-and-a-half feet tall, with another half foot to his hat, he eyed me up and down with a quick decisive glance, followed up by a study of everyone in our group.

His energy filled the room—it was obvious why he was the ringmaster. He radiated power and demanded that we give him our attention.

Dust kicked up as we trudged across the sawdust on the ground. My shoes would never recover.

"Are you all trying out, then? Mike told me a girl and a boy?"

"That's us!" I piped, trying not to nervously glance at Ethan, warm and sturdy at my side.

"And what is it that you do, young lady?"

"We, um, we walk the high wire."

"WE?!" Ethan hissed in my ear.

"Yep!" I chirped. "We're very good, as good as the girl you got up there. We could be a trio, and that would be even better, don't you think, three people instead of one risking their lives on the high wire in the spotlight—"

Ethan squeezed my hand to stop the vomit flow of words. "We'd be happy to join her, is what we're saying."

The ringmaster ran a hand over his moustache. "I like the idea—local performers always bring in the hometown crowd. Okay, we're here through the end of this week. Be here tomorrow afternoon, and I'll introduce you to your new potential teammates, and we'll see how you do. You could even start tomorrow night, if you're good enough. But what happens when the circus moves on? Surely you're ready to quit school and come join us for the summer?" He looked straight at me and smiled.

Suddenly, I could see it—traveling on the road, new towns every night, an adoring audience and fun teammates, the spotlight, over and over—

Ethan said flatly, "Probably not. But you never know."

I blinked, suddenly aware that I had been actually daydreaming about leaving my favorite place in the world, with my favorite people, all for… what? A traveling circus job? At just under fifteen years old? With no security or anyone who could know about my secret? Not to mention no actual circus skills. That was… weird.

But I still wanted to go. It made no sense.

Avery made a weird gargle sound in her throat, grabbed my elbow, and pulled me back. "We'll see you tomorrow then, thanks."

She steered us out of there while I was still shaking my head, with visions of circus life dancing like sugar plums in my head.

"I tried to read him, too," Avery hissed as we hurried out of the tent, into the cool night air. "And I picked up something dangerous from him, something about a choice he'll make and a gift… and I got the vibe the message meant *psychic* gift. Did you sense anything from him?"

Gifted? Well, that explained that crazy impulse, then. Two new gifteds in one place? Then again, we did tend to find each other. It wasn't like there were a ton of us in the world, but we'd learned we were far from alone.

We slowed our pace when we hit the street that led us back into town. Others were walking home, too, clumped in family groups and throngs of loud, raucous friends.

I whispered. "Well, honestly… I did feel a suddenly strange pull to really join that circus. I could just *see* it, and I never felt such an urge to do something rash in my life."

Maybe I wasn't the only one who could make people feel things around here.

Avery frowned. "You haven't been hiding some secret circus ambition, have you?"

"Never had a circus dream before," I said. "Scout's honor."

She tapped her fingers together the way she did when she was problem solving. Our Avery's got a great brain. "But you still felt a strong pull to join up, out of the blue. Were you shielded?"

"Probably not as good as I should have been," I admitted. "It's been a long night with a lot of emotions. My shields start to chip a bit after a while. Like cheap nail polish."

"And most people don't have any psychic mental shields at all. I wonder if that's how he has so many talented people in what is otherwise a pretty small circus, you know? They were all super talented. Why are they with him? They can't be pulling in that much money, going from little town to little town. And a few of them looked almost as young as us."

Ethan asked, "Think he's an empath like Parker, or something else?"

That's when it really hit me: another empath? *Finally*, someone I could ask for advice about my own gift, and if there was a way to tame the wilder, more dangerous parts of it?

I was dying to find out. I bit my lip to keep from blurting out my real feelings. I knew it was a bad idea. But still. When would I get another chance?

Avery said. "I don't know, but I didn't get any messages from the future about him. I do know that girl is in trouble. So, Parks, I hope you're ready to try your high-wire walk tomorrow, for real. Bring your old ballet slippers. And get a lot of rest. You'll need your best psychic shield anytime you're around that guy, for sure, until we know what he's up to."

I shuddered. I loved a good spotlight, just not one a hundred feet in the air. But it looked like that was my next step—out onto a freakin' wire.

But if it meant learning more about fully using my gift, I'd cross a high wire that was on fire.

When I told my dad that I needed to get back to the circus the next day for an audition, I tried to play it off as no big deal, but he wasn't having it.

"You are doing WHAT?" My dad's voice went very high. He knows I'm awesome, but I guess any parent might freak out some at the thought of their baby that high off the ground. Even when that baby has psychic powers. Maybe *especially* when that parent didn't have any special abilities on his own.

My dad would do anything for me, which helped balance my mom. She'd always been weirded out by me and my abilities, though we were finally doing better these days.

"I can handle it, Dad, and they have nets—think about it! How many times does a girl get a chance to be in a high-wire act?" I left out the bit about maybe going up against another empath and trying to pick his brain.

He went paler. "High wire? Parker, you faint up high!"

I gulped. "Not today. Dad, there's two psychics there at least, and one of them needs our help."

He groaned. "Then I'm coming, too."

"I wouldn't have it any other way."

"In fact, our parent meeting is right before then, so we could all come over together. I think you'll have a bunch of concerned parents watching out for you."

My dad had started a parenting group for the secret psychics. While we are all undeniably awesome, parenting one of us admittedly involves challenges no one else could understand. There were even parents from other states that joined them online, including some whose children had disappeared, just like we feared would happen to us... word spread quickly when you had telepaths among you.

I nodded, unsurprised. We had an awesome group of parents, overall. "Cool. I bet you'll all enjoy the show."

"If you're performing? No doubt." His confidence in me helped soothe all the thousands of butterflies crowding in my stomach at the thought of the tightrope.

With a laugh, I gave him a high five.

Aside from the whole don't-fall-off-the-high-wire thing, I'd clearly need to brush up on my blocking others out before I dealt with the ringmaster again. I had solid shield skills, hard-won, but I felt better after an hour focusing on building a solid steel wall around my mind and heart.

I'd probably just been off my game from the constant tidal waves of emotions from everyone at the circus. Keeping out that many people with strong feelings felt like juggling not two or three balls, but twenty-five at the same time. It was tough not to drop any, and sometimes, a few feelings snuck through, especially the strongest ones.

But I could do it. I did it all the time at football games. Have you *been* to a football game in Texas? Emotions run high, let me tell you.

I didn't sleep very well, despite Avery's order, but my makeup carefully concealed that the next day.

Ethan and I showed up at the big tent early, along with my dad and at least ten other parents. Not suspicious at all. I rolled my eyes at us, but I was glad for their support.

My knees felt shaky, which was very unusual for me. I'm an actress and used to performing on stage. But I like my feet planted *on* that stage, not above it.

We were directed to a smaller tent behind the big one, where a very tattooed lady told us, "Try on these costumes until you find one that fits." She looked bored.

"When will we get to meet our co-star?" I asked, hoping to bypass all of this if we could get to Belinda the Brave fast enough.

"She's practicing now. You can join her after you've picked out your costume. Show starts in just a few hours, so I need time to make any alterations in case you're accepted right away."

"Does he move that fast, usually? With new hires?"

The woman smirked. "Most times, people just can't wait to get started. They're ready to dive right in. Never seen so many dedicated, hard workers."

We'd all discussed the fact that if he could manipulate emotions and didn't feel bad about doing so, he could be keeping her there against her wishes, sort of. I mean, she might want to stay, but only because of his gift. We had to find out and free her if necessary.

And hopefully, somewhere along the way, I'd get a chance to talk to him myself.

It didn't take too long to find the perfect outfit. I spun in front of the cracked mirror. The gold spangly leotard had long sheer sleeves and a little skirt with more sequins. It really made my blond hair glimmer. "I look good, at least."

Ethan came up behind me, in spangly white pants and a sparkly gold tank top. "When *don't* you look good?" He smiled.

"Look who's talking."

He bowed. "I feel like I'm about to go perform in the Ice Capades. We match."

"We look fantastic, on ice or tightrope." I gave him a quick kiss, adjusting his shirt a bit. "Are we crazy, Ethan?"

He laughed. "No question about it."

"Welp. Let's do it, then."

The floor was still sawdust-y and smelled of hay and cedar. Performers were dotted throughout the tent, practicing their skills. The guy with the sharp-shooting gun kept shooting tin cans off of tiny stands, and I jumped with each shot.

Our little crowd of parents sat on the benches near the front of the short bleachers, looking a lot less excited than the prior audience. Despite trying to pep talk myself, I felt the same as the parents.

We were shielded from the ringmaster's psychic control, at least. Avery would know if something truly awful was about to come down. No more excuses. Time to step out into the ring.

"Relax," Ethan whispered. "We're just trying out. Probably he won't even let us get halfway across before he tells us we suck, but at least we can talk to her up there without anyone overhearing."

I craned my neck up. She was already up there: Belinda the Brave. Stretching out her legs on the top platform. "Time to go up."

I tried not to look down. Whenever I did, my vision swam and my grip loosened on the rungs.

"Easy, Parker," Ethan whispered, and I felt the air pushing me gently behind me, giving me a sense of being held.

"Thanks," I told him, slowing my breath. Not for the first time, I wished my empath powers worked on myself, but alas. Luckily, anxiety didn't strike me like this very often.

I searched for the girl above with my gift and tasted—pure panic and desperation, smelling like burned coffee grounds. My foot slipped off the rung, and I shrieked. Ethan grabbed my waist with one hand, coming up behind me, so that his body pressed against mine like a shield. "What is it?"

I shook as I clung. We were only halfway up there. The ringmaster had sauntered out into the arena. I pushed myself to move a little further up. Almost there.

"Okay, newbies. Let's see it," he hollered up at us. "Belinda, show them the ropes."

Belinda reached her hand down to help haul me up. I steeled myself for what would come next. The moment our skin touched, I dropped my shields completely and searched her, ruthlessly seeking the truth.

I got a little too close… her emotions were just too strong. Following the bright trails of psychic pain, I stepped right into Belinda's memories. It wasn't like watching a movie, as it is for me sometimes. For that moment, I became Belinda.

I sat alone in a field, a suitcase beside me. How did I ever get there? I'd gone to the circus last night… I knew that for sure… and then Mom and I had fought… wait, why—

A man stepped close. I shaded my eyes against the sun. The ringmaster from last night? The tall hat was unmistakable.

The ringmaster leaned down, gazing at my eyes, and I fell into them, moving like a puppet as I signed a contract for years of my life, even grateful for the chance, then woke in a web, trapped!

No! I remembered now. He'd stolen my will, stolen my future. I had plans for my life, good ones—finish high school, go to college, become a teacher. I had friends who loved me and family who would miss me. Family he'd said I'd never see again.

Inside, I was screaming. But outside, I picked up my suitcase and followed him with the others.

Fear and grief boiled up around me, the emotions so strong that the smell of garbage and rancid food rushed over me, snapping my psychic connection with Belinda. Thank goodness. It'd been a long time since I'd gotten sucked into a memory like that.

Scented memories happened with the strongest of emotions, but fear was the worst. I gagged.

Her hand was strong on mine, but her feelings were fragile, raw, and almost broken.

I wanted to hug her right away, but I knew better. She hadn't relived that memory with me, but she was still a fancy porcelain bowl, ready to shatter in an instant. The worst case I'd seen in a long time. I'd have to be at my most charming to get her to open up and save her from whatever doom lurked in the future.

Ethan popped up on the platform behind me. "Hi! We're Ethan and Parker!" He gave a little wave.

"I'm Belinda." Her voice was huskier than I'd pictured from the small frame. "Listen, have you done this before? Because, no disrespect, but falling into the net from here requires some skill, you know. You could land funny or bounce out."

I met her eyes. They were dark, almost empty. I recognized that look in them. She felt hopeless. I cracked my shields again and patted her arm to judge her current mood. "We're actually here just to talk to you. About something really important."

The pain was tucked away, numbed and cold.

Ethan looked at me, startled, but then shrugged. "We know your secret."

Belinda took a step back, right near the wire.

I reached my arm out. "No, no, we have the same secret. Only I doubt our gifts are the same. I can feel emotions—make people feel things, too, though I don't. And Ethan here is telekinetic. And he's the only way I'm going to get out on that wire. What about you?"

The ringmaster yelled up, "I haven't got all day! Let's go!"

She stepped out on the wire as easily as if she were stepping out onto a ship's plank. "Metal knows me. It's like I am magnetic when I want to be. I cling to the wire with my feet with my gift. And the ringmaster knows it, so be careful. He'll never let me go. I've been with him for a year. He took me away from my family and made me run off with his troupe. He didn't physically force me to run away, technically, but he did something to me that made me stay with him. He stole my will, my choice. And if he finds out about you, he'll trap you, too. That's *his* gift. A freakin' pied piper."

She turned and walked to the center of the wire, arms held wide, though I had no doubt that part was just for show. She didn't need help to balance.

"I'm going after her. You ready to hold me?" I asked Ethan.

"I won't let you fall."

I won't look down. I won't look down. I stepped out onto the wire, my shoes soft enough to bend on either side. I stood like a dancer, one foot in front of the other, mimicking her pose. I felt the air under my toes and heels firm up, thanks to Ethan's power. I didn't know how long he could hold it while also doing his part. I hurried across the wire, my breath loud in my ears.

Focus, focus, focus.

"Do you want to stay here with us?" I whispered to her when I got close enough. "We'll help protect you."

She lifted one leg, like a ballerina. Wavering exactly zero. *Dang.* "I can't leave. I want to, but whenever I try, I can't. I don't know how he does it, but every time I try to leave, the ringmaster makes me stay. It's like he takes over my emotions and even my thoughts, against my own wishes. He can't change me deep down, but he might as well have put me in handcuffs."

Ah hah! "Like the pied piper, you said! Yeah, I felt it too!" I got excited and wobbled as Ethan struggled to keep up. "Sorry!" I called back over my shoulder. One more step, and I'd be able to touch her. Physical touch amplified all gifts.

I added, "When he looked in my eyes, I was suddenly ready to run away from everything I loved and join up. That's not like me at all. But we know how to shield ourselves from other people's gifts and can teach you, too. Come with us afterward, and we'll keep you safe."

She walked backward to the other platform. The audience applauded her as she stepped off the wire. "If only it were that easy…"

"But it is!"

She turned away, began to climb down the ladder of that side's platform.

"Something bad is going to happen to you if you stay!" I said, moving toward her platform. "My precog friend saw it! Please! You can stay with me for a while! Those of us who are different have to stick together!"

Belinda smiled sadly. "The circus is also full of different people who stick together. I can't abandon the others now that I know that most of them want to leave, too. Just like me. They may not have psychic talents, but they're very skilled, and most of them are here because he made them join him."

She disappeared under the platform. And I looked down, without thinking.

The ground was so far away. It was miles and miles and miles away.

My knees went weak. I wanted to kneel, but the wire was too thin for that sort of thing.

"Parker!" Ethan called. "Snap out of it! Look up!"

My eyes rolled back in my head. My feet slipped off the wire. And I fell.

The air rushed through my hair and fluttered my skirt. My stomach was left far behind. A loud shriek filled my ears, and then I landed softly in the net, almost like landing in a bed. I'd thought it might hurt to fall that far, at least knocking the wind out of me or bouncing me off the net entirely. It wasn't like I'd prepared myself for it. But as I forced my eyes open, I saw

Ethan looking down from over the platform, hands in a fist.

He'd saved me.

Things went dark.

I woke in a little room in the ringmaster's trailer. It was clear from the spangly jacket hanging on the hook by the door. Without thought, I sent my gift searching, tasting the room for the mood. Ethan was holding my hand, silent behind his own mental shields. Belinda sat still beside me, looking and feeling profoundly anxious. The ringmaster, though, he felt… hungry.

He met my eyes for a split second before I closed mine in response. No more falling into his eyes. No wonder he drew such big crowds. He was able to mesmerize with his gaze.

He must have gotten to my dad and the other parents, too. There was no way they'd leave us alone in here now, otherwise. They were a lot more vulnerable than anyone gifted.

"Ethan?" I asked.

"We've just been talking with Ringmaster Kane here about joining up. The contract is a good one. Ten years of service, and we get room and board."

I did a double take. Ethan sat staring at the ringmaster, a small goofy smile on his face.

Oh, no.

I whispered, "You've got Ethan hooked somehow." And Ethan had *excellent* mental shields. Better than mine, most days.

Oh, no.

"Somehow?" the ringmaster said. His voice was warm like hot chocolate, and I wanted to look his way, but nope. I could out-stubborn a donkey. The miracle man didn't know who he was messing with.

I built up the thickest mental wall I could. With the ringmaster this close, Ethan was caught in this man's web, just like Belinda.

Like I almost was, too. Me, Parker Mills, Persuader Extraordinaire, nearly got out-persuaded. He wanted us both, no doubt. I had to think fast.

"Is your gift based in empathy?" I asked him, staring at the ground.

"My gift?" his voice was coy.

My eyes felt pulled up. Gritting my teeth, I looked at his jawline, refusing to meet his gaze. "Yeah, this manipulation you've done to these two here, making them feel like they want to run off with you, when their hearts don't want to. Why do it?"

He sighed. "Oh, dear. You really are young, aren't you? How do you think amazing circus stunts have been performed? Do you really think that all those disappearing acts were illusions? That all those lion tamers were just using behavioral science? If you want to find the gifted, child, you look among the most astonishing of us all, and there you will find us. You belong with us. You and your beau. I feel things and make others feel things, too, yes. But I also know psychic cheating when I see it. Your feet were inches off that wire, yet you stood firm. Not even a good illusion, by the way, and not something I could use. But I bet you could learn. And you'd make my show stronger."

"Would you tell me how your gift works? So I could master mine?" The words slipped out. I hadn't meant to really tell him that, but I so wanted to know.

His swift intake of breath made my heart stop for a second. "A little empath, is that it? Well, maybe in due time, I could teach you."

My heart sped. To have full control of my wild gift... "You could?"

"Most certainly, though that is not truly what I am. I'm bigger than an empath. I'm a *fascinator,* more about capturing interest than reading emotions or steering them. I only steer one way—to me. But I'm very good at what I do, and our gifts are certainly related."

Disappointment coated my mouth like sour lemons. He didn't have anything to offer after all. He didn't see controlling people as a problem. He'd never understand me.

"So will you join me?" He held out his palm. "You could be my junior ringmaster—you have the charm for it, even without a gift—and find out what it's like to control an entire crowd with your empathy. I assure you there's nothing like it."

I furiously turned from the pull of his gaze—wow, I wanted to look in those eyes. I guess he could compel interest and fascination because he was veeeery fascinating. I found my eyes tracing the golden lapel of his shirt, his short-trimmed beard, the square jaw of a surprisingly young man…

At the last second, my eyes flipped up to his face, and he caught me. His dark eyes glittered, full of secrets, of hidden chambers that he wanted me to seek out. I stepped into the darkness, hearing an echo around me.

"What are you doing?" I whispered.

"Showing you what I am," he said. "I have a contract for you just over here. I think you'd like to sign it."

"I'm not old enough to legally sign anything like that."

"I have an excellent forger who will make you eighteen in a heartbeat. People like *us* are above such mundane things as petty human law."

My legs stood of their own volition. *No!* My mind shrieked, but it was like I was behind a pane of glass.

Step. Step. Step.

No. I would not do this. This man would not run over my emotions like this. I was Parker Mill, and emotions were MY thing.

His hand was close, gesturing to the table. Through the loud sound of ocean waves filling my mind, I reached deep inside me and found the part of my gift I'd let lie dormant all this time: the ability to control what others felt. It came with a big price tag and was morally wrong, but what other choice did I have?

I put my hand in his. His smile was broad and victorious. Carefully picking through my emotions to find the emotional link between us, I sent my gift down that connected channel of our palms, pushing it more and more, until emotions exploded into his heart.

RELEASE US AND BE AFRAID! I commanded with my empathy. *STOP THIS!*

He gasped and jerked away from me, cowering. "What was that? Why did I feel so horrible—I still want to run… was that… you?" His gaze turned from smug to uncertain to angry, like various clouds passing before the sun. His eyes no longer glittered and no longer held me.

I was the ringmaster in this room.

I sent another burst of emotion through that forged connection. It was a complex emotion, a desire to leave, a desire to help others, a desire to do better.

It made me feel… powerful. Strong. Euphoric. And scared—because I remembered this feeling. It had led me down a bad path when I once controlled others' feelings, even with the best of intentions.

He groaned and fell to his knees, hands on his head. "Get out, get out of my mind!"

"I'm not in your mind. I'd say I'm in your heart. Except you don't have one."

But I cut off the out-pouring of emotions to him, steadying myself. It felt too good to do to him.

I knew that while he might have the power to fascinate, I had the power to not only fascinate, but to enrage, terrify, entice, or excite. And I had my answer about my gift. He'd taught me after all.

There were some things too powerful to train or use. Changing how others felt was off the table, permanently. The wistful hope of one day controlling it fell away in that moment. Looking at the trembling man on the ground, I knew I never wanted to be anything like him.

Tossing my hair back, I said to him, "No thank you to your job offer. I don't want to control crowds with my gift. Been there. Done that." I stood up and grabbed Ethan's hand. "Ethan, we need to go. Now."

Ethan blinked at me, his dark eyes cloudy and unfocused. Clearly, the spell or whatever lasted a while. I opened my shield and sent a pulse of emotion to him, just sharing my own love for him, pushing through his confusion, letting it soak in. "This is who you are, Ethan Kwan. You belong with me."

He shook his head and blinked, standing. "Parker? Did I almost just agree to run off with this circus?"

"Not your fault, but we've got to go."

The ringmaster stood, glaring from beneath slanted brows.

A loud knock sounded on the door, and then a redheaded whirlwind busted in, eyes wild. "Let my friends go, you big buffoon!" Avery yelled. "How dare you!"

"Hey, I've got it, Avery. Don't worry!" I hurried to her, thankful that she was able to fight off his gift, too.

My dad followed right behind her, literally dragging a guard hanging onto his legs. He still looked dazed, but he was doing an impressive job of fighting back, for a non-psychic. "Or we're going to blow this tent down!"

Pride sang through me. My dad first taught me how to shield, not through a gift but from careful study and practice. And love.

The ringmaster's eyes lit up as he straightened, brushing off his pants. He'd recalibrated fast, but that made sense for another emotion-based talent.

"Ooh, your dad knows about you, too! Oh, do please tell me you will all come along! I'll give you a trailer all to yourselves, one big happy group! Can't you see it?"

And I could. Even without his magic, it sounded like such fun. All of us laughing, performing, becoming famous all over the world…

But then I imagined my dad alone at his table. He was a professor. The circus? Life without my dad? No way. My heart skipped a beat. The vision faded from my mind. "No. I have ties here. And besides, we can't trust you. You've used all of your staff, against their wishes. But you need to let them go now if they want to go."

I sent another pulse of emotion to him, and he shuddered. He spoke through gritted teeth. "But I need them with me."

That's how he's gonna be? Fine. I squared my shoulders. If he wouldn't release them, I would. Grabbing his hand again, I traced along our psychic link until I found his other connections to everyone he could control, sitting like a spider in a web.

Sending a surge of righteous fury and determination down our shared link, I used my emotions like a sledgehammer, shattering all of those psychic ties, freeing those he'd fascinated.

Shouts came from the big top, but I couldn't even turn to see what was happening.

He lifted his hands in a sign of surrender, grimacing. "Fine, fine, just stop that. It's far worse than mine, I must say. I at least make people feel good."

"Only for a little while. Then you feel worse than you can imagine." That was Belinda the Brave, trembling in the doorway. "But I quit."

She said the words like she was afraid they'd hurt. When they didn't, she stood taller and smiled. "I QUIT."

Other voices came from outside his trailer door. "We're all walking, Kane! You can take this tent and shove it right up your—"

"I can see when I'm not wanted." The ringmaster smirked, bowed low. He'd managed to cut off his emotions from me—he was a fast learner, all right. But I had the sense that he was far from humbled. A man like that never was.

He started packing, and we stepped back to the tent. Various circus performers hugged Belinda, thanking her for her help and her work.

Our parents crowded around us, with our friends, hugging us.

My dad said, "You did good, Parks."

I almost hadn't, though. I'd been cocky and almost got owned for it. If not by his gift, then by mine. I'd be wiser next time. If there was one fascinator out there, there could well be another. The parents got busy arranging rides for all the circus performers who wanted to leave town. My dad knew how to take care of people.

"It's a little stuffy in here," Avery said. "Let's wait outside."

When we stepped outside the tent, the ringmaster walked up, carrying a suitcase. He said, "So the little bundle of emotions managed to disrupt all of my connections with her own. Too bad you can't stay with me. I would have very much enjoyed using you to excite the crowd."

Avery laughed. "Parker using her gift like *that* doesn't always go the way you think it would, trust me."

He stroked his moustache again. "Interesting. Well, Parker Mills, maybe in five more years, you will feel differently about living in this little town, while the big, wide world goes on without you. You were built for adventures, don't you think?"

His eyes glowed, dark and powerful. I didn't want to push back with my gift again—I might not be able to resist it a second time—but he was too mesmerizing—

Then Ethan stepped in front of him, eyes locked on mine. "We'll make our own adventures, Parker." Then he kissed me.

All the big tents in the world vanished in a cloud of love and comfort. This was where I belonged, here in Divine, with my boyfriend, best friends, and the world's best dad.

"Sorry, Ringmaster Kane. We're not available. And it looks like your circus is out of performers."

All of them had quit as soon as his fascination had been broken by my intrusion into his emotions. Right down to the costume designer. They'd grabbed their stuff—including those cute little dogs—and left faster than I could have imagined. Now that they weren't under a compulsion, they could drive their cars and trailers wherever they wanted. And they did.

"So I am, but not for long. You can't follow me everywhere, little empath."

"No, but you'd better not come back here again." I glared at him.

He grinned, but he left. It was a win. I'd take it.

Belinda let out a long sigh. "I can't believe it's finally over. I wonder what my parents think happened to me. I've worried about them for so long, but I could never even send them a letter."

"We have a phone you could use?" I suggested. "And if you can't remember their number, my dad has all kinds of connections. Did your parents know about your… abilities?"

"Oh, yes," she said. "It was a problem for us, because I kept destroying all our televisions and radios and stuff."

She laughed shakily, and we all laughed with her. Avery gave her a hug, and I felt the emotional shift. *Ahhh*—the smell was the scent of rain just before a storm.

Belinda started crying. I felt the jagged scraping of grief mixed with relief, a strange sweet-and-sour taste, but a fresh, clean scent. I strengthened my shield, glancing over at Dad, who smiled with relief.

I waved him over. "Dad, can you help Belinda contact her parents? She's one of us, you know."

He nodded. "We'll put a call out through the parent group online—I bet we'll be able to find them in short order, if they know about her gift. We've got a pretty good reach into the secret psychic community by now. She's not the first one who's gone missing and been found. I'm sure they've never given up on you, Belinda!"

Fresh tears fell, and they stepped away to make a few phone calls.

Belinda was going to be okay. We all were. At least for now.

As secret psychics, we needed to always be on guard. This had been a good reminder for all of us.

When my dad and Belinda returned, they were both beaming. Their joy brushed my shields, so strong I could taste it, sweeter than the cotton candy sold in the stands. They had a good lead on reaching Belinda's parents—and in the meantime, Avery's mom had invited Belinda to stay in their spare room until the family could be reunited.

As we left the circus grounds, Avery bumped my shoulder. "At least this means you don't have to get up on the high wire, Parker. Which is a good thing, since you passed out from it."

Ethan squeezed my hand.

I laughed. "No kidding. I'd better keep my feet on the ground from here on out."

After all, I had everything I ever wanted, right here by my side.

You can read more about Parker, Ethan, and their friends
in the Secret Psychics series.

a SPECIAL THEORY of CIRCUS
ADRIANO

A Special Theory of Circus

MARY FAN

Indiana, 1891

Newton's Third Law of Motion states that for every action, there is an equal and opposite reaction. He was talking about forces in physics. For example, when you sit down, you exert a force on the chair, and the chair exerts one on you. I was certain a similar, less scientifically explicable law must have been at play when my twin sister and I were born.

She was the force—a vibrant, energetic whirlwind of a human being—and I was the reaction—a quiet, studious bookworm. People often commented that I acted more like a sixty-year-old schoolmarm than a sixteen-year-old girl.

The differences between us couldn't have been more obvious than when I stepped into the big top, having been directed there by a roustabout upon arriving at the grounds of the Bicker Family Circus, which was setting up for the shows that would begin the following week. There I stood, in my humble trousers, plain white shirt, and boring brown vest, with the only interesting thing about my appearance being my round, brass-rimmed spectacles, which had several lenses that allowed for different levels of magnification. And there was Lulu, swinging from the flying trapeze, her spangle-covered leotard and colorful tutu glittering and flouncing with every move. A rainbow of ribbons flowed behind her from her elaborately twisted black hair. My own dark locks hung in an unassuming braid down my back.

"Hallie!" Still flying across the trapeze rig, Lulu grinned at me. "It's so good to see you!"

Very much right-side up, with both feet planted firmly on the ground beside my trunk, I waved. "Good to see you too. Where's Ma?"

"I'm here," came a voice from behind me.

I turned to find Ma, an elegant woman often mistaken for decades younger than her forty-five years, approaching from behind a house-shaped set piece used in one of the clown acts.

She embraced me tightly. "I'm so glad you agreed to spend the summer with us. I'd always hoped that someday, I could show you my world."

I didn't have the heart to reply with the truth: that I'd only agreed to leave New York and my beloved science books because Ba had been invited to an academic conference in London and had feared he'd be too busy to look out for me in a foreign city.

The enormity of differences between myself and Lulu had been obvious even at the age of five, when our parents had agreed that Ma, who'd chosen to leave the theater and join a traveling circus, would take the spritely Lulu with her, and Ba, whose career as a legal scholar was rooted in the city, would keep the bookish me with him. Though Ma and Ba had grown up together in New York City's Chinatown, they couldn't have been more different. I supposed it made sense that my sister and I would be similarly contrasting. And I supposed it was only fair that I should spend a summer with Ma and Lulu's circus, since they returned to New York each winter while the show was on hiatus.

Lulu released the trapeze bar, bounced into the net, and threw a somersault. Grinning, she flipped onto the ground and ran up to me. Though we'd been born on the same day and shared the same pale gold complexion and dark brown eyes, we were not identical. Whereas Lulu had inherited Ma's square-ish face and pointy chin, I had what our Chinese aunties called a "duck egg" face—oval with round cheeks and a soft chin.

"Want to take a swing?" Lulu gestured at the rig. "It's easier than it looks, especially since we'll put you in safety lines."

I shook my head, terrified by the very idea. "No, but I'll watch you and Ma rehearse."

Lulu shook my shoulder. "Oh, please give it a try! It's so much fun!"

"Now, now," Ma said. "Don't pressure Hallie. Come, let us run through our routine."

I sat down on my trunk, figuring I could worry about settling in after Ma and Lulu were done rehearsing, and watched as Lulu threw trick after trick into Ma's waiting hands. I recalled the advertisements for the thrilling mother-daughter trapeze duo that I'd seen on my way over from the train station, and a twinge of jealousy bit me.

Perhaps I could give it a try. I narrowed my eyes in concentration as Lulu jumped off the platform again. *It's only a pendulum, after all.* Lulu swung forward toward Ma, released one hand, and turned around. I noted that she'd waited for the top of the swing, where the gravitational forces were minimal, to let go. She would have felt weightless—and perfectly safe—releasing one hand. *But if she'd chosen the wrong moment and lost her grip, the gravitational forces would have thrown her across the rig... That's probably what would happen to me if I tried.*

"It's going too fast!" A panicked, high-pitched voice caught my attention.

I turned to see a little girl who looked about eight sitting in an aerial hoop. Her red hair whipped around as she spun a few feet above the ground.

A blond girl, who appeared the same age, reached up as if to grab the hoop.

"Don't!" I exclaimed. "A force in motion stays in motion—if you stop the hoop too suddenly, she could fly off!"

The blond girl retracted her hand. "What do we do?"

I looked up at the girl in the hoop, who sat with her knees crossed. "Straddle your legs as wide as you can. That will slow it down."

The redheaded girl obeyed. Soon, the hoop slowed enough to safely grab it.

"Thank you." The girl hopped down, blinking quickly. "How did you know that would work?"

I shrugged. "Conservation of angular momentum."

"Huh?"

"Here, I'll show you." I might not have been an acrobat like Lulu, but I'd climbed my fair share of trees. Pulling myself into the hoop, which was low enough that a hop was all it took, was easy enough. I sat with my legs crossed. "Give me a push."

The redheaded girl complied, and the hoop spun.

"If no external forces are applied, this hoop could spin forever," I said. "Angular momentum is rotational inertia times angular velocity, so when one goes up, the other must go down." I straddled my legs, and the hoop slowed. I then crossed my legs again, and it sped back up. "See?"

"Sort of," the redheaded girl said, while the blond girl gave a noncommittal head nod.

I jumped down from the hoop, a little dizzy but too excited about getting to explain something I enjoyed to care. "Friction is also a factor in this case. The swivel is well greased but still exerts a force on the system."

Lulu approached with a twinkle in her eye. "I don't know what you're talking about, but if you can do that"—she gestured at the hoop—"you can certainly do trapeze."

Ma approached and eyed the two little girls. "Olive, Ruth, you should know better than to play on the equipment while your parents are busy setting up the—"

She broke off and whirled toward the big top's entrance with a look of concern.

I followed her gaze. The noises of frantic shouts soaked the air and grew louder by the moment. Lulu and I exchanged a look and then both rushed outside to see what was causing the commotion.

Several boys in dirty overalls and worn flat caps raced about with buckets of tar, splattering the sideshow tents and game stalls, as well as the workers who tried to stop them. A few knocked over equipment and tore down posters.

One, who had a striking dark brown face with high cheekbones and a sharp chin, climbed onto the popcorn machine, a giant automaton that doubled as an exhibition and a food vendor, and smashed his brush against the sign above it. He grinned as he drew black Xs across the words "Wonder of Science at Work."

Perhaps because it felt like an attack on science itself that this particular hooligan riled me the most. Without thinking, I ran to the machine and climbed after him. "How dare you?"

The boy whirled to face me, and his laughing amber eyes, which had sharp corners, met mine. He flicked his brush, sending sticky black splatters at me. Gasping, I grabbed at him. He dodged with a smug smirk and then jumped off the machine, flipping in the air before landing on both feet.

"Stop!" I started to jump but froze when I realized I was higher up than anticipated. Inertia kept my spectacles going, though, and they flew right off my face.

The boy snatched them out of the air and tossed them back up to me. "You'll need those to catch me, miss!"

With a wink, he raced off.

By the time I reached the ground, he'd vanished into the commotion. The other ruffians continued splattering tar and causing mayhem.

"That's enough, boys." A man's booming voice shot through the noise. "I think we've made our point."

A large man in a well-tailored waistcoat that spoke of impressive wealth strode toward the big top. A slighter but similarly dressed man followed, and I wasn't sure which had spoken.

Madam Bicker, the matriarch of the Bicker Family and the woman in charge of the circus's affairs, emerged from the large canvas tent with her hands on her hips. Despite her gray hair and small stature, she carried herself with authority. Her long skirt swished by her ankles as she marched up to the two men.

"Mr. Prescott." She glared at the large man. "Mr. Philbert." She turned her icy brown eyes toward the slighter man. "What is the meaning of this?"

Mr. Prescott looked down at her. "We warned you not to schedule your circus for the same week as the Prescott & Philbert Greatest Show. Delay your opening until after we leave town, and you will have no further problems."

"Do not think that because your show is bigger and wealthier that you can intimidate me." Madam Bicker pointed at each man in turn.

"Consider your options carefully." Mr. Prescott swept his arms at the ruffians, who stood amid the chaos they'd caused. "Come along, boys. We have much work to do."

He and Mr. Philbert stalked off, and the gaggle of hooligans followed, including the amber-eyed boy who'd splattered me. He glanced back at me and tipped his gray flat cap in a mocking manner.

Ma approached, with Lulu close behind, and shook her head. "I'm sorry this happened on your first day here, Hallie. The Prescott & Philbert Greatest Show has been our rival for years. This isn't the first time they've sent their young roustabouts to cause us trouble."

Lulu scowled. "We can't keep letting them get away with this. One of these days, we'll get back at them."

"No, Lulu." Ma gave her a chastising look. "That will only make matters worse."

I glanced around at the mess. "Can't the police do anything?"

Lulu shook her head. "There's never enough damage for it to be considered a serious crime. Each time Madam Bicker has gone to the police, they've always laughed her off."

Ma sighed. "Come along, girls. Let's help clean up."

I glanced at the tar-covered automaton, and anger churned in my gut. Lulu was right: We couldn't let them get away with this again.

By the following day, we had managed to clean, replace, or cover up everything that Mr. Prescott and Mr. Philbert's band of ruffians had marred with tar. Tedious as the task of tidying up was, it did give me an excuse to take a closer look at that popcorn-vending automaton, which I'd volunteered to scrub. Though I'd freed its bronze gears of the last sticky flecks some time ago, I remained beside it just outside the open entryway to the big top, examining the machinery with the magnifying lenses attached to my spectacles.

"It's like magic!" A high-pitched voice caught my attention, and I recognized it as belonging to Olive, the little red-haired girl.

I glanced over to see her and the blond girl, Ruth, watching my sister rehearse on the flying trapeze. At the top of the swing, Lulu turned upside down and hooked her legs on the bar. After the trapeze swung to the other end of the rig, she released both hands.

The two little girls gasped.

"I could never be strong enough to do that," Ruth said with a sigh.

"Yes, you could." I ducked into the big top. "You don't really need much strength at all. Centripetal force pulls you down at the bottom of the pendulum, but you'd feel like you weigh almost nothing at the two peaks. The closer you get to ninety degrees from the bottom of the swing, the less gravitational force is pulling you down."

The girls gave me confused looks.

"I don't know what all those science words mean, but she's right." Lulu dropped into the net and glanced at me with glinting eyes. "You know, Hallie, you could prove it to them right now. You could do this trick, even though the most you use your arms for is carrying books."

I rubbed the back of my head. "I don't know…"

Lulu flipped down to the ground and arched an eyebrow. "You had no problem demonstrating on the hoop yesterday." She turned to Olive and Ruth. "What do you say, girls? Do you want Hallie to show that even a bookworm with no circus experience can hang by her knees from a flying trapeze?"

Olive looked at me with her hands on her hips. "I don't think you can do it. You don't have the muscles to pull yourself up like that."

"It's not about muscles—it's about timing." I huffed. "As I was saying, the gravitational force—"

"You're speaking in tongues, Hallie." Lulu grinned. "The only way to help them understand centipede force or whatever you were talking about is to demonstrate."

"*Centripetal* force." I glanced up at the rig. I *was* rather envious that my mother and sister shared this art form, while I'd never so much as touched a trapeze bar. It still looked intimidating, but less so than yesterday. I drew a breath. "You said there were safety lines, right?"

"Yes!" Lulu jumped up and down with excitement. "I'll go get Ma. She would be so cross if you took your first swing without her here!"

Half an hour later, I found myself standing on the trapeze platform, some thirty feet above the ground, with a safety belt cinching my waist, attached to two long ropes on either side of the rig that came together via a pulley system and were hooked to a thicker rope trailing down to the ground. Ma, wearing thick gloves to protect her hands from the friction, held that rope while Lulu, beside me on the platform, gripped the back of my belt. I'd left my spectacles with Olive and Ruth, and while I only needed them to read small texts, I felt odd without them.

"Ready?" Lulu asked.

"No." But looking down at Ruth and Olive's skeptical faces, I knew there was no backing out. I wanted them to understand that it was science, not magic, behind flying trapeze.

All right, so perhaps I was trying to convince myself as much as I was them.

Using a long hook, Lulu swung the bar up to me and instructed me to hold on with both hands.

I lifted it as high as I could. The higher the bar, the more potential energy—that is, the energy held by the bar that would be released once I swung. And the more potential energy I could give it, the higher I would fly, and the lighter I would feel at the top. Since I certainly didn't have the brute strength to swing my legs above my head, I would need all the help physics could give me.

At Ma's call, I jumped off the platform. An exhilarated feeling whooshed through me as I swung. Ma gave another call as I approached the top of the swing, and I lifted my legs. Though I'd known in theory that I would feel weightless, it was different actually *feeling weightless.* My heart skittered as I hooked my knees onto the bar the same as Lulu had. The trapeze swung toward the platform, and as it reached the back, that weightless feeling filled me again. I let go on Ma's signal.

The next thing I knew, I was dangling upside down from a flying trapeze by my legs alone. Part of me was terrified I would either fall or be stuck in this position—the bar looked desperately far from my hands, and I didn't trust my ability to crunch up and grab it. But I reminded myself that physics meant I needed no strength at all; I only had to wait for those moments of weightlessness.

Grabbing the bar at the back of the swing felt as easy as tapping my knees from a seated position. I lowered my legs on Ma's instruction. At the top of the swing, she called for me to let go. Because I was once again in that weightless part, I fell straight down without careening across the net as I'd feared.

By the time I made it down to the ground, my heart was pounding. But not in a bad way.

I turned to Ruth and Olive. "I told you it wasn't magic or strength. It's simply physics."

The two little girls stared at me in awe.

"This is a trick, isn't it?" Ruth asked. "You've done this before."

Ma turned to her. "I assure you, she has not."

"But how?" Olive asked.

I started again to explain about centripetal and gravitational forces, doing my best to break down the concepts, but soon realized it would be easier if they experienced the weightlessness themselves.

I gestured at the rig. "Do you want to give it a try? If Ma says it's all right, of course."

Ma shrugged. "I see no harm in a little bit of fun."

The girls looked at each other with wide eyes. "Yes!" they squealed at the same time.

Just then, a loud cracking noise exploded from outside.

Ma whirled with a look of concern. "Oh, what now?" She quickly took off her gloves and ran out.

Lulu scurried down the ladder and followed. "Come on! I'll bet it's Prescott and Philbert again."

I raced after her. The moment I left the big top, a scene of mayhem greeted me. Dogs and monkeys and horses and pigs—all trained for animal acts—ran amok across the circus grounds, chased by those same hooligans who'd thrown tar the previous day. The frenzied creatures jumped onto stalls and knocked over the displays we'd just finished cleaning.

"Those no-good scoundrels!" Lulu started forward, but I seized her arm.

"What are you planning to do?" I demanded.

"I'm going to show those brutes—"

"Ma would have your hide if you got into a fight!" I looked around, but Ma was nowhere in sight. She must have gone to get help.

Moments later, she returned with two of the animal trainers in tow. But though they did their best to round up the creatures, the boys continued agitating them with loud noises: clapping their hands, blowing whistles, and shouting. One even set off firecrackers—a closer look revealed him to be the same amber-eyed boy who'd splattered the automaton.

Irritation sparked in my chest, and part of me yearned to release Lulu and join her in pommeling these good-for-nothings.

"What is going on here?" Madam Bicker rushed onto the scene.

The amber-eyed boy turned to her with a smirk. "We've been sent to deliver a message, ma'am. Mr. Prescott and Mr. Philbert kindly request that you delay your show's opening, or they'll keep sending us back for more fun."

Madam Bicker balled her fists. "You tell those two yellow-bellied hornswogglers that we'll do no such thing! And you tell them that if they're afraid of fair competition, then they have no business running a show!"

"I'll pass on your message, ma'am." The boy tipped his hat mockingly.

"Why are you doing this?" I strode up to the boy. "We haven't done anything to you!"

"Mr. Prescott and Mr. Philbert think you're stealing their audiences." The boy shrugged. "I don't much care myself. I'm only here for the fun—and because they pay us extra. When you're a roustabout, you need those extra pennies." He winked and grabbed the reins of an escaped horse. With a few expert moves, he leaped onto its back.

My eyes widened. He certainly knew a lot of tricks for a roustabout.

"Let's go, boys!" he shouted. "We've done what we came to do!"

As the ruffians scampered away, Madam Bicker let out a long sigh and surveyed the damage. Several booths had been completely knocked over, and two of the sideshow tents had collapsed. "Well, the papers will have plenty to write about at least. I'm afraid we'll have to spend another evening cleaning." She walked off.

Lulu glared at the chaotic scene. "This has gone on for too long. It may be only your second day, Hallie, but they've been doing this to us for years. I can't tolerate it anymore. At the very least, I want to cause them as much annoyance as they've caused us."

Based on the tightness in her jaw, I could tell she was not simply speculating. And I knew better than to think I could stop her when she had her mind set on something. Besides, she had a point. I could throw a bucket of tar as well as any paid hooligan.

I turned to Lulu. "Whatever you're thinking, I want to join you. As long as there's no fighting."

A wicked glint lit her eyes. "Oh, I wouldn't be so foolish. But I do have something in mind…"

With only the light of a single candle to see by, the big top of the Prescott & Philbert Greatest Show—abandoned since it was past midnight—looked more like a mausoleum than a circus tent. Empty seats encircled a wide ring, and the tiny flame flickering above Lulu's hand made the shadows shudder and squirm. The end of the rope she'd brought, coiled over her shoulder, swayed like a snake as she made her way to the center.

I clutched a bucket of red paint in one hand and a brush in the other. That we'd managed to slip onto the grounds of the rival circus without being seen felt like something of a miracle, especially since I was not the most graceful of people and had made a racket slipping behind the various tents and stalls. I could only attribute our success to the overconfidence or laziness of the few night watchmen Mr. Prescott and Mr. Philbert employed.

Lulu lifted her candle. A great banner spanned the tent, spelling out the show's name. Her idea of revenge was to cross out the word "Greatest" and replace it with a giant red "Worst." Childish, to be sure. But she'd found the idea to be amusing and satisfying, and as far as pranks went, it was pretty harmless. Just enough to irritate our rivals but not so much as to cause true damage. Which was more consideration than they'd given us.

Lulu frowned up at the banner. "That's higher than I expected." Her gaze wandered over to one of the two wooden posts holding up the banner, and she handed me the candle, which we'd only lit once we'd been sure the big top was unoccupied.

I accepted it and followed her to the post. The plan was for her to climb up, take a seat on the beam from which the banner dangled, and lower one end of the rope down to me. I would then tie it to the bucket for her to pull up.

Unfortunately, the gleaming, polished post was too slippery for even my acrobatic sister to climb. She cursed as she slid down.

I looked around for anything she could use as a source of additional friction. A few substances came to mind—tar, or perhaps rosin, like from a violin bow—but I couldn't glimpse anything that would serve our purpose.

What I did spot, however, was a pile of flat boards and round posts and other such materials—likely pieces of a set that hadn't been assembled yet. They included two A-frames with a beam between them, which put me in mind of a teeter-totter, except without the actual board a child would sit upon.

I bit the inside of my cheek as an idea wafted through my head. I'd seen acrobatic acts use teeter-totters before; one person would stand on the end on the ground, and two would jump onto the other end, sending the first person flying. The flyer would usually throw a few somersaults or twists before landing, sometimes on an elevated platform. I would never attempt such a thing, but Lulu was a flyer…

I glanced at my sister, who was still attempting to climb the slippery post, and then back at the frame. It didn't look too heavy. We could easily move it under the banner and place a board across it. Ordinarily, a teeter-totter was supported by a single pivot point located at the midpoint between both ends, meant for two children of roughly the same size to play on. If that were my intention, then my sister and I would have been perfectly matched. But I had something else in mind. Those throwing circus tricks would have two people jump on the other end in order to increase the height of the flyer. I was, of course, only one person. However, if we adjusted the teeter-totter so that the point on which it rested—the fulcrum—was closer to one end, and Lulu stood on the shorter side, then my mass alone would be able to give her the height she needed to reach the banner. And if I carried the paint bucket and perhaps another item of bulk, then that would increase her height even further.

"Lulu!" I ran up to my sister. "Stop climbing. I have a better idea."

She slid back to the ground—not that she'd made it very far upward—and whirled to face me. "Oh?"

I quickly explained my idea. Part of me expected her to protest my jumping onto an unsecured board to launch her into the air.

Instead, she grinned. "Genius!" She dumped the rope on the ground and ran to grab a board. "I always wanted to try flipping off a teeter-totter. Being thrown to the top of a tent is the next best thing!"

I put down the candle and paint bucket, tucked my spectacles into my pocket for safe-keeping, and went to go help her. At the same time, I quickly ran through a few simple equations. Taking into account the length of the board as well as Lulu and my own weights—plus those of the paint bucket and a heavy metal toolbox I found—I determined where to place the flat piece of wood in such a way that when I jumped onto one end, it would send Lulu up to the beam holding up the banner.

Of course, without proper measuring tools, my calculations were approximate at best. Nervousness bit me as I stacked a few wooden crates atop each other to give myself adequate height to jump onto my end of the teeter-totter. If this went wrong, Lulu could be seriously injured. But she had no qualms about standing on the lower end, waiting for me to launch her upward. And, I reminded myself, she'd grown up in the circus. Flying came to her as naturally as walking did to me.

To increase my mass, I held the paint bucket in one hand and the metal toolbox in the other. Lulu, waiting on the other end of the teeter-totter with the rope wrapped around her waist, nodded to indicate that she was ready.

I took a deep breath and jumped, hitting the longer end of the teeter-totter.

Lulu flew upward. As I stumbled to the ground, she gripped the beam holding the banner.

"It worked!" She pulled herself on top of the beam with a laugh. "That was so much fun!"

She lowered the end of the rope down to me, and I tied the paint bucket to it.

As she sabotaged our rivals' banner, giggling with each stroke of red paint, I held up the candle to give her some light and kept an eye out for any watchmen who might stumble upon us.

Soon, Lulu's handiwork glimmered in fresh red paint across the Prescott & Philbert Greatest Show's enormous banner—now renamed "Worst Show." I shook my head at the foolishness of it all, but I had to admit, it was satisfying to see after all the trouble they'd caused us. I fought to contain a few giggles of my own as Lulu tied her rope to the beam and then climbed down.

She'd made it about halfway to the ground when a gruff voice called out, "What's that light in the big top?"

Gasping, I snuffed out the candle. But it was too late—a second voice shouted, "Someone's here! Get the others!"

"Fantastic," I grumbled.

Lulu slid the rest of the way down and grabbed my arm. "Run!"

We raced out of the big top through the same entryway we'd come in from. That turned out to be a mistake—we found ourselves face-to-face with two men carrying lanterns.

Lulu dodged as one tried to grab her. I stuck out a leg and threw myself into a roundhouse kick, aiming at the other's shin. I might not have had much strength, but momentum meant I was nevertheless able to generate plenty of force. My leg, unaccustomed to combat, protested the impact, but at least my adversary fell as intended. The one who'd tried to seize Lulu, meanwhile, tumbled forward as he missed, undone by his own inertia.

We sprinted across the grounds, but the shouts of angry men surrounded us from every direction. It was only a matter of time before we were spotted again, and as much as I trusted momentum and inertia, I couldn't count on physics alone to save us.

As Lulu and I ducked behind a stall, I looked around to assess our situation. Those working for Mr. Prescott and Mr. Philbert ignited the gas lamps lining the walkways. Soon, the whole place would be as bright as downtown on a holiday.

"This is bad," I muttered. "They're all looking for us. The moment we make a run for the exit, they'll hear us."

Lulu blew out a breath. "We need a diversion. Any ideas?"

I stroked my chin. A tent touting the Most Marvelous Mechanical Men lay immediately to our left. *That must be an exhibit of automatons*, I thought. *It's fortunate I know a thing or two about those…*

I inclined my chin toward the tent. Lulu's eyes widened, and she nodded.

We slipped inside the tent and were greeted by a sea of metal faces. Skeletal bodies with exposed gears and machinery, each at least eight feet tall, gleamed in the vague light sifting through the canvas tent. Control panels sat on the back of each bronze human-shaped figure. I'd observed enough both from books and from the popcorn-vending automaton back at the Bicker Family Circus to know how to activate and adjust each. I set them up to walk out of the tent and wander in random directions. They would crash into stalls and signs the same as the escaped animals at our circus had, which seemed rather fitting. With any luck, Prescott and Philbert's men would be too busy trying to stop them to notice me and Lulu escape.

It worked—or, at least, it led to the desired result. I hadn't intended for the automatons to walk into the tent's canvas with such force as to cause the whole thing to collapse. Fortunately, Lulu and I had both exited by the time the beams came crashing down. As I'd hoped, the men soon turned their focus toward stopping the rogue machines rather than searching for intruders.

"Who is responsible for this?" Mr. Prescott's enraged voice pierced the air through the ruckus.

Lulu could barely contain her giggles as we made our escape. We'd nearly reached the edge of the circus grounds when a hand seized my arm.

"Got you!"

I spun. It was the same amber-eyed boy I'd encountered previously.

"Nice work back there." An amused smile curled his lips. "Almost makes me feel bad about bringing you to the bosses."

"Let my sister go!" Lulu shoved him, but he was at least ten inches taller than her—not to mention broad and muscular from a lifetime of physical labor. She might have been strong enough to hold up her own mass, but she was still significantly smaller than he was, and the push didn't even cause him to teeter.

He reached out to grab her as well, but she was too quick.

"Get out of here!" I exclaimed.

"Not without you." Lulu raised her fists.

The boy sighed, still looking entertained rather than angered. "You're half my size. Either listen to your sister and run, or come with me to meet Mr. Prescott and Mr. Philbert."

I narrowed my eyes. The boy might have been bigger, but like a bullet, Lulu was tiny yet powerful. She only had to use her body in the right way.

"Force is not mass alone." I arched my brows at Lulu, hoping she would take the hint.

Confusion briefly crossed her face. Then she spun on her heel and sprinted away into the night.

The boy let out a derisive noise. "Well, I didn't expect that. It's too bad your sister wouldn't stand by—"

Fast as a locomotive, Lulu reappeared and launched herself at the boy. He fell backward. Though he pulled me down with him, his grip slackened as soon as he hit the ground.

Lulu, who'd somehow managed to stay on her feet, grabbed my hand and yanked me up. "Let's go!"

The two of us sprinted off, though I struggled to keep up with her pace.

"I'm glad you remembered Newton's second law," I said between breaths.

"Huh?" She threw me a quizzical look.

"Force is mass times acceleration. I thought you understood since you compensated for your lack of mass by running so quickly."

"Ah. Well, I didn't know all that, but I do know that running into something really fast causes a big impact."

We made our way back toward the Bicker Family Circus's grounds, and soon, the noise from the commotion we'd caused vanished into the night.

Even the thick walls of the brightly painted train car that served as Madam Bicker's office couldn't keep the entire circus from hearing what Mr. Prescott and Mr. Philbert had to say. Impressively, we could hear her responses just as clearly.

Through the small window, I glimpsed Mr. Prescott's face. It was quite purple.

"This is outrageous!" he bellowed. "I demand that you compensate us for the damage your ruffians caused!"

"My ruffians?" Madam Bicker sounded unimpressed. "I did not dispatch anyone to your show's grounds. Though I hear that the trespassers merely adjusted your banner to speak the truth."

Lulu, who along with every performer and worker at the Bicker Family Circus, stood outside the train car to witness the verbal battle, let out a snicker. I shot her a warning look. Though at least three people had seen us and knew we were the guilty parties, we didn't have to make it obvious.

"Only someone with your show would have had reason!" Mr. Philbert's voice shook with anger.

"Suppose they were with my show." Madam Bicker stood, and the top of her head became visible in the window. "I would assess the damage they did to be roughly equivalent to that caused by the hooligans you admitted to paying extra to cause me trouble. A little paint, a few wayward creatures and fallen tents—I'd say we're about even at this point, so let us put an end to the whole affair and call a truce. After all, we're both due to open in three days' time and should focus on delivering quality shows. What do you say?"

"You will compensate us for the damage." Mr. Prescott's voice rose, though I wasn't sure how that was possible considering how loud he'd already been. "And you will delay your show until we are out of town. Otherwise, there will be consequences."

"I will do no such thing." Madam Bicker's voice was firm. "And I challenge you to provide proof that I was the one who sent people to graffiti your sign and set your automatons loose. If it's only the word of a few roustabouts you have, then let's hope those men remain quiet when asked why someone would do such a thing to you in the first place, and what the complete scope of their duties for you might have been."

The train car's door burst open. Mr. Prescott and Mr. Philbert emerged with identical expressions of rage and indignation. The crowd quickly scattered. I grabbed Lulu and headed back toward the big top.

I glanced over my shoulder and caught the poisonous looks Mr. Prescott and Mr. Philbert gave Madam Bicker, who stood in the doorway, watching them leave. Ice filled my gut. It seemed the two men were taking our childish prank far more seriously than Madam Bicker had taken their provocations.

If the trapeze were a simple pendulum, then Lulu would be a point mass. Back in the big top, watching my mother and sister rehearse, I scribbled a few diagrams and equations into my worn notebook, my spectacles perched on my nose. Ma dangled by her hands from the catch trapeze, doing a few warm-up exercises by lifting her legs and curling her torso, while Lulu swung back and forth across the rig. With a few well-timed kicks, she managed to use the force of her body to make the swing higher each time, and I tried to make sense of how that was possible given conservation of linear momentum. *Of course, Lulu isn't a point. She behaves as a pendulum herself relative to the fly bar. So, really, it's a coupled pendulum system…*

At the back of the swing, Lulu pushed her feet against the bar and arched through, creating a round shape that made my back hurt just watching. She waited for the top of the swing, then released, falling face-first toward the net. But halfway down, she twisted midair, like a cat, and landed on her back instead. I scribbled a few notes into the margins.

Lulu flipped off the net. "Hallie, are you analyzing me again?"

I lifted my notebook. "Naturally."

She walked up to me and peered at the diagrams and equations twisting in black ink across the yellow paper. "Can you teach me all that when you're finished? It might help me improve if I understood the science behind what

I'm doing."

I grinned. "I would love to."

Ma pulled herself up onto the catch trapeze and started pumping her legs, causing it to swing. "No dawdling, Lulu. Our show opens the day after tomorrow, and you're still not breaking hard enough on your layouts."

"Yes, Ma." Lulu started toward the rig.

Suddenly, a great cracking noise, like thunder, exploded through the big top. One of the posts holding up the tent split in the middle, the next thing I knew, the entire structure was collapsing. Panicked screams and alarmed shouts from the other performers and workers buzzed through the air in a chaotic cacophony.

Lulu grabbed me and tried to run, but there wasn't time. The next thing I knew, I was trapped beneath the big top's thick fallen canvas.

Lulu and I pushed at it, searching for an opening. We crawled beneath the canvas until finally, after what felt like an eternity, we made our way out.

"Lulu! Hallie!" Madam Bicker, who along with several others had rushed onto the scene, reached out a hand and pulled me up. "Thank goodness you're all right!"

I turned and stared at the scene I had just escaped. The entire big top had collapsed. The red-and-white striped canvas, which moments ago had stood with impressive grandeur, now lay in messy bunches across the audience stands and performance equipment it had housed. *What about the trapeze rig? Ma was thirty feet in the air when the canvas fell…*

"Ma!" I looked around wildly.

Lulu and I searched and searched, hoping to find her amid the mess of cloth and fallen set pieces. Several people emerged shaken but otherwise unhurt. Others were not so lucky and had to be carried away. A few shouted for help from beneath the fallen tent and were greeted by peers who sliced open the canvas to let them out.

"*Ma!*" I cried.

"Hallie?" A weak voice wafted toward me.

I rushed toward it. Lulu had obtained a knife from someone, and with her cutting and me pulling on the canvas, we managed to create a hole. Ma lay on the ground, groaning. Bruises dotted her limbs, and each breath she drew sounded pained.

She gave me an encouraging smile. "I'll be all right, girls. I think I might have broken a few ribs when I fell, but I'll heal."

Tears streamed down my face. "How could this have happened?"

"Prescott and Philbert." Lulu's expression darkened. "Their goons must have sabotaged the tent in a way that would cause it to collapse hours after they left."

Weakening one point in the object while letting the forces of gravity work against the system… I inhaled sharply. "How could they do such a thing?"

Madam Bicker approached with several others, two of whom carried a stretcher between them. A scowl contorted her usually friendly round face. "Those pigeon-livered scoundrels have gone too far this time. It's time to get the police involved."

"We have no evidence," Ma mumbled. "Without solid proof, they'll say it was an accident and brush us off as they always have."

I huffed. "There must be something we can do."

"There is." Lulu balled her fists. "We can take down *their* big top—"

"No, Lulu." Even injured, Ma managed a piercing glare.

Lulu sobbed. "This is my fault, isn't it? If I hadn't painted their banner…"

"Now, now." Ma put her hand on Lulu's. "You mustn't blame yourself."

I bit my lip, searching for a solution. Ma was right—we needed evidence.

A movement caught my eye, and I whirled in time to see a figure dart behind a cart full of equipment. If I hadn't encountered him three times previously, I might not have recognized the amber-eyed boy. He must have been among those who'd sabotaged the big top.

Anger surged through my veins. In the absence of evidence, a witness would suffice.

I launched myself in his direction, running as quickly as my legs would allow.

Everyone else must have thought I'd run from the scene of the collapsed big top because I was upset. That was the only explanation for the fact that I alone chased after the one member of Mr. Prescott and Mr. Philbert's team of saboteurs who'd been foolish enough to remain on the Bicker Family Circus's grounds. I supposed that wasn't an unreasonable assumption considering I'd taken off without a word.

I chased the amber-eyed boy past the circus's designated borders and into the flat fields of dry grass on the outskirts of Indianapolis. Only the force of my anger could have given me the speed to catch up to him, given his superior height, strength, and pretty much everything physical. But with my heart racing and my lungs bursting, I knew I wouldn't be able to keep up my extreme pace for long.

And so I pushed off the ground as hard as I could and launched myself at him like a torpedo—a more aggressive version of what Lulu had done to escape him previously. In that moment, I didn't much care what would happen after I took flight.

I crashed into the boy's back, knocking the breath from my own lungs. He lost his balance and fell face-first into the grass. For a moment, he lay there stunned. I took advantage of those few seconds to seize the leather boot from my foot and hold it above his head, waving it like a bludgeon.

"If you try to escape, I'll clobber you!" I shouted.

He flipped over and attempted to push me off, but I managed to pin him down again. I slammed my boot into the ground beside him.

His eyes widened. "Was that blow intended for my face, or was it only a threat? Either way, I'm glad you missed. I rather like my nose the way it is, miss."

Keeping my knee pressed into his chest, I held up my makeshift weapon. "How could you do that to us? My mother was badly injured because of you—she could have died! And there were others, too! I don't even know how many were hurt!"

"I'm so sorry."

"Sorry? You think a simple word like that is enough after what you did?"

"No, of course not." A heavy look descended on his face, robbing it of any trace of the mischievous merriment I'd come to expect from him. That was when I noticed the deep blue tint across one of his dark brown cheeks. A bruise—and a bad one at that.

Furious as I was, I couldn't help a twinge of guilt. I hadn't meant to cause injury—not yet, at least.

His fingers wandered up to his cheek. "Oh, don't worry, that little fall didn't cause this here shiner. No, this was courtesy of Mr. Prescott. He didn't like that I tried to stop the others from sabotaging your big top. I'd hoped to get to your grounds sooner to warn someone, but it took a while to break out of the train car they locked me in."

I frowned, unsure whether to believe him. "You tried to stop them? You're lying."

He held up his hands in surrender. "I may not be respectable, but I'm also not foolish enough to wait around by the scene of a crime I committed. I swear, I only came to try to warn someone. But by the time I arrived, the tent was already falling."

I narrowed my eyes. "You had no problem doing Mr. Prescott and Mr.

Philbert's dirty work before."

"That was different! Splattering tar and releasing well-trained animals? No true harm would have come from that. I thought they were playing up our rivalry for publicity, especially since a few newspapers actually wrote about it. But what you did with the banner and the automatons really angered the bosses. They're not accustomed to people striking back at them. They wanted to send a message to Madam Bicker and those who work for her. It was their idea to make it so the big top would collapse during a rehearsal. I would never agree to do anything where people could get hurt, and I told them if they didn't back down, I would go to the police. Of course, they weren't about to let that happen."

I lowered my boot. If he was lying, then he was doing an awfully good job. "Why did you run away when I spotted you, if you weren't guilty?"

He shrugged. "Instinct, I suppose. Each time we've met before, one of us has been chasing the other."

I couldn't help a slight laugh. "That's true. Would you be willing to go to the police now and tell them what you know?"

He hesitated. "I would, but what if they don't believe me?"

I thought for a moment. "Let's go talk to Madam Bicker. She might have some ideas."

"Before I agree to anything, I want you to put that boot back on. I'd feel much better if you were unarmed."

Rolling my eyes, I got off him, pulled the boot back onto my foot, and stood up. "Happy now?"

"Very much so." He scooped something up from the ground and held it up to me. I recognized my spectacles, which must have fallen off when I'd tackled him. "By the way, what's your name?"

"Hallie." I accepted the spectacles. "What's yours?"

"Charlie."

I reached down and pulled him up. "Well, Charlie, it's nice to meet you."

It was Madam Bicker's idea to ask Charlie about the details of what had happened to the big top. Fortunately, Charlie had waited for Mr. Prescott and Mr. Philbert to outline every part of their wicked plan before expressing his refusal. Since he was able to describe precisely what the others had done to cause the big top to fall several hours after they'd left our grounds, the officers Madam Bicker called in believed him. Charlie also gave them the names of other roustabouts who'd be likely to flip on their bosses in exchange for leniency.

Between the witnesses and evidence he was able to present, the authorities actually had enough to arrest Mr. Prescott and Mr. Philbert for the damage and injuries they'd caused. Enormous headlines blazed across every paper in Indianapolis, and probably several across the nation as well. It was one of the biggest scandals ever to hit the circus world.

Madam Bicker sighed as she held up one of the papers. "This is the greatest publicity I could have asked for. And with our rivals' reputation in shambles, we should fare well. Yet it's all to our disadvantage, since we no longer have a show." She gestured at the plot where the big top had stood. The workers had cleared away the canvas and the broken posts, but a lot of the equipment, including the trapeze rig, remained.

Lulu and I had gone with her to survey the situation, mostly because Ma had grown tired of us hovering over her bed. She'd ordered us to stop feeling sorry for her and instead come up with a solution to our problems. The circus was scheduled to open the next day, and while we still had game booths and sideshows and such, people would be disappointed by the lack of a big top spectacular.

"Most of the equipment survived, but half the acts have injured performers, so it won't do us much good." Lulu rubbed the back of her head.

"I can still fly on the trapeze, but without Ma to catch me, it won't be a good performance."

"We still have most of the animal acts," I said, trying to sound optimistic. "And the audience stands are still set up. We could simply do a pared down outdoor show."

"I don't mind the outdoor aspect," Madam Bicker said. "But 'pared down'? People don't go to the circus for 'pared down'! And if they're disappointed, word will spread, which will affect our ability sell tickets in the next city, and the one after that, and so on, even after we get a new big top."

I glanced around, combing my mind for ideas, and noticed little Olive and Ruth helping their parents pick up splintered wood from the big top's broken posts. Charlie worked nearby, reinforcing the supports on one of the stands. Out of guilt, he'd volunteered to work for Madam Bicker for the remainder of the circus's stay in Indianapolis.

Seeing him reminded me of how I'd first encountered him—when he'd drawn Xs across the "Wonder of Science at Work" sign.

Pieces of an idea clicked together in my mind. "I have a radical proposal."

Madam Bicker turned to me. "Let's hear it."

I cupped my hands to my mouth. "Olive! Ruth! Charlie! Can you come here for a moment?"

The two little girls looked at their parents and, upon receiving nods, scampered over. Charlie approached at a leisurely pace, a look between skepticism and curiosity twisting his face.

I turned to Lulu. "Remember how I was able to hang from my knees on the flying trapeze even though I'd never touched a rig before? And remember how I explained that it wasn't magic, it was physics? Well, here's what I propose: We perform a similar demonstration for the audience… and then let them try it for themselves. Why simply watch a circus when you can be *part* of one?"

Madam Bicker's eyebrows flew up. "My, that *is* radical."

"Olive and Ruth, you said you wanted to give it a try." I nodded at the trapeze rig. "You two, with your parents, can pose as ordinary audience members, and when we call for volunteers, you can be the first to go up. Once everyone sees two little girls demonstrate how easy it is, then more will volunteer."

"Not a bad idea," Charlie said. "Where do I come in?"

I turned to him. "Lulu will need to be at the top of the platform to demonstrate the trick and to see audience members take off safely, and I'll be busy explaining things. I need someone strong to hold onto the safety lines from the ground."

Charlie flexed one arm. "I can handle that."

Madam Bicker gave me an appraising look. "This could work. We could get some of the other acts to participate as well. People could try spinning in the aerial hoop, or posing on the rope, or walking on a low version of the high wire…" A spark lit her crinkled eyes. "Yes, this could work."

"It isn't magic. It's simply science." Standing before a large poster, upon which I'd drawn bigger versions of my trapeze diagrams and equations, I pointed at the figure representing the flyer. The "Wonder of Science at Work" sign stretched above me. I'd just finished explaining the basic physics of flying trapeze.

Behind me, Lulu took off from the platform, swung across the rig, and demonstrated hooking her knees onto the bar. When she finished, she dropped into the net with a flourish.

"Lulu, of course, is a trained acrobat," I said. "But because of the lack of gravitational force at the top of the swing, it takes almost no strength at all to tuck up into a ball and hook one's knees onto the bar. Why, even a little girl could do it."

I eyed the audience, pretending to search for a volunteer. I found Olive and Ruth sitting with their parents a few rows back and gestured at them. "Girls, would you care to give it a try?"

Olive and Ruth did a fairly good job of feigning surprise and nervousness considering we'd practiced the night before. But they were still new enough to flying that they didn't have to fake much confusion or awkwardness. I pulled a safety belt onto Olive while Charlie helped with Ruth's, and then we sent both girls up the ladder.

The audience muttered with skepticism at first, then gasped and applauded when Olive successfully hung by her knees, moving to Lulu's shouted instructions. Ruth went next to equal success.

I sent the girls back to their parents. "Who would like to volunteer next?"

Charlie turned to the audience with a big grin. "Come on, folks! If even these little girls can do it, what are you afraid of?"

"They're plants!" a smug male voice called from the back. "I saw their parents putting up posters for the show downtown! I'll bet they've been training for this since they were born!"

I froze. I wasn't prepared for hecklers.

Charlie, on the other hand, didn't seem the least bit fazed. "Thank you for volunteering, kind sir! Come on down! Why, the whole point of this demonstration is to prove that any fool can do flying trapeze, and you, mister, are certainly qualified. Unless you're too yellow to try?"

I suppressed a snicker.

A man with straw-colored hair stood up and made his way down. "I ain't afraid of nothin'."

"Then, come!" Charlie waved his arm in a beckoning motion. "Oh, and let's make this more interesting. Hallie, *you* hold his lines."

The man froze. "What are you playing at? You think I'm going to trust my life to that tiny young woman?"

Charlie arched his brows. "Why not? I would! Hallie, throw me a belt and explain to these fine folks how a pulley system works."

I shook my head. This wasn't how I'd intended for the show to go, and I was willing to bet that Charlie only wanted a turn on the trapeze himself. But the audience was watching enthusiastically. If this little drama would get them further invested in our demonstration, then I wasn't about to object.

"A pulley system changes the direction of an applied force and can reduce the force needed to lift a weight." I pointed up at the round mechanisms at the top of the rig and the ropes wrapped around them. "Because we have a two-wheel pulley here, I only need to exert half the amount of force to lift the same amount of weight as I would ordinarily."

Charlie walked up to me, standing shoulder-to-shoulder to highlight the difference in our sizes. "I'm nearly a foot taller than Hallie and at least fifty pounds heavier. And trust me, she's no strongwoman. I mean, look at her."

I made a face. "True, I can barely carry more than a stack of books. Yet thanks to these pulleys, I'm going to lower Charlie down nice and slow after he's done with his trick. Now, some of you may not believe me"—I gave the straw-haired man a pointed look—"but Charlie has never flown on a trapeze before. Yet like he said, any fool can do it." I glanced at Charlie with lifted brows.

He barked out a laugh. As he pulled off his gloves, put on a safety belt, and made his way up the ladder, I went into a few more details about the pulley system.

Once he was at the top, I put on the gloves and grabbed the rope that was hooked to the pulley system, which in turn was hooked to the ropes attached to Charlie's safety belt.

On Lulu's cue, he hopped off the platform and let out an enthusiastic cheer.

Like Olive and Ruth, he successfully hung by his knees and let go with his hands. Unlike those two, he didn't manage to *keep* his knees on the bar. He slid off and started plummeting head-first into the net. And since that happened midway through the swing, the force of the pendulum kept him flying forward as opposed to dropping straight down at the top of the swing as he was supposed to.

The audience gasped and shouted in alarm.

I yanked hard at the safety lines, even letting them lift me off the ground briefly. Though it took some effort, I—with my skinny, muscle-less arms—managed to lower the tall, broad Charlie slowly into the net.

He laughed as he made his way to the edge. "And that, folks, is the power of physics!"

I narrowed my eyes. After the show, I'd have to interrogate him on whether he'd purposely fallen.

Even though it was possible for me to hold the safety lines, I was glad to hand the rope back to him. Physics did not account for fatigue.

The straw-haired man went up next. Watching him go from frowning at the top of the platform to grinning as he made his way off the net after a successful trick was worth the trouble he'd tried to cause earlier.

After that, we had no problem with volunteers. Audience members eagerly rushed up for their turns on the flying trapeze.

Elsewhere, others tried spinning on the aerial hoop, posing on the rope, and walking on a high wire that wasn't all that high—only a foot or so off the ground. Delighted laughter and enthusiastic chatter made the air sparkle.

"This is almost better than a regular show," Charlie said.

"I agree," I said.

"I wonder if Madam Bicker would let us continue doing these demonstrations at the next stop."

I arched my brows. "'Next stop'?"

"Madam Bicker appreciates that I'm a good worker, and that I stepped up when it mattered. She said I could come along if I wanted. Who knows, maybe someday I'll get an act of my own."

"Just stay away from the tar buckets." I gave a teasing smile.

"Hallie!" Lulu shouted down from the top of the platform. "You've spent all this time talking about the science of flying trapeze. I say it's time you showed these folks that you can do it, too!"

I shot her an annoyed look. "That's not part of the plan!"

"Oh, come on!" Lulu turned to the audience. "What do you say? Would you like the lecturer to do as she lectured?"

Cheers rose from the audience. Charlie tossed me a safety belt.

With a half-amused, half-exasperated sigh, I put it on. "Very well, then."

I climbed the ladder, and Lulu clipped the safety lines to my belt.

"We're going to have a lot to write to Ba about," she said. "He'll wish he came with you instead of going to that boring academic conference."

"Maybe I can come back next summer," I mused aloud.

"Yes!" Lulu grinned widely. "Are you ready to fly?"

I nodded and held out my hand for the bar. She swung it up, and I gripped it tight.

Lift the bar up to eye level to increase potential energy, I reminded myself. *At the top of the swing, gravitational force will decrease, and I'll be nearly weightless…*

On Lulu's call, I took off into the air.

REVIVAL FALLS

LEIGH HELLMAN

Max died on a Tuesday, the first Tuesday after Thanksgiving. It'd been a strange, warm harvest season, and the corn fields hadn't quite gone dry and tough. Birds rattled out harmonies come dusk and dawn—except for the sparrows who hadn't come south yet.

The first Tuesday after Thanksgiving, Drew's father was still carving turkey scraps off the bone when the phone in their cramped kitchen rang.

Drew shuffled in from the living room, still groggy from his afternoon nap.

"Get it," his father had said without looking up. "My hands are all greasy."

A Tuesday evening, dark with the November night, and the voice on the other end of the phone shook like the last leaves on an old maple branch. Drew heard the words but couldn't fit them together in his mind.

When his mother and little sister came home, they ate a meal of holiday leftovers in silence.

Illustration by Martina Localzo

"Ah, que poca… it's a damn shame," his father offered, finally. He shook his head as he sawed through the last slice of meat on his plate, eyes never leaving the chipped porcelain.

And that was that.

The Tuesday after the Tuesday Max died, out past where the Union Pacific and Burlington Northern Santa Fe lines crossed, a small tent went up.

The winds had shifted and blown in the first frost, slicking over concrete doorsteps and tricky patches of asphalt on the back roads. Coats started being zipped over flannel button-ups. The birds got quiet.

Wreaths and garlands and lights started popping up in store windows and front yards, late for the season because of the business with the funeral. It wasn't gonna be a big service, but most folks in town tried to keep the mood somber until it passed. For the family's sake.

Drew'd been invited, of course. *You were his best friend*, Max's stepmother had assured him with wet, streaky cheeks. *He'd want you there.*

What Max would want. He couldn't really agree with that, but he wasn't gonna argue with Mrs. Cao. Not now, not like this.

He went but stayed in the back, tried to stuff himself between the floral arrangements. Nodded along with reminiscences and condolences. Gave Mr. Cao an envelope with the cash he'd saved from his part-time work with his uncles, landscaping around town between the spring thaw and the winter snow.

He kept away from the casket, closed like it might have secrets to tell.

Before he could be hustled back to Max's house for casseroles and dumplings and more swallowed tears, Drew slipped out of the church and headed out toward the edge of town. He wasn't walking anywhere in particular, just away. Away from the sidelong stares, the smothering hugs, the words of comfort that stank sweet like a bowl of fruit left to rot in the sun. Away from the nosy pity, the whispered rumors, the small-town game of telephone.

He wasn't walking anywhere in particular, but somehow, he ended up in front of the small tent out by the railroad crossing.

It wasn't much bigger than a garden shed. Looked like someone had taken the frame of a park gazebo and tied it up in weatherproof canvas, the kind that started out white but stained gray within the first season. The loose flaps were anchored to the ground with rusted spikes, and the split opening was knotted shut up and down the seam. A faded wooden board had been stabbed into the dirt, chipped-paint message reading:

COMING SOON!

Drew kicked at the gravel and watched it roll under the tarp. He thought about trying a knot or two, just to see if they'd open easy. See if he could get a look inside. He didn't think anyone was there; he couldn't hear footsteps or talking or any other signs of life, but it seemed strange to leave a tent up on the side of the road without anyone keeping an eye on it. Even if there was nothing but rocks and weeds inside, there were still plenty of folks around who could find a use for the canvas and lumber.

But something about it made Drew pull away. Made him shove his hands in his dress pants pockets and scuff his heels back toward town.

A train horn drifted from the horizon, somewhere in the distance, and Drew picked up his pace to try to beat it home.

When they were young, they used to race trains. See how many cars they could keep up with before their legs buckled. See how many times they could jump the tracks before the engine barreled through. And if the train was one of the long, slow freights that chugged out of Chicago on its way to the Quad Cities, they'd see if they could hop on and off any low ladders and ride until the town started to fade from view.

Drew couldn't remember if it'd been his idea or Max's first. That was usually how it went with them—every plan seemed like it'd been shared between them before it ever got brought up. Two peas in a pod, that was what everyone said about them when they were minding their manners. Partners in crime, when they weren't.

"Where d'you think this train's going?" Max had asked one day as they watched an Amtrak glide by, too fast to do anything else.

It'd been the summer between seventh and eighth grades, between the single-story elementary school they could walk to and the combined middle school they'd have to get bused to a few towns over.

Drew shrugged. "I dunno. West, so maybe Dubuque or Cedar Rapids?"

"I've never been there," Max said, almost too quiet to hear over the grinding of the metal wheels against the rough tracks.

"Where?" Drew looked at him, watched the shadow of the passing train cars flutter across his face.

Max glanced back at him, mouth pinched tight at the corners. "Anywhere."

Drew thought on that for a minute. He'd never been much of anywhere either. A few trips to DeKalb and Rockford, a weekend in Milwaukee meeting some cousins he hadn't grown up with. He'd heard that eighth graders got to go to Springfield to learn about the state government, but only if their parents could afford the fees.

"Let's go on a road trip," Drew decided.

Max scoffed. "We can't even drive yet."

Drew rolled his eyes. "Not now, dummy. Let's do it after we finish high school. To celebrate."

Max paused, chewed his lips like he always did when he was mulling something over.

"Where would we go?"

Drew grinned at him, slinging an arm over his small shoulder.

"Anywhere."

Four days after the funeral, Drew drove his dad's rattly old pickup down Route 38 to get an order of bulbs and mulch for the winter landscaping stock. The sun was creeping low when he started heading back, and the sky had lost most of its glow by the time he crossed the tracks into town.

The tent was still there, still solitary. Still tied shut.

Drew pulled the car up next to the ditch that cut the road from the fields and idled there for a second. Examined the tent, counted the ropes and spikes, and tried to remember how many there had been before. It seemed bigger, but not by any obvious scale. Just slightly wider, slightly taller. Just enough to make someone stop and wonder if their eyes were playing tricks on them in the dull twilight.

On top of the tent mast a little flag flew, sputtering in the bursts of wind. Drew couldn't make out the colors or design, but he was sure of at least one thing: That hadn't been there before. He would've noticed the movement, heard the strip of fabric whip back and forth to break up the rest of the silence around it.

It meant that someone had been here, after the tent went up.

Of course they were. Drew shook off the vines of suspicion. *The sign says*

"COMING SOON" after all.

He put the truck back into gear and drove toward home, the top of the tent and its flag waving at him in the rear-view mirror long after he thought they should've been out of view.

When they were young, there were two churches in town: the one where the old white folks went and the one where everyone else went. The white folks' church was right off the town square, a historic building anchoring other historic buildings. It had a Saturday evening service, two Sunday morning services, and a Wednesday evening potluck. It rang bells every day at noon and then again at sunset, but otherwise, it was silent and empty. The old white folks didn't seem to need church any more than that.

The other church—that went through half a dozen names during their childhood before finally settling on Iglesia Nueva Creación—was out by the factory that packaged frozen popsicles and various brands of puddings. It was in a commercial garage that had been repurposed back before either of their families got there, with concrete floors and an altar built up with discarded plywood and wooden pallets. The insulation and plumbing were never really up to code, so the toilets worked as often as they didn't, and it was extra layers in the winter and propped-open doors and windows in the summer.

There were services twice a day during the week, before and after work, and then services that merged into meals and fellowships for most of the day on the weekends. Drew's mother and his aunts spent most of their free time there, and, despite his protests, he had to attend at least one service a week until his homework and the landscaping jobs got to be too much.

"Ah, mijo, school is important, but so is your soul," his mother had argued at first, simmering two pots of menudo—one for the family and one for the church.

His father set the bowls and silverware out on their small kitchen table. "I'm sure God sees Andrés's heart wherever he is, right cariño?"

"Of course." His mother waved off the bait. "But God likes to see his children at home sometimes, too."

In the end, Drew had said that he'd go when he could, but most mornings, his mother didn't seem to have the heart to wake him out of his brief sleep. Instead, she'd go and light an extra candle for him, which she only reminded him of when she was really irritated with him.

When they'd first met, Max didn't go to church. His parents weren't religious, or at least weren't any kind of religious that Drew recognized. They'd burn sticks of incense and wrap gifts in red paper and set out a table full of food that no one ate, and it reminded Drew of the ofrenda his family set up before Halloween each year that was covered in candles and colorful papel picado and burning copal. Sometimes, he'd sneak a pan de muerto for Max and get an IOU for half a mooncake come winter.

Max's mother left during their first year of high school; she drove her car out of the driveway one morning and never came back. Sent a letter to Max along with the divorce papers, but he'd never told Drew what it said. And Drew hadn't asked.

The whole town ran with rumors when most of them hadn't even bothered to talk to Max's mother before she'd gone, and Drew didn't want to add to the sideshow. He shot his aunts dark look when they gossiped over afternoon coffee and told his cousins to shut up if they started to ask too many questions.

It lasted a season, then another scandal hit that wiped it clean from everyone's minds. A councilperson's sister who crashed her car into the library after one too many beers at the local happy hour, or the school cafeteria serving rancid food, or something like that. Drew couldn't remember.

Several more scandals came and went by the time Max's father announced he was getting remarried to one of the nice local ladies who had brought him pans of lasagna and biscuits and gravy to make sure he got good, home-cooked meals without his wife around to make them. She cleared out the incense holders and money plants, and there were no more tables of food left out for Max's ancestors around the holidays.

Instead, she went to the old white church every Sunday, like she and her family always had. Sometimes, Max and his father joined her.

"What's it like?" Drew asked him as they sped through the town square on their secondhand bikes.

"They're all very polite," Max answered without looking back at him. "She says it's godly to welcome non-believers into the fold."

"But, like, do you want to go into the… fold?" Drew skidded but caught himself before he fell.

Max shrugged his shoulders, balanced evenly on his bike. "I don't think what I want really matters to your God."

Drew stopped pedaling for a moment, lost his rhythm, and tripped to a stop. Something itched at the bottom of his brain, something about his mother's—*his*—God not caring about what he wanted. What his best friend wanted. Only caring that they believed. That they obeyed, no matter what it cost them.

Max pulled his brakes and looked over his shoulder, confusion twisting all the delicate features of his face.

Drew's eyes dropped, suddenly embarrassed and not sure why.

"Got some rocks stuck in my treads, is all." He kicked his front tire for emphasis then sped off without waiting for Max to catch up with him.

The first snow came about a week before Christmas, settling like a hush over the town. Shovels and plows came out, but it wasn't more than a couple of inches, so the job was quick. Main streets and sidewalks were cleared, but unused lots and back roads were left for folks to make their own way. A jumble of footprints crisscrossed between front doors like trails of breadcrumbs that mapped out comings and goings.

Crisp, undisturbed yards and walkways stood out, raising eyebrows and setting off murmurs and that gave Drew an idea. He laced up his thickest boots and trudged out to the crossing and the tent for the first time since he'd seen the flag. The tracks were cleared, with gray slush piled around them, but otherwise, the ground was smooth and clean. No footprints, human or otherwise, just a hazy white expanse all the way to the far tree line with only dead stalks poking out and breaking up the sweep of snow.

The tent rose out of the bright, untouched ground like a monument. As Drew approached it, he could tell for sure that it'd gotten bigger. It'd been just a few inches taller than him when he'd first stood by it; now, it was almost double his height, with two smaller tents jutting out the back of it. The first flag was now flanked by two others, and he could see that they were black with haphazard white designs that seemed to rearrange themselves like an inkblot test with each new gust they caught.

The front flap was still tied shut, but one of the top ties had unknotted. Drew didn't know if that'd been the wind or something with more purpose, but it hung open like an invitation. If he stood on his tiptoes and stretched up as far as he could, he'd probably be able to grab the next one down and pull the knot loose.

He reached up but stopped short. Didn't know why, something just didn't want him to pull. What that something was—the mysterious owners who probably wouldn't appreciate trespassers, his own gut intuition, or maybe the tent itself—Drew couldn't say. He pulled his hand back but leaned in, trying to hear if there was anything waiting for him on the other side.

It was still—the rustle of the tent, the rush of the wind, the crunch of the snow beneath his boots. He could hear his own breath puffing out into the winter cold, could feel his own blood pumping in his numb ears.

He should've worn a hat.

Just as he was about to turn around and hustle his way home, something beyond the flap shifted. Something exhaled, then whispered but got muffled in the canvas. Something started to hum, a tune that Drew knew but couldn't place. Something swayed, and, although Drew couldn't see it, he knew it was miming his own steps as he backed away.

He followed the single set of prints he'd made until it joined with others and got lost in the town traffic.

That night, he didn't sleep much, but when he did, he dreamed that he and Max were sitting in the first pew of the old white church, listening to a choir of nice town ladies sing about how merciful their god was.

Drew had girlfriends, starting with the classmate he'd asked to their fourth-grade spring dance. He had girlfriends who he kissed and fooled around a little with, though nothing that'd get a lecture from his father or—even worse—his mother. He had girlfriends to kill time with, to brag about during pickup soccer, to give his uncles something to tease him about other than how little he could carry and how bad his Spanish was.

He had girlfriends because that was what teenage boys were supposed to do. Except for Max, who never had any girlfriends.

"I don't get it," Drew told him one afternoon as they practiced soccer drills after school. "Why'd you say no to Maggie?"

Max blocked him from a shot. "I don't like her like that. It's not that hard to get."

Drew recovered and went for a goal, but it swung wide. "Yeah, but that's what you always say. You can't not like any of these girls that way."

"Why not?" Max pushed him to get the ball, hands gentle on his back. "Should I lie and lead them on? Would that make me a good boyfriend?"

"No." Drew carried the ball to the corner. "But maybe you just don't know that you like them yet? Maybe you'd like them if you went out with them?"

"Or maybe I wouldn't." Max crossed his arms and huffed. "You sound like my stepmom."

Drew winced, deflecting that comment with a long kick.

"I just—" Drew ran to get the ball but was too slow. "If you had a girlfriend, then we could double date and hang out even more."

Max stole the ball and dribbled it for a few seconds. "Do we need girlfriends to hang out more?"

"No." Drew paused, let the ball dance between Max's feet. "But it would just make it easier, right?"

"Easier than what?" Max passed the ball.

It stopped in front of Drew, but he didn't bring it in.

"Easier than explaining why we're always just hanging out together. Alone." Drew scuffed the grass with his cleats. "Folks might get the wrong idea, you know?"

Max stood still, fists clenching and unclenching. He didn't ask what Drew meant, who these folks were, or what kind of wrong ideas they might be getting.

His head was down, not looking at Drew anymore.

"Sure, yeah," he finally muttered. "Whatever."

Max was upset; a random stranger in the park could've figured out as much. And Drew wasn't a random stranger—even though, at times like this, he felt like he'd lost a key to a door he'd walked through a million times before. A door that should've been unlocked to him, and he didn't quite understand why it wasn't.

"C'mon Max, what's up with y—" Drew started but was cut off by Max swiping the ball away from him and running toward the goal.

And that was it, the end of the conversation. Max beat him easy that day, and when the sky started to streak like fire, they drifted off home. After a few minutes of bumping elbows, Drew slung an arm across Max's shoulder, loose and casual like he'd done on most of their walks home over the years. He felt Max go stiff like he'd just been stung—by a wasp, not a bee—then he shrugged Drew's arm off and put a few extra inches between them.

They walked the rest of the way in a jittery silence, up to the street where Max turned left and Drew went right.

They didn't talk about it again. Any of it. But Drew stopped asking about girlfriends, and Max initiated high-fives where there used to be hugs, and they stopped leaning, brushing, reaching for each other like they had before. Drew didn't even realize they'd been doing it until they stopped. Didn't even know he had something to miss until it was gone.

But it didn't matter how far apart they stood, how rarely they touched each other. It didn't matter how little time they spent together—*alone*—after that. The wrong idea was still out there, like a patch of bull thistle too spiny to pull out. The locker room jokes, the hallway looks, the lunchroom rumors. About them, but more often about Max. About the sports he didn't care about, and the poetry club he joined. About the clothes he wore and his smooth skin and how that wasn't the way a boy was supposed to look. About the girls he turned down for dates but agreed to be friends with. About who he watched when he thought no one else was looking.

Drew tried to defend him, tried to discredit and dismiss, but it seemed to do more harm than good.

Of course you'd try to protect your boyfriend, the wrong idea would sneer.

Still, he tried his best until one day after an especially nasty gym class when Max cornered him by the equipment closet.

"Stop it, Drew," Max hissed as they shoved the cracked mats into the room.

"Stop what?" Drew hoisted two at a time, and they hit the back wall with a dull smack.

"All of this," Max ground out. "Trying to be a white knight, fighting my battles for me. I don't need it."

Drew stopped, dropped a mat. "I'm just trying to help."

"Yeah, well, don't bother." Max kicked the dropped mat into the closet and pulled the door shut.

Drew wanted to scream at him, wanted to curse and shout and ask why he was being such a dick about this. And not just about this. He wanted to take a swing at him, wanted to knock some sense back into him before someone else took the chance. He wanted to grab him, wanted to pull him back and make him explain what the hell was going on with him. With them.

He wanted to go after him, wanted to tell him: *Don't go. Just stay here a little longer with me.*

After that, Drew started dreaming of knocking on locked doors and hearing nothing but a hollow echo behind them.

Christmas came and went in a blur of cooking and singing and arguing and drinking. His family hopped from house to house to house, aunts to uncles to cousins and back around again, until everyone was so sick of each other that they didn't want to visit again until Easter. His mother usually nagged him to go to a Christmas Eve service, but this year, she let it slide.

Probably because of Max. The thought sloshed around, sour with the alcohol in his brain.

He sat out in the garage of his youngest uncle's house on a wobbly lawn chair, plastic cup filled with whatever his family had dumped into a large bowl and called Christmas Punch. He couldn't drink at the local bars, at least not legally, but his parents made an exception for the holidays.

The garage door was halfway open, and a space heater was plugged in right near his feet. He watched the snowflakes fall like feathers, light and soft without any wind to churn them around.

"What're you doing out here?" His sister's voice cut through the haze just on the edge of drunk. "The cousins want to play lotería."

Drew didn't answer, just shrugged and took another gulp of punch.

"This is healthy," she snorted.

When that didn't get a response, she walked over to the chair and put a hand on the back of it.

"Do you want to talk about it?"

Drew blinked at how white the snow was, even in the dark. "Talk about what?"

His sister shifted her weight onto her other foot. "About whatever's going on with you."

The words poured into Drew's mind, and he swam around in them. Whatever was going on.

With him.

They were supposed to go to college in the fall. They'd decided to take a year off, earn some money, get some work experience. Take a road trip. Drew had planned it for the late spring—cutting down through Kentucky and Tennessee, hitting Nashville before heading into the Great Smokies. Stopping at Pigeon Forge to see Dollywood and winding through the Blue

Ridge Parkway, then driving straight through until they hit the Outer Banks. They'd stand in the ocean together, see if it ebbed different from the Great Lakes.

They'd get Nashville hot chicken and Carolina barbeque and soft-shell crab in Ocracoke. They'd drive Drew's dad's old four door—the one he'd kept in their garage for years because it still ran well enough and he never knew when he might need it again—and stay at little mom-and-pop road motels with shag carpets and vintage knickknacks. Maybe drive through a night or two, or pull off and sleep in rest stop parking lots to save some cash.

It was supposed to be their big adventure before heading out into the world. Not the end, just a turn in the road. Time together, just the two of them, to get back to where they'd been. Move past all the whispers and misunderstandings. Say what needed to be said. Figure out who they were with each other now.

Drew was gonna tell him. Was gonna surprise him at Christmas with the itinerary and the money he'd saved up landscaping over the past two years. And Max would've been confused, flustered. But then a warm flush would creep up his neck and across his cheeks, and he'd smile at Drew like he did when they were dumb kids, watching the passenger trains whizz by.

They were supposed to be okay. Here. Together.

"I wonder when the rest of the circus will come," he said instead. "It's been more than a month now since that tent went up."

"What tent?" His sister's hand moved to his shoulder, squeezed like she was trying to keep him from slipping away.

He turned to look up at her. "The tent out by the railroad crossing. The only tent in town."

Her eyebrows knotted together, and her lips twisted, like what he'd said had tasted bitter.

"There's no tent out by the railroad crossing," she said, slow and deliberate. "I mean, I haven't seen any tent out there, and I just drove past it last week."

Drew paused, closed his eyes. Tried to clear the fuzzy edges of his thoughts.

He hadn't been out to the tent since before Christmas, and it was almost New Year's. Maybe they'd packed up; after a month of nothing, maybe they'd figured this was a dead stop for a circus. Or maybe the rest of their troupe had gotten stuck somewhere else, and they'd decided to go meet up with them. Or maybe some of the locals had gotten fed up with an unoccupied tent being up for weeks and took it down themselves. Maybe it'd been a prank—a strange, kind of pointless one—done by some kids with too much time on their hands.

For some reason, Drew was sad that it was gone.

"Hey." His sister poked him, a bite of alarm in her voice. "Are you sure you saw a tent out there?"

He shook his head and smiled, like maybe it'd all just been a silly joke. "Huh, I guess not."

On a Tuesday morning, the first Tuesday morning after Thanksgiving, Max texted him.

Meet me at the old sugar maple?

North of town—following drainage ditches that lined gravel farm roads running away from I-88—there were spider-leg creeks that burrowed through crop soil and under asphalt bridges. Out west they fed into the churning Rock River, but here they were thin and narrow and dry as many months as not. Anchored alongside one creek bed was a broad, weathered sugar maple that rose like a pillar out of the flat stretch of Midwestern earth. It hung heavy with thick green shade in spring and summer then caught fire in September, bright leaves rustling like flames before falling. Even in the winter with nothing but its naked dark bark, it still held its presence against the snow drifts and biting winds.

It'd been a marker of sorts for them growing up, a boundary line between far and too far. Back when their boundaries weren't so blurry. It was a guidepost when they lost track of where they were, which way was home. As long as they could see the old sugar maple, they knew they'd be able to find their way back.

They hadn't met out there in years; Drew couldn't even remember the last time he'd driven past it. His work routes never took him up that way, and he didn't have any other reason to go out there. No one to go out there with—not these days, when he and Max barely spoke to one another.

He'd checked and double-checked the message but didn't answer it. He had a bad feeling, a gut twist like something was about to happen.

Maybe Max was gonna tell him that he'd decided to go somewhere else for college, another state where they'd get to see each other once a year if he came back over the summer. Drew didn't have money for more than a local community college, or a state school if he could get a scholarship. He had to be nearby to help with the family business anyway. Max had talked about Rockford or DeKalb or Davenport, maybe even Chicago—nothing more than a couple of hours away. But maybe that'd changed.

Maybe he was gonna tell Drew about something he'd been hiding, some terrible secret that'd made him act the way he'd been acting. Something that would explain away the swampy distance that was festering between them. Maybe it was something Drew wouldn't want to hear, or something that Max was afraid would hurt him. It'd be a hard conversation either way, and one that Drew wasn't sure he was up to right after the holiday.

Or maybe he was just going to cut it off between them. Their history, their friendship, their future. Maybe this was a breakup text, and Drew knew he wasn't up for that.

So he'd pushed it aside, flipped through TV channels that had nothing worth watching, and eventually fallen asleep on the living room couch. He didn't wake up until his father called him into the kitchen to help set up for dinner.

Drew's father was still carving turkey scraps off the bone when the phone in their cramped kitchen rang.

"Get it," his father had said without looking up. "My hands are all greasy."

Drew picked it up on the third ring.

It was Max's dad, his accent folded carefully around the corners of his voice. Drew knew he sounded off but couldn't quite place it. Almost too formal, like he was making a business call instead of talking to his teenage son's best friend.

"I'm sorry," he said, tone even like a knife. "It's about Max."

The holiday flurries turned into a bona fide winter storm that snowed the town in for the first week of the new year. Drew kept himself busy inside, downloading college applications that he wasn't gonna fill out. Reading through the requirements for places he wouldn't go, like Boston and San Diego. Zooming in and out of maps and tracing how he'd get to those places he'd never go, which highways to take and which exits to pull off of along the way.

He searched for:

acetaminophen overdose accidental
tylenol cough syrup alcohol how long death
suicide signs and reasons

He searched for:

lgbt chinese culture
what happens to souls in china religion
chinese heaven and chinese hell

He searched for:

what if my best friend is gay

He searched for *in love with best friend* but closed the browser before the results loaded.

After they finally dug out from the storm, Drew went for a walk. He had to get out of the house, crawl out of his brain and do something—anything—that he didn't have to think about.

"Where are you going, mijo?" his mother asked as he headed for the door.

Drew shrugged. "Just taking a walk."

The air was frigid, biting his face as he made his way down the street. But it was still, no wind whipping through to give it teeth. He shuffled along, directionless, kicking chunks of snow with each dig of the toe of his boots.

Eventually, he ended up at the end of town, out past where the Union Pacific and Burlington Northern Santa Fe lines crossed. A cluster of several white tents were pitched up, a few probably too close to the tracks, and the largest one stretched tall and wide like the congregational hall of the white folks' church. The same inkblot flags flew above it; they dotted the other tents now, too. No footprints in the snow, no trailers or cars parked out behind, no illumination except from the washed-out sun straining through the gray winter clouds.

Drew stared at the tents, blinked over and over, expecting them to disappear each time he opened his eyes again. They never did.

No voices came from the tents, but Drew thought he could hear a pull of something tinny and melodic. Not quite a song—more like the tune that announced an ice cream truck a few streets away. Mechanical and repetitive and strangely hypnotic. Like a memory that wouldn't quite come into focus.

The knots that had kept the front flap of the big tent shut were untied now, hanging limp. Like an invitation. Like permission.

Drew took a step closer, then another. He reached out and slid his fingers into the open seam, then pulled the flap back in one swift, violent move.

It was dark inside. Pitch black. Void of anything—but Drew could feel it moving, heaving and twisting and creaking. His body was rigid, tight, and sparking, screaming at him to close the flap and leave it be. Run and not look back, never look back.

But he couldn't stop himself. He had to know.

He pushed in and hit resistance like a curtain wound with thick, sticky webs. He clawed through it, choked on the threads tightening around his neck and stuffing their way down his throat. His wrists and ankles were tangled; he lost traction on the ground and started to thrash, bone-chilled with panic. The blackness was swallowing him whole.

Suddenly, a sliver of light cut through; he shut his eyes against the burn. Something pulled him, or loosened the dark around him, and he was spit out onto a dusty ground. He frantically tore at the webs he could feel still clinging to him but found nothing, not even broken strands.

When he finally looked up, he realized that he was in the middle of a circus ring. Rows of wooden bleachers lined the edges in one continuous circle, but they were empty. The flap was gone, sealed up and blocked off somewhere behind the seats. There was no way out.

In front of him, anchored in the middle of the dirt floor, was a collection of junk—spare lumber, pipes, wires, cuts of fencing, and jagged tears of tarp—molded into the shape of a tree. Wide, sturdy trunk building up to curls of branches that almost reached the top of the tent.

Sitting on one of the far branches, legs dangling, someone was watching him. Drew couldn't quite make out the face in the shadows, but the shape felt familiar.

"Hello?" Drew called out, his voice raspy from the smothering darkness.

The figure stiffened, then jumped down onto the ground. Made its way toward Drew, slow like an oil spill.

"You came."

Drew recognized the voice before he recognized the face. Blood pounded in his ears, and ice seeped into his veins. He watched the figure come closer, eyes wide open and terrified of what would happen if he closed them.

"Max?" He whispered it, not sure if he was allowed to ask.

The figure stopped in front of him. He looked a little sallow, like he hadn't been out in the sun for a while, and his clothing hung loose on his body. Drew wondered if he'd been eating enough, then shook the thought out of his head.

Ghosts don't eat.

That was what this had to be, of course. A ghost, or maybe a hallucination. Maybe he'd tripped and fallen in the dark, and this was just his mind drifting through a blackout. Or a coma. Maybe his body was lying unconscious inside an empty, dark tent, where no one would think to look for him until it was too late.

"You came," Max repeated, lips softening into a small smile. "I've been waiting for you."

Max's eyes were sweet and dark like they'd always been. His cheeks flushed like there was still blood in them as he pulled at the worn cuffs on his sweater. Almost like he was shy, embarrassed to see Drew here.

Just my dying brain playing tricks on me.

"At the old sugar maple, right?" Max closed in, near enough to feel the breath that shouldn't have been coming from his mouth. "I knew you'd find your way."

Drew's stomach lurched, his skin itched, a shiver crawled up his spine and stroked the back of his neck. This wasn't right, couldn't be right. He had to wake up, had to scream out, had to drag himself back—

A gentle, warm hand cupped his cheek, wiped away the hot, wet streaks that were running down his face.

He didn't know he'd been crying.

Max's hand was firm, solid as the ground beneath their feet. Not like any ghost Drew'd ever imagined.

This was wrong. A lie, a trick, a trap. It had to be.

Drew leaned into the warmth and let out a sob that echoed hollow off the canvas walls.

"I-I'm sorry," he sputtered out. "I'm sorry, Max, I'm so sorry."

"Shh," Max soothed him, tracing tiny circles under Drew's eye with his thumb. "It's okay. You're here now and that's all that matters, right?"

Drew nodded, watched everything go blurry with his tears. He was choking again, heaving with the blackness that pulsed just around the edges of his vision. It was hungry, waiting to swallow him if he stepped back into it.

Max's hand fell from his face, traced down his neck and his shoulder and his arm, stopped at his wrist. Gripped Drew tight and led him to the shade of the junk tree.

And Drew went, without a struggle or a fight. Went willing and calm, with the void lapping at his heels.

Drew followed Max without saying another word, silent as the grave.

The Tuesday after Drew disappeared, his parents drove out to the county sheriff's office to file a missing persons report. His aunts and uncles went door to door asking if anyone had seen him, while his cousins stapled posters with his smiling graduation photo to every telephone pole in town.

And out past where the Union Pacific and Burlington Northern Santa Fe lines crossed, the cluster of tents was gone. They left nothing—not even an outline of flattened weeds and snowless earth—behind.

CIRCUS IN THE SKY

LISA TOOHEY

Kaleigh sighed as she cleaned the muck out of Rooter's stall for the last time. She brushed the bangs away from her eyes, grimacing as she realized that all she'd done was spread more dirt over her face. Rooter, the anteater-like creature, had not been happy unless they'd half-filled the enclosure with dirt; keeping it sanitary had been the hardest part of looking after the strange creature. He'd been cute, for all that he'd smelled, and easy to work with. The minor sniffles he'd developed at Tera4 had turned serious, and the executive decision from the Ringmaster had come down. In the confines of a spaceship, any illness could spread fast. No one wanted to leave something to spread to the other animals—or worse, the humans.

Rooter had been old, she reminded herself. Arthritic in his hips, barely able to perform, and, as the Ringmaster had told her before, anyone that couldn't work on his ship didn't belong on his ship. She'd done the lethal injection herself, since her boss, the Beast Master, wouldn't have bothered with humane euthanasia. He preferred older, cheaper methods. The rest of his underlings followed his lead. Kaleigh was alone in truly caring about the creatures under their charge.

She scraped the last of the muck out of her wheelbarrow, dumping it into the waste recycler at the end of the aisle of pens. Their plexiglass fronts exposed the array of exotic and alien creatures. The Beast Hold was the second biggest room on the ship, after the Big Top. Rows of square pens, interrupted only by the training ring in the center of the room. Kaleigh set about sanitizing the enclosure. Making sure her water was hot enough to sterilize. The hot water stung her hands, but at least she was less dirty, too.

The Ringmaster had already found a replacement for Rooter. The new creature would be arriving soon, and everything had to be perfect for his precious new specimen. Since she'd made the modifications to Rooter's stall to make him more comfortable, it was up to her to undo those changes before the newest creature arrived.

Kaleigh had been born on the ship, always living among the stars, traveling endlessly through them instead of under them on a planet. She'd known no other life. As the daughter of two of the most successful acts, everyone had expected her to develop an act of her own. To take to the circus life with ease and grace. She might have looked like her slender mother but wasn't like her at all; she had no head for spinning through zero-g in acrobatic air dance, and while she had her father's dark eyes, she hadn't inherited his daredevil skills; he thrilled his audiences with death-defying falls through artificial gravity.

With no act of her own, the Ringmaster had found her something else to do: She worked under the tyranny of the Beast Master. It hadn't been her first choice. Nor was she convinced that it was her only option in life. She'd spent her time with the animals learning more than just how to cajole them into performing. On the long days journeying between space stations, she'd researched all she could about the creatures under her care. Kaleigh wasn't a talented performer, but she didn't consider herself a shirker. Everyone on the ship had a job, and in time, she had come to love her beasts. She had begun implementing little changes, making her animals happier and more adjusted to space, like the dirt in Rooter's enclosure. As an Aereosnophlepod, he would have spent most of his natural life below ground. The inability to dig had had an adverse effect on his mental and even physical health. The Beast Master tolerated her little ecological "upgrades" as long as the animals continued to perform for her. Her changes worked; her creatures were the best behaved and the best performers.

She dreamed, though, of leaving the circus behind and experiencing these creatures in their natural habitats, of observing and adding to the scant information known about so many of these species that had been ripped from their homes for the entertainment of the masses. Somehow, seeing them like this made the animals less… alive.

Kaleigh was determined that someday, she would see them as they were supposed to be: free.

"Bring it this way. Careful now, the tranquilizer will be wearing off."

Kaleigh stepped out of the enclosure and moved out of the way. All her charges were restless as the new animal was brought in. She could hear the big insect across the aisle clicking its feelers. She buried her instant frustration; it had taken her months to find the perfect neighbors for her charges, and it looked like all that work was about to be undone.

Six of the circus's strongmen half-carried and half-dragged a bear-like creature. For a moment, Kaleigh thought it might be a rare polar bear from Earth, the original home planet, but a second glance changed her assessment. This creature's long, silky fur was silver, not white, and its forearms were oddly long and slender for its large body. Its small head was waving from side to side with its black nose sniffing the air. It seemed alert, though it didn't resist its captors at all. Its sheer size intimidated her.

The men threw the beast unceremoniously into its new prison and quickly moved off. They were all like that, spending the least amount of time with their charges as possible. It made Kaleigh sick to think of how little anyone cared for these living beings.

The Beast Master hovered over his newest possession, not out of concern, but out of glee. A rare and unusual creature would bring big crowds.

"Kaleigh!" He barked for her.

"Yes, sir?" she asked, coming to join him at the glass door that fronted the cage. She always felt like a midget standing next the almost seven-foot-tall man, even though at 5'6" she really wasn't that short for a girl.

"Ever seen one before?" He didn't glance away from the semi-conscious creature.

"No, sir," she said. She'd never seen anything like it. The more she examined the creature, the more impressed she became. The beast was massive, yet somehow, she knew it was more than just a brainless carnivore.

"It's a Kogen. Extremely rare, extremely dangerous. Its home planet has a danger rating of eight. Almost no expeditions set foot there. Too many casualties. Do your thing: Figure out what it likes, and figure out how you're going to make it perform."

He turned and walked away, whistling a tune. The Beast Master didn't bother to glance back at the rude face she was making. Which was probably for the best; he had a short fuse and a heavy hand. It was good he was happy, but if she couldn't figure this beast out, that mood would sour fast. Then either she or this strange creature would get the brunt of it. Being different only made Kaleigh more of a target to the intolerant drunkard. Being better with the animals than him made her his favorite target.

"I have got to get out of this place." She stared into the cage. The creature, which had been lying prone on the floor, sat up. It looked very bear-like with those long paws tucked between its legs and that tiny nose sniffing about. It didn't look all that dangerous curled into a ball like that.

"Well, Mr. Kogen, what would you like to eat?"

The silver-furred creature turned to stare at her. Its dark eyes met hers, and an incredible craving for blueberries—or at least something that resembled blueberries—hit her. She was halfway to the circus's pantry before she could get the image out of her mind. She stopped in the middle of the narrow metal hallway, causing a minor traffic jam. A crew member shoved her roughly from behind. Startled, Kaleigh moved to the side and tried to figure out why she'd rushed out of the hold in the first place. She was never impulsive when it came to her creatures.

"Well, it does look like it could be an omnivore—blunt claws, smaller fangs," she reasoned to herself, drawing on her knowledge of other animals. "Fresh fruit is a natural thought. I should mix it up, though. Just straight fruit doesn't make a balanced diet."

Kaleigh turned back to the Beast Hold for the wheelbarrow she used when feeding the larger creatures before heading to the storeroom. She lined the bottom with less perishable items, making sure to take from the stocks that had excess. The Ringmaster and Beast Master were okay with her special diet plans for each animal, but only if it didn't affect any person's eating habits. More often than she liked, their limited pantry meant the circus beasts were fed leftovers and scraps. Unsure of the creature's diet, she grabbed a little bit of everything, even some of the more processed foods she normally avoided for her creatures, like bread and cheese.

She trundled her full wheelbarrow back. The Kogen was still sitting in the same position. Not knowing anything about the creature, Kaleigh decided to use the small window built into the enclosure wall to feel her new charge instead of entering the pen. Her boss had said it was a dangerous beast. She giggled as the Kogen approached on all fours. It reminded her a bit of a cross between a big monkey and a bear when it walked. For its size, it seemed graceful, although she could already tell the enclosure was much too small for the kind of exercise the creature would need. The creature seemed unsure on the metal floor and shuffled instead of using a longer, more open gait. Its slender nose stuck through the round window, smelling her barrow. She once again pictured the strange berries.

"I brought you a bit of everything to try, Mr. Kogen." Kaleigh tried to speak to the animals as much as possible when she worked with or fed them. Her reading had told her that it would make a positive connection between herself and them.

The Kogen used its long arms to gracefully accept each item she pushed through the hole with a dexterity that surprised and pleased her. It sniffed them, and then set them aside. It had long, dull claws on its paws and no opposable thumbs. She noticed, though, that it used its dewclaws quite effectively. When the barrow was empty, she shut the little porthole window and retrieved her tablet from her locker at the entrance to the Beast Hold. The Kogen had returned to its sitting position in the center of the pen, its pile of food untouched beside it.

Kaleigh frowned and opened up her tablet. It was unlikely they were close enough to a hypernet node to download anything, but she had a lot of books on her tablet already. If she was lucky, something might tell her about her new charge. The Beast Master would not be happy with her if the thing wouldn't eat.

She leaned back across the aisle and kept one eye on the Kogen as she scrolled through her tablet. It sat perfectly still, black eyes fixed on her. Every now and then, its nose twitched, and Kaleigh hoped that meant something she'd offered it was appealing.

Her mind kept returning to the image of that strange fruit, and it made her research difficult. It wasn't even a fruit she could name, so she couldn't fathom why was she kept thinking about it. It had to be connected to the Kogen somehow. It had been after the beast arrived that the image had embedded itself in her mind. She finally connected the dots.

"I don't have any berries like that," she said angrily, looking up from her tablet and meeting the beast's gaze solidly.

It huffed and reached for the grapes. The image faded from her mind, and she was finally able to focus. There was not a single reference in all of her books to a Kogen. She couldn't even figure out what planet it came from.

"You're a mystery, Mr. Kogen," she said finally. "I'm going to have to wait until we're in range of a node to learn more about you, it seems."

It crooked its head to the side when she spoke. Kaleigh sighed and returned her gaze to the tablet. The time in the top left-hand corner told her just how "late" it was now. Here on the ship, there was no true day or night. Most of the performers had secondary duties, working in shifts to keep the giant circus ship running smoothly, supporting the crew of mechanics and pilots. The Ringmaster was cheap; he kept his crew to a minimum. She was used to adjusting her internal clock for whatever spaceport or planet they happened to land on.

The idea crossed her mind to return to her parents' quarters and catch a few hours of sleep, but she knew if she didn't, no one would care. It wasn't like she could get into much trouble trapped on the ship. They knew she would turn up eventually. She hated her cramped little berth in their cramped little quarters. She also hated the endless bickering between them, or worse, the lectures when they joined sides to insist that she try to be a performer like them. So, like she so often did, Kaleigh just didn't go back, but stayed in the Beast Hold instead.

An image drifted across her mind, pushing back the unhappy thoughts of her complicated family. The sensation reminded her of a bad radio signal at first, all choppy and distorted, but as the image in her mind cleared, it became more and more real. She stood on an endless plain, and the moon high in the sky turned the rippling grasses silver in the night. A soft breeze blew across her face—sweet fresh air, so unlike the stagnant recycled air of space stations and ships. The soft ground was cool under her bare feet. Her hands ran across the soft tops of the grasses. She could smell damp earth as if it had rained recently, but the sky was clear now. Thousands of stars gleamed in the endless sky above her. No walls in sight. No limits on her world. The sense of freedom swept over Kaleigh.

The Kogen crooned, a little song rising and falling like the wind in the field. The song bled into the vision of the endless plain until she couldn't separate the two anymore, and it carried her away into a peaceful sleep…

The sound of shift change woke Kaleigh. The crew that worked in the engineering room tromped right past the Beast Hold on their way back to the crew quarters. Nothing could sleep through the avalanche of noise that created. The metal corridor reverberated and echoed into the Beast Hold. All around her, she could hear animals complain as the sound disturbed them. She took a peek at the Kogen, which had curled up in a corner of its pen, the food almost completely untouched. Despite sleeping on the cold metal floor, she felt somehow more relaxed than she would have sleeping in a bed.

"I'll be back soon, Mr. Kogen," she whispered. Her friend Frank performed with the clowns during shows, but during flights, he was part of the comms and navigation team. His shift should just be starting, and Kaleigh needed to know when they'd be passing the next hypernet node.

The hallway outside the Beast Hold was dimly lit. Most of the crew had grown up on the ship and could navigate it in pitch blackness. A childhood of exploring the twisting corridors had left them all with an innate ability to find their way. No one ever complained about the poor lighting. The ship was an unintentional maze, designed around its dual purpose of spaceship and circus tent. Most of the larger useable areas had been devoted to the circus, and the ship's primary functions came next. Things like living quarters came last, and people had found some interesting nooks to set up their homes in.

Kaleigh slipped into the communications room, tucked into the highest reaches of the ship, above the Big Top. It was a long, narrow space lined with workstations. The dim space was lit almost entirely by the light from their terminal screens. Several crewmembers murmured into their microphones, heavy headsets clamped over their ears. She had no idea why there had to be more than one comms operator at any time, but like with many other systems on the ship, she had never really bothered to find out. Caring for the beasts was one of the few jobs on the ship that didn't stop between shows. She spied her friend's blond mop of hair sitting near the far wall and noticed the seat next to him was unoccupied.

Kaleigh slipped into the chair and waited for him to finish his call.

"Hey, Kally-Bally." Frank tousled her hair affectionately. He was a good eight years older than her and always treated her more like a little sister than anything else. "How's the new charge?"

She smiled. Comms guys always knew the gossip before anyone else. "He's more interesting than Rooter, but I have no idea with this one. None of the books in my library or the ship's library have been any help. I was just wondering when we'd be in range of a node."

He checked the screen in front of him, scrolling across a star chart.

"We won't encounter another node until we're within striking range of Keptermine Station. About a week."

Kaleigh frowned. Keptermine was a big station. Her boss might want the Kogen to perform… but she couldn't even get it to eat right now.

"You all right there?"

"Yeah. Worried about my new beastie, but thanks for the help, Frank."

"Any time, kiddo. I gotta get back to work, but maybe I'll drop by and see the beast after my shift."

Kaleigh's hands trembled as she reentered the Beast Hold, a bit scared that something had gone wrong with her beast. A glance showed no change. She tried to ignore the Kogen as she cared for the rest of her charges.

Moving back and forth between the food storage and each pen, she could tell the other beast "tamers" had been in to feed their own charges while she was out. Once again, it looked like they'd done the least amount of work possible. None of them cared about their creatures like she did. They'd be back later today to train, but only if the Beast Master made them. On the whole, they were a lazy bunch. She fully expected at least one of them to get killed by their creatures soon. It was a callous thought, but a lot of the animals they worked with had been born wild. Putting them in a cage didn't make them easier to work with, a concept the boys didn't seem to understand. In contrast, there was never any concern that her charges would attack her. Kaleigh had a way with the beasts.

The Circus in the Sky had one of the best varieties of exotic animals, and she'd come to know them all well. Not just her own charges, though; she couldn't *not* help the other creatures. There were the dogs from the home world, tiny creatures that danced on their hind legs and yipped with joy when they saw her approach. She checked over the female. Kaleigh suspected the little creature was pregnant again. She'd told its handler, Keifer, that it was a bad idea to leave the male in the same cage, but he'd laughed her off.

The Beast Master would be mad when the female stopped performing to have her litter.

Some of the cages had become elaborate habitats, like the one for the Rockhawk from Cyrmore. She had screwed special dense foam to the walls, then shaped and painted it to make it look like a mountainside. The beast of prey had been bored nearly all the time, plucking at his own feathers until bald spots had appeared. Kaleigh had convinced the Ringmaster to set live traps for rodents and pests. The fierce bird now "hunted" its dinner to its heart's delight within its artificial environment.

When Kaleigh looked around, she could see her touch on almost every cage. She'd transformed them into little habitats for the creatures. There was the python-like snake with the amazing patterns on its scales, sunning on its rock under the heat lamp. It got live prey too; her books said it would just keep on growing as long as it had heat and food. The bigger the snake, the bigger the draw. The Beast Master had been happy about that tidbit. Kaleigh had been worried they would run out of rats at first, but then realized every spaceport they docked at re-infested the ship. Over in the next pen, the Franta Monkeys skittered around on their artificial tree, playing with the little toys she'd tied to its branches. They could be a noisy bunch, rambunctious but, with proper rewards, very tractable. She didn't understand why Sullivan had run into so much trouble with them. She figured he'd tried to force them and never thought to appeal to their inquisitive natures.

Finally, when she could avoid it no longer, Kaleigh returned to the Kogen. The food had been picked over, but she couldn't tell what might have been eaten. The Kogen was now sitting in the far corner of its bare enclosure, its face almost pressed against the back wall.

"Help me out here, Kogen," she said, exasperated. "My boss doesn't listen to excuses—he expects me to just magically discover how to care for you."

The Kogen turned to look at her, its long paws dragging on the floor as it twisted its hips. She couldn't get over the look of desolation in its little eyes. She racked her brain for something, anything, she could do to make the creature more comfortable, then her mind settled on her strange dream from the night before. The wide-open plain.

"Was that you?" she asked, not really believing it. "Was that your home?"

The beast crooned softly.

Kaleigh's fingers tapped against the glass for a moment while she thought.

"Okay, I got it, Mr. Kogen. I'll be right back, okay?" She thought back to the dream of the night before, sure that the Kogen had somehow, just like the berries, shown it to her. It seemed strange, but then again, her giant insect used prisms embedded in its chitinous shell to make rainbows. Her books said it used the electromagnetic spectrum as a form of communication. Telepathy wasn't much stranger than that.

She didn't wait to see if the creature responded; she took off running across the ship. People yelled as she dashed by them in the narrow hallways and scrambled up and down the narrow shafts, the strange passages that helped bypass the Big Top that filled so much of the ship. She worked her way deeper and lower into the ship, until she was underneath both the Big Top and the staging room below it.

Kaleigh was winded when she reached her destination. While the ship overall wasn't gleaming, one could see the neglect in this section more than any other. Few people bothered to tread all the way down here. Besides, none of the crew would bother to clean areas of the ship visitors would never see. It wasn't that circus folks were lazy; it was just that their public image was the only thing that mattered. Kaleigh had realized the analog between the maintenance of the ship and the psychology of the crew a long, long time ago.

A door opened, light spilling out into the narrow, poorly lit hallway and breaking her reverie. A dumpy-looking old woman waved to her from the doorway.

"Kaleigh, honey, I wasn't expecting you until next week. The vegetables aren't ready yet!"

Kaleigh approached and joined the woman in the far room. She breathed deeply, smelling the dirt and the fresh air made by the green growing things of the hydroponics lab. It was a surprisingly large room, but it still felt crowded by all the plants. Rows of raised beds filled the room. LED bulbs bathed it in bright light. The dripping water pipes added to the humidity. It was a pale comparison to an endless field, but perhaps something like this could make her Kogen happy.

"I have a new charge," Kaleigh said. "It's just a hunch, but I'm hoping something… nature-y in its enclosure might help it relax."

The hydroponics tech frowned a bit. "I don't have space for a lot of superfluous plants. Ringmaster's always telling me this place isn't profitable enough for the light and water that it uses."

"Good thing that carbon recyclation is so important, and those new carbon scrubbers cost so much more than they're worth! I don't need anything fancy—even something like grasses might help?"

The woman sighed. "Give me a few hours, and I'll get my assistant to bring it over to you. It won't be much!" she warned as Kaleigh hugged her.

"Thanks so much! I'll go get the pen ready!"

Kaleigh detoured on her way back to the Beast Hold. She'd need the master's permission to enter the Kogen's enclosure. He agreed grudgingly, but insisted on being present, his dart gun in hand. The plants were waiting in the aisle when they arrived, a mix of tall ferns and long, slender grasses. The

Kogen was still staring at the back wall.

"Be careful, girl," he told her, his finger already on the trigger of his tranquilizer.

Kaleigh took a deep breath. So far, the creature hadn't responded to their presence at all. She took a moment to close her eyes and focus on the green plants. *Stay still—these are for you.* She tried to think the thought as hard as she could at the Kogen. It seemed able to place images in her head, but could it read her mind, too?

She slid the glass doorway open just far enough for her to enter, dragging one of the bigger potted plants in behind her. Its bobbing ferns tickled the back of her neck. Quick as she could, Kaleigh tucked it into the corner closest to her and backed out again. The Kogen turned to stare at her but otherwise didn't move. She wondered if that was just its nature, or if it really could see the mental images she was trying to send it. She repeated the process several times until the aisle was empty and the Kogen was half hidden by the plants.

"Two more days, and then we need to start its training," the Beast Master warned her. "Ringmaster and I agree: By the time we reach our next show, we want to at least display the beast."

"That's only a week away, though! He's not even eating yet."

"I don't care if he eats as long as he'll perform! No freeloaders on this ship!"

"But sir!"

"You will do as you are told!" he yelled at her.

The sound of a meaty fist on the glass made them both jump. The Kogen had left its corner and was standing at its full height, looming over them. It splayed its long claws against the glass, its small nose pressed in, its teeth bared.

"Get on with ya!" the Beast Master roared at the Kogen, and then he turned to leave the hold.

After the man had disappeared into the corridor, the Kogen slumped back down. Its large paws brushed the green leaves of the ferns, and its little black nose sniffed them.

Kaleigh finally unfroze. "Were you… defending me?" She drew closer to the glass, watching, entranced, as it continued to examine the changes to its environment.

"I'll make it better," she promised. "With enough time, I can maybe even grow you a whole bed of grasses. If I can find a way to get the prop guys on my side, I could paint you a horizon, too. It won't be real, but I can at least make it close." She tried to picture the finished product in her mind for the creature, feeling silly, still not knowing if it could see things in her head, or just put them there.

Her belly growled. Almost a whole day had passed since she'd acquired the Kogen, and in all that time, she'd never stopped to eat. The Kogen stared at her for a moment, and its head once more cocked to the side. Then, it reached behind itself and grabbed the scuffed loaf of bread she'd given it the day before, obviously offering her the food. The image of berries came with the offering of bread, and Kaleigh laughed. She opened the porthole, and the creature slipped the bread through. It reminded her of a child playing a puzzle slot game as it tried to fit the loaf through the hole. It stuck its nose through the little porthole after fitting the bread through, snuffling the air outside its cell.

"So this is your new beast." Frank walked into the Beast Hold.

The Kogen withdrew its nose, and a silent snarl crossed its face. The fur on its back bristled, and she could see it hunch its shoulders forward.

"It's okay, Mr. Kogen," she murmured to it. "He's a friend." She turned to Frank. "Yeah, Frank, meet Mr. Kogen."

The Kogen dropped to all fours and began shuffling around its cage. It settled in behind one of the ferns, which provided a comical amount of cover for the large beast.

"Poor thing," Frank said. "I can't imagine being locked in a cage and stared at all day."

"Seriously?" Kaleigh said. "I've lived my entire life trapped on this ship while people come to stare at us at every stop."

"Still going to clear off as soon as you're eighteen, then? What's that, two more years?"

She sighed and leaned back against the pen's glass door. "As much as I hate it here, I can't imagine abandoning all my animals. No one else will look after them properly."

Frank shrugged his shoulders, still watching the Kogen with fascination. "They survived before you came into their lives, you know. You've gotta take care of yourself. You were born to this life, but I can't say you ever took to it."

"None of these creatures were born to live in cages."

"I have a surprise for you," he told her, changing the subject.

"Frank, I'm sorry, but I'm really not in the mood, and I only have six days to figure out how to show this guy off."

"Well, then, my surprise is even more perfect. One of the comms guys from Keptermine Station and I were chatting—"

"Get to the point, Frank!" she said. He was the worst for beating around the bush.

"Some hoity-toity biologist is at Keptermine, and she's agreed to get on the line with you, see if she can help you out."

"What!" Kaleigh jumped and hugged him. "Frank, I owe you."

"Yeah, yeah." He grinned at her. "Just helpin' a friend."

Kaleigh perched in Frank's chair, using her hands to hold his headset onto her head.

"Don't forget, there is a delay," he warned her as he pressed some buttons on the keyboard. She heard static crackling in the background of her headset.

"Hello?" Kaleigh said.

"Announce who you are, silly!" Frank said.

She nodded at him. "This is Kaleigh Gattling, Animal Handler on the First Galactic Circus in the Sky."

"Over," Frank said.

She nodded again. "Over."

They sat in silence for a moment. "Hey there, Kaleigh, this is Anita Farling. I hear you have a Kogen there on board. Over."

Kaleigh sighed in relief. "Yes! Please, I can't find any information on how to help him. It's not really eating and just spends all its time sulking, and if I can't get it to perform, my boss is going to be so mad. I don't know what to do! Over."

The silence while they waited for the woman's reply was maddening.

"Kaleigh. The Kogen is a dangerous, dangerous creature. It has never been successfully domesticated or even trained. They either die in captivity or are killed. Please advise as to the temperament of your specimen. Over."

"It's never been aggressive toward me," Kaleigh said defensively. "Although it doesn't like the Beast Master. We've only had it a few days. Please, can Kogens make you think things? Over."

The silence stretched even longer this time. Just as Kaleigh was beginning to think they'd lost their connection, the biologist spoke again.

"It is extremely rare that a Kogen chooses to share its empathetic and telepathic skills with someone outside their race. You must be quite amazing, Miss Gattling. Your Kogen trusts you, and that is something no other animal handler I can think of can claim. I'm being told we need to clear the line, but please contact me as soon as you're within hypernet range. We can talk without jamming up the deep space lines and have a proper private conversation. Until then, just keep doing what you're doing, because you must be doing something right. Over and out here at Keptermine."

Kaleigh pulled off the headset as Frank closed their end of the connection.

"You look down, Kally-Bally. Couldn't she help you?"

Kaleigh shook her head. "She didn't have much to add, just that no Kogen has ever been successfully kept in captivity. I'm supposed to contact her when we're in hypernet range."

"We'll be in range about a day before we hit the station," he informed her.

She nodded. "I'm gonna get back." She didn't want to tell him that being away from her Kogen made her nervous, especially after what the biologist had told her. If the Beast Master tried to butt heads with the Kogen… Well, one of them wouldn't survive. Despite her desire to get back, she did make a pit stop in the kitchen to grab some berries.

The Beast Hold was still empty when she made it back. With less than a week left until they touched down at Keptermine Station, she knew the quiet wouldn't last. Everyone would be practicing their acts up in the Big Top, both animal handlers and regular performers.

"Hello, Mr. Kogen," she said. It had pushed its potted plants into a row and lain down behind them. Its antisocial behavior scared her. It still hadn't eaten any of the food scattered around its cage. Indecision waged war in her mind. Feeding it through the window had gotten her nowhere, but everyone kept telling her the Kogen was dangerous. But it'd never been aggressive to her, and that made up her mind. She grabbed her broom and dustpan and cracked its cell door open, slinking inside.

Instantly, the Kogen sat up, a low snarl humming in its throat.

"Hey, it's me!" she said, a bit scared, but she tried not to show it. Animals could respond badly to fear.

The snarl softened and turned into a wavering note. The Kogen sat up, and its little black nose sniffed the air.

"Yes, I brought you every single sort of berry that I could find." She latched the gate behind her.

It tucked its paws between its legs and waited patiently. She reached into the bag on her back and pulled out the first container of berries.

"Blueberries," she told it. She cracked open the clamshell container and held them out through the ferns. "I think they're the closest to what you want. Don't tell anyone I gave them to you. They're supposed to be saved for circus treats."

The Kogen leaned forward and sniffed the container, then delicately buried its face in the food, eating the berries and licking the container clean.

"Okay, blueberries are good." One by one, she pulled the different berries out of her bag and offered them to the Kogen. It liked the strawberries so much, it actually took the container from her to scarf them down faster. It was indifferent to the grapes, but also liked the raspberries.

When her bag was empty, it settled back on its haunches, waiting.

"That's all I've got," she said. "The berries are hard to get. Like I said, they're for circus treats."

It cocked its head to the side and made more humming noises, but it seemed to understand there were no more berries. She quickly swept up the food from her first attempt at feeding, then turned to leave.

The creature crooned again, and she looked over her shoulder. In her mind, she saw a picture of herself.

"You want me to stay?"

It hunkered down lower to the floor and somehow looked pleading. She set down her dustpan and broom. Her stomach flipped butterflies as she once again approached the Kogen, keeping the potted plants between them. It leaned its head through the ferns. She could see her reflection in its black eyes. Her hand came up and gently scratched its head. The Kogen crooned. Its eyes closed as she continued to scratch.

"You're like me, you know," she told the beast. "You weren't born to live in a cage, just like I wasn't born to live on this ship."

For the next week, Kaleigh spent every free moment she could in the pen with the Kogen. It still refused to eat anything but fresh berries, and she could see the weight loss on the creature's frame. Its silver pelt had lost its shine and seemed to hang loosely off the creature. It was also growing more and more lethargic. She'd programmed a timer into her tablet; the alarm would go off the second the ship came in range of the hypernet node.

When it did, Kaleigh's fingers fumbled over the keys as she connected to the hypernet, frantic to contact Anita Farling, but no one answered her call. She tried again three more times before giving up. Patience, she was learning, was harder than it looked.

She was in the pen with the Kogen when her tablet vibrated, indicating the incoming communication. The Kogen watched the tablet warily while Kaleigh scrambled to pick it up. She'd been leaning against the Kogen's side, and she settled back into her old position when she answered.

A middle-aged woman appeared on her screen. She looked nerdy, with the big glasses and the tied-back hair and everything.

"Dr. Farling?"

"Hello, Kaleigh! Wait, is that the Kogen?" The woman nearly squeaked.

The Kogen craned its head around to see what was making noise in its pen.

"Yes." Kaleigh grinned, petting the silver fur. "We've become good friends, Mr. Kogen and I."

"Astounding. Just astounding. How is your creature doing?"

Her smile faded. "Not well. All it'll eat is berries, and if my math is right, even just lying here, it requires upwards of three thousand calories a day."

"He's eating at all—that's big. His breed has never survived in captivity. I can't believe he lets you so close."

"He is a he? I thought so, but I wasn't sure. He doesn't like when I go. He asks me to come back with pictures in my mind."

"Astounding. Just astounding. Kaleigh, do you know how amazing this is? No one has ever managed to form a bond with these creatures. It's a shame."

Kaleigh didn't need an explanation; she knew if he stayed here, he would die. He would only die quicker if they put the creature on display in the Big Top. The Kogen didn't like when any of the crew came to stare at him. She could only imagine how poor his response to hundreds of people yelling and staring would be. She'd known almost since the creature came under her care that he would never survive in a cramped little enclosure on a ship hurtling through space. He needed room to run—he needed to be free.

"Dr. Farling, could you… I mean, uh… Well, I want to save him, if I can, and um…"

"I was waiting for you to ask, dear. I've already started making inquiries in the hopes that you'd feel this way. My ship, *The Pilgrim*, is stocked and ready to depart. We just need to get the Kogen on board. There's one more thing about your Kogen you may not have discovered yet: Did you know that they can blend?"

"Blend what?"

"No, blend in with their surroundings. They do it in their wild habitat. No one has quite figured out how, but they're almost impossible to spot in the wild."

The noise of the other beast handlers approaching the hold reached Kaleigh's ears. "I have to go. I'll message you with a plan later." She terminated the call and crept to the door of the Kogen's cage. So far, none of the others had seen how close she could get to the Kogen. He crooned weakly as she left.

"I'll be back soon, Mr. Kogen, I promise," she whispered as she closed the gate behind her.

She left the hold to seek out Frank. She wanted to ask his advice. People moved at top speed through the halls. Preparations for landing at Keptermine were in full swing, which meant he was back to practicing with the clowns. Kaleigh turned, heading back to the Beast Hold, then stopped mid-step as a realization dawned on her. Everyone was running around like chickens with their heads cut off trying to get everything ready. Kaleigh had helped dock the ship more times than she could count. She knew everyone's job, and, just like a well-oiled machine, everyone would be in the right place, at the right time, and since her place was with the beasts, no one would be looking at her.

She detoured to the kitchen, empty at this hour, and filled her bag with as many berries as it could hold, then repacked the clamshells in the fridge to hide the empty containers behind them. She didn't return to the Beast Hold, though. Instead, she detoured back down to the belly of the ship, where there was less traffic. This was also where the majority of the ship's escape pods were docked.

Kaleigh crawled through the pods. They were a mottled assortment salvaged from other ships and rigged to work with the circus. Even if every pod fired filled to capacity, there were still too few for the burgeoning crew of the First Galactic Circus in the Sky. Several of the other emergency launch bays had been converted into quarters for crew members more years ago than Kaleigh could remember. No one on board seemed concerned with the safety violation; after all, the circus had been traveling for years and years without ever needing the pods.

Ignored by the ship's maintenance crew, Kaleigh could tell at a glance that her plan was going to hit hiccups. One was clearly visible to her already. The auto loader was rusted, meaning she would have to manually move the tubular pod onto the launch gate. The pod itself powered on for her, though, and that gave her hope.

She moved like a ninja over the next day, using all the graceful movements and acting her parents had tried to drum into her head over the years to remain unnoticed by the crew, sneaking first food and then her personal items down into the pod, stealing lubricant from the maintenance department, as well as various other tools to try to get the rundown pod ready. Down in the emergency launch bay, she'd set the plan with Dr. Farling. Timing would be key.

Once everything was set, she returned to the Kogen. There were a few hours left until docking at Keptermine, and the most difficult part of her plan was ahead: Moving a half-ton bear-like creature through a crowded ship. The Kogen perked its head up as she slid open the gate.

"Mr. Kogen." She put on her most serious adult face. "You need to be free. You weren't born to live in a cage. I want to help you get home, but you need to follow me. I don't know how much you understand, but this is really important. We need to leave now, and you need to be really quiet. Okay?"

He crawled onto all fours and sniffed at her backpack.

"Yes, I have berries." She pulled out a handful. "Follow me for the berries."

He trundled slowly after her as she backed out of the Beast Hold. Her route to getting the Kogen down to the emergency pods was not ideal. He didn't fit through many of the same crawlspaces she did, which drew out the length of the trip. This close to docking, any non-essential personnel were resting, and the public areas of the circus were eerily empty. She'd been betting on that as a safe route. Her biggest concern was running out of berries before she got him down there.

They were crossing the Big Top when she heard arguing voices approaching. Her eyes grew wide and darted back and forth, trying to find someplace to hide the beast. The Kogen was a step ahead of her, trundling toward the shadows at the edge of the ring. Her panic grew; even the deep shadows against the wall would do nothing to hide his massive silver form. The voices drew closer, and her eyes darted toward the doorway. In the instant she looked away, she almost lost sight of the Kogen. His coloring had changed to match the blues and blacks of the shadows. She rushed toward the beast, grateful that Dr. Farling had mentioned the blending. It was a little less freaky knowing that this was a normal thing for the large creature. She crouched next to him as he flattened himself to the floor, hiding behind the giant beast.

"She's been shirking and disappearing off to hell-knows-where." The Beast Master was furious.

"She's what, man, fifteen? Sixteen? She's probably found herself a boy or the like."

"You're her father, and you don't even know! It's your lack of discipline that ruined her. Probably told her she could do anything she dreamed of."

The men continued to argue as they moved past Kaleigh and the Kogen. He growled deep in his throat. Kaleigh produced a handful of berries and rubbed the soft fur on his head. It didn't bother her much, her father and her master fighting over what she'd become. She had no respect for either of them. Her father, who'd told her all she could aspire to be was a circus performer, who'd never made time to get to know who his daughter really was. And the master who'd beaten her until she got good enough at her job to rob him of the excuse, who'd taken credit for every successful animal she'd trained or tamed. It crystallized to her just why she wanted to leave. Despite soaring freely through the skies on the circus ship, she'd been like her animals, confined in the cage of the ship and performing to other people's drums.

Once the coast was clear, she led the Kogen off again. They reached the pod without encountering anyone else, but the Kogen took one look at the small space and began kicking up a fuss, making its whistling and humming noises. He sat back on his hind paws, balking at her every attempt to lead him to safety.

"Shh, Mr. Kogen, please. Stop. This is the way home. I promise." She did her best to focus on the wide fields in her mind. The ones he had shown her in the dream. "You don't need to go in yet. First, I need your help."

A smooth voice cut in over the ship's intercom system.

"This is a ship-wide alert: Docking will commence in twenty minutes. Please stand by as we complete the pre-check procedures."

"Okay, Mr. Kogen. I really, really need your help right now." He crooked his head to the side, watching her. "We're moving the pod, okay?" She pictured it in as much detail as she could: the Kogen lifting the pod and gently setting it down on the bay door in the floor. She screwed her eyes shut and imagined it harder. She kept imagining it until she heard the scrape of claws on metal. Her eyes snapped open, and she watched as the Kogen dragged the pod over to the spot she'd been picturing.

"Oh, you're such a smart beastie!" she exclaimed as it settled into place. This part of the plan had hinged strongly on her being able to let the beast know what she needed. Her relief was palpable that he really could see the pictures in her mind like she'd thought he could. She opened her bag and pulled out the biggest handful of berries she could. The Kogen daintily took the berries from her and sucked them down.

Kaleigh climbed into the pod, powering it on from the tiny little console. The escape pod couldn't be steered, but if Dr. Farling was waiting, they wouldn't be in space for more than a few minutes.

"Okay, Kogen, now you need to come in. Come on, you can have the rest of the berries!" She opened up her bag and showed him the gleaming pile of blackberries inside. He hesitated, then trundled inside. Kaleigh sighed in relief and flipped the switch to close the hatch.

"Okay, here goes. Opening Gate One." She fiddled with the controls, and the ship lurched downward, falling into the airlock it had been resting on. "Closing Gate One." She tuned out the crooning and growling of the Kogen. Technology like this wasn't her strong point—before being assigned to the beasts, she'd done a rather disastrous stint in maintenance—but she had to get it right.

"And… Opening Gate Two." The pod fell again, and the rush of air escaping the hatch pulled them out into space. The windows of the pod showed the wall of the station close by on the left. Kaleigh craned her head upward to catch a glimpse of the Circus in the Sky from the outside. The brightly colored ship was so large that at first, she could only see a portion of its hull as they drifted away. As the ship moved closer and finished its docking, she got a better look. Painted in a rainbow of colors, with giant pictures showing the various acts on the ship, it was a somewhat garish sight, but instantly recognizable to the people of a space station, which was the whole point. The ship had never been designed for speed or good looks. No, the massive, bulbous creation was downright ugly.

Lights on the far bank of windows drew her attention; a smaller ship, more streamlined than the giant circus ship, was bearing down on them as they drifted out into space. Clearly emblazoned on the side in white was the name of the ship. *The Pilgrim* had found them.

"This is it, Mr. Kogen. This is the first step to getting you home." She rubbed his fur as he buried his head in the bag of berries. As the little pod was picked up by *The Pilgrim*, Kaleigh realized for the first time that she'd done it. She'd left the circus behind and was about to begin the greatest adventure of her life. She was about to join an ecological survey ship with one of the best biologists on board. She was going to take the Kogen home… and then?

She smiled to herself and snuggled against her beast. Then she was going to learn all about him the right way, in his natural habitat.

THE GRUDGE MATCH

MILAN OBRADOVIC

Day 13

On a rainy September day, 1993, in a smoke-filled pub in Hanover, Germany, I sat opposite "The Madman from Waco, Texas," Jody Scott, nursing my beer and my neck.

When I had committed my life to becoming a professional wrestler, after seeing The Ultimate Warrior pin The Immortal Hulk Hogan in front of sixty thousand screaming fans in the Toronto Skydome over three years earlier, I had envisioned my future differently.

Athletic, bright-eyed eighteen-year-old Jason Cantwell had turned into prematurely disillusioned twenty-three-year-old Jason Jagger. Cooler name, much worse morale. A soon-to-be never-was, I feared.

But not because of Jody. I liked Jody, even before he changed my life. At the time, I had no idea whether he felt the same.

The legendary Jody Scott—sometimes billed as "Sniper" Jody Scott, "Texas Terror" Jody Scott, and often called "Scotty" or "Scotsman" by his peers—had been paired with me by local promoter Klaus Hartmann, himself a retired wrestler, or rather "Catcher," as we were called in Germany by the older fans who had been attending since before American pro-wrestling was on TV.

Nobody has more nicknames than a veteran wrestler. There's your real name, your wrestling name, your real nickname, your wrestling nickname, the nickname for your wrestling nickname, your nickname in Germany, your nickname in Japan, and, of course, there's always that one special unfortunate nickname that somehow stuck after "Pretty" Rico Cargioni once saw you eat beans straight from a can backstage at an independent show in Des Moines, Iowa, that was attended by 143 people, and now, twenty-nine years later, there's at least two dozen adult men who still call you "Beans."

I called Jody, "Jody." Thankfully, he called me "kid," not "Beans."

We were two weeks into a sixty-day run. Yes, sixty shows in sixty days, all in the same place. Madness when you think about it today, but that's the way the CWF, the Catch-Wrestling Federation, had been doing it for decades.

All the action took place in the CWF *Festzelt*, a big tent on the Hanover fairgrounds, where the city staged one of the world's biggest fairs every summer. Right now, we were the only attraction.

I could see the rectangular blue tent in the distance from the pub window. It was topped by a white dome and fronted by a jagged, neon-lit marquee. It didn't look much like the Skydome when viewed through crocheted curtains.

I took a swig of beer. Everything hurt, especially my neck.

"Are your ribs okay?" I asked Jody. "I'm sorry about earlier."

"Don't worry about it, kid. It only hurts when I'm breathing." Jody left-handedly downed a *Lüttje Lage*, a combo drink of the local colorless liquor and beer, drunk by pouring the shot into the beer as you finish it in one go. He took a deep drag from his cigarette and gave a left-handed thumbs-up to the sponsor of our refreshments, an older gentleman at the other side of the bar.

"*Morgen macht ihr sie fertig, Madman!*" the man yelled across the room.

"What's that?" I asked softly. "My German's still terrible."

"Tomorrow, you'll get 'em." Jody rolled his cigarette back and forth between his thumb and index finger. "Well, hopefully he'll be back next week, too. Crowd's been soft. Let's enjoy the free drinks while we can."

I pushed the shot over to Jody. "I don't really drink liquor."

He shrugged and drank, again using his left.

I had nailed him in the ribs earlier tonight, and he had kept his right arm close to his body ever since. Although we were a tag team, a planned spot of miscommunication led to our loss. Unfortunately, I got him good with my knee, right above the liver. And in 1993, I still moved fast. That was why I had a spot—dynamic moves, muscular build, good hair, a young face. I looked a bit like the wrestlers on TV and a bit less like the veteran troupe the people of Hanover had seen in the tent for years.

But nobody had ever heard of me, while Jody, a former world champion, was still a true star, even in the twilight of his career. He had the crowd in the palm of his hand every evening. My association with him was nothing less than a gift to me.

Mentor and rookie, always an easy story. And the best stories in wrestling are simple and rooted in truth.

Unbeknownst to me, my coach in the U.S., Jax Stevens, had finagled for Jody to attempt to put my game together. They had traded the world title twice in the seventies and stayed friendly.

Jax, God bless the bastard, would die of a heart attack in 1999 and hadn't done a nice thing for anybody since at least 1973. But if I had to venture a guess, it was either pity or personal pride that made him try to save my career.

In the spring of '93, I had tried out for the World Wrestling Federation, the world's biggest wrestling organization and the place that had made me a fan. I stunk up the joint. I stunk all the way from the ring to the mats outside, up the ramp through the curtains, and then all the way back to the dressing room.

The *Wrestling Observer Newsletter*, basically the *New York Times* of the wrestling world, had this to write about my match:

In a dark match before the TV taping, Thomas "Trashman" Traeger beat highly touted prospect Jason Jagger with the compactor in 4:53. The match was described to us as a train wreck. Jagger, real name Jason Cantwell, is being trained by Jax Stevens in Buffalo.

The overuse of alliterations in wrestling was the least of my problems.

"Seasoning in Europe," Jax had said about CWF after the tryout disaster. "A change of pace!"

I would have to generate some buzz over here and put my game together, or my career was doomed. Business had tanked in the U.S. over the last couple of years, and the two big leagues hired no rookies except the promoter's son.

Meanwhile, in Europe, business boomed with the advent of cable television, but people only wanted to see the colorful U.S. version that was failing to draw big crowds stateside. Just my luck, an American in Europe while American business boomed, but I'm stuck working for the failing local holdovers.

"It's the stupid tent," I told Jody, who still droned on about how half the people as usual attended the show these days. "People see the Skydome on TV, and then they see us in a tent next to a row of porta-potties. Nobody wants that."

"Don't knock the tent," Jody said. "Keeps you honest. Never forget that we're the whole circus for these people. Right now, you're only the acrobat, but if you really want to make it, you also have to be the animal and the tamer, the director, the juggler, what have you. And when the time is right, you gotta show some ass and be their clown, too. In this tent, it's only us."

Call it nonsense or wisdom, but Jody had been around the block. Independent wrestling outside of the big touring organizations was holding on by the skin of its teeth all over the world. And its biggest remaining stars like Jody were held together by spit and duct tape. But they persevered, made money, and still brought paying customers into a tent on a rainy September day in Northern Germany. You had to respect that.

At the time, I thought less philosophically. Not being able to turn your head will do that to you. Our opponents had really put the hammer down on me.

"Why'd you let the Hunters get away with their shit?" I asked Jody. That sore neck would bother me for at least another week. "I couldn't say anything, but they would have listened to you!"

"That's their whole shtick. They're just protecting their spot. Did you see how hard I hit *them?*"

We had fought in the semi-main against the British twin tag team of "The Hunters," Darren and Desmond "Dez" Hunter. I was a nobody and Jody was untouchable, so they really stiffed me during the match. Their *shtick.* Nearly took my head off with a clothesline. In the end, Jody made the big comeback, but after our "miscommunication," they threw him outside and pinned me with their finisher, a stuffed piledriver. I didn't have to pretend that my neck hurt on the way to the back.

"It's so unprofessional. I hate these guys. Selfish pricks."

"Look, you're not the promoter, you're the wrestler. *I'm* only the wrestler." Jody sounded impatient.

The Hunters were legit tough guys, coming up as carnies in Manchester. Their dad was serving a life sentence back in the U.K., and nobody really talked about why. Hardened brawlers, born and bred.

As teenagers, they had fought drunk wannabe wrestlers at the carnival while I watched Saturday Night's Main Event on NBC in my E.T. PJs and tried to convince my parents to pay for wrestling school. We were not the same.

After the match, Jody had shaken hands with them and said, "Great match, thanks." I'd bit my tongue.

"They took liberties out there!" I felt slighted. "Klaus said they're challenging for the titles next weekend, but that was still some BS."

"Could you stop with the whining for one minute?" Jody said. "I'm trying to have a beer in peace."

"Oh, sorry," I snapped back. "I just didn't want to get paralyzed because the Hunters forgot wrestling is fake."

Yes, I used the f-word. That itself didn't bother Jody, though.

"Let me tell you what you gotta do, son!" He wagged his finger at me. "You gotta stand up for yourself when it's time, but right now, you gotta shut up and worry about yourself, not the Hunters. I'm a humble man, but you were put in there with me. That still means something around here. Klaus sees something in our program, but I don't know if you can hold up your end. When you nailed me with that running knee, I know you were worried about me in real life, but who cares if they can't tell? Or they don't believe?

"You gotta make him"—he pointed to the guy who'd bought us drinks—"believe you were worried. And maybe he's in the last row. You go big in that ring if it's part of the story. You turn the other cheek if it's not. Nobody cares about my actual ribs or how hard Dez is hitting you. Hit him back, tell your story. Forget my ribs and tell your story. It's not the actual moves or the actual pain unless you make them believe."

Jody tried to take another sip, but his glass was empty. He put it down emphatically. "I want Hans and Franz over there to come back next week. What are *you* doing to make them come back? Complaining about the

Hunters laying it in? People pay to see them kick ass. Today, it was your ass. You gotta make the people feel something for you. Real life must be less interesting than our story. I don't want an ounce of real pity in that ring if it's not part of the story. They hit you for real? You gotta get sympathy, you gotta sell *our* story. The Hunters kicked our asses for fifteen minutes, and then they beat us. The end. Right now, that's all everybody remembers because you didn't make an impression, you didn't connect."

Day 20

"Big day for everyone," Klaus told us in the dressing room before our match. "The Twins are going to win the tag titles, but you're challenging next. Make them want to see it, *ja?* Show the fire."

The Hunter Twins were penciled in to take the titles from the popular German duo of Michael Ilic and Christoph Schulze while we faced the makeshift team of Croatian youngster Zoran Antic and American veteran Jim Masters, whose claim to fame was a brief stay as a jobber for the WWF in the mid-80s. The winners, us, would go on to challenge the Hunters with the bigger picture idea being that we carried a grudge from last week and went for revenge by taking their titles.

Oh, I had a grudge, all right. I still couldn't move my neck freely.

But finally, a breakthrough on the horizon, a tag team title reign. Maybe a write-up in the *Observer*? I could see it in front of my mind's eye:

Jody Scott and Jason Jagger beat the Hunter Twins for the CWF tag team championship in 18:42 when Jagger pinned Darren Hunter after a top rope splash.

Later that night, after we won our alleged warm-up match, reality struck.

I had never seen Jody this irate before.

"You're the worst babyface in the world." The scars running across his forehead lit up with anger. "What the hell was that sell of the chicken wing?" He mocked me casually reaching out for the tag with a pained expression. "Uh, Jody, I'm in a bit of a bother over here… Please take my hand. Boo-fucking-hoo."

I had tried to make the fans believe, I thought, but they just weren't into my stuff. I didn't *connect*. Jody did his thing, but people didn't care about *me*, and the match turned into a dud.

"Playing the phoniest goody two-shoes out there," Jody rambled on. "What have I been saying? They're only going to care if they think it's real. Not the violence, the emotions. You're dragging me down. Nobody out there believes I'd take you dork under my wing. I'll talk to Klaus. This isn't working."

Later that night, I lay in bed, wondering if I should quit the tour and stop wrestling. Nobody in the U.S. would even take a look at me after a failed run with Jody, of all people. I put on my clothes and went out for a walk in the dark. I needed to see the tent, feel whether it wanted me back, whether I wanted to go back.

As I stood there like an idiot, staring at the place of my latest failure in the middle of the night, a twelve-year-old boy walked past me with his dad. They had been in the front row a few times over the last couple of weeks.

The boy's face lit up when he recognized me, and he tugged at his dad's arm. "*Papa, Papa, da ist Jason Jagger!*"

The smallest thing, but it meant a lot to me. Maybe I wasn't destined for greatness in the U.S., but at least one kid in Hanover, Germany, recognized me!

Then he flipped me the bird and said in heavily accented English, "I hope ze Hunters kick your ass!"

His dad pulled him away quickly, admonishing him in German.

Day 35

Jody sprung it on me in the morning over breakfast. Some of the international talent stayed at a bed-and-breakfast run by the promoter's mother-in-law. Including me, since I knew nobody in Germany and couldn't afford a hotel for two months.

"The Madman from Waco" sat down in a tattered bathrobe. He could have afforded a fancier place, but as the frugal veteran type, he had been coming here for two decades, and everyone doted on him.

"Thank you, love," he said to the smitten proprietress, who handed him a cup of coffee. She never had as much as a smile for any of the other wrestlers.

He turned to me. "I talked to Klaus. We're losing tonight. And we're gonna split after that. I'm going singles. Gotta get people back in the tent."

They had weighed me and found me lacking, even for the fairgrounds. At the news stand, I had counted twelve different wrestling magazines in German. Every single one had a WWF star on the cover. People wanted the circus, but not the tent. And I wasn't even good enough for that.

The rest of the day went by in a trance. I filled out imaginary college applications and saw myself stocking cans of beans at the grocery store.

Sure, I could always take indie dates in the States and get my bell rung for 40 bucks and a slice of Pizza Hut, but if you couldn't launch off of being in a tag team with Jody, you could shelve any higher aspirations than that.

Later, we went over the match with Klaus and the Hunters in the locker room. I let Jody do our talking.

When the Brits got up, Klaus told us to stay. "I have an idea for you guys. Something spicy."

As he explained, I sat up straight, a current of anticipation creeping up my spine.

"You know I always do business," Jody said after Klaus finished, "but I don't think Jason's ready for *this*. People aren't gonna buy it."

"I'll just have to prove you wrong," I said calmly, silently vowing to make damn sure people would buy it. If not, I'd quit and go back to the States. *My time, now or never.*

Our main event match with the Brits went smoother than last time.

I hit them a little harder than the first time, and somehow, their punches hurt a little less. I ran on adrenaline and excitement, meeting their signature beating with stubborn resilience and occasional high-energy flurries.

Ten minutes into the match, Darren grabbed me in a headlock to slow things down and whispered, "Take it easy, kid. Don't blow me up."

After he caught his breath, I powered out of the hold, hit a stiff shoulder block to send him flying, and got the fans on my side for what felt like the first time.

Dez illegally tripped me again to cut me off, and the fans jeered, but after five more minutes of spirited struggle, I made the hot tag to Jody, and he ran wild. The tent believed in the Madman, and maybe even a little in Jason Jagger.

I came back into the ring to prevent another two-on-one, then held up a dazed Dez for one of Jody's patented haymakers. The Brit ducked, and Jody clobbered me in the face as hard as I've ever been hit in my life.

One of the surprising things about wrestling is that your friends hit you much harder than your enemies. Apparently, Jody considered me his best friend in the world.

My knees buckled for a split second, but I had rarely been more clear-headed in my life. *Here we go.*

The other Brit grabbed Jody by the neck and threw him out of the ring.

When I turn around, they double-team me with their signature piledriver, and I look up at the lights. Again. *One, two, three.*

Thunderous boos. Stomping. We had them. The people actually wanted us to win.

Where had that enthusiasm been for the last thirty days?

The Brits leave with their belts.

A distraught Jody helps me to my feet.

I touch my face and feel a gigantic mouse forming under my left eye. *Thanks, Jody.*

He sees my reaction and gesticulates apologetically, then raises my arm.

The fans give me a respectful hand. They appreciate a spirited losing effort, and Jody's endorsement still means something.

But I'm tired of losing. And I'm especially tired of Jody and his well-meaning advice. I touch my bruise again. My fingers come back bloody. Jody turns and steps over the second rope to leave the ring.

"Jody!" I yell.

He turns his head to me, straddling the rope.

"Screw you." I kick the rope as hard as I can. I'd feel bad, but Jody already has two daughters at home.

The crowd gasps as he crumples to the mat.

"*Hey, hey, Jason, was machst du da?*" The German ring announcer admonishes me over the house mic. "*Lass Jody in Ruhe.*"

I'm sorry, but I'm not going to leave Jody in peace. I'm not trying to hurt him, but I'm telling my story tonight. The frustration, the anger, the anxiety.

The crowd turns on me in a split second, showering me with boos, almost drowning out the sound of my own heartbeat. I leave Jody tied up in the ropes and stalk the ring.

I'm so in the moment, I wouldn't be able to identify my mother in the crowd. Everything is a blur, except that one kid in the front row. The one from my night walk. He points his thumbs down and yells in German.

I grab Jody by the hair and drag him over to the kid's side of the ring. Under the ring apron is a metal chain among the tools used to put up the ring. I pull it out and present it to the crowd. They boo in anticipation.

Everybody knows what's coming, and I'm not going to disappoint. I wrap the chain around my fist and pull Jody's head up, facing the kid on the outside.

"Here's your hero!" I rear back and hit Jody in the forehead. He drops down to the mat and buries his head in his hands.

I look the kid straight in the eye. "That's what you wanted, isn't it?" I spit on the floor in front of him in disgust.

Now the kid's dad jumps up and yells at me in German. Security takes a step closer, but I turn toward Jody.

His eyebrow is covered in blood as he tries to get up, but his legs give out, and he falls back down. I get on my knees next to him and cradle his head in my left arm. I whisper, "Thank you," in his ear, before I open up the cut on his forehead with rapid-fire punches, until the blood flows freely and his face turns into a crimson mask.

Day 45

I had kept away from Jody since my heel turn by being curt at the B&B and keeping to myself in the locker room. I knew he had done me a huge favor, but I didn't want to spoil the vibe. I had discovered my edge; no reason to dull it.

And Jody had been impressed by my intensity and our crowd reaction that night. At least, that's what Darren Hunter told me, and he didn't have to butter me up for no reason.

Over the last few shows, I had torn through all the other babyfaces to keep me hot until Jody's big revenge.

I clawed, I scratched, I cheated, I kept winning. One older German lady tried to hit me with an umbrella at ringside after I raked local favorite Olaf Reichardt's eyes and rolled him up, holding the tights outside the view of the referee. One day, I left the locker room late in the evening and a teen flipped me off from across the street. Things were going swimmingly.

Until Day 45. The box office had stabilized with the Brits as ass-kicking champions and people intrigued by how and when Jody would get revenge on me, but then Klaus got a chance to bring in "Fronk" for a reasonable rate.

Fronk, real name Frank McGriffith, had gotten himself over in the WWF with a full-on sad clown gimmick, only to get fired over some backstage kerfuffle with one of their main eventers, but he'd featured in enough of the dozen wrestling magazines on sale at the train station for Klaus to jump at the chance to book him. God knows why, but Fronk chose me from a list of potential opponents, and he wasn't in town to lose.

For the first time in my whole stay in Hanover, I questioned the booking. "Won't this derail my program with Jody? If Fronk beats me, how much is Jody's revenge gonna be worth?"

Klaus remained unperturbed. "We sold an extra 250 tickets since I started advertising him. People know him from TV. It'll be fine."

"People know him from TV," I objected, "but he won't be here next week."

Klaus waved it away. "It'll be, like, an exhibition, a special attraction. There's people who've never seen you. Show them what you're about!"

I didn't want exhibitions. I had tasted blood. I wanted things to mean something.

But he had sold 250 tickets.

As Jody liked to say, the winner wasn't the person whose hand was raised but whose performance you remembered on your way home. The one you'd pay money to see again. I vowed to give them something to see *me* again, not him.

I went over the match with Fronk, grudgingly but amicably. Before we went out there, he parted with, "Just take it easy. I got a signing in Pensacola on Sunday, and I'm flying coach."

I got it. *I get it.* He had a family, a life, bills, somewhat of a career, a few hundred bucks coming in from a car dealership in Pensacola. But to be frank, Fronk's Pensacola signing was far down the list of my personal priorities.

"I got ya," I told him, before I went out to the boos of the audience. And I took good care of him. I worked my ass off, in the ring and outside. I even took a hip toss over the railing onto the concrete between spectator rows. I clawed, I scratched, I cheated, I lost. He outsmarted me and reversed a rollup. I jumped up and complained to the referee, but the decision stood. I lost. The fans went crazy for Fronk.

After he leaves the ring, I grab the ref by his collar. "Two! That was two!" No, he holds three fingers high up in the air, and the fans roar. The ring announcer warns me not to touch the ref lest I be suspended for the rest of the festival. I let go of him and plead my case to the fans. "That was two. That's a fluke!"

There's a kid in the front row I know all too well by now. He holds up three fingers. "*Das war drei, du Arschloch!*" My German is good enough for that.

At the wrestlers' entrance, Jody steps out into the tent and points at me. The announcer draws everyone's attention to him, and he gives me the thumbs down to the roar of the crowd. The fans cheer, and I cover my ears. He'll have his revenge next.

Day 60

The final day. There had been a tournament the last ten days for what they called the CWA Champion's Cup. It was made up, naturally, but so were all other titles and trophies. Jody and I had both lost in the first round when we interfered in each other's matches. Now, everyone was looking forward more to our grudge match than the Champion's Cup finals.

Good. I considered this a promoter-problem, not a me-problem.

Of course, I would be losing. Jody was *Jody*, one of wrestling's living legends. I was Jason Jagger, obnoxious, ungrateful rookie. The whole point of it all was for him to vanquish me at the end. That was the story. I knew it, intellectually, and I didn't mind. Yet I was sincerely, shall we say, *irked?*

It was the end of my run in Europe. I had won a lot lately, but all my biggest matches—the Hunters, Fronk, now Jody—I'd lost. It shouldn't have mattered, yet somehow, it did.

Hanover, Germany—October 27, 1993. Jody Scott beat Jason Jagger in 21:49 with the Indian Deathlock in a no-holds-barred match.

Not good enough to get noticed in the *Observer*, I feared, but it just wasn't up to me. The morning of the big match, I vowed to go out on my shield. *May the chips fall as they may.*

Jody and I went over our match in the closest interaction we'd had since my turn.

He sensed my annoyance. "Are you okay?"

"I'm just ready to go."

He nodded. "Go with the flow."

We have the crowd all the way through. Nobody sells a beating like Jody. I bust him open after ten minutes by running his head into the post on the outside. He stumbles all over the ring, parading around a pained expression through a veil of caked blood. I lay in punches to his cut with overt glee. The tent hates me.

In this scenario, I would eventually take too much glee in punishing Jody, passing up the opportunity to pin him in favor of inflicting more pain, leading to his big win. Rookie hubris defeated by veteran guile and perseverance.

But when the time comes for him to punish my arrogance and put me into his finisher, the dreaded Indian Deathlock, he collapses to the mat, holding his knee and waving the referee closer.

I turn to the audience to gloat, giving them time to discuss whatever needs discussing. When I move back in, the ref pulls me close and says, "Jody can't move, go home."

Going home meant ending the match, but the planned finish is him submitting me.

He writhes on the mat, looking at me challengingly.

The penny drops. I kick his ostensibly injured knee before applying a leg lock and leaning back in a strained effort to rip his knee apart.

Jody struggles and writhes, waves to the ref. He's submitting, but it takes a stern look to convince the ref this unplanned ending is truly happening.

Finally, the bell rings. I immediately release the hold and throw my arms up in triumph. The outcomes are fake, but any wrestler who tells you winning doesn't feel good is selling you something else.

I've beaten Jody, and nobody can ever take that away from me. Yet I turn around to put the boots to him. He'd expect nothing less.

The Hunters come running from backstage, and I flee the ring.

I pass the kid in the front row. "I won, you little shithead."

Dez clotheslines me from behind, and I tumble into the front row, sending everyone scattering. Dez then holds me up, and Darren forearms me in the face to the kid's pure delight.

I cowardly flee backstage and catch a stray beer cup on the way. Moments later, I peek back out through the curtain to see what Jody is up to. He refuses all help and pulls himself upright on the ring ropes before saluting the crowd and staggering to the back on his own accord, cursing me and vowing revenge every step of the way.

The *Observer* writes:

In a big upset, Jason Jagger beat Jody Scott in a no-holds-barred match via submission in 17:55 on the final day of CWF Catchfest in Hanover, Germany. We got reports that Jason had a true breakthrough performance as a heel and would be someone to watch over the next year.

Later that night, Jody and I had drinks in his room. We couldn't be seen in public together anymore.

"Remember the kid in the front row?" Jody asked me.

"Sure do."

"He'll be back next year." He took a sip of his Jack Daniels. "He'll be back, I guarantee it."

FLYER, FLYER

MARY FAN

For most, the circus is at once alluring and frightening… a weird, mysterious place full of otherworldly wonders and dangers, that draws you in and doesn't let go. But to me, it's home.

Which is why I'm always bummed to leave the studio after my aerial silks class is done, and especially so today. I plop down on a bench beside the cubbies, under a cheery red-and-white sign for New Heights Aerial. My tank top and leggings are soaked in sweat, and soreness settles into my arms and shoulders. I'd be disappointed if it were any other way.

"Nice splits today, Skylar!"

I look around, confused—I skipped the splits today because of a sore hamstring. Then I glimpse one of the other students waving at my classmate Regan from across the room. She shrugs, and I shake my head. People have been getting us mixed up since we both started coming to this after-school program freshman year. It's not hard to see why—we're the exact same height and have nearly identical builds. Plus, we both keep our long, straight black hair in high ponytails, so from the back, it's impossible to tell us apart. Probably doesn't help that we're both Asian—though she's half Japanese, half white, and I'm the daughter of Chinese immigrants.

Though we have similar face shapes—high cheeks, pointed chin—you'd never mistake my round eyes for her sharper ones, or my finer lips for her cherry mouth.

Regan settles down beside me. "Can't believe that was our last class… ever."

"It's not our last class." I throw her an annoyed look. Regan has always been dramatic. "Sure, we won't be in the youth program anymore, but they have adult classes."

"Will you have time for them in college, though?"

I purse my lips. *I'll make time… it's money that'll be the problem.* My parents made it clear that if I wanted to continue my circus studies after high school, I'd have to pay for them myself. Which, fair. They could barely afford to send me in the first place. I don't feel like getting into that, though, so I only shrug in response.

Regan pulls the phone from her leggings pocket and lets out a long sigh as she checks her notifications. A half-sad, half-angry look clouds her eyes.

I peer into her face. "Okay, what's up? You've seemed bummed out all afternoon."

She twists her mouth, then turns her screen toward me. "A bunch of my friends are talking about this wellness retreat in Arizona that they're all going on. One of their cousins owns the place. I was invited, and I really, *really* wanna go. It's supposed to be *life changing.* I want some clarity before deciding what to do with the rest of my life, you know? Do some soul-searching and whatnot."

"Isn't that why you deferred college?"

She shakes her head. "My mom told me to so I could pursue a performance career like the one she used to have, back when she did ballet. Don't know why I went with it… guess I'm too used to listening to her."

"And she doesn't want you going on a wellness retreat."

"Hell, no. That'd mean time off from training, and if you take time off, you get sloppy!" Regan lets out a cynical laugh. "Besides, I'm already enrolled in the Gravity Arts intensive, and it's at the same time."

"Oh, poor you." A disgruntled feeling rumbles in my gut. I would *kill* to attend the Gravity Arts Institute—a prestigious circus school in Vermont whose student showcases attract talent scouts. Lots of professional circus artists got their starts there. I used to dream of going, and if Regan can get in, then I'm pretty sure I could, too. But I didn't even apply. It's the money thing again… if after-school classes at our local New Jersey studio are barely within reach, then a fancy two-week residential program is totally out of the question.

"Yeah, yeah, I know. 'Poor little rich girl.'" Regan smiles at me.

I give a sheepish look. "Sorry…"

"Don't apologize. I know how much you wanted to go. Trust me, if I could give you my spot at Gravity Arts, I would."

"Did you say Gravity Arts?" Zephyr, one of the other advanced students, reaches past us to grab their bag from a cubby. Their long, rainbow-dyed bangs sweep their ivory forehead. "I'm so excited. After two summers of silks, I'm finally gonna focus on rope. You're sticking with silks, right, Regan?" They turn to me for an answer, and their eyes widen. "Oh, I'm sorry! You're Skylar!" They whip around. "*Regan*," they say, addressing the correct person this time. "My bad, my bad. Anyway, silks, right?"

Regan gives them a thumbs-up. "One apparatus is enough for me."

"To each their own. See you in Vermont!" They stride to the door and exit.

I grab my shoes from a cubby. As I tug them on, Regan abruptly grips my shoulder.

A wild spark lights her dark eyes. "Skylar," she says in a conspiratorial whisper. "I think I can actually do it."

I furrow my brow. "Do what?"

"Give you my spot! At Gravity Arts!"

"Huh?"

"People have been getting us mixed up forever—remember that one teacher who thought we were twins?"

I blink. "You're not saying…"

"You go to Gravity Arts as me, while I go to Arizona with my friends."

A quick laugh escapes me. "That'd never work!"

"Yeah, it would! Just tell your parents that you got a last-minute scholarship, and don't let them see you check in with my ID."

"What about *your* parents?"

"They'll be traveling. My dad's got all this business in Japan, and my mom's going with him for, you know, social functions and stuff. My boyfriend was always gonna be the one to drive me up."

"And what about him?"

"I'll tell Ethan I got another friend to do it. He'll be happy—means he'll get to go to his young leaders summit in DC a day early."

"Other people from this studio will be there, like Zephyr."

"Not in the silks program—I checked when they sent us the welcome email. Don't you see? It's perfect! You'll just have to feed me info so when my parents call me, I can tell them about *your* day. Oh, and you'll have to update my public Instagram and TikTok accounts. My mom keeps an eye on those."

I start to protest again but pause. Regan's social media videos are often shot from a distance, and she likes using filters. We *do* resemble each other… I've accidentally sent her videos of myself that I took in class, instead of the ones I took of her.

Regan's lips curl. "You're in, aren't you?"

I'm gonna regret this. But I'd regret it more if I chickened out. "Sure, I'm in."

Even as Mom pulls into the line of cars waiting to enter the Gravity Arts Institute and drop off their kids for the summer, I still can't believe Regan and I are actually making this scheme happen. Her drivers' license and phone—she's gonna use her laptop for everything—sit heavily in my pocket, and I keep checking to make sure they're still there, as if they might have evaporated during the eight-hour drive from our house in Central Jersey to the school in northern Vermont.

Mom, a small woman with a graying bob, glances at me. "Are you all right? You've been antsy this entire drive. Nervous?"

"Of course I'm nervous!" Thank goodness going to such an elite circus program, under any circumstances, gives me good reason to be. I try to smile. "But also excited. Coming here was my dream, and I don't wanna screw it up."

"You'll do wonderfully, sweetie." Mom glances out the window with an impatient look. "If we ever get there…"

That's the opening I've been waiting for. "I can walk the rest of the way. I've only got one suitcase, and some of these divas brought so much, it could take *hours* to get to the front."

"Oh, it won't be that bad…"

I gesture at the clock. "It'll be nearly midnight by the time you get home as it is. I don't think it's worth waiting just so you can say goodbye at the Institute's doors instead of here."

She hesitates, but I know I've got her. She's been complaining for the past week about how she'd have to make the marathon drive back to Jersey then work tomorrow. I still can't believe she's making the whole roundtrip in one day, but she had work yesterday, too. At least she got a day off, unlike Dad—the restaurant where he works as a line cook is short-staffed and needs him constantly.

"Very well." Mom puts the car into park. "If I make good enough time, I might even be able to start early and finally begin cleaning out Mrs. Dunn's basement."

"Since when do home health aides clean basements?"

"Since their clients' daughters offer them two thousand dollars to do it. Now, don't forget to text as soon as you're settled in. I want photos of your dorm!"

"Sure, Mom."

I give her a quick hug and kiss goodbye, then hop out of the car, grab my suitcase from the trunk, and start walking up the road toward the school. I'm not the only kid who gave up on the drop-off line—several others wheel along ahead of me.

Mom pulls the car out of the line, then waves from the open window and yells, "Love you, Sky!"

My eyes widen. *No one was paying attention, right?*

"Welcome, Sky!"

I jump as a young woman with honey-brown skin and tight black curls, streaked with pink highlights, approaches holding a tablet. "What?"

"Sorry, didn't mean to startle you." The woman sticks out her hand. "I'm Avery Johnson, and I'm interning with the office for the summer. Basically, that means I do admin-y things and social media. What's your full name, please?"

"Um… Regan Takahashi. 'Sky' is just something my mom calls me. No one else calls me that. It's kinda embarrassing, actually." I'm babbling. I've gotta stop babbling… "Anyway, I should check in."

"Oh, sure. But first, can I get a photo for our Insta? Documenting the move-in process, you know." She waves the tablet.

"No! Uh… I mean, I've been sitting in the car forever, and I'm a mess.

I've got no make-up on, my hair's all tangled…"

She laughs. "All right, I get it. I'll catch you next time."

"Sure." I give an awkward grin and rush off. Note to self: Keep an eye out for Avery. Last thing I need is a pic of my face on Gravity Arts' socials. Regan told me her mom follows that account.

The Institute's main building—which, according to the website, used to be an early 20th-century hotel—towers ahead, its brick facade surrounded by bright green trees. This is where the dorms, offices, cafeteria, and various storage closets are, and where ground classes like stretch and conditioning workouts take place.

I stride through the double doors and glance around for where to check in. For the millionth time, I stick my hand in my pocket to make sure Regan's ID and phone are still there.

"That's right, everyone, I'm here at the greatest youth circus program in the world, Gravity Arts Institute, and they ain't prepared for what they 'bout to get!" A loud, obnoxious voice reverberates through the wide atrium. "Oh, and hey, welcome to those of you just tuning in! In case you don't know for whatever reason, I'm Diego Ramirez, he/him, your next circus star, and I'll be taking you along on my journey this summer…"

Great, an "influencer." I duck my head, wishing I'd thought to wear a hat or something. It doesn't take long to glimpse the tall, dark-haired boy with a selfie stick.

I twist away and free my long hair from its ponytail, letting it fall over my face. I probably look like some horror movie ghost, but whatever.

The word "Registration" splashes across a paper sign taped to the wall with an arrow pointing to the corridor on the left. I head toward it, dragging my suitcase.

"… and here we have—what the—?!"

Something bumps into my suitcase, and the patter of desperate footsteps sounds behind me. I glimpse a pair of sneakered feet trying desperately to regain their balance. This Diego guy must've backed into me. That's what happens when you're too busy staring at your own face in a screen to look where you're going.

He laughs. "Sorry about that, everyone! But hey, now you get to meet one of my classmates—"

Oh, no. I dodge as he swings the selfie stick around.

"C'mon, don't be shy! Say hi to my followers!" He tries to angle the phone toward me again.

I leap behind my suitcase and curl up into a ball behind it. A ridiculous hiding spot, but I didn't see any others. "Get away from me!"

"Whoa, okay… Sorry, everyone, seems my new classmate doesn't like the spotlight. Kinda weird for a circus artist, but hey, we're all weird here."

Irritation bursts through my chest. "If you have something to say, say it to *me*, not your random followers."

"Oh, and she's a little irritable—wait, sorry. I never asked your pronouns."

"She/her. Go away."

"Gimme a moment, everyone, seems someone needs a little soothing."

Still ducked against my suitcase, I peer at the floor, trying to get some inkling of what's going on.

Diego's sneakers appear beside me. "I paused it. You can come out now."

Warily, I glance up, and when I see that the selfie stick is now by his side—with the phone screen off—I stand and finally get a good look at the guy. Tousled black curls frame majestic cheekbones, which cut across a bold-featured face with an amber-tan complexion and blunt chin. Warm brown eyes stare at me from beneath thick black brows. I won't lie—he's hot. Of course he is. He's got *followers*.

I roll my eyes. "You shouldn't record people without their consent."

"What's the big deal?" An irritated—and irritating—smirk lifts his lips.

"Don't tell me you aren't posting videos of yourself all up and down the internet anyway."

"Sure, I post stuff for my friends and family, but that's my business—"

"Regan!" Avery waves to me from across the atrium. "Your dorm counselor was asking if you'd checked in yet. Can you go find her when you're done?"

"Sure," I say.

Diego gives me a funny look. "Wait… Regan? As in Regan Takahashi?" A harsh laugh escapes him. "So, you're *not* camera shy. Just a hypocrite."

"Excuse me?"

"You don't remember me, do you? Aerial Dreams Circus Camp? Summer after seventh grade? You were always taking photos and videos for your socials." He lifts an eyebrow. "Unless you've deleted your accounts since?"

"Um… no…" I scowl. "But that still doesn't mean you can just stick your phone in my face!"

"Whatever." He furrows his brow. "You look different…"

Alarm seizes me, and I channel it into an indignant look. "Well, *yeah*. It's been, what, five years? Of course I don't look the same as when I was thirteen." Sensing that he's searching my face for the Regan he used to know, I scowl. "Stop staring at me. It's creepy."

"I wasn't staring. Still think everyone's obsessed with you, huh?"

"Look who's talking. Don't you have followers to get back to?"

"Yeah, I do, actually. I'll see you around." As Diego marches off, he turns his camera back on.

I duck into the corridor to make sure I won't get caught in his shot. Seems he didn't get along with Regan back in the day, and I certainly didn't help matters.

That's fine. If I have my way, that's the last I'll see of that vain, self-centered jerk.

How're things going?

The text from Regan pops up as I'm about to grab my tote bag and head to the aerial studio, which currently has no scheduled activities but is open for anyone who wants to train on their own. It comes from her private, secret Instagram account, only for family and friends, to the public one that she left unlocked on the phone she gave me.

I give her a brief summary of yesterday afternoon and evening—how I kept anyone from catching me on social media, how I posted photos and videos of the campus that I took but wasn't in, how otherwise, everything seems to be going smoothly.

She responds with:

Awesome. My mom texted saying she'd seen the photos and was glad I seem happy with my room and stuff, but she wants to see pics of me, so make sure to get some of yourself. Also, she's totally tracking my phone like I knew she would… had to come up with a wild tale for why I didn't leave NJ till the morning of drop-off… so if you plan to sneak out or anything, make sure you leave it in your dorm.

I chuckle to myself. I'm not the type to sneak out—Regan must know that.

I'd actually seen the text from her mom—Regan gets them on both her phone and laptop—and was already planning to post some videos during my workout; if I put the phone on the ground while I'm doing stuff near the ceiling, no one will see my face. It's a little weird reading texts that're meant to be between her and her mom, but she doesn't have a problem with it. Said she never really uses her texts anyway. Her parents, being in Japan, are mostly using WhatsApp; the lone text must've been a force of habit. And she's using her secret Insta, which she did log out of on her phone, to keep in touch with her boyfriend and the friends going with her to Arizona.

I head out of my room and down the stairs. The aerial studio is actually an enormous white tent that sits in the middle of a wide field behind the main building. Beyond that lie the green trees and mountains after which Vermont was named.

I round a corner. The back door, which is just ahead, swings open. Zephyr walks through, along with two others from New Heights Aerial.

Crap! I whirl and head back the way I came.

"Regan?" Zephyr says.

Footsteps patter behind me. I don't want to say anything—I don't know if my voice sounds enough like Regan's to fool someone we both know.

So, I speed to a run instead.

"Hey, girl, where're you off to?" A laugh colors Zephyr's voice. "Regan!"

This is ridiculous—I have no idea where I'm going! Any second, Zephyr and the others will catch up to me, and then what?

Salvation comes in the form of an open door ahead. An equipment closet full of aerial supplies… and costumes.

A wild idea strikes me. I duck inside, snatch the first mask I see—some red feathery Venetian thing—and pull it on.

"Whoa, nice!" Zephyr sounds like they're literally right behind me. "So, this is where they keep the cool stuff. What're you doing here?"

I draw a breath and turn. "Good evening, gentlefolk," I say in an exaggerated showman voice. I bow deeply. "Welcome to the Closet of Wonders."

A weirded-out look twists Zephyr's face. "Regan, what're you doing?"

"It's… Re-*gahn* the Magnificent." Some strange accent colors my voice. I must sound like a kindergartener's impression of Dracula. "And I'll thank you to address me as such."

"Oh, I see, we're in character." Zephyr gives a whimsical smile. "I beg your forgiveness, Madam Magnificent." They bow deeply. "What're you up to now?"

"Open workout… I must… hone my art."

"I've never seen you do a character piece before. It's always 'look at me, I am a perfect, be-*yoo*-tiful aerialist.' Didn't think you'd be bold enough—respect."

The other two nod and comment in agreement.

"If you'll excuse me." I brush past them, keeping my head high as I imagine my newly made-up character would. *Whew, that was close.*

Though the mask itches, I keep it on even after I leave the building. Regan said no one we know is in the *silks* program. Well, Zephyr and the other two are in rope, and I have no idea who's signed up for trapeze, hoop, or anything else. Best to stay incognito for now.

My phone pings—it's Regan.

Hey, my mom is really bugging me for a pic. Can you snap something? Like, back-of-the-head or whatever?

I can do better than that. I hold her phone out, turn my face to the sky, and snap a masked three-quarter selfie with the studio and the sign stating *Gravity Arts Aerial Studio* clearly visible in the background. I send it to Regan, and her response is:

PERFECT!!!

I grin. Yes, this is all going to work out…

No one I recognize is in the studio when I enter, and so I relieve myself of the mask, find the nearest set of silks, warm up, and pop in a pair of wireless ear buds. Soon, I'm lost in my head as I improvise to one of my favorite songs, twisting through poses and sequences, playing with choreography, and letting the music carry me to another dimension.

Day One was for settling in, orientation, and open workout if you wanted. But Day Two is when the scheduled activities begin. And following breakfast and a morning stretch class—which, fortunately, none of the New Heights people were in—I head to my first real silks workshop at the studio.

The enormous tent is big enough to house more than a dozen aerial points, from which various apparatuses can be suspended. Multiple classes occur at once, and I had a moment of panic when I realized my workshops could be concurrent with those of people from New Heights. But then I reminded myself that everyone is there to focus on their own training, not watch me. Besides, the points are spread out enough that classes occur on opposite sides of the structure. I still brought a hoodie, just in case.

"… and I'm so excited to be starting the first class in our performance workshop, which will culminate in a showcase at the end of the program!"

Great. Diego. Though it's pretty warm in the tent, I pull on the hoodie in case his camera swings in my direction.

"… everyone, there's gonna be scouts from Cirque Céleste attending, and if they like me, they could send me to one of their elite training camps, which are feeders for their world-famous shows. Suffice it to say, this is an important one…"

A shudder runs through me. I've been so busy worrying about being "Regan" that I nearly forgot that I have something else to be nervous about. Cirque Céleste… they've got half a dozen traveling shows, plus residencies in Vegas, and are generally known as the best of the circus world. I know I have a long way to go before I could perform with them, but to even pass their training camp—which lots of people attend multiple times before being hired—would give me the credentials I need to start auditioning for professional circuses. Yeah, the reward for doing well in training is more training, but that's what it takes to perform this gorgeous, thrilling, dangerous art at a high level. And I intend to take it as far as I can go.

"Welcome, everyone!" A small, muscular woman with a brown topknot strides toward us. "I'm Rebecca, and I'm excited to work with you all on our piece for the showcase!"

"Gotta go, everyone, teacher's here." Diego hastily puts his phone and selfie stick away.

Rebecca gestures for us to gather, and the twelve of us in this workshop huddle around or plop down on the blue crash mat in front of her. "For those of you who were here last year, yes, this will be the same choreography. However, I challenge you to find new interpretations. For those of you who are new, this piece consists primarily of partnering—so, two people on one pair of silks, and all the pairs doing the same, or similar, things simultaneously. Though there are a few solo sequences, so you'll each get a chance to show off. I've watched all of your application videos and assigned partners based on those, but we can switch if necessary."

In my case, she picked based on Regan's video, but that shouldn't be an issue. Sure, her splits are better, but I've got a bendier back... she's got stronger hip keys, but my inverts are more consistent... it'll even out.

Rebecca starts calling out pairs. Eventually, she says, "Regan Takahashi... and Diego Ramirez."

Of. Course. I don't think I've ever rolled my eyes so hard in my life. The universe is totally having a laugh at my expense.

I glance over at Diego, who stands with his arms crossed. I'll have to ask

Regan what happened in junior high to make him dislike her so much. Not that it matters. I don't like him, either. Plus, that annoying live-streaming habit of his could screw me over.

Rebecca did say we could switch. Maybe I'll screw up on purpose to make sure that happens.

"All right, let's start with some basic partnering warm-ups." Rebecca gestures at the six pairs of silks, arranged in two rows of three. "Bases—cross-back straddles. Flyers—pikes, splits, broken arrows. You know the drill."

In our pairing, Diego's the base—which makes total sense, since he's about six inches taller and way broader in the shoulders. Like it or not, size matters in partnering. Though it isn't necessarily gendered—the pair beside us consists of a female base and her much-smaller male flyer, and the pair beside them is two girls.

"All right, let's do this," Diego grumbles as he climbs the bright red silks.

I pull off my hoodie—coast seems clear for now, and all that clothing will get in my way. "Sure you don't need to set up your phone for your followers first?"

The corner of his mouth flicks. "Hey, I've got no problem with live-streaming warm-ups and compiling my screw-ups into blooper reels. It's my partner who can't stand to be seen unless she's *perfect*."

I dunk my hands in the rosin bucket; the same stuff violinists use on their bows makes your hands sticky so it's easier to grip things. "At least I don't need random internet people watching my every move to feel important."

"You're one to talk." He wraps his feet—one on each fabric—twists around so they form an X on his back, and then turns upside down, supported by that X, his legs stick-straight in a wide straddle. With his arms now free, he reaches down.

Just be a pro. I school my features into a neutral expression, approach, and reach up.

He pulls his arms back. "Okay, let's hear it now, before I've gotta try to respond with you pulling down on me."

"What're you talking about?"

"You seriously don't remember?"

I shrug. "Junior high was a long time ago."

He starts to say something, then huffs. "Fine. Yeah, you're right. Bygones, and all."

I reach up again. "Can we just warm up?"

"Sure. Still, pretending you don't remember is kind of a jerk move."

I choose not to reply. *Regan, what the hell did you do to him?*

He grips my forearms, and I grip him back. He's as sturdy as I'd expect for an aspiring circus artist—all hard muscle and rough skin. I hate to admit it, but he's probably the best base I've worked with that wasn't a teacher. When I invert between his arms, I feel as secure as I would on solid ground. And when he pulls me up, it's as if I weigh nothing at all.

He's not the only one working, though. I hold myself tight as I push into a split. Right now, my apparatus is a person, and that person will feel every move I make, so I'd better keep steady. I bring my legs into a V-shape and arch my back while he pulls up with one arm, tipping my head upward.

That's when I glimpse Avery, with her tablet up in front of her, obviously taking photos or videos.

Panic spirals through me. I'm not sure what exactly happens—my whole body flails, and my grip loosens. My foot smacks into something and, the next thing I know, I'm plopping down on the crash mat.

"Oh my God!" Rebecca rushes over.

I point at Avery. "Turn that thing off!"

Avery lowers the tablet. "Don't worry, I'll delete the video."

"Do it *now!*"

"Okay, fine!" With an irritated look, Avery taps the screen.

"Is everyone all right?" Rebecca asks, then turns to Diego, who's descending from the silks.

"Yeah." He rubs his cheek.

I gasp. So that's what my foot hit. "I'm so sorry!"

Rebecca furrows her brow. "What happened?"

"Isn't it obvious?" Avery says. "He dropped her."

Diego whirls to Rebecca. "I didn't—"

"It was completely my fault." Standing up, I give both Diego and Rebecca apologetic looks. "I freaked out when I saw Avery with the camera. I went… noodle-y… and accidentally kicked my partner… in the face. I'm fine, though. We're both fine… right?"

"Yeah." He gives me an odd look.

Rebecca sighs. "Glad no one got hurt. And if videos make you uncomfortable, I'll ask Avery not to take them during our class." She approaches the young woman.

Diego shakes his head at me. "You really don't like being filmed unless you're doing it yourself, do you?"

I shrug. "When I do it myself, I control my image."

He frowns, then nods. "I get that."

I blink. I thought he'd call me—or Regan—a hypocrite again.

But something about him seems more relaxed as he turns back to the silks. "Let's try again."

It's not until I'm reaching up to him that I realize I blew my chance to switch partners. But… it would've been wrong to blame him when the fall was literally my fault, and I'm not *that* desperate. Plus, he's a really good base.

You've gotta post more! Mom's getting suspicious—she asked if I was doing okay because I haven't updated my social media as much as usual!

The message from Regan's private account pops up on her phone, which sits on the desk in my dorm beside the sandwich I grabbed from the caf earlier. Couldn't risk eating there in case Zephyr or someone else from New Heights spotted me.

Annoyed, I remind Regan that I've already posted the masked pic to her Instagram grid, plus a compilation of drops and spins—where I'm a blur—to her TikTok. Apparently, though, that's not enough. I assure her that I'll do more. Diego will probably call me out again for constantly updating Regan's social media while dodging everyone else's. Speaking of Diego…

I type:

Say, do you remember Diego Ramirez? Because he seems to remember you and has some kind of grudge.

After several moments, her answer appears:

Ugh, probably because I was a total control freak in junior high. He was my base at this summer workshop, and I was always yelling and nitpicking at him… was afraid he'd make me look bad. Pretty sure I made him cry once. I wanted so badly to fulfill Mom's dreams of me being the most perfect aerialist in the world or something that it made me a huge jerk… Tell him I'm sorry?

I twist my mouth. Sounds like Regan used to be something of a bully… glad I never knew that version of her.

A notification pops up before I can reply. I furrow my brow. Someone is messaging Regan's public account… her boyfriend, Ethan, saying he misses her and sending rose emojis.

I wrinkle my nose. Pretending to be Regan to her boyfriend was *not* part of the plan. I message Regan's private account to tell her what's going on, and I can practically see her rolling her eyes when she replies:

I TOLD him not to message me there! Don't worry, I'll take care of it. BTW I just got a message to this account from Zephyr. They invited me—well, you—to sneak out after curfew with a few others to check out a nearby swimming hole.

I cock my brow and type:

You told them no, right?

To my dismay, Regan's answer is:

I told them yes! It's me! I never say no to that kind of thing, and they know it! So you've gotta show up or they might realize something's going on.

My jaw drops.

WHAT?!

Regan replies:

You'll be fine! It'll be dark. Just stay in the shadows.

I can't believe the nerve of her. My mind whirls with ways to get out of it... but if Regan has been messaging Zephyr directly, then anything I do might only make things worse. I could text, but Zephyr would be weirded out if "Regan" was both texting and messaging at the same time, and saying contradictory things. I definitely can't speak to them in person... the "in character" bit might not work a second time.

Sighing, I ask Regan where and when I'm supposed to meet Zephyr.

Thank goodness it's a cool night, so my zip-up hoodie won't look out of place. I didn't think to pack a swimsuit, so my oldest, cheapest leotard will be getting soaked tonight.

About half a dozen kids are already waiting by the back door where Zephyr told Regan to meet them. With all the exterior lights switched off for the night, only a few cell phone flashlights illuminate the space. The good news: More people means it'll be easier to avoid talking to Zephyr directly. The bad news: The two others from New Heights are with them.

"Regan? That you?" Zephyr turns their flashlight toward me.

I duck my head. "Yup." The less I say, the fewer chances for anyone to recognize my voice.

"You okay?"

I nod.

"Are you—"

"Hey, hope I'm not late!" A shadowy figure rushes up to us—Diego. *Great.*

Zephyr turns to him. "Not late, but you are the last one we were waiting on. Let's go!"

They lead us across the backyard of the Institute and onto an overgrown trail in the woods behind it. While the others chatter excitedly, I hang back to avoid being caught in someone's flashlight.

After a few minutes, we arrive at a dark swimming hole—a deep pool at the bottom of a waterfall that spills down from the wide creek above. Moonlight skitters across the ripples, and cell phone lights flash off gleaming rocks at the edges.

Zephyr, Diego, and a few others ditch their clothes right away and jump in with whoops and shouts. I put one hand into the water and snatch it back. This pool might as well be an ice bucket. *Nope. Absolutely not.*

Diego looks around, damp hair clinging to his forehead. "Hey, can someone take a video of me?"

"I will!" I answer a bit too quickly, but being behind the camera guarantees I won't get caught in the shot.

"Thanks!" He climbs out of the water and grabs his phone from the shore. I don't know how he isn't shivering. He hands me the device, with the camera already open and flashlight on, then points to a large rock. "I'm gonna do a flip off that. Hit record on my signal."

"Are you sure that's a good idea?"

"Yeah, it'll be fine."

He climbs up the edge of the rock, shouts down to the others below to clear out of the way, and then turns to me with a thumbs-up. I aim the camera at him. The flashlight glints off his toned torso and gives his brown skin a ghostly tint as I hit record.

A cheesy grin spreads across his face. "Hey, everyone! Got a new trick for you. Now, you've seen me do flips before, but not like this!" He rushes to the edge of the rock with a "*Wooooo!*" and dives over the edge, tucking his knees to his chest.

I follow him with the camera as he rotates—not just once, but twice. I have to admit, it's impressive.

He hits the water with a cry, and his head vanishes beneath the surface.

"Diego!" I drop the phone and rush into the water. My breath seizes at the cold, and I search frantically.

Diego pops up with a gasp. "*Ow!* Felt like my whole body got slapped!" He glances at me. "Where's my phone?"

My jaw drops. "Are you serious? I thought you were dead!"

"Get the phone! Keep recording!"

"You—"

"Do it!"

"Fine!" I stomp back to shore, grab the phone, and aim it at him.

Diego gives the camera two thumbs-ups. "Not bad for the first time, right?"

I roll my eyes as he continues with his usual influencer spiel—like, subscribe, blah, blah, blah.

"All right, I'm done," he says, and I stop the recording. "Thanks for that. Your dramatic rescue attempt will make this video even better."

I hand him his phone, still shaking my head in disbelief. "You're ridiculous."

"Yeah, I know." He scrolls through the footage. "But it's the only reason I can do any of this." He gestures broadly toward the Institute.

"Thought you loved the attention."

He shakes his head. "My parents can barely afford our rent—no way they're shelling out hundreds of dollars a month for me to train. I work part time, but it isn't really enough. So, I create content and do brand ambassador-type stuff to make up the difference. When something's your passion, all the ridiculous things you do to sustain it feel worthwhile."

A grin creeps across my face. "I get that."

"Yeah, right. Don't tell me you've ever had to throw yourself off a rock hoping to keep your stats high enough to keep getting paid. Everything gets handed to you."

The grin twists into a grimace. I want so badly to say, *Actually, I had to lie to my parents, my classmates, and everyone here for a chance Regan didn't even want.*

Diego must have mistaken my discomfort for hurt, because his eyes soften and he says, "Sorry, that was uncalled for."

"I mean… you're not wrong," I mumble. "It's not fair, how some people simply *get* the things that others have to fight for."

He looks at me for a long moment, and something shifts in his eyes. "You've really changed since junior high."

"Thanks?" I hesitate, then decide I might as well try to clear the air, even if it means lying. "Hey… sorry for what happened back then." Recalling what Regan told me, I say, "I wanted so badly to fulfill my mom's dreams of me being the most perfect aerialist in the world or something that it made me a huge jerk. So… uh… sorry." It feels so, *so* weird to apologize for something I didn't do—didn't even know about until, like, five minutes ago. But if we're going to be partners, then I don't want Regan's past screwing us up. "I can't take back what happened, but I can offer an apology?"

To my surprise, a soft smile lights Diego's face. "That's all I ever wanted, Regan. And… I have to admit… you *were* pretty perfect, and trying to keep up made me better, too. Still feels like that."

My stomach twists. I shouldn't have said all that… shouldn't have brought up a past I didn't live. But what did he mean by "still feels like that"? I try to think of a reply, but then a great splash douses us both.

I gasp. Zephyr and the others are in the middle of a splashing war, and clearly, they don't care about collateral damage.

"Hey!" I cry.

Diego bumps me with his elbow. "Let's go get them for that. C'mon, you're already soaked!"

I hesitate. *Oh, screw it.* "Sure, let's go!"

"Woohoo!" He races into the water.

I yank off my hoodie and jump in after him, yelping at the biting cold.

Water suddenly splashes into my face. "Argh!"

A guilty grin spreads across Diego's face. "Sorry, was aiming for Zephyr…"

"Liar!" I splash him back, and a laugh escapes me.

"Okay, so it might have been revenge for that time you made me cry."

An uncomfortable feeling snakes through my gut, but another icy torrent—courtesy of Diego's flicking hands—distracts me.

Instinct takes over, and I bombard him with water. He bombards me right back, and our laughter rings through the night.

For a few moments, I forget all about the cold, but then a huge shudder runs through me. I'm suddenly aware of how chilled my insides are, and I spin away, toward the shore.

"What's wrong?" Diego asks.

"Too… cold…" I crawl out of the water, shaking.

He follows me to shore, then grabs my zip-up hoodie. I hold out one quivering hand but can't seem to grasp it.

"Here, let me help." He wraps it over my shoulders and starts rubbing my arms. His touch sends heat coursing through my veins—a comfortable heat, a gentle heat. Like that of a fireplace on a snowy night.

A quiet bliss descends on my mind, and I lean into him. Our eyes meet, and a strange energy crackles through the air. The next thing I know, his arms are wrapped around me, and my head is resting against his shoulder.

Above, wispy clouds veil a timid, almost-full moon, and a clean breeze rustles the sweetly scented trees. With Diego's warmth surrounding me, all worry melts from my heart.

After two whole hours of stretching and conditioning, I'm glad to have the rest of the day free. Still sweating from all those pull-ups, leg lifts, planks, and such, I head toward my dorm.

"Regan!" Avery waves at me from ahead.

My eyes widen as she holds up her tablet's camera, and I whirl away from her.

"Hey, Regan!" Avery's footsteps quicken behind me. "Your mom's been sending the Institute angry notes about you not being featured on our social media—I promised I'd fix that. Can you just—"

"No!" I speed away from her, tugging the scrunchie out of my hair so my long locks will shield my face in case she decides to snap some pics anyway. "I-I just got out of conditioning! I'm a mess!"

"That's okay! It'll be good to showcase the realness and let everyone know how much work goes into circus arts—"

"I'll send you some pics to post, okay?"

"Well, see, the Gravity Arts Institute has certain brand guidelines for our social media pages, so I need to be the one who takes the photos. Will you—"

"Nope!" I quicken to a full-blown sprint.

"Regan!"

I rush down the corridors, until I find myself facing the building's exit. The tent where aerial classes are held lies beyond. I don't know if Avery's still following me, but just in case, I head out. At least in the tent, I'll be able to climb something to get my face away from that camera.

I burst into the space, out of breath. Avery doesn't seem to have followed me… maybe I overreacted. But I don't want to risk encountering her in the building again. Might as well hang out here, where open workout is going on.

Enough of the bright midday sun seeps into the tent that lights aren't necessary. I meander along the edges, searching for a spot to drop my tote bag and loiter until I feel like training.

A movement above catches my eye—Diego, in the middle of wrapping for a pose. His eyes are shut, and he's got Bluetooth headphones secured to his ears with medical tape. Seems he's running a solo routine, and I watch, mesmerized. From our time in workshop, and from what I've seen of his Instagram and TikTok, I thought he was one of those "power" aerialists who mostly throw drops and flips and other dynamic tricks, thrilling the audience with the possibility of danger.

But it seems he has a lyrical, balletic side… the routine he's working on involves no drops at all, only graceful poses and smooth choreography that makes every movement, no matter how mundane, look like art.

He's so lost in his act that he doesn't seem to notice any of his surroundings, and soon, I'm lost, too.

Which is why I'm startled when his eyes catch mine.

The corner of his mouth flicks, and I look away quickly. *What was I doing again? Right… setting down my stuff… C'mon, Skylar! What's wrong with you?*

Since going to the swimming hole a few days ago, we've been working well as partners, and I've tried not to think about what happened as anything more than two people making peace with each other. He's been perfectly friendly, and that's all I can expect—all I want, really.

I amble awkwardly to a bench along the tent's side, dump my bag, and busy myself with restoring my ponytail.

"What'd you think?" Diego saunters over.

"Hm?" I turn to him.

"Of my new routine."

"It was… um… really nice. Are you submitting it for a show?"

He shakes his head. "Too simple. I just put it together for myself, as a challenge. I wanted to see if I could create something more dance-like, without always hiding behind stunts, you know? Anyway, since you're here, wanna work on our partner routine?"

I hesitate. "Um… I'm pretty tired from conditioning, but I also need all the practice I can get… do you think it's safe to train without a teacher? I don't have much experience with partnering, so a lot of what we've been working on is pretty new to me…"

Diego furrows his brow. "Seriously? It's pretty similar to what we learned back in junior high, and you've done other partnering workshops since, right?"

Crap, I forgot that Regan's done a ton of partner stuff! Realizing my mistake, I give an awkward grin. "Well… I mean… I dunno, I just don't feel that confident? It's not my favorite… makes me nervous."

"Wow, the great Regan Takahashi admits to being bad at something."

"I didn't say—"

"Kidding!" His lips lift, and an admiring look fills his eyes. "I like this version of you. The old Regan would never admit to being less than perfect."

Guilt trickles down my gut, but I manage to smile. "Let's just say I'm not the same person you met in junior high."

"You know, I meant what I said the other day at the swimming hole… about how you're kind of perfect."

A flutter runs through my chest. "Um…"

"I mean as an aerialist!" he says hastily. "You look like you're floating up there… like you live in those silks, and gravity has no meaning." He rubs the back of his head. "In fact, I… uh… I might have asked Rebecca to pair us."

I blink. "You did? Thought you hated me."

"I mean… yeah, I was pissed about how you treated me in junior high, and I was planning to avoid you at first. But then I saw you at open workout on the first day, doing your character piece with the mask." He glances around uncomfortably. "You have a really expressive style, and I was like, 'That's what I need in a partner.' And so, I told myself to get over what happened a long time ago and made my case to Rebecca until she agreed."

"You spied on me?"

"You weren't exactly in private!" Diego crosses his arms. "And you're one to talk—you were staring at me for my entire run just now."

My cheeks grow hot. "Right… yeah. Sorry."

"Well, it's not like I minded." His eyes glint.

My mind is still stuck on the fact that he *requested* me as a partner. Not Regan—*me.* "For what it's worth… I think you're pretty amazing. On silks, I mean."

"Thanks." He brightens. "What is it about partnering that makes you nervous?"

"I don't love that I'm climbing a person instead of the apparatus," I confess. "When you're doing a solo thing on silks, you get to wrap yourself into the fabrics to feel secure. When you're a flyer, though, the base is the one attached to the silks, and you have to rely on them in order to not fall."

"You're afraid I'll drop you… I guess I kind of did our first day in workshop. But hey, that's only because I was startled, and I know to pay better attention now. Next time, you can go as noodle-y as you want, and you wouldn't fall. Here, I'll show you." Diego holds out his hand to me.

I reach back, more by instinct than intentionally.

He grips my forearm and smirks. It's a really strong grip—and he knows it. "Try to wiggle away—flail as much as you want. You can even kick me in the face again if you'd like."

I laugh. "I'm not gonna do that!" I do yank back as hard as I can, though, and then shake and twist to throw him off. Impressively, none of that makes him budge.

"See? You've got nothing to worry about up there."

"I believe it." I smile.

He loosens his grip, but I don't withdraw—and neither does he. A shimmering heat seems to flow from his touch. As partners, we've had plenty of contact with each other. But something feels… different now.

The next thing I know, I'm staring into his eyes and leaning toward him—

A buzzing sound emits from the bench. Diego jumps, then chuckles nervously. "I think that's mine." He rushes over and picks up his phone from beside his gym bag. An apologetic look comes over his face. "It's my mom. She always talks for an hour, and then I've got my work shift later. Maybe we can practice tomorrow?"

"Yeah, sure," I say.

"Looking forward to it." He starts to turn away.

"Hey!"

He pauses. "Yeah?"

I blink. I have no idea what I meant to say. He lifts his brows, waiting.

The heat in my face could melt the polar ice caps. Finally, I manage, "I… I mean… wanna hang out sometime? Other than training, I mean?"

A smile blooms across his face. "Yeah, I'd love to."

I grin.

Diego answers the phone in Spanish, slings his bag onto his shoulder, and heads out of the noisy tent.

As I watch him leave, that grin seems stuck on my lips. If he brings that lyrical, balletic side he just showed to the choreography, and I bring the expressiveness that apparently impressed him enough to request me for a partner, then we have a good chance of creating something beautiful enough to impress the scouts. I can already see it in my head… the fluid way we'd move together…

But it's not just our skills that seem to be coming together. I've tried not to think about it, told myself to focus on aerial, but…

"Regan!"

The sound of "my" name snaps my attention back to reality.

A blond boy in a varsity jacket waves from the door. For a moment, I'm puzzled… he isn't one of my classmates…

Then I recall where I've seen that square-jawed face before, and my chest seizes.

Ethan. Regan's boyfriend.

"Hey, babe! Thought I'd surprise you!" Ethan strides into the tent.

I spin away from him. *Crap, crap, crap!*

My eyes land on the silks Diego was just training on, and an escape route opens up in my mind. I kick off my shoes and grab the fabrics.

I've never climbed so fast in my life.

"Regan! Hey!"

Clinging to the top of the silks, which spin from a metal swivel, I deepen my voice into something I hope sounds more like Regan's. "Oh… hi… honey!"

"'Honey'?" Though I make sure not to face Ethan, I can practically see his confused expression from his tone. "You never call me that. Also, you sound funny… are you okay?"

"Yeah." I clear my throat noisily. "Just… a little phlegm-y. It's cold out here."

"Should you be up there if you aren't feeling well?"

"I'm fine." I should do something to justify being in the air… Ethan's probably weirded out enough that his girlfriend hasn't come down to greet him. I scissor my legs and wrap the silks over my hips, then grab the tail, tuck into a little ball, and start spinning—the whirling will also keep him from getting a good look at me.

"Hey, well, I know how seriously you take your training, so I can wait down here until you're done."

"No! I mean… could be a while… what are you doing here anyway? Aren't you supposed to be in DC?"

"We didn't have any important activities this weekend, and my aunt in Burlington has been begging me to visit her at her lake cabin, so I came up and figured I'd see you while I was at it. She let me borrow one of her cars. Thought we could hang out by the lake and then go somewhere for dinner. I know you're busy with Institute stuff, but you can take one day off, right? You don't have anything official scheduled—I checked with the office before coming. And… well… I miss you. I really wanted to see you in person again."

Dammit, Regan, your boyfriend actually seems sweet. And persistent…

The spinning is starting to make me dizzy, so I stretch my legs to slow down, thread one between the two fabrics, and adjust myself until I'm in a cradle of sorts. "That's… uh… nice of you… but… I can't. Need to train. Show's coming up."

"I get it. We can skip the lake, then, and just meet for dinner? You need to eat, after all, and there's a place down the road." Ethan circles the mat below, trying to get a look at my face.

I twist away from him. "I… don't have time. I want everything to be perfect for the scouts, so I can't get distracted."

"C'mon, babe, even you can't train nonstop. It'll only be a few hours."

Ugh! What do I do? WHAT DO I DO?! "Well… I mean… my mom! She'd kill me if I went off campus instead of doing something to prepare for the show. Like, studying other peoples' performance videos, or reading up on theory, or… I just can't leave, okay? You know how she is."

"Yeah, fair."

For the briefest of moments, triumph skitters through my chest.

Then, Ethan says, "I'll call her, how's that? She loves me! I'm sure I can convince her to let you—"

"*No!*" Oh God, if Ethan calls Mrs. Takahashi, then I'm finished. "I mean… she's in Japan, and it's the middle of the night there, so she's probably asleep."

"You told me she's a night owl who never goes to bed before two in the morning."

"But, but, but—" Realizing how panicked I sound, I interrupt myself with a loud cough followed by a fake sneeze. "Ugh, sorry." I draw a breath. Regan wouldn't panic. "So much rosin and chalk in the air…"

"Maybe you should come down." Ethan sounds worried.

"I'm all right. Anyway, you can't call my mom… she's got important… business."

"I'm sure she won't mind. Last time you took me to see her, she said point blank that she wanted to adopt me." He chuckles.

He's not gonna take "no" for an answer, is he? And the longer this conversation goes on, the more chances there are for me to screw up and reveal myself. "Okay, I'll go to dinner!"

"*Yes!*" In the corner of my eye, I catch him pumping his fist with all the excitement of a boy who's just landed a first date with his biggest crush.

Dammit, Regan, why do you have to have such a devoted boyfriend?

"I gotta finish training," I say. "Text me later."

"Sure thing, babe! See you tonight!"

Finally, he departs. I don't come down from the fabrics until well after he's left the tent.

Crap, crap, crap! How am I gonna get out of this one?

I rush over to the bench, grab my phone, and start typing out a message to Regan. Maybe she'll have an idea for what to do…

Regan didn't answer my messages. Not a single one. Which means that either all hundred million of the frantic notes I shot off got lost in cyberspace, or she's off the grid. *Stupid retreat!*

I considered standing Ethan up and letting her fix their relationship later—would serve her right for vanishing on me at a time like this. But then he might get suspicious… maybe even suspicious enough to reach out to Mrs. Takahashi.

So, after a lot of cursing and pacing and digging my hands into my hair, I came up with a plan.

I emerge from the Institute's building and approach the car idling by the curb.

Ethan sits behind the wheel, confusion plain on his face. I guess he's not used to seeing his girlfriend in a giant feathered mask that covers her entire face except for her mouth, which is shadowed by the long beak of a nose.

He reaches across the passenger seat and opens the door. "Babe, why are you dressed like that?"

"Call me Re-*gahn* the Magnificent." Hey, it worked on Zephyr.

I said I had a plan… not that it was a good one.

"Okay… Re-*gahn*." A perplexed smile twists his lips. "What… why…?"

"An immersive assignment—I'm to remain in character for the remainder of the day, and perhaps even into tomorrow." I speak with an exaggerated accent that bears absolutely no resemblance to any real one.

"Dedication. I like it."

As I climb into the car—which is harder than it should be in the long, sequined skirt I nabbed from the costume closet—he leans over with his lips puckered.

I dodge the kiss and hold up a hand. "Back, peasant! The Magnificent One is not to be touched!"

"Whoa, intense." Ethan withdraws with a bewildered smile. "Who's this character supposed to be?"

Hell if I know! "I am… many things. I also understand if you would prefer not to spend an evening with one so… odd…"

"Are you kidding?" Excitement fills his bright brown eyes. "You never let me see your creative process! I love getting to know this side of you. It's fascinating."

Freaking Regan couldn't have picked a jerk-ier boyfriend? "Well… I'm… glad you think so." I close the door. Guess there's no escaping now.

Ethan revs up the car, and soon, we're on our way to the restaurant. Luckily, I'm able to get him talking about his summer program, so all I have to do is throw in the occasional "uh huh" or "cool" or "that's so funny."

Now, if I can only keep him talking about himself for the rest of the evening…

We arrive at the restaurant and are seated immediately, since Ethan made a reservation. Guilt digs at me. I hate that I'm lying like this, that I'm deceiving someone who really seems like a nice guy and maybe wrecking Regan's relationship. What's gonna happen when he finds out? Or will we keep up this lie for the rest of our lives? What if she and Ethan end up getting married, and he starts telling their future kids the story of how their mom once went to a restaurant as a weird character, and she's forced to lie to them, too, and—and—

Stop spiraling, Skylar! Just… get through dinner…

Ethan pulls out a chair for me—what a gentleman—and then takes a seat across the table. "So, is this the character you'll be performing as at the showcase?" He gestures broadly at my costume.

"No, it is merely a creative exercise—" My phone buzzes. Frowning, I reach into my bag and grab it. My eyes widen—my mom's the one who's calling. That's when I realize I should have brought Regan's phone instead of my own… I was so busy panicking, I didn't think when I grabbed it. I shove the phone back into my bag. "Spam call."

"Ugh, I hate those." Ethan takes a sip of his water. "So, how does this creative exercise work?"

I scramble for ideas. "Well, it begins with—"

The phone buzzes again. And again. And again. I can't say more than three words without it going off.

Ethan's brows gather. "Do you wanna get that? Seems like it might be important."

I squeeze my eyes. *Seriously, Mom, you had to call NOW?*

I grab the phone and am immediately bombarded with half a dozen text notifications, all from Mom, with messages like *Skylar! Why you not picking up?* and *I'm worried! Call mom!!!*

The phone goes off yet again, the word *MOM* yelling at me across the screen. Doing my best not to grimace, I pick up. "Hi, Mom."

"Skylar! What's wrong? I thought you were dead! Why didn't you respond?" Her voice is so loud, I fear for a moment that Ethan might have heard her yell my name.

But he must not have, because he leans across the table and calls out, "Hi, Mrs. Takahashi! Hope you're enjoying Japan!"

"Skylar, what was that?" Mom demands. "What was he talking about?"

"Nothing… just… I'm someplace crowded." I keep the deepness in my voice to prevent Ethan from hearing my real one, though I've dropped the weird accent.

"Why do you sound like that? Are you sick?"

"No, it's the mountain air… doing weird things to my throat."

"You need to take better care of your health!" She goes on to lecture me about getting enough of the right nutrients and avoiding cold foods and so on and so on.

The waiter comes by, though I'm too busy trying to stop my mom's TED Talk to pay attention.

"Hey… hey, Mom, can we talk about this later?" I plead. "I'm in the middle of something."

"I'll have a ginger ale, please," Ethan says to the waiter. "And she'll have a Diet Coke with lemon. I'm her boyfriend—she always gets the same thing."

Mom stops in the middle of her latest sentence, and there's a brief pause. "Boyfriend?! Skylar, you have a *boyfriend?*"

"Don't pay attention—it's just background noise." My heart races. "Please, Mom, can we—"

"Don't lie to me, Skylar! You're on a date, aren't you? That's why you don't have time for your mom! Why didn't you tell me about this boy?"

I nervously clench my skirt under the table. "I'll explain everything later, okay? I just… I…"

"Fine, fine, have your date." She huffs loudly. "But you call me as soon as you get home!"

I exhale. "Thanks, Mom. Love you!"

"Love you, too, sweetie. Talk later." Mercifully, she hangs up.

An involuntary sigh escapes me, and I slump against the back of my chair.

"You okay, babe?" Ethan reaches for my hand.

I quickly withdraw it and straighten, attempting to resume character. "Of course. Apologies for any… confusion."

Concern fills his eyes. "Hey, I know you're taking this character thing seriously, but… you seem stressed, and I can tell it isn't the acting. C'mon, talk to me."

"I'm fine, really."

"It's the program, isn't it? The way you've been so worried about perfecting your routine, and now committing to a character assignment all night… Regan, I knew this place was intense, but I had no idea it was that bad."

I draw a breath. *Be calm. If Ethan gets worried, he could call Mrs. Takahashi. So, let's not give him a reason to worry.* "It's not bad, really. Every performer gets nervous before a big show."

"You're doing a partner piece, right? Is that what's stressing you out? I know what a perfectionist you are. You're afraid he'll make you look bad. 'A terrible base will ruin an act, no matter how good the flyer is'—that's what you told me."

"Well—"

"Would you like to order any appetizers?"

I jump at the waiter's voice. *It can't be…*

I glance up, and my stomach sinks. That's Diego, wearing a T-shirt with the restaurant's name and holding a pen and pad. *He said he had a work shift…*

and of course, it had to be at this restaurant…

I swallow hard. "I—"

"I'll give you a few minutes." He walks off with a stormy expression.

I didn't say any of that stuff Ethan mentioned! I want to call out after him, but then Ethan might realize that I'm not Regan. *What a freaking nightmare.*

Ethan starts going on about how I—well, Regan—have nothing to worry about because of how beautiful and talented I am, how many times I've proven myself before, etc., etc. I nod along but keep looking for Diego, waiting for him to return to earshot. I need him to know that I'd never insult him behind his back.

Eventually, he makes his way back to our table. "Are you ready to order?"

"Hey, uh… I…" My words stumble, and my brain can't seem to recover. "Look, I didn't say…"

"Just let me know your order, miss."

Ethan gives him an apologetic smile. "We need a bit more time to decide."

"No problem." Diego goes over to the next table.

I'm so busy kicking myself that I barely hear what Ethan says next. I keep glancing over at Diego, wondering what I can do to make this right.

The third time he returns, we finally put in an order for appetizers, and I once again fail to say anything meaningful.

He starts to walk off but pauses. "So, how long have you two been dating?"

I look to Ethan, expecting him to respond, but instead he nods at me. "Oh, we have differing opinions over what counted as our first date, so I'll let her answer first."

Oh, no. I have no idea… I didn't expect to run into Ethan… ever… so I never asked Regan for any of these details. "I…"

Ethan tilts his head. "What's wrong?"

"Uh…" I have to get out. I don't care how—I just have to get out.

My gaze lands on my soda. I lift one arm. "So, here's the thing—" With each word, I gesture emphatically, until I knock that glass right onto myself.

Cold soda seeps into my costume, and I let out a horrified gasp. "My costume! Oh, no, I have to get back, or it'll be ruined! Let's go!"

Ethan stands and approaches with a napkin. "I'm sure it'll be fine. Let's get some club soda—"

"This was hand-made and can't just be cleaned with club soda! It needs specialized products, and… and the material is delicate, so the longer we wait, the worse it will get, and… I have to go!"

Ethan nods. "Okay, all right. We'll go."

I squirm uncomfortably as he settles up with the restaurant. Diego sets about cleaning the mess, and I feel awful for causing it. He won't look at me, and I can't blame him. If someone had been talking trash about me to their boyfriend…

Boyfriend… He didn't know Regan has a boyfriend… and I've been acting like I don't because, well, I don't…

My mind flashes back to earlier this afternoon, how something electric passed between us when he was holding me.

Skylar, you're the biggest idiot in the universe.

The next few days pass normally. Well, as normally as they can for someone pretending to be another person. I eventually heard back from Regan, who sent me a long missive about how stupid my plan was before laughing it off and saying she managed to smooth things over with Ethan. Clearly, she's much better at this than I am. Because I haven't been able to break the ice that's formed between me and Diego.

He's perfectly respectful as we rosin up and prepare to run our part in the show for Rebecca, who will be scrutinizing each pair individually now that we're a week away from performing. And when we get on the silks, we do every move correctly.

But I might as well be performing with a robot—and him, too. I feel it each time he grips me to hoist me onto the apparatus, each time I descend into his arms and hold a pose… these were all moments choreographed to convey a connection between two performers, and yet, even as I go through them, I feel… hollow.

What am I supposed to do? He thinks I was flirting with him while hiding a boyfriend… well, maybe not flirting, but… you know what I mean. There was *something* between us that day in the tent, before Ethan showed up and ruined it. But even if he hadn't, what was I going to do, start dating someone while lying about my identity?

My mind is in chaos, but my body remembers the choreography I've put it through so many times. Wrapping one wrist around a single fabric while Diego does the same with the other, and then spinning around each other. Gripping his arms while he's secured in an upside-down straddle on the silks and then turning into an upside-down split. Holding each other's waists while he grips the fabrics with one hand and moving our legs in sync as if walking on air.

Finally, Diego lowers me to the ground, then descends from the silks, and we strike a final pose on the floor to end the piece.

The others in our workshop clap politely, as we've been doing after each pair's run.

Rebecca does as well, but disappointment clouds her eyes. "Well, it certainly was… precise. But where's the passion? I know you're both expressive aerialists—I've seen you working on solo material during open workout."

Diego stares at the ground, and I shuffle my feet.

Just then, Avery marches into the studio. "Regan?"

What now? I thought she'd given up on trying to capture my face for social media.

But there's no tablet in her hand this time, and a serious expression fills her face. "Regan, Director Haley needs to see you in her office—immediately."

My face goes cold. "What… why?"

"She didn't say. Just… come with me." Avery gestures for me to follow her out.

I glance at Rebecca, who gives a curt nod before resuming the workshop as if nothing happened.

The other students throw odd glances in my direction, and Diego watches me leave with furrowed brows.

They've figured it out. That's the only explanation…

I breathe hard to calm myself. Maybe I'm overreacting. Maybe it's something mundane, and I'm spiraling again. Maybe—

Any hope vanishes when Avery opens the door to the Director's office.

Three others are already inside: my mom, Mrs. Takahashi, and Regan… the real one.

Director Haley gestures at me. "Hello… Skylar. Please, shut the door, and have a seat."

Swallowing hard, I comply and take the empty chair next to my mom, doing my best to avoid the poisonous look she's giving me.

The Director clasps her hands and places them on her desk. "Well, this is an unusual situation. Care to explain yourselves?" She looks from me to

Regan and back again.

I jitter. "How—how did you—?"

"Did you really think you could get away with this deception?" Mrs. Takahashi, a regal blonde in a burgundy power suit, gives Regan a pointed look, then turns to me. "Ethan messaged me after your unusual 'date' and told me he was worried, since you were acting strangely. So, I did a little digging, and I found a TikTok that one of Regan's friends posted from Arizona—with Regan in the background. Well, you can imagine my surprise when I realized my daughter was in the wrong state! I flew there immediately to retrieve her, then found Mrs. Huang's information and let her know what had transpired."

Regan twists her hands and gives me an apologetic look. "I wanted to warn you, but she confiscated my laptop."

"It's okay," I mumble. Seems she didn't smooth things over with Ethan as well as she'd thought. But I'm the reason she had to try in the first place. "I screwed up, too."

"I am very, very sorry about all this." My mom, looking mortified, gestures emphatically with each word. "I should have looked closer when Skylar claimed she received a last-minute scholarship... we'll get her things and leave immediately."

"No!" The word bursts instinctively from my lips.

Mom glares at me. "You shouldn't be here in the first place, Skylar! I thought I raised you better than this! I don't care how badly you wanted to come—you shouldn't have lied!"

I bite my lip. I have no good response.

Mrs. Takahashi turns to the Director. "Ms. Haley, I understand that these circumstances are, as you said, unusual, but the fact is that I already paid for this program in full. There is still a week left before the show, and Regan should have the opportunity to complete the workshop and perform. I guarantee, she can learn the choreography in time."

The other hesitates. "Well…"

"I should remind you, Director, that it was your security failure that allowed Skylar to impersonate my daughter in the first place. You should have been more thorough, and if Regan is not allowed—"

"No." Regan gives her mother a firm look. "I don't want to."

Mrs. Takahashi waves her hand dismissively. "Oh, don't be nervous—"

"I'm not nervous, Mom." Regan rises from her chair. "I don't want to do this program. I never did. That's why I gave my spot to Skylar."

I watch her with admiration. I've never seen her stand up to anyone like this before.

Mrs. Takahashi gives an uncomfortable smile. "Listen, darling—"

"I've *been* listening. It's you who hasn't." Regan's voice takes on a pleading tone. "All my life, you told me how important it was to be perfect and beautiful… You would know. You were a professional ballerina. And when I couldn't cut it at ballet, you sent me to circus school instead. It was fun, sure. But I never wanted to be a pro… I couldn't realize that, though, with you always in my head. That's why I had to run away to Arizona, away from all this. My time at the retreat, exploring my true inner self, made me realize I don't wanna be a performer. All that perfectionism has been eating away at my mental health." Tears fill her eyes. "I need to stay out of any kind of spotlight for a while, so I can figure out who *I* am, when no one's watching."

Mrs. Takahashi looks taken aback for a moment. Then, she stands and embraces her daughter. "Oh, baby, I had no idea you were this unhappy! Why didn't you tell me?"

"I tried, Mom. I tried so many times." Regan wipes her eyes. "I can't do this. But you know who can? Skylar." She turns to me with a small smile. "Skylar loves being in the air more than anyone else I've ever met. She knows what she wants—and she should get to finish what she started here."

I stare at her with a mix of disbelief and gratitude. "Regan, you don't have to do that."

"Yeah, I do. This whole thing was my stupid idea to begin with." A nervous chuckle escapes her. She turns to my mom. "I'm so sorry, Mrs. Huang. I'm the one who told Skylar to lie to you."

Mom glares at me. "You shouldn't have done as she said."

"I know." I stare at the ground. "I just… I wanted this *so bad*." Drawing a breath, I manage to look her in the eye. "Aerial is my passion, and performing is my dream. This felt like my only chance to make it happen. I'm sorry I lied… I just didn't see any other way."

Mom's mouth remains pursed, but her eyes soften.

"So." Director Haley glances uncomfortably between the four of us across her desk. "What I'm hearing is that Skylar will finish out the program—with records amended, of course. Is that correct?"

Mrs. Takahashi looks at Regan, then turns to the Director and nods. "I am amenable to this—but I want paperwork stating that Skylar's tuition was sponsored by the Takahashi Foundation so I can write it off as charity."

"That can be arranged." The Director turns to my mom. "Mrs. Huang?"

Mom watches me for a long moment. "When you get home after the program, you will be the one to clean Mrs. Dunn's basement. That will be your punishment."

A relieved smile spreads across my face, and I throw my arms around her. "Thanks, Mom!"

"Don't thank me. She has sixty years' worth of junk down there."

"I'll help," Regan says. "Since this is my fault, too."

I give her a grateful look. "I don't know how I could ever thank you. For everything."

Regan grins. "Just name one of the circus cats after me when you're touring with a professional show."

It feels weird to go back to workshop after all the drama in the office, but the sooner I can come clean to my teachers and classmates, the better. Already, a great weight has been lifted off my chest. No more hiding from cameras, no more dodging classmates from back home, no more putting on weird characters and voices… finally, I can just be *me.*

I rush across the tent, to where Rebecca is wrapping up her critique of another pair's routine.

When she finishes, she turns to me with a puzzled look. "What was all that about, Regan?"

I twist my hands. "Well… this is awkward, but… I'm not Regan Takahashi. My name is Skylar Huang. I'm one of Regan's friends from New Heights Aerial back in Jersey, and I've been pretending to be Regan these past few weeks." Gasps and mutterings scatter though the air. I wait for them to die down, then explain, as best I can, what Regan and I did, and why. "I'm sorry for lying to all of you." I glance at Diego, who sits on a bench, staring at his clasped hands. "Especially to my partner. To do what we do, we have to trust each other, and I broke that trust. I'm truly, deeply sorry, and I know there's nothing I can do to take back what I did, but… I hope we can at least start over?"

Diego doesn't answer. He doesn't even look at me.

A swell of tears rises behind my eyes, and I blink hard to keep them back.

Rebecca places a hand on my shoulder. "Thank you for your honesty… Skylar." She turns to the others. "Well, I don't think any of us will be able to focus after that. Fortunately, we're finished with the critiques anyway. Feel free to do any exercises you feel you need to on your own with the remainder of our time. Tomorrow, we'll run the whole thing in sync."

The others scatter, but Diego remains on the bench, glaring at the ground with his mouth tight. I approach him tentatively. "Diego?"

When his eyes finally flick up, they're unreadable. "Well, now I know the real reason why you were so mad when I tried to introduce you on the live stream. Was anything you said to me true?"

"Yes! So much of it! I… I meant everything I said about how good you are, and that thing Ethan said at the restaurant—it wasn't about you. Regan—the real Regan—must've said it about someone else—"

"I don't care about that." He shakes his head. "I'd better go condition. Let me know if you want to meet at open workout later and run anything."

"Diego…"

"The show must go on." With that, he turns away from me and heads to the silks.

I thought I'd feel fantastic after revealing my true identity. I thought I could finally enjoy the Gravity Arts Institute the way everyone else does, rather than constantly worrying about being exposed. The way things played out in Director Haley's office was practically a miracle, and I should be basking in it.

Instead, I don't think I've ever been more miserable.

Sure, I get to practice the performance art I love, and sure, my classmates and teachers have turned the whole switcharoo thing into a big joke and campus legend.

But Diego and I still look like robots when we run our routine, and I know it's my fault. He's doing his best to be professional, but I can tell I've really hurt him. And he can't take the space he needs to process what I've done—how can he when I'm climbing on him every day?

I hug my arms as I leave the tent, after yet another practice session where Rebecca critiqued our lack of artistry. The show's in two days, and if we can't change something, then all the scouts will see are two boring aerialists going through the technical motions, with none of the passion and expression that makes our art form so beautiful. They won't select either of us, and it'll be my fault.

I brought this upon myself, but Diego… he doesn't deserve to have his chances ruined because of me.

I know what I have to do.

I enter the main building, find my way to Zephyr's dorm, and knock.

They open the door and, upon seeing me, give a joking grin. "Oh, hello, *Regan.*"

I throw them an annoyed look. "Can I talk to you?"

"Sure." They gesture for me to enter. "Still can't believe you managed to avoid me all that time you were pretending to be her. What's up?"

"You did the silks workshop last year, right? And it's the same choreography, right? You were the flyer? And you still remember how it goes? You could do it again right now if you needed to?"

"Whoa, slow down! Yes, to all of that. Are you looking for tips?"

I shake my head. "I… have a huge, *huge* favor to ask. I… I can pay you, even. Depending on how much, I might need a little time, but—"

"What are you talking about, Skylar?" Concern comes over their face.

"I need you to take my place in the show." *There, I said it out loud.* "I can't finish the program after all, and Diego needs a flyer who… who… well, he needs a flyer that isn't me. It's too awkward between us, and… this is his future. I can't be the reason he loses his shot."

Zephyr gives me a sympathetic look. "Not gonna lie, I've seen you two practicing, and… yeah, something isn't working. But I don't think this is the answer."

"Yes, it is. If you're okay with it, I mean. I know you've got your rope act, too, but I just thought… you and Diego are friends, and you're an awesome performer. You'll work well together, and the scouts will get to see the best of him."

"Wow, you *really* like him, don't you?" Zephyr raises their brows.

My ears burn. "That's not why—"

"Yeah, it is." They smile. "This is really sweet of you. He should know how much you care. If I take your part in the show, I'm gonna tell him why."

"No! Just tell him—"

"Don't you think he's been lied to enough?"

My jaw drops. "I-I—"

"Those are my terms. I won't take your money, Skylar, but I will take your truth."

I nod. "Fine… okay. Fine."

They place a hand on my arm. "If you change your mind, that's all right, too."

"Thanks." I leave Zephyr's room, grab the phone from my bag, and call my mom. "Hey… Mom? Look… I… I can't finish the program after all. Can I come home?"

"First, you make such a fuss to stay, and now, you want to quit?" Mom sounds exasperated. "You don't have to do anything you don't want to, sweetie, but I have work. I took off the day after tomorrow to see your show, but I can't come earlier than that."

"I understand… thanks. I'll see you the day after tomorrow, then."

I hang up, make my way to my dorm, and flop onto the bed.

"Skylar, hey!" Regan calls out to me from the passenger seat of a BMW convertible. From behind the wheel, Ethan gives a small wave. Whatever issues they had, they've clearly made up if she convinced him to drive her back to the Gravity Arts Institute after everything.

Standing on the curb with my suitcase—Mom's supposed to arrive any minute now to pick me up—I give Regan an odd look. "What're you doing here?"

"Had nothing else this weekend, so me and Ethan are hanging at his aunt's cabin. Figured I'd come out for the show and cheer on my friends while I'm here. What are *you* doing?" Her face twists. "Shouldn't you be warming up?"

I shake my head with a sigh, then quickly explain why I'll be skipping the show.

Before Regan can reply, Mom arrives and pulls up behind Ethan's car. She gets out and greets me with a hug.

"Well, Sky, I hope you at least had fun these past few weeks." She shakes her head at me. "So much driving for me, though!"

"Wait." Regan leans out the car window. "You should at least stay and watch the show, too. Seems wrong to just… sneak off."

"I'm not sneaking off!" But I see her point… it does feel a bit rude to ditch everyone without a goodbye. I glance at Mom, who shrugs.

"I wouldn't mind watching your friends," she says. "It'll be a nice break from the driving."

Regan opens the car door and hops out. "Great, it's settled!" She hooks her elbow into mine and glances back at Ethan. "Babe, can you go park the car and meet me inside?"

"Yeah, sure." Ethan pulls the door shut and drives off.

Mom grabs my suitcase. "I'll put this in the car and meet you inside, too. Save me a good seat."

"Do you need help?" I ask.

She waves me off.

Regan strides onto the walkway that leads around the main building and to the tent in the back, which is being repurposed from a practice studio into a makeshift performance venue. "So glad you changed your mind about staying. Though I wish you'd change it about performing, too."

"I—"

"There you are!"

For a moment, I'm not sure what Regan's talking about, and then I see the figure appear from around the corner of the building, rushing toward us.

I furrow my brow. "Diego?"

Regan unhooks my elbow. "Told you I'd stall her."

I give her a perplexed look. "What…?"

"You have to come back." The words tumble out of Diego. "To the show, I mean. Zephyr's great, but… I can't do it without you."

My frown deepens. "Why? Did they not remember the choreography—?"

"It's got nothing to do with that. I…" He puts his hands in his pockets—he isn't in costume yet—and looks away. "I know I've been cold to you. First, because I thought… well, when you were pretending to be Regan, and at the restaurant… I mean… and then after you said who you really were… There was a lot going on in my head, and I kept telling myself to just be a pro and suck it up. And when Zephyr came to replace you, I repeated that thought to myself over and over. But… it's *wrong*. You worked so hard for this chance. You shouldn't have to give it up because of me, and I'm sorry I made you feel like you did."

I shift my weight uncomfortably. "Did… did Zephyr tell you…?"

He shakes his head, and his lips lift. "They did some pretty heavy implying but held back, said it should come from you. I… kinda figured it out."

My heart jitters. "I-I…"

"I'll go first, then." He looks me in the eye and holds out one hand.

Without thinking, I take it.

A smile blossoms across his face, and he gives my fingers a squeeze. "I really like you, Skylar. It's why I was so out of sorts when I thought you had a boyfriend, why I was so pissed when you revealed the truth. I thought the person I liked might have been an act—might have been someone who didn't exist. I mean, we talked about things Regan did, and it really messed with my head. But you were always *you*, weren't you? Only your name was different… and some stuff you said about junior high, sure. But, like, your personality… that was all you."

Biting my lip, I nod. "I… I'm so sorry…"

"No, *I'm* sorry. I never gave you a chance… could you possibly give me one?" He angles his chin down and looks up at me, closing his mouth into something of a pout.

I giggle. "Stop that! You look ridiculous!"

"Oh, you ain't seen nothing." He holds my hand with both of his and drops to his knees. "Skylar Huang, will you do me the honor of being my silks partner tonight?"

I snatch my hand back. "Oh my God, get up!"

He stands with a grin, but it drops into an earnest expression. "Seriously, I wouldn't feel right performing without you. We might not have been able to rehearse properly, but… I know we'll be great together. Please, give me a chance to prove it."

My pulse must be louder than a drumroll by now. My head starts nodding before my mind has a chance to catch up. "Okay… yeah, let's do it."

"Hustle, you two!" Regan—who I'd completely forgotten about—points emphatically at the tent. "Show's in an hour, and you've still gotta get your costumes on and warm up!"

I narrow my eyes at her, then at Diego. "You two planned this, didn't you?"

Regan shrugs. "Zephyr may have told me about you dropping out, and I may have told Diego he'd be an idiot to let you, and he may have told me that he'd already realized it but couldn't find you, and I may have gotten that text right as Ethan was driving me here… But seriously, get moving!"

Struck by a sudden sense of urgency, I rush down the sidewalk. Then, it hits me that I never told Diego how I felt, and I stop in my tracks.

He runs smack-bang into my back. "Whoa! What—?"

"I like you, too." I give a helpless grin. "Sorry, just realized I didn't tell you."

He smiles back. "Yeah, you did. C'mon."

He takes my hand, and we both rush to the tent and enter through the side entrance, which leads to an area that has been curtained off to serve as a backstage area.

Zephyr sits waiting in a chair, wearing the outfit for their rope routine and holding a costume. They toss it to me with lifted brows. "About time."

The main lights go down, and ethereal ones illuminate the six pairs of sky-blue silks. The twelve of us in the workshop file out from behind the curtain as an atmospheric synthetic soundtrack whooshes through the tent.

The *circus* tent. No longer a training ground—a stage.

I try not to think about the scouts sitting in the bleachers alongside the students' friends and families.

The concept of this act is a simple one: The angel who falls in love with a mortal. Played out in tandem by six pairs—the bases in long, earth-toned costumes as the mortals, the flyers in shimmering white bodysuits as the angels. Though we were all given the same choreography, Rebecca left us plenty of room to be expressive.

I climb the silks first, rolling my spine and reaching my limbs with each move, until I arrive at the top. There, I turn upside down, wrap my legs around the fabrics, and cross them behind my back.

When I'm secure in place, Diego climbs the loose silks below me. His weight yanks down on the fabrics wrapped around me, tightening them. But I barely feel it.

His movements are intentionally rough at first, as he tries to reach me, so high above him. Halfway there, in sync with the weary music, he stops and bows his head. If I didn't know better, I'd think he was too exhausted to continue the routine.

The music strikes up again, and he winds himself into an upside-down straddle position that locks both legs but leaves the arms free. It's one of the most basic poses on silks—something a lot of aerialists consider a warm-up— yet he turns it into art with a combination of purposeful lines and heartfelt gestures.

I shift my position on the silks above and reach down to him, as he extends an arm toward me. Our eyes lock, and for a moment, I forget where I am.

And then, the beat drops. That's my cue.

This is the part I usually hate, the part where I have to rely on my partner instead of the silks. I climb down and eventually slide down into Diego's arms, where he holds me in a cradle. Our eyes lock again, and he smiles.

I've never felt safer in my life. And part of me wishes I could stay here forever.

The show concluded an hour ago, but none of us have left the tent. We're all anxiously waiting backstage for Director Haley to tell us who the scouts are interested in.

Finally, she enters through the curtain, holding her tablet out before her. Avery stands beside her, camera ready, and, for once, I don't try to dodge it.

"Thank you for your patience, everyone." Director Haley taps the tablet. "You all did a wonderful job today, and…" I barely process the encouraging words she says next. I just need to know what's on that tablet. "…as you know, there were scouts from several reputable circuses and schools here. I'm happy to say that Cirque Céleste would like to extend invitations to their official training camp—a feeder for their internationally renowned shows—to the following students."

I give Diego a nervous look, and he slides his hand into mine and gives it a squeeze.

The Director names a few students, including Zephyr, who burst out in cheers and laughter and tears of joy. Then finally…

"Diego Ramirez… and Skylar Huang."

An excited scream bursts from my lips, and Diego leaps into the air with an elated fist pump.

This is it… I'm going to be a real circus artist. I'm going to learn from the best, so I can become one of the best, perform with the best. I can already see it—traveling shows in arenas across the country, Vegas residencies, international performances.

And in each one of these visions, Diego is right there with me.

I'm not sure who grabs who first—the next thing I know, our arms are wrapped around each other.

I place a hand on his cheek, and he brushes the hair off my forehead. Pulling him close, I press my lips to his.

I didn't think there could be such thing as a perfect moment, but as I stand here in his arms, lost in his kiss and the joy swirling around us, I know I've found one.

About the Authors

AMY BEARCE writes magical escapes for young readers and the young at heart. She is the author of the *World of Aluvia* series, the *Secret Psychics* series, and the *Wish & Wander* series, for ages 10+, as well as *The Worst Villain Ever*, for ages 8 and up.

She is also a former reading teacher and school librarian. As a military kid, she moved eight times before she was eighteen, so she feels especially fortunate to be married to her high school sweetheart. Together, they're raising two daughters in San Antonio.

You can find her online at amybearce.com.

New York-based circus legend HOVEY BURGESS is a multifaceted performer and educator, renowned as a juggler, acrobat, clown, and author. At 17, he embarked on his circus journey by joining a small traveling show as a juggler and unicyclist. Over his career, which spans more than half a century, he has performed with numerous circuses, including Big Apple Circus, Circus Flora, Circo dell'Arte, The Electric Circus, Toledo Zoo Wild Animal Show, Flying High Circus, Hagen Bros. Circus, Patterson Bros. Circus, Bindlestiff Family Cirkus, among others.

Hovey served as a professor of Circus Arts at NYU for 51 years, teaching 100 semesters from 1966 to 2017. He has also taught at prestigious institutions such as Juilliard and the Ringling Brothers Barnum & Bailey Clown College. Additionally, he is the author of *Circus Techniques: Juggling, Equilibristics, Vaulting*.

PAIGE DANIELS is the author of the *Non-Compliance* series, the *Singularity Wars* series, *Agents of the Consortium*, and a number of short stories. By day, she works as an electrical engineer. When she's not busy with working and writing, she's hanging out on her hobby farm with cows, goats, dogs, and cats.

DOROTHY DREYER is a Philippine-born American living in Germany with her family. She is an award-winning, USA Today Bestselling author of fantasy, romance, and horror, which usually have some element of magic or the supernatural in them. Aside from reading, she enjoys movies, binge-watching series, chocolate, take-out, traveling, and having fun with friends and family. She tends to sing sometimes, too, so keep her away from your Karaoke bars.

MARY FAN is a sci-fi/fantasy author hailing from Jersey City. Her books include *Stronger Than a Bronze Dragon*, the *Starswept* trilogy, the *Flynn Nightsider* series, the *Jane Colt* trilogy, and the *Fated Stars* series. She is also the co-editor, along with Paige Daniels, of the *Brave New Girls* anthology series about girls in STEM. Her short fiction has appeared in numerous anthologies, including *Magic at Midnight, Sing, Goddess!*, *Thrilling Adventure Yarns*, *Phenomenons*, and *Tales of the Crimson Keep*. She is a contributor to *Star Wars Insider* and *The Workprint* and has previously written for the official *Star Trek* website.

In addition, Mary is an amateur circus artist. Her apparatus of choice is aerial silks, though she also trains on flying trapeze, dance trapeze, rope, and lyra. Occasionally, you might glimpse her attempting hammock, straps, or handstands.

Find her online at www.MaryFan.com.

Growing up in the Black Forest as a hopeless dreamer with an overactive imagination, JANINA FRANCK began writing at a young age to give a voice to the stories living inside her head. As a teenager, she moved to Ireland, where she went on to study Modern Languages and Multimedia. Since then, she has also lived in France and Brazil. While her surroundings changed, her desire to create stories did not, which she now pursues across various types of media, while traveling to quench her thirst for new impressions and adventures.

LEIGH HELLMAN is a queer and non-binary writer, originally from the western suburbs of Chicago, and a graduate of the MA Program for Writers at the University of Illinois at Chicago. After gaining the ever-lucrative BA in English, they spent five years living and teaching in South Korea before returning to their native Midwest. They are currently located in Bellingham.

Leigh's short fiction and creative nonfiction work has been featured in *Hippocampus Magazine*, *VIDA Review*, and *Fulbright Korea Infusion Magazine*. Their critical and journalistic work has been featured in the *American Book Review*, the *Gwangju News* magazine, the *Windy City Times*, and *Bellingham Alive!*. Their debut novel, *Orbit*, is a new adult speculative fiction story available through Snowy Wings Publishing. They also have a historical fantasy piece included in the SWP anthology *Magic at Midnight* and a cyberpunk sci-fi piece included in the SWP anthology *Sing, Goddess!*. They have been writing erotica for over 20 years and have participated in both fan and original spaces for erotic and romance work.

Leigh is a strong advocate for full-day breakfast menus, all varieties of dark chocolate, building a wardrobe based primarily on bad puns, and bathing in the tears of their enemies.

Growing up with a fascination for space and things that fly, JAMIE KRAKOVER turned that love into a career as an Aerospace Engineer. Combining her natural enthusiasm for science fiction and her love of reading, she now spends a lot of her time writing middle grade and young adult science fiction and fantasy.

Jamie lives in St. Louis, Missouri with her husband, Andrew, their son, and their dog, Rogue (named after the X-Men, not *Star Wars*, although she loves both). When she isn't being a rocket scientist by day and a writer by night, she can be found catching up on the latest sci-fi TV, books, and movies, as well as spending time on social media (maybe a little too much time :-P). And no, the rocket science jokes never get old!

Through Snowy Wings Publishing, Jamie is the author of *The Tracker Sequence* duology. She also has two female-in-STEM short stories published in the *Brave New Girls* anthologies and two engineering-centered nonfiction pieces published in *Writer's Digest's Putting the Science in Fiction*.

KARISSA LAUREL is a science fiction, fantasy, and romance author living in central North Carolina. Her favorite things are *Star Wars*, Southern cuisine, and being outside on the water or on the back of her Yamaha TW200. Karissa has served as an assistant editor at *Cast of Wonders*, a young adult speculative fiction podcast that is part of the Escape Artists family. Most recently, she is the author of *Serendipity at the End of the World*, a young adult story of steampunk, love, and zombies. She's also the author of numerous novels and short stories about monsters, magic, and intrepid young women. Find out more on her Facebook Page at www.facebook.com/karissalaurel, or check her out on Instagram @KarissaLaurel.

ADRIANO MORAES is a multifaceted Brazilian artist who has worked in comics, animation, illustration, cartoons, and production art, employing a variety of styles.

He is currently the resident artist at the Slipper Room—a neo-burlesque theater and lounge that features an eclectic mix of dance, drag, comedy, magic, and circus arts—where he draws performances live, often producing three drawings during a single five-minute act. Additionally, he has drawn various burlesque, cirque, and sideshow acts in New York and Philadelphia.

Follow him on Instagram at @liveartbyadriano.

MILAN OBRADOVIC is the L.A.-based author of the time-bending young adult adventure *Jasper Faulks and the Passage of Time*, available everywhere. Decades ago, he dipped his ticket stub into the spilled blood of a pro wrestler in a dingy high school gym in rural Germany, but he also rode with Owen Hart and Davey Boy Smith, saw WrestleMania in Hollywood, the Royal Rumble in New Orleans, Double or Nothing in Las Vegas, and witnessed the Battle of Los Angeles. Watch out for the sci-fi novel *Sky Skraper 1*, a second Jasper Faulks adventure, and more pro wrestling stories. Find him online at milanobradovic.com and on all social media @1milanobradovic.

SELENIA PAZ loves to write stories containing elements of mystery and of the supernatural. When not writing, she loves to read and spend time with her family. She received her Master of Library Science degree from Texas Woman's University in 2010 and has been a librarian ever since. Selenia is also the author of the middle grade fantasy *Leyendas* trilogy from Snowy Wings Publishing.

LISA TOOHEY lives in Ontario, Canada, where she spends her free time riding horses, hiking, and gardening. She works in Marketing as a day job. In her writing, Lisa enjoys exploring present-day themes in futuristic settings. You can find additional stories from Lisa in the Brave New Girls anthologies.

www.ingramcontent.com/pod-product-compliance
Lightning Source LLC
Chambersburg PA
CBHW021231190726
48289CB00005B/1274